"WOULD YOU PLEASE NOT HOLD ME SO CLOSE?"

"Why not?" he asked in a low tone that sounded disturbingly sensual at these close quarters.

"Because it isn't right," Susan answered, trying to breathe normally.

There was a testing movement of his hand on her back. "It feels right," murmured Mitch.

"Well, it doesn't look right," she replied in an almost desperate whisper.

He tipped his head downward, his mouth moving against her dark hair as he spoke. "To whom?"

"To everyone." Her heart was thudding against her ribs, a traitorous weakness flowing into her limbs. She glanced wildly around the room, pulling away from the warm breath that teased the hair at her temples. "Mitch, please don't do that."

A finger touched her chin to draw her gaze back to his face. There was no laughing curve in his mouth. The bronze tan of his cheeks, smoothly shaven from cheekbone to jawline, invited her caress. The teasing glitter was absent from his eyes, but their darkening blue fire made Susan feel warm all over.

"Do you have any idea how long I've been waiting to hear you say my name?"

Books by Janet Dailey

CALDER PROMISE

SHIFTING CALDER WIND

GREEN CALDER GRASS

MAYBE THIS CHRISTMAS

SCROOGE WORE SPURS

A CAPITAL HOLIDAY

"The Devil and Mr. Chocolate"
in the anthology
THE ONLY THING BETTER THAN
CHOCOLATE

ALWAYS WITH LOVE

BECAUSE OF YOU

CAN'T SAY GOODBYE

DANCE WITH ME

EVERYTHING

FOREVER

BECAUSE OF YOU

Janet Dailey

ZEBRA BOOKS
KENSINGTON PUBLISHING CORP.

http://www.kensingtonbooks.com

CONTENTS

THE INDY MAN

Chapter One

The candle flame flickered briefly despite the colored, pear-shaped glass that rose protectively around it to keep away the drafts. It was a touch of intimate atmosphere in an otherwise well-lit lounge.

As Susan sipped a margarita from a salt-rimmed, handblown glass, the wavering light caught and reflected a red gleam in the sleek curls of her dark brown hair. Discreetly, she licked a grain or two of salt from her full lips as she set the drink down and looked at the man sitting opposite her.

For the thousandth time, Susan studied his aloof, almost arrogant features: the firm jaw, the thin, hard mouth, the aristocratically straight nose. His eyes were impassive, nearly black beneath thick brows that were equally dark. His hair was the same dark brown as hers but it had a raven-black sheen in this light, without the touch of fire hers possessed.

Warren Sullivan was not looking at Susan, though. His intent gaze was moving about the lounge in that ever-alert manner of his. He seemed suddenly withdrawn and remote, not actually with her but apart.

Leaning forward, Susan reached out to touch the long, masculine fingers that held his glass. The movement caused the vee of her shimmering Lycra top to open, revealing a tantalizing glimpse of her lacy bra. The nearness of her hand to the candle flame illuminated the gold ring and its brilliant diamond. Her fingernails were impractically long and manicured, the way Warren liked them.

The touch of her hand against his brought his dark gaze to center on her face, cameo-smooth in tenderness. A semblance of a smile curved his lips as Warren released the glass to let his fingers close over the tips of hers. Susan ignored the lack of warmth in his expression because she saw the look of approval in his eyes.

"We're going to have a good marriage, Susan." The matter-of-fact announcement was issued quietly as if he had been pondering the question and was now satisfied with his conclusion.

Susan smiled, letting her dark lashes flutter down. She had become accustomed to Warren's statements. They were rarely romantic but she didn't mind. He had never actually proposed to her—merely told her they were getting married. Her acceptance of his decision was taken for granted.

"I hope so. But why are you so sure?" Her tone was untroubled and softly teasing, as if she already knew what his answer would be.

"Because, Susan, during the day you're level-headed and efficient. There's only the slightest trace of the womanly, feminine creature that you can be at the moment. That's why we'll have a good marriage—you're like me. You don't get private emotions mixed up with business."

"Or business mixed up with private emotions."

"That too, of course." His broad shoulders moved in an agreeing shrug as that was of secondary importance. Susan held back a sigh.

There were times when she wondered if Warren really loved her. Fortunately, there were times when he convinced her of it very thoroughly. She silently wished they weren't here in this public place so he could take her in his strong arms and convince her again.

Her fingertip trailed around the salted edge of her margarita glass. Glancing up, she noticed his gaze wandering around the room again. Almost as if he felt her watching him, he met the soft adoration of her look.

"I often wonder," he mused, "why it took me so long to actually notice you. It wasn't until my father became ill and I had to stand in for him at the office Christmas party. You'd worked there for how long—two years?"

"Four years," corrected Susan gently. "Two years in the marketing division and two years as your administrative assistant."

"I always thought you were very attractive," Warren continued, not in the least perturbed that he didn't have a clue as to how long she'd been working for his law firm. "But you were always so practical. I didn't realize how warm and vibrant you really were until you suddenly became the life of the party."

"That party went down in history," Susan murmured. "Did you know that the female employees of Sullivan, Sullivan, and Holmes cheered when they heard you were going to attend?"

"Did you?"

"Loudest of all." She grinned at him, remembering the day. "I told you I had a crush on you from the moment I first saw you. But with all the socialites that paraded through your life, I never thought I had a chance."

"Oh, yes. Blonde and blonder." He laughed in derision. "I wasn't interested in any of them. I was looking for someone like you, intelligent and understanding, capable of appreciating the demands of my career and supporting my ambitions. Until I got to know you, I thought all women threw tantrums if legal work interfered with the time I spent with them."

"You should have dated a doctor's daughter before," Susan laughed. "I don't remember any school function my father saw through to the end. Somebody's baby would always decide to be born by the middle of every performance and the hospital would page him, and that was that. Yes, it hurt my feelings now and then, but my mother taught me patience and understanding. She'd had plenty of time to learn."

Susan knew Warren was listening to her, yet his head was half-turned to glance around the lounge. They weren't expecting to meet anyone tonight and she wondered fleetingly why he was so interested in the other customers. But her budding curiosity didn't last longer than it took for his look to return to her.

"I'm glad you understand," he said. Was it her

imagination or was his expression sterner than before? "It's going to be hell at the office next week when my father goes into the hospital for surgery."

"I'm sure the doctors will find that the tumor is benign," Susan offered, realizing Warren's harshness had probably been a show of concern for his father's health. They were very close.

"Of course it will be," he said curtly, sliding a glance again to the side, his mouth tightening grimly. "Though they'll have to do a biopsy to know for certain."

"Warren." Susan tilted her head to the side, a tiny frown drawing her brows together. "What's wrong?"

Impatience laced his expression. "The man at the second table—no, don't look now," he reprimanded her in a low, sharp voice. "He's been staring at you for the last ten minutes."

"At me?" she repeated in disbelief. "Are you sure?"

"Of course I'm sure," Warren retorted.

"Maybe I know him. Maybe he's someone I went to school with and he just found my yearbook picture on Classmates.com. I never liked that picture," Susan said flippantly, hoping to ease Warren's irritation. "You said he's at the second table—"

"Yes. Take a look but don't be obvious about it," he commanded, an order that was much easier to give than carry out.

With forced nonchalance, Susan leaned back in her chair. She let her gaze wander idly about the lounge until it was caught by the man at the second table and held by his intent regard. There wasn't any doubt in Susan's mind that he was looking at no one else but her.

The man was alone at the table, leaning some-what indolently back in his chair. A thumb was hooked in the waistband of his suit trousers, hold-ing the jacket open to reveal a vest in the same unusual tobacco-brown color as his suit. Even at this distance, Susan could recognize the expensive tailoring.

His hair was a tawny shade, brown gilded with natural streaks of dark gold, and a trifle long judged by the clean-cut standards Warren adhered to. Its careless style gave the man a look suggesting the untamed. His lean, handsome face held deeply grooved lines around the mouth and eyes that said he smiled often. *Boyish* was the initial adjective that Susan wanted to use to describe the man, but he was much too virile and masculine. That faintly boyish charm she detected was really the rakish air of a rogue. His sensual good looks and devastating smile had probably overwhelmed many women.

Her inspection finally stopped at his eyes, blue and glinting with undisguised amusement. Susan couldn't shake the feeling that there was some-thing about him that was vaguely familiar. She stared at him a minute more while she tried to place what it was.

The stranger used that minute to inspect her insolently. As his blue eyes took in her figure, Susan felt as if her clothes were being stripped away little by little. The caressing quality of the sensation sent flames shooting through her veins but without any feeling of annoyance or anger. She looked away before she could figure out where or when she'd seen him before.

"Well?" Warren demanded impatiently.

A black anger was in his expression and Susan

knew that he had recognized the stranger's intimate appraisal of her for what it was. Perhaps the only major fault that Warren possessed was his foul, brooding temper. She almost wanted to say that she knew the man, but at this point she didn't think Warren cared whether she did or not.

"I don't think I know him, although I have the feeling I've seen him someplace before," she replied evenly. It wouldn't do to let Warren see she'd been embarrassed.

Warren flashed another glance at the man, his jaw tightening ominously as he let his gaze slide back to her. "He's got some nerve," he muttered angrily.

"Just ignore him." Susan shrugged.

"How can you ignore rudeness like that?" he snapped. "It's about time someone taught him some manners."

"Then you would be behaving as boorishly as he is," she pointed out. Logic was the only way to cool Warren's hot temper. "Besides," she glanced out of the corner of her eye to see the man rise from his seat, "he's leaving anyway."

Warren didn't seem satisfied with Susan's word that the man was leaving and had to look for himself. His eyes were dark as pitch as they swung back to her, narrowing suspiciously. "You sure you don't know him?" he demanded.

"I—" Susan hesitated, then invisibly shrugged away that vague sensation of something familiar about the stranger who had eyed her so appreciatively. "I'm sure," she concluded with a firm nod of her head.

"Then tell me why," Warren continued in the

same ominously low tone, "he's walking to our table."

Her brown eyes widened with bewilderment as her hand moved to the dark hair at her temple, smoothing it back before she glanced surreptitiously at the man. He was approaching their table with a rolling, supple walk totally unlike Warren's firm, almost military stride. There was the faintest suggestion of a smile on the man's face, but his eyes were decidedly crinkled at the corners, a wicked glitter in their blueness. She had barely met his mocking look and she was glancing swiftly away.

She didn't know him, did she? How could anyone forget someone like him? She didn't know him, she was sure of it. Yet why was he coming to their table?

He was suddenly standing very near but Susan wouldn't look up. Her hands were trembling and she clasped them together, silently praying that Warren wouldn't notice how unnerved she was, and that he wouldn't make a scene.

"Excuse me," the man spoke in a voice that was low and musically pitched.

Unwillingly, Susan lifted her chin, determined to show the man how completely indifferent she was to his presence. But his laughing blue eyes weren't looking at her. The man's falsely solemn expression was directed at Warren, whose head tilted challengingly toward the man.

"You don't know me," the man continued, erasing at least one of Susan's doubts. "My name is Mitch Braden." A bell rang in her memory, but not loudly enough for her to know why. A hand was extended to Warren in greeting. "I came over to offer an apology for my rudeness. I'm afraid I might've offended you by staring at your date."

For the briefest of seconds, the man's gaze swung to Susan before it centered again on Warren. His hand remained outstretched. Warren grudgingly shook the man's hand, obviously not mollified by the apology but unable to disregard it without displaying bad manners himself.

"Apology accepted," Warren responded curtly, releasing the man's hand at once.

"Thank you, Mr.—I'm sorry, what was your name?" A smile flashed across Mitch Braden's face, deepening the grooves around his mouth and proving as devastatingly attractive as Susan had thought it would be.

"Sullivan, Warren Sullivan," was the reluctant reply. At that moment Warren had released the man's gaze so he missed the sudden twinkle that sparkled in the man's eyes, but Susan saw it. As if feeling her gaze, the man named Mitch Braden looked at her.

"I don't suppose you need me to tell you what a very beautiful woman your date is, Mr. Sullivan. Obviously you've had more opportunity to appreciate her looks than the few moments I've spent admiring her. It isn't often that a face as beautiful as hers has a figure to go with it."

Susan breathed in sharply, unable to believe the man could speak so audaciously. Warren seemed momentarily stunned by the man's boldness as well.

"Mr. Braden," he said cuttingly, "I don't like your comments."

An eyebrow of golden brown, the same color as the man's hair, raised in surprise. "Don't you think she has a beautiful shape? I would say she's almost perfectly proportioned. Maybe you haven't taken a good look at her recently—"

"Susan is very beautiful," Warren interrupted angrily, black fire flashing from his eyes. "But I certainly don't appreciate you saying things like that—"

"I see," Mitch Braden interrupted calmly. His laughing gaze moved to Susan's face, taking note of her heightened color. When he was looking at her, the man didn't attempt to conceal his mockery with pretend innocence. "You're afraid too many compliments will go to her head, is that it?" He studied Warren's smoldering expression. "Susan, did you say her name was Susan?"

"It happens to be Mrs. Sullivan. She's my wife!" Warren snapped.

Partially angered by the man's flirtatious remarks, which were obviously intended to rile Warren, Susan still found herself hiding a smile. But the tiny dimple in her cheek vanished at Warren's announcement.

"Congratulations," Mitch Braden responded easily to the news, not displaying disappointment or surprise. "You're a lucky man, Mr. Sullivan."

"Thank you," Warren returned acidly.

When Mitch Braden glanced again at Susan, his expressive blue eyes said it was such a pity she was married, but his smiling voice spoke of something else.

"May I buy you two a drink and we can toast the happy couple?" he offered with a flashing smile.

Susan's heart accelerated slightly. "No, thank you, Mr. Braden," she replied swiftly.

"We were just going into the dining room to

eat," Warren said, as if to rescue her. "Thanks just the same."

The man inclined his head in shrugging acceptance. "Least I could do to make up for my earlier bad manners."

Warren rose to his feet. Susan was faintly surprised to see that he was an inch or two taller than Mitch Braden. Mitch's presence had so completely dominated the table that she had presumed him to be the taller of the two. Even now Mitch Braden was the more compelling.

"Your apology has been accepted, Mr. Braden," Warren said coolly, touching Susan's shoulder to prompt her to her feet. "Now please excuse us!"

"Of course." The stunning smile seemed permanently carved on the handsome face, the sparkling blue eyes directed at each of them in turn. "I hope you two have a long and happy marriage. If not—" the wicked glint returned as his gaze rested momentarily on Susan, "I hope I'm around to pick up the pieces."

Susan slipped her hand under Warren's elbow. "We're very happy, Mr. Braden, as you can see. Good-bye."

With a curt nod in the general direction of Mitch Braden, Warren turned Susan toward the door. The muscles in his arms were rigidly hard as his striding walk practically carried her out of the lounge. She guessed at the taut hold he had on his temper. There was no need for them to turn around because she could feel Mitch Braden's eyes watch them leave.

Free of the room and of Braden, Warren's rein on his temper relaxed. "Unbelievably obnoxious!" he muttered beneath his breath. "He apologizes, then tries to steal you from under my nose. It didn't even faze him when I told him you were my wife!"

"That was a little extreme, wasn't it?" she asked gently. "I mean, we aren't married yet."

"Simply because it isn't convenient right now," Warren snapped. "And August is only a little over two months away and we're getting married then."

"Yes," Susan agreed but Warren's white lie bothered her.

Warren continued as if he hadn't heard her. "Do you know this is the first time I've wanted to beat up another guy since I was in high school and punched out the local bully?"

She had heard the story several times before, so she merely nodded and was secretly relieved that Warren hadn't embarrassed her tonight by trying to repeat his high school heroics. Warren, embarrassing her? The idea was so ludicrous considering how proper and polite Warren usually was that she nearly laughed aloud.

"Let's forget about that man," she suggested instead, and wondered why she didn't believe her own words.

"You're right, of course." The taut lines of anger vanished as Warren looked down his nose at her. "I suppose there's no need to let his rudeness spoil our evening. Shall we dine here as planned? He won't bother us again."

Susan wasn't as certain about that as Warren seemed to be but she agreed with his suggestion anyway. Besides, she told herself as the dining room hostess led them to a table, she should look on the bright side of the unfortunate episode. At least she had learned that Warren was capable of jealousy.

Sometimes he was so self-contained that she wondered if she aroused any feelings in him at all.

They were studying the menu when the sound of loud, laughing voices invaded the dining room. Susan's back was to the entrance but she didn't need to turn around to learn who had entered.

"Oh, no," Warren exclaimed with disgust. "It's that guy Braden again and his buddies! The hostess is leading them this way. Pretend not to notice them, Susan."

How could anyone fail to notice the boisterous group coming nearer? Susan tried to obey Warren's crisp command by concentrating on the list of entrees, but as the men filed past their table, she couldn't resist peering above the leather-bound menu.

There were six men in the group, counting Mitch Braden. If he had noticed Susan and Warren, there was no indication of it now. He was laughing at some comment from the gangly youth bringing up the rear. It was an odd assortment, average men running from short to tall, skinny to thin, young to old. None of them possessed the strikingly handsome looks of the man leading the way.

The large table the hostess led them to was not far away from Susan and Warren. Susan breathed a silent sigh of relief when Mitch Braden took a chair that faced away from them. She doubted if she could have eaten with him watching her at his leisure. Warren, too, seemed to relax.

After hearing Susan's choice for her meal, Warren gave the waiter their order, spending a few minutes choosing a wine from the dining room's wine list. He prided himself on being a connoisseur with very discriminating tastes, but Susan had difficulty telling one wine from another.

When the main course was served, the waiter uncorked the chilled bottle and offered a tasting portion to Warren. ''Sir—'' the waiter began.

''This isn't the wine I ordered,'' Warren interrupted immediately, not allowing the man a chance to finish. He reached for the bottle still in the waiter's hands. ''This wine wasn't even on your list.''

''No, sir,'' the waiter agreed. ''It's from the owner's private stock. Compliments of the gentleman at the large table.'' Mitch Braden. Both Warren and Susan darted a look at him. He had turned in his chair and briefly inclined his head in acknowledgment.

''The owner?'' Susan breathed, glancing curiously at the waiter.

''He's a friend of the owner, I believe,'' was the courteous reply.

Indecision held Warren silent for an instant. Susan guessed that he wanted to refuse the wine. It must have been an excellent vintage because he did not.

''Please thank the gentleman for us,'' Warren said tautly.

''Of course, sir''

Perhaps if Mitch Braden had not sent the wine to their table, Susan might have been better able to ignore his presence in the dining room. As it was, her eyes strayed often to his table, focusing on his lean masculine form and the dark, golden-toast shade of his hair. Never once during the entire meal did she encounter the laughing blue eyes with the crinkled lines at the corners.

There was constant laughter and chatter from the table of six. In comparison the silence between Susan and Warren seemed unnatural. But Warren didn't care for any discussions during a meal. The time for talk was before or after, but never during a meal. By the time coffee was served, a tiny pain had begun to hammer at her temples, from tension, Susan guessed.

More laughter punctuated the air, coming from Mitch Braden's table. Warren cast a censorious look in that direction.

"It would have been an excellent meal if the atmosphere had been more peaceful," he commented.

Lifting her chin slightly, Susan refused to let her gaze wander to the other table. "I imagine the only place you can be absolutely sure of eating a quiet meal is in your own home."

"True enough," Warren agreed dryly. "Are we ready to leave?" At Susan's nod, he signaled their waiter for the bill. When he rose and walked to the back of her chair, Susan noticed one of the men nudge Mitch Braden. She could barely see his lips move, but she knew instinctively that he was telling Mitch that she and Warren were leaving. One shoulder lifted in an uncaring gesture and some comment was made in response by the man. A stout, balding man guffawed and said, "When did that ever stop you?" Mitch Braden's low answer brought laughter from the rest of the group.

Holding her breath for fear he might have heard the exchange too, Susan glanced swiftly at Warren. He merely looked inquiringly back and she smiled with false brightness.

From the restaurant, Warren drove her straight

home with no stops in between. It was a weeknight, which meant that they both had to be at the office in the morning. Warren didn't believe in keeping late hours when he had to work the next day. For that matter, neither did Susan. On Tuesdays and Thursdays, the only weeknights they went out, it was strictly for dinner, then home. The weekends were quite different.

This night Susan was glad to have the evening end quickly. It hadn't been as enjoyable as other outings—mostly because of Mitch Braden.

Their good-night embrace in the parked car outside her home didn't last long. Lingering kisses were saved for the weekends when they had more time to indulge in them. At those times, Warren was masterful and passionate. Susan had never considered it odd that those were the times when she was most aware she loved him.

Only when she was in the house and watching his car drive away did she wish for the first time that the pattern of their relationship hadn't become so predictable. A surprise now and then would be nice.

Of course, Mitch Braden, whoever he was, had provided a surprise this night and it hadn't been so nice. Oh, Warren had displayed jealousy, but Susan still wished that the encounter had never occurred. Just why she wished that, she didn't know.

"Is that you, Susan?" her mother called.

She turned away from the window. "Yes, Mom, it's me," she answered, before shedding her spring coat and hanging it in the closet. She walked down the hallway to the large family room.

"Hello, honey, did you have a nice time?" Her

father, Dr. Simon Mabry, greeted her with a wave as she entered the room. His burly frame was settled into a reclining chair, a medical magazine unopened on his lap.

"Of course." Susan smiled.

"Is *he* here?" Her younger brother Greg, a week away from turning seventeen, twisted away from the television set and MTV's latest bikini-and-baby-oil party to glance at her.

"No, Warren didn't come in tonight." Susan picked up a pillow from the couch and then threw it at her brother's lanky frame sprawled on the floor. Warren and Greg had disliked each other on first sight and the months since their first meeting hadn't changed either's opinion.

"Ouch, Mom! You're pulling my hair!" the youngest of the Mabrys exclaimed angrily—Amy, age thirteen.

"Well, if you would just hold still . . ." Beth Mabry sighed.

"You'd pull out every hair in my head," Amy squeaked, her hands moving protectively to her long auburn hair.

"I have to get the tangles out somehow, unless you'd rather do it yourself." Beth firmly pulled her young daughter closer to her chair. "After all, you were the one who got into this mess, climbing that tree like a tomboy."

"I told you," Amy protested with an innocent look. "I had to get Peggy Fraser's kitten. Ouch!"

"Want me to comb it for you, Amy?" Susan offered, knowing the tug-of-war could go on for a while between her mother and her little sister. As her mother had put it the night before when she and Amy had argued, Amy was "going through that difficult stage," crazy about boys and becoming a woman but not quite able to stop climbing trees.

"Oh, yes, please, Susan!" Amy agreed fervently.

"Will you guys pipe down?" Greg protested impatiently. "I'm trying to watch MTV Spring Break, and this babe's really hot." He stared fixedly at a girl wearing very little besides a thong and a tan until his father swatted him gently with the rolled-up magazine.

"Don't you have homework to do or something?"

Greg nodded vigorously. "This is my homework."

"Amy, keep it to a low roar." Simon Mabry sighed.

"Greg's getting much too bossy, Dad." Amy stuck out her tongue at her brother as she walked to the couch where Susan sat.

Slowly and carefully working the snarls free from Amy's hair, Susan smiled to herself. It was no wonder that Warren found it difficult to relax when he came here. He had been an only child and the constant wrangling that went on between brother and sister and parent was something he couldn't accept. He would adjust to it when they started having children of their own.

Her father commandeered the remote and switched to a police drama. Susan managed to grasp most of the storyline without giving the picture her complete attention. The local Indianapolis news came on as she brushed the last snarl from Amy's long hair. She listened to the headlines and the weather, but when the subject shifted to sports, Susan uncrossed her legs and stood up.

A familiar face appeared on the television screen. She stared at it in disbelief. It was Mitch Braden, the man she had so disastrously met with Warren tonight. Only on television he wasn't wearing that perfectly tailored suit and vest. He wore a T-shirt that stretched like a second skin over his chest and snug-fitting Levis. The interview was being taped outside and the wind was ruffling the dark, tawny gold of his hair.

"Is . . . is that Mitch Braden?" Susan forced the question out, too stunned to hear what the sports anchor was saying,

"Yep," Greg replied. "He's totally awesome."

The smiling, handsome face left the screen and a rundown of baseball scores began.

"Who is he?"

"Dude, he's Mitch Braden." Greg frowned at the dumbness of the question.

"Don't call your sister dude," Beth said automatically.

"Mom, it's just an expression."

"But—what does he do?" Susan asked hesitantly.

"What does he *do*?" Greg exclaimed with a taunting hoot. "He's just about the most famous race car driver around. He's in town for the Indy 500 Memorial Day race. What does he do? Boy, what a dumb sister!"

"I thought he looked familiar," she commented, but more to herself than anyone in the room.

"Well, you just saw him on the television screen." Greg shook his head in despair at her strange remark.

"No, I mean tonight at the restaurant," Susan explained absently, still slightly stunned that Mitch

Braden had turned out to be such a famous personality.

"You saw him? You saw Mitch Braden?" Her brother bounded to his feet. "Did you get his autograph? Did you talk to him?"

"Well, yes, I talked to him in a way, but I didn't recognize him. I knew he looked familiar but I didn't know why."

"You didn't get his autograph!" Greg moaned. "I can't believe it."

"Mostly he talked to Warren," Susan answered truthfully enough, wishing suddenly that she hadn't mentioned that she had seen him. "He's good-looking." More so than on camera, she thought silently, because videotape couldn't capture the magnetism he exuded.

Her father included himself in the conversation with a slight clearing of his throat. "I wasn't aware that Warren was acquainted with anyone involved with the Indy 500. Let alone a champion like Mitch Braden."

Greg's hair, a dark brown like Susan's, fell shaggily across his forehead. He flipped it away from his eyes with his hand. "Me neither," he agreed forcefully.

Susan bit into her lower lip. She wasn't about to explain what had really happened. "Warren doesn't know him."

"You said he talked to him."

"They were simply in the same restaurant at the same time." Susan walked across the room, hoping for an end to the uncomfortable subject. "It was just a case of two strangers exchanging casual conversation. I wouldn't even have mentioned it if I'd known I was going to get the third degree." She started for the hall with Greg dogging her heels.

"Don't suppose Wonder Warren knew who Mitch Braden was either."

"Will you stop insulting my fiancé?" Susan demanded impatiently. "And no, he didn't know who he was any more than I did."

"That figures," Greg responded derisively.

Sometimes she regretted her decision to live at home after college, and this was one of those times. Her kid brother knew just how to push her buttons, and something inside her snapped.

"There are more important things in the world, Greg—" Susan stamped her foot on the floor, knowing that it was a childish action for someone approaching her twenty-fourth birthday but doing it anyway, "—than knowing some idiot who drives around a racetrack at a hundred and fifty miles per hour."

"Yeah?" her brother challenged.

"Greg!" came her mother's warning voice.

"Ah, gee, Mom." He turned impatiently away from Susan. "There's only a chance in a million of meeting someone like Mitch Braden and my sister blew it!"

Susan didn't wait to hear what arguments her mother would offer on her behalf. She escaped to her room while she had the chance, knowing that she probably hadn't heard the last of her brother's recriminations—or Mitch Braden's name.

Chapter Two

"Susan, is my son busy?"

Glancing up from her computer screen, Susan encountered the solemn face of Robert Sullivan, the senior partner of the law firm and Warren's father. The resemblance between the two was striking. Both were tall and ruggedly handsome, though Warren's hair was jet black while his father's had turned iron gray.

"Yes, he is," she nodded. "You can go on in, Mr. Sullivan." She gestured fleetingly toward the closed interoffice door behind her, wondering if she would ever be able to address the man less formally even after she and Warren were married. Robert Sullivan always seemed so remote and unapproachable, the way Warren did sometimes.

With a sigh, Susan turned back toward the computer screen, rereading the last page of the corporate agreement for typos and any other mistakes.

Warren had spent a small fortune on the latest in legal software but she still made it a habit to check everything twice. Satisfied that there were no errors, she clicked Save and then Print, and waited while the printer churned out copies. The hall door opened as she started to staple the multi-page document together.

"Hi." Greg ambled into her office, hands stuffed into the pockets of his baggy sweatshirt.

"Hello." Her surprise at his unexpected appearance was clear in her voice. "What are you doing downtown?"

"I had to take care of my car insurance," he answered with a shrug of his shoulders. "Thought I'd stop by to see if you wanted a ride home."

Susan glanced at her watch. It was only a few minutes before five o'clock, which was her normal leaving time. "Warren was going to take me home, but—" She looked at the closed interoffice door. With his father in there, there was no telling how long he would be tied up.

"Oh, that's okay. I just thought I'd check." Greg started to turn back toward the hall door.

"Greg?" The atmosphere had been tense between Susan and her brother since she had lost her temper two nights before after his disparaging reference to Warren. She guessed his offer of a ride was a conciliatory gesture. He stopped and pivoted toward her. "I'm not sure—" she began, only to come to a halt as the door to Warren's office opened.

"Susan . . ." Warren walked in, an absent frown clouding his wide forehead. At the sight of her brother, he paused and nodded. "Hello, Gregory. I didn't expect to see you here."

Susan knew how much her brother disliked the use of his full name. No matter how tactfully she mentioned it to Warren, he still persisted in using it.

"I stopped to see if Susan needed a ride home," her brother explained tautly. His chin was thrust defiantly forward and there was a belligerent darkness in the gaze that met Warren's.

"Well, that's opportune." He smiled coldly, and Susan despaired of the two ever becoming friends. Warren's obsidian eyes looked toward her. "I was just coming in to suggest that it might be better if you left without me. My father and I have some legal work to go over, cases I have to handle while he's in the hospital. It might take considerable time."

"I understand." She smiled. "I'll go home with Greg." She hesitated, not wanting to mention dinner that evening since he hadn't. "What about dinner tonight?"

"I'll phone you at home. I don't know how long I'll be," he answered, not expressing any regret in words or his tone of voice that their plans for the evening might be canceled.

"Of course." Susan turned away, a barely audible sigh of disappointment escaping with the words she spoke.

"Since Gregory is already here and it's nearly five, you might as well leave whenever you've straightened up," Warren stated in dismissal.

"I've finished the Hoxworth agreement," she said, picking up the document she had just stapled together. "Did you want it now or in the morning?"

"I'll take it now." He reached for the papers in

her hands, briefly leafing through them as he turned again toward his office.

"I heard you met Mitch Braden the other night," Greg spoke up unexpectedly.

Warren stopped short and glanced piercingly over his shoulder at Susan, condemnation in his look.

"I forgot to mention to you, Warren," Susan hastened to explain how Greg had known about their meeting with Mitch Braden, "why he looked so familiar to me. Mitch Braden is a race car driver. He's in town for the Indianapolis 500 race."

"A race car driver?" There was a faintly contemptuous curl to Warren's mouth. "I suppose that explains his behavior."

When the door to his office had closed behind Warren, Susan could feel Greg's eyes watching her. "What did he mean by that?" he asked finally.

She didn't look up but continued clearing her desk in preparation to leave. "Let's just say that your idol Mitch Braden behaved a little rudely the other night and leave it at that."

"With a snob like your boyfriend, I wouldn't blame him," her brother retorted.

Susan counted slowly to ten. "You don't know what you're talking about and Warren is not a snob," she replied patiently. "And I have no intention of arguing about it or discussing it any further. Okay?"

"Okay," Greg said grudgingly.

A quarter of an hour later, Susan was gingerly sliding into the passenger seat of Greg's vintage Chevrolet, a tactful term for a worn-out used car. She carefully avoided the jutting edge of broken plastic ribbing on the seat that was trying to snag her pantyhose.

"I thought you were going to buy new covers for the seats," she commented as she brushed her olive-and-black plaid skirt.

Her brother grinned and turned the key in the ignition. "I'm hoping Mom and Dad will buy them as a birthday present. Then I can use the money I saved to buy some hubcaps."

"Maybe you should just save up for a down payment on a new car," Susan suggested when the motor grudgingly growled to life. "It might be a better investment."

"This car is practically an antique. It's going to be worth a lot of money someday."

"Yes, but will it be worth as much money as you put into it? That's the question," she teased, but with a thread of seriousness.

"She runs like a top," Greg said defensively.

Her brother was almost fanatic about his beloved Chevrolet. He and his friends spent hours tinkering with it after school and on weekends. As they merged into rush hour traffic on the freeway en route to their home on the outskirts of Indianapolis, Susan admitted that outside of a grumbling reluctance to start, the car ran quite well.

They were nearly halfway home when Greg murmured a worried "Uh-oh," and began to edge the car into the outside lane of traffic.

Susan glanced curiously at his troubled frown. "What's wrong?"

"The engine's overheating," he answered, slowing the car to a stop on the wide shoulder of the freeway.

"Why?"

"That's what I'm about to find out," Greg answered grimly as he opened his door and walked to the front of the car to raise the hood. "Do you have a cell phone?"

A misty gray cloud swirled into the air when the hood came up. Alarmed, Susan realized that she had left her cell phone on her desk. Whatever the problem was, they were stuck here for the time being. She quickly opened her door and joined her cursing brother now standing several steps from the front of the car. "Is it on fire?" she asked anxiously, not seeing any flames that might be causing the smoke.

"No, that's steam," he sighed heavily. "The radiator hose has a leak."

"Can you fix it?" Susan followed Greg as he moved closer to inspect the problem when most of the steam had dissipated. She was careful not to come too close to the car in case the condensing vapor stained her skirt or the tailored jacket in matching olive green.

"Even if I could fix it temporarily," he grumbled, "there isn't any place to get water to replace what the radiator has lost, which looks like about all of it."

"Which means?"

Greg propped his hands on his hips and looked disgustedly past the car in the direction they had just come. "Means I'm going to have to hike to that service station a mile and a half back, and see if they have a tow truck. And that means I'm going to have to spend the money I was saving for my hubcaps."

"Greg, I'm sorry," Susan offered sympathetically. "I'll pay the towing fee as part of your birthday present. I—"

"Hello, Susan. Are you having trouble?"

Whirling around, Susan felt her heart skip a beat as she saw the winning smile of Mitch Braden. His supple, rolling walk was carrying him from the cobalt blue sportscar parked ahead of theirs.

She noticed absently that his twinkling eyes just about matched the color of his car or vice versa, but mostly Susan simply felt stunned amazement. The traffic had been so heavy that she hadn't noticed any cars even slowing in response to their breakdown, let alone hear one stop.

"How . . . how did you know it was me?" she breathed, still in a state of confused astonishment.

His gaze swept her from head to toe and back. "I pride myself on never forgetting a figure," he grinned wickedly, "or a face."

His suggestive reply disturbed her heartbeat, making it pulse much too fast. Susan turned away, momentarily unable to counter his remark. Out of the corner of her eye, she caught a glimpse of her brother's open-mouthed stare, as if he couldn't believe his eyes. For that matter, neither could she. Who would ever have dreamed of Mitch Braden stopping to help?

A sickening thought knotted her stomach. What if he mentioned her supposed marriage to Warren in front of Greg? She would never be able to endure that man's mockery if he learned Warren had lied.

"What's the problem?" Mitch Braden was directly behind her, his voice low and amused.

"Oh . . . er . . . a leak in the radiator hose." Greg pulled himself out of his trance with a supreme effort.

Mitch Braden leaned forward to look under the hood and verify the problem. Susan moved quickly to the side of the car. The man was a wolf. She wasn't going to allow any accidental physical contact between them—he would be too quick to find a way to take advantage of it.

He straightened, his expression serious as he darted her a twinkling look. "It's a busted hose, all right."

"Hey, I never introduced myself. I'm Greg Mabry, Susan's brother." Greg's words came out in a rush, as the shock of meeting a world-famous race car driver finally wore off. "Boy, I can't believe I'm actually meeting you in person, Mr. Braden. I've watched you drive hundreds of times, on television mostly, but—wow, this is really a thrill for me!"

"I'm happy to meet you, too, Greg." Mitch Braden offered his hand, which Greg shook with obvious enthusiasm.

"Well, this was worth breaking down for," her brother said with a grin, a quaking excitement trembling beneath the surface of his voice as if he still wasn't sure this was really happening to him. "I was mad because my sister forgot her cell phone but now—"

Mitch nodded. "And the battery on mine just went dead."

Yeah, right, thought Susan furiously. "Greg, it's getting late." It was high time someone reminded him of the problem at hand.

"What?" He looked at her blankly for an instant. "Oh, yeah."

Mitch Braden decided to take charge. "Greg, what if I give you a lift to the nearest service station and we'll make arrangements to have your car towed in?''

"Would you?" Greg breathed excitedly. "I mean—wow, dude, that would be terrific!"

Susan felt an overwhelming desire to give her brother a hard shake. His blatant hero-worship of the man was getting on her nerves. More than that, however, she wanted to bring this meeting to an end.

"Lock up your car and we'll go," the man ordered easily.

"There's no need to," Susan said quickly. "I'll stay here and keep an eye on it until Greg comes back with the tow truck guy."

"I can't let you do that." Mitch Braden shook his head, a mocking glint in his blue eyes. "A beautiful woman like you, stranded on a highway, that would be asking for trouble. I would never be able to face your husband if something happened to you while your brother and I were gone."

Husband. There it was. And Greg picked up on it immediately as Susan's heart sank to her toes.

"Husband?" He frowned. "Susan isn't married."

There was no mistaking the gleam in Mitch Braden's eyes as they swung to Greg. "She isn't? This Warren—"

"That creep!" her brother grunted.

"Greg!" Susan warned through gritted teeth.

He paid no attention to her. "She's engaged to him all right," her brother acknowledged in the same contemptuous voice, "but she isn't married to him yet"

"Doesn't sound like you're exactly in favor of the marriage," Mitch Braden observed.

"That's putting it mildly," Greg replied, indifferent to his sister's daggers.

"Maybe you and I will have to join forces to see what we can do about it," Mitch suggested with a crooked smile.

"That's a good idea," her brother laughed, suddenly seeing himself in the role of matchmaker and liking the idea of Susan and Mitch Braden together.

"If you don't mind—" Anger trembled through her into her voice.

"You're right." Mitch Braden nodded, his brown hair glinting golden as it caught the fire of the setting sun. "This conversation isn't getting your car fixed."

"Right," Greg agreed. "I'll lock up."

He shut the hood and walked around to the driver's side to lock the doors. Susan wanted to dig her heels in and refuse to leave the car. Meeting Mitch's challenging look, she knew she couldn't leave Greg alone with him. There was no telling what kind of a scheme he would talk her gullible younger brother into trying.

Her brown eyes snapped with frustrated anger as she stalked past him to the blue sportscar. Of all the motorists on the highway, why had he been the one to stop? She paused beside the passenger door of the low-slung sportscar and Mitch Braden was instantly beside her, his lazy, rolling stride covering ground with surprising swiftness.

"You'll have to wait for your brother," he murmured in a mocking tone. "It'll be easier for him to crawl into the back than for you with your skirt."

She stared through the tinted glass window at the bucket seats in front of the half-seat behind them. What he said was irritatingly correct, and Susan wondered why he couldn't drive a car with full seats front and back. Impatiently she glanced back to see her brother jogging toward them. His eyes widened in admiration as he approached the sportscar.

"A Ferrari!" Greg whistled, touching the shiny blue surface almost reverently.

"She's a beauty, isn't she?" Mitch smiled understandingly as he opened the door.

"I'll say!" her brother agreed fervently, ducking his head inside to look around before crawling automatically into the compartment behind the bucket seats.

Susan's lips tightened grimly as she slid into the bucket seat, keeping her gaze straight ahead while Mitch closed the door. She picked up the cell phone on the dash as he went around the car and turned it on for a second, just to see if he'd been telling the truth. The little screen stayed black . . . the battery was indeed dead. She put it back quickly, hoping he hadn't seen. Score one for Mitch.

She was squeezed to the right as Greg leaned forward to inspect the instrument panel, a marvel of state-of-the-art automotive engineering, and the gearshift on the floor between the two seats.

"Awesome," he said breathlessly. "I've only seen these babies in magazines. Now I'm actually in one. My wildest dream just came true."

Mitch grinned and slipped behind the wheel, turning the key in the ignition and savoring the sound of the powerful motor roaring to life. "This one has been modified to meet United States emissions standards," he explained solemnly.

As if her little brother cared, Susan thought. Anything that vroomed impressed him. But she refused to seem in the least impressed, instead looking uninterestedly out the window. The car accelerated quickly into the main stream of traffic, the hand near her thigh smoothly shifting the gears. She sat very still in prim silence.

"I saw you on television the other night," Greg offered after they had traveled some distance.

"Did you?" Mitch responded absently as if it was a commonplace occurrence that didn't warrant any special mention.

"How do you think you'll do in the time trials for the Indy 500?"

"If the car keeps running the way it did today, it ought to finish somewhere up in the top ten," he replied.

"The Indy Web site says you have the fastest car," Greg pointed out.

"Maybe," Mitch shrugged, "but a race as long as the Indy 500 is unpredictable. Just owning the fastest car doesn't mean winning is a sure thing."

"Yeah," her brother agreed eagerly. "A lot depends on the driver behind the wheel and you're the best driver on the circuit."

"With you and luck on my side" Mitch grinned, "I won't need a cheering section to win. Of course, there are some other guys in the race who are just as hell-bent on making that victory lap as I am. And a couple of women, too."

Even Susan had heard of them and had to admire their courage—both for entering the race and going up against arrogant superstars like Mitch Braden. But she said nothing and just let Greg do the talking.

"Hey, forget about them. You'll win. I know it."

"Greg, if I do, you can come down to the winner's circle and help me and my pit crew pour the champagne. But no drinking the stuff."

Susan forgot her annoyance for a moment, and wondered at his friendliness and lack of pretension. Racing was big, big business in Indianapolis and elsewhere, with millions of dollars in sponsorships and endorsements going to the winners, as well as the prize money. Yet Mitch talked to Greg as if he were a member of the family. . . . Don't go there, she told herself sternly.

Mitch chuckled at something her brother had just said. Susan reluctantly acknowledged to herself that it was an attractive sound, warm and caressing like his voice. Her fingers tightened on the handle of her purse, not wanting to like anything about this man.

Out of the corner of her eye, she studied the strong hands gripping the wheel. Muscles rippled in the tan arms, bare below the short sleeves of his shirt. She considered the strength that the fingers, hands and arms had to possess to manhandle a race car traveling a hundred eighty miles or more.

Yet something told her they could be gentle, too. The prospect of them ever touching her with that gentleness was disturbing and she mentally shook the thought away. They had made the turnaround on the highway and were driving into the station that had been Greg's destination when he had intended to walk for help. Cutting the motor, Mitch stepped from the car and Greg scrambled over the driver's seat to follow him.

Taking a step, Greg turned back, glancing into the car at Susan. "You might as well wait here until I find out whether they can help me now."

Susan had turned slightly, reaching for the door handle, but at her brother's words she subsided into the molding cushions of the leather seat. With Mitch Braden there, they would receive speedy service, she thought with a sigh.

The cynicism in the thought surprised her. What was there about the man that acted on her like two opposing fields of a magnet? She was unquestionably drawn by his charm and stunning looks. It was only natural that she found him physically attractive.

Yet something inside her insisted that she keep a safe distance from Mitch Braden. Susan wanted to believe it was a sense of fidelity to Warren, but that was only a part of it. There was a feeling of guilt, too, that she would be attracted to a man who was not her fiancé.

Propping her elbow on the door, she rested her chin in her hand, trying to discern why she couldn't bring herself to trust Mitch Braden, and why she was so determined not to let herself like him.

The door on the driver's side was opened. Susan turned with a start as Mitch slid behind the wheel and closed the door. The motor growled at the turn of the ignition key and he shifted the gear into reverse.

"Where's Greg?" Susan looked frantically for her brother.

Deftly they had turned around, the car fluidly changing from a reverse motion to forward with barely a break. The car was responsive to Mitch

Braden's slightest touch, its power an extension of the man who commanded it. Turning in her seat to look out the rear window, she saw Greg waving a casual good-bye.

"It'll be ten minutes before the tow truck driver can get your brother's car," Mitch finally explained when her frantic gaze riveted itself on his profile. "Then they still have to install the new hose. I offered to give you a ride home."

"Don't I have some say in it?" Susan protested with astonishment at his high-handed manner.

"I have your brother's permission." He sent her a wicked smile. "And I thought by the time you had finished all your objections about why you didn't want to ride with me, I would have you home."

Susan breathed in deeply and finally expelled the breath in a frustrated, angry sigh.

"What's the matter?" he mocked. "Don't you think I'll take you straight home?"

"Will you?" she returned acidly.

"No side trips," Mitch assured her with a mock promise, his blue eyes sparkling with an audacious light. "Of course with such precious cargo, I'll take my time."

"I think, Mr. Braden, that you're impossible," she retorted tightly.

"Call me Mitch. And what warm-blooded male would deprive himself of such beautiful company sooner than he had to?" He grinned.

Susan turned her head away, a faint warmth creeping into her limbs. She had to remind herself how easily he issued compliments. She mustn't let them go to her head.

"Would you please not talk to me that way?" she

requested icily, her fingers nervously clutching the purse in her lap.

"You don't like me to say that I think you're beautiful, is that it?" He rephrased the compliment with infuriating calm.

"That's it," she tried to reply in the same vein.

"Okay," Mitch agreed with a faint shrug.

They drove for a time in a silence that was unnerving for Susan. She simply couldn't seem to relax. Every muscle was taut with her inner tension.

"Do you know something, Susan?" he spoke finally in a thoughtful tone. "You're the first woman who's kissed me today."

"That must be a record," was her initial reply, until she realized what he had said. Her head pivoted sharply to stare at him. "I haven't kissed you!"

"Haven't you?" A wicked light flickered in his brief glance. "That's okay, there's still time."

"In case you've forgotten, Mr. Braden," she snapped, "I am engaged."

"But you're not married," he reminded her. "Why do you suppose your fiancé told me you were?"

An uncomfortable flush began to warm her cheeks, and she averted her face so he wouldn't see.

"I really wouldn't know," she answered haughtily.

"Maybe he didn't feel secure enough about your affection to risk any competition?" Mitch suggested.

"Warren is very much aware of how much I love him and how eagerly I look forward to our marriage," Susan told him in no uncertain terms.

"But to claim you were married?" An eyebrow

arched with faint arrogance. "Surely it would have been enough to admit that you were engaged."

"Unfortunately, Warren couldn't guess that you wouldn't respect the bonds of matrimony any more than an engagement ring," she flashed.

"Hey!" He laughed softly. "You're aiming those blows below the belt, aren't you?"

She tilted her head to the side in defiant challenge. "I thought I was only speaking the truth."

"You don't think much of me, do you?" drawled Mitch.

"Actually, I don't think of you at all," she said coolly.

"Ooh—ouch!" He made a mock grimace of pain. "Now you really are trying to upset my ego!"

"I think it's of sufficient size not to suffer any lasting harm."

Susan directed her gaze out the window at the rows of homes on the residential street. "Our house is the two-story brick home, the second from the corner on the next block."

Mitch Braden didn't comment as he swung the car into the driveway, stopping in front of the two-car garage. Her hand had closed over the metal door handle when her other wrist was seized.

"Will you let me go?" She looked at him coldly.

"You remind me of a racing car," he said thoughtfully, his gaze sweeping her appraisingly. "All classic design and beautiful to look at, with a lot of fire under the hood. Fire that could be amazingly responsive with the right man at the controls."

Her pulse thudded a little faster. It was impossible to remain passive any longer and she strained to free her wrist from his firm grip. Applying only the slightest pressure, Mitch pulled her toward him.

His other hand reached out to cup the back of her neck, entangling itself in the silky curtain of her dark hair. "You forgot to kiss me, Susan," he said softly.

Susan forgot to struggle as the sensual line of his mouth moved closer. Then it was closing warmly over hers and her lashes fluttered down, the craziest sensation rocking her body. Almost before the kiss began, he was ending it, moving away to his own side of the car.

She blinked at him once and turned hurriedly away, opening the car door quickly, needing desperately to escape his presence. It only occurred to her when she was standing in the driveway, the car door slammed shut, that she should have slapped him for taking such liberties when he knew she was engaged.

But of course she should have offered some sort of protest, too. Slapping him after the fact would have been equal to locking the door after the house had been burglarized.

The driver's door opened and closed, too. Susan stared in disbelief when Mitch Braden walked around the car to her side.

"I'm home now. You can leave any time," she said huskily.

The grooves around his mouth deepened although he didn't actually smile. "I promised Greg I would stick around until he came back. I think he intends to invite me to dinner. Naturally I'll accept."

Susan breathed in sharply, ready to demand that he leave. At that same moment a car pulled into the drive. A quick glance said it was her father. Recognition of Mitch Braden was already flashing in his face, and Susan knew any hope that she would soon be rid of this man was lost.

Chapter Three

An explanation as to why Mitch Braden had brought Susan home had been required by her father as well as an introduction. Then Susan had had to repeat the same thing again for her mother with an added word from Mitch that Greg had asked him to stay until he returned. The expected invitation to dinner had immediately come from Beth Mabry.

The glitter in the blue eyes had mocked Susan's tight-lipped expression as Mitch Braden had murmured politely that he didn't want to inconvenience Mrs. Mabry before he allowed himself to be talked into staying.

It had irritated Susan, the way her mother treated him like visiting royalty. Amy hadn't been much better, practically swooning at his feet when she saw him, as if he were a movie star. Her father had seemed to be the only one in her family to react normally, but then few things had ever ruffled him.

As for Susan, she had made an escape to the privacy of her room as soon as she decently could. Changing out of her office clothes, she had donned a cotton robe of cranberry red, offering a silent prayer that Warren's meeting with his father would not cancel their dinner. The digital clock at her bedside had displayed the passing minutes with infuriating slowness.

Downstairs the telephone rang. She unconsciously held her breath until her mother called, "Susan, it's for you!"

It had to be Warren. With fingers crossed, she hurried down the stairs, the long robe swinging about her ankles. Her mother was near the base of the stairs in the living room alcove that served as an entrance hall, the phone was in her hand.

"It's Warren," she told Susan. "You aren't going out tonight, are you? Not with Mr. Braden staying for dinner?"

"Mitch Braden is Greg's guest, not mine," Susan answered airily, reaching to take the receiver from her mother's hand. Her moving gaze was caught by the man seated in the living room talking with her father. She quickly turned her back on the secretly amused gleam as she brought the telephone to her ear.

"Hello, darling," she spoke into the mouthpiece with forced brightness.

Her greeting was not returned. Instead, Warren's harsh voice demanded, "What did your mother just say? What was that about Mitch Braden staying for dinner?"

"That's right," Susan breathed softly and hesitantly.

"What's he doing there?"

"I'll . . . I'll explain later," she stalled.

"Does he know—of course he knows," Warren answered his own half-spoken question in a disgusted voice. But Susan knew what he had been going to ask, whether Mitch had learned they weren't married. "Has he been bothering you?"

"No, of course not." That was a lie, but the last thing Susan wanted was for Warren to make a scene. "What about dinner this evening? Will you be free?" There was a slightly desperate ring to her voice in spite of her effort to reassure him that everything was all right.

Warren hesitated. "Yes," he said, then more firmly, "Yes, I'll be free. I'll be at your house in the time it takes me to drive from the office."

"I'll be ready," she promised, knowing that didn't give her a great deal of time.

"See you then," he said with his usual clipped shortness, and hung up.

After Susan replaced the receiver in its cradle, her mother approached again. "Susan—?" she began.

"Excuse me. Mom," Susan interrupted quickly, "but Warren is on his way here now and I don't have much time to get ready."

Without giving her mother a chance to reply, she hurried up the stairs to her room. The cranberry-colored robe was tossed onto the bed and a classically straight dress of beige knit was taken from the clothes closet.

Dressing in record time, Susan dashed to the single bathroom on the second floor to repair her makeup. Amy was there in front of the mirror, carefully stroking her eyebrows with a tiny brush.

"Do you mind, Amy?" Susan said impatiently. "I have to get ready. Warren will be here any minute."

Her sister stepped sideways so she would be occupying only one small corner of the mirror. "No, go ahead. You can use the mirror, too." She set the brush in the makeup tray and picked up a tube of lip gloss.

Susan shook her head in despair and made use of her larger portion of the mirror. Sharing the bathroom with her teenage sister was something she probably should start becoming accustomed to.

"Do you think Mom would notice if I used some mascara?" Amy asked thoughtfully as she touched the corner of her mouth where some gloss had smeared.

"I'm sure she would," Susan answered, hiding a smile while she remembered how eager she had been to wear makeup.

Amy sighed and picked up the hairbrush to run it through her long auburn hair. "He likes long hair. Did you know that?"

A tiny frown of confusion knitted her eyebrows as Susan glanced curiously at Amy's reflection in the mirror. "Who's 'he'?" she asked, retouching her eyeshadow.

"Mitch," was the prompt answer. "He asked me to call him Mitch."

"He did?" Susan responded dryly.

"Yes." Amy leaned forward to fluff her bangs. "He said he had a fondness for redheads, too. Of course, he said there was nothing wrong with brunettes," she hastened to add as if suddenly worried that Susan might have felt insulted.

"I think Mitch Braden likes women, period." Susan added a touch of peach blusher to her cheekbones, unable to keep the sarcasm out of her voice.

"Well, women like him, so I guess that makes the feeling mutual," Amy declared with an airy toss of her head. "I suppose I'd better get downstairs. Mom is almost ready to put the food on the table."

That was an understatement, Susan thought as her sister went out of the room. Mitch Braden's sex appeal seemed to know no age barriers either. Her thirteen-year-old sister had just toppled under the spell of his charm. Unless she was careful, there was no telling who might be next.

When she was finished, Susan didn't go downstairs to wait for Warren. She chose to watch for him from her bedroom window that faced the street. As soon as she saw his car drive up, she hurried downstairs to the front door, calling good-bye to her family in the dining room.

There was a chorus of answering good-byes including Mitch Braden's mocking, "Have a good time, Susan."

Warren had just emerged from his car when she darted out the front door. She saw him eye the blue sportscar in the driveway and the black scowl that had appeared instantaneously on his face.

"I suppose that's his car," he said contemptuously as he held the passenger door open for Susan.

"Yes." She nodded.

"It's disgusting the amount of money those racing drivers win," he muttered almost beneath his breath. He closed Susan's door and walked around to the driver's side, but didn't speak again until he was behind the wheel and they were driving away from the house. "Now tell me how you ran into that Indy man again," he commanded.

For the third time Susan repeated the story about Greg's car breaking down and Mitch Braden's arrival to help. Then she tacked on Greg's request that Mitch wait at the house for him and her mother's subsequent invitation to dinner.

"What did he say to you?" Warren asked when she had finished.

Susan glanced at his stern profile with some confusion. "When?"

"When he found out about—the marriage thing?"

Taking a deep, considering breath, Susan knew she couldn't repeat Mitch's response, so she chose to lie tactfully instead. "When he said he thought I was married, I simply told him that he had misunderstood you. That what you'd actually said was that I was to *be* your wife."

"Good thinking." The look in his dark eyes was almost grateful, except Warren was much too proud. "I should have known I could count on you."

The topic of Mitch Braden was dropped for the time being, although Susan longed to ask why Warren had lied in the beginning. Yet his name cropped up the entire evening, usually in derogatory comments made by Warren. Fortunately the blue sportscar was gone when Warren brought her home.

At the office the following morning, Warren questioned her very thoroughly about what her family had told Susan concerning Mitch's visit.

Since Susan had not questioned them herself, she could answer very little. She had gathered the impression that possibly Greg planned to see Mitch Braden again, but since she wasn't positive of that, she didn't tell Warren.

By Saturday evening Warren seemed to have forgotten Mitch Braden's existence completely. Susan was relieved because she had been uneasy discussing him with Warren. She constantly felt she had to be on guard in case something slipped. And she didn't want to have to watch her words when she was with the man she was going to marry.

After a quiet dinner, Warren had told her that they were going to have to attend a party being given by one of his clients. Normally Susan didn't object to the mingling of business with their evenings together.

After all, when they were married, she would need to know the people Warren associated with outside of business hours. Yet tonight she had wanted them to be alone so she could be the center of his attention. Warren had indicated they wouldn't stay long, but they had already been at Grayson Trevor's house for an hour. Susan was standing on the fringe of a group of men gathered around Warren, all of them deeply embroiled in a political discussion.

She had been with some of the younger women, but had become bored with their never-ending gossip. She had hoped to catch Warren's eye and suggest that they leave. He had seen her, but he was quite plainly not ready to leave.

Dance party music was coming from the glassed veranda of the ultramodern home and Susan gravitated toward it. She stood quietly near the wall watching the rhythmic, swaying motions of the couples dancing on the tiled floor. Hidden by her long black skirt, a toe tapped in time with the music.

A young, attractively dressed woman entered the room, ash blond hair coiled in a sophisticated bun at the nape of her neck. Susan smiled in warm recognition. Anna Kemper was two years older, married with two small children. Since Susan had started dating Warren, she had met Anna at many functions such as this.

Anna spotted Susan at almost the same instant. "Hello. Where's Warren?"

"In the other room talking politics," she answered, smiling wryly. "Where's Frank?"

"By now he's probably joined Warren," Anna laughed.

"How are the children?"

Susan never learned the answer. At that moment a man came up behind her friend, his arms circling her waist. Brown hair flashed golden as the man bent his head to place a kiss in the hollow of Anna's neck. Susan's mouth opened in disbelief.

"Anna—still breathtakingly lovely, I see," Mitch Braden murmured as he allowed her to turn in his arms.

"Mitch!" she exclaimed gaily. "I might have known it was you. How are you? All in one piece?"

"I'm fine." He smiled lazily, and loosened his hold so Anna stood free. "Looks like you are, too."

Anna turned to Susan, her hazel eyes dancing with pleasure. The words of introduction were forming on her lips, but Mitch didn't allow her to get them out.

"I knew if I looked long enough I'd find the

most beautiful girl in the house," he said softly. "Hello, Susan."

"Mr. Braden." Susan stiffly tilted her head in acknowledgment, placing emphasis on the formality of her greeting.

"Do you two know each other?" Anna asked with a frown of surprise.

"We've met," Susan admitted in the same rigid tone, "but I didn't know he'd be here tonight."

"Sorry about that, Susan," Mitch said mockingly, his eyes crinkling merrily at the corners. "Well, listen, I'm the proverbial bad penny. I always turn up."

"So I'm beginning to learn," she said coolly.

"Do I dare ask," Anna hesitated, laughing nervously, "what the problem is between you two?"

"There isn't any problem as far as I'm concerned, but you might ask that question of Susan later when the two of you are alone," Mitch suggested, the directness of his gaze compelling Susan to look at him. His voice became husky, losing its amused quality to become caressing. "Dance with me, Susan."

It was neither an order nor a question. Not even a challenge. There was a small, negative movement of her dark head.

"No, thank you," she refused, but the firmness in her voice wavered.

He reached out and lightly closed his fingers over the wrist of one of the hands clasped in front of her. There was something very winning in the boyishly pleading tilt of his handsome face.

"One dance won't hurt," he coaxed.

"Warren—" Susan began, glancing self-consciously over her shoulder.

"Warren isn't here." With slight pressure, he disentangled her hands and drew her toward him. "And while he's away, the cat is going to play—with the mouse."

Susan cast a helpless look to Anna, seeking aid from her friend as she unresistingly allowed Mitch to lead her away. But Anna was lost in some silent speculation of her own and missed the wordless plea for help.

At the edge of the impromptu dance floor, the upbeat song ended and the music changed to a slow, romantic tune.

"This couldn't have worked out better if I'd planned it." Mitch smiled slowly, and drew Susan around into his arms. For several steps, she allowed her mind to concentrate only on following his lead. Then gradually her physical sense began to register impressions in her brain and she was unable to ignore him.

There was a clean, fresh scent about him that was definitely pleasing. His fingers were spread across the small of her back, molding her gently against him until she could feel the muscular strength in his legs and narrow hips.

She was staring at the knot of his black tie, yet she was very conscious of the strong-columned throat and the width of his shoulders beneath the black evening suit. The caressing warmth of his breath was near her temple. There seemed to be a steady increase in the rate of her heartbeat.

Her hand stiffened against his shoulder in protest to the way he was affecting her. "Would you please not hold me so close?" she requested softly.

"Why not?" he asked in a low tone that

sounded disturbingly sensual at these close quarters.

"Because it isn't right," Susan answered, trying to breathe normally.

There was a testing movement of his hand on her back. "It feels right," murmured Mitch.

"Well, it doesn't look right," she replied in an almost desperate whisper.

He tipped his head downward, his mouth moving against her dark hair as he spoke. "To whom?"

"To everyone." Her heart was thudding against her ribs, a traitorous weakness flowing into her limbs. She glanced wildly around the room, pulling away from the warm breath that teased the hair at her temples, but only Anna appeared to be watching them. "Mitch, please don't do that."

A finger touched her chin to draw her gaze back to his face. There was no laughing curve in his mouth. The bronze tan of his cheeks, smoothly shaven from cheekbone to jawline, invited her caress. The teasing glitter was absent from his eyes, but their darkening blue fire made Susan feel warm all over.

"Do you have any idea how long I've been waiting to hear you say my name?"

"I—" Susan faltered. No man should be so handsome! His gaze became riveted on her lips and she couldn't think straight.

"This is a fine time to be in the middle of a dance floor, isn't it, darling?" A faint smile curved his mouth.

She breathed in sharply. "Don't call me that!"

"Why not?" he asked complacently. "That's the way I think of you. Honey, darling—"

"Stop it!" Susan quickly lowered her gaze to the white of his shirt collar. "You forget I'm engaged."

"I haven't forgotten."

"Then please leave me alone!" she protested, filled with a strange anger that she didn't understand.

"Do you mean here, right this minute?" A quick glance revealed his expression was serious in spite of the teasing lightness in his voice.

Susan looked around at the other couples, knowing eyebrows would rise if she and Mitch parted company in the middle of a dance. Her wandering gaze was caught by Warren standing in the veranda doorway. His withdrawn expression was cold with displeasure. At that moment Anna approached Warren and Susan's gaze was released. She wanted to hide in the black cloth of Mitch's jacket.

"Warren is here," she muttered nervously.

"Am I supposed to quake in my shoes?" he asked in an amused tone.

"Oh, Mitch, would you be serious?" Susan demanded impatiently.

"Believe me, I'm very serious."

She let the double meaning of his comment sail over her head. "I don't want there to be any trouble."

"You mean that you don't want any fights started," Mitch defined. "Most women would be secretly flattered to have two men coming to blows over them."

"I wouldn't, so please don't. . . don't rile him."

"Are you afraid I might get hurt?"

She had felt the sinewy strong muscles in his

chest, arms and thighs. Warren might have a weight advantage, but Mitch Braden was in much better physical condition.

Susan shook her head. "I just don't want any trouble."

"I wouldn't worry," Mitch replied. "Your fiancé is an attorney. He fights with words."

"And you believe that actions speak louder?"

He shrugged indifferently "Let's just say that former opponents know that I'm experienced with both."

There was little doubt in her mind that he spoke the truth. She remembered the first meeting when his mock-serious comments had demolished Warren's composure to the point that he had lied about being married to Susan.

"Please, Mitch, don't start anything for my sake," Susan requested humbly.

The glint of humor left his gaze as it traveled over her upturned face. His solemn expression made her suddenly aware of an unrelenting quality in his handsome features. Beneath the surface charm and roguish air was a man of iron determination, incapable of wavering once he had set his mind on a goal.

"You have my word," he answered evenly, "for this once." And Susan knew instinctively that Mitch would keep his promise. She breathed an inaudible sigh of relief and smiled. A corner of his mouth quirked in response. Their steps automatically ceased as the last note of the song faded. The lull in the music made Susan aware of the voices and laughter that filled the house.

The smile left her face before she turned to make her way toward Warren. Mitch's arm was curved lightly across her back, his hand resting on the side of her waist. The light embrace ended when they reached Warren.

"Hello, Warren." Susan smiled with an attempt at naturalness as she moved to his side and slipped a hand beneath his elbow. His dark eyes gave her a sense of guilt even though she knew she had done nothing wrong.

"Susan," he acknowledged her, with a cool smile.

"I've returned her to you safe and unharmed, Mr. Sullivan," Mitch said, inclining his head with mock politeness.

"Thank you, Mr. Braden." Susan could sense Warren's tense anger.

"And thank you for the dance, Miss Mabry." Cynical laughter glittered in the blue eyes that were turned to her. "Is that polite enough for you?"

"Y-you're quite welcome," Susan replied before glancing anxiously at the frown of confusion in Warren's face.

"Forgive me, Mr. Sullivan," Mitch apologized. "Susan has been giving me a lesson in manners."

A black brow arched inquiringly at Susan, the imposing arrogance of Warren's stance commanding her attention. Then his dark gaze slid back to Mitch Braden.

"I hope you didn't find it too difficult to learn," he said condescendingly.

"It wasn't easy to accept, Mr. Sullivan, believe me," responded Mitch, dry-voiced. He glanced at Anna and her husband Frank Kemper. "Anna, Frank," he greeted them with a nod of his head. "Excuse me, won't you? I think I'll go find the refreshment bar."

With that Mitch moved away, walking lightly as always. An uneasy silence followed his departure, one that neither Susan nor the couple standing next to her were willing to break.

"How did he crash the party?" Warren muttered, staring after Mitch.

Frank Kemper ran a hand through his curling hair, hiding the glitter of amusement that appeared briefly in his brown eyes. "I would guess he came with the Colesons. Their son is one of his chief mechanics and design engineers."

"Do you know him, Frank?" Warren glanced curiously at his friend.

"Yes, although actually he's more Anna's friend than mine."

The reply had Warren raising a brow of surprise at Frank's ash blond wife. Anna glanced hesitantly at her husband as if asking him just how she should explain before replying.

"Mitch and I grew up in the same small town in Michigan. Of course, he's older than I am, but our parents were always good friends. We've been more or less like cousins," Anna concluded.

"I see," Warren drawled.

But Susan wasn't certain if she did. That hadn't been exactly a cousinly kiss Anna had received on the neck from Mitch. Perhaps they had been more than cousins. Susan didn't have time to consider the thought further as Warren claimed her attention.

"I certainly hope you put him in his place once and for all," he said.

"I doubt if anyone could do that," Anna commented. "That's supposing Mitch Braden had a place."

Susan agreed, but she did so silently.

"Are you ready to leave, Susan?" Warren's hand closed possessively over the slender fingers resting on his arm.

"Yes, if you are." She glanced into his face, seeing that the remoteness and coldness were gone. The ardent light in his dark eyes said she was forgiven for whatever it was she had done wrong.

"I am." He smiled, his rugged features softening for a moment.

"So soon?" Anna sighed, then smiled understandingly at the engaged couple. "Very well, I'll walk with Susan while she gets her coat."

"I won't be long," Susan promised Warren before leaving to get her wrap. As she and Anna left the glassed veranda for the main living area of the house, she took a deep, calming breath. "You never did tell me how the children are."

"And you never did tell me how you met Mitch." Her friend's hazel eyes twinkled back.

Susan paused for a second. "It isn't a pleasant memory."

"I can't believe that." Anna laughed shortly. "Tell me about it."

After relating an accurate version of the first encounter in the restaurant, Susan tacked on a shortened version of Mitch stopping to aid them on the highway. She didn't know why she hadn't refused to discuss it with Anna.

"No wonder Warren was livid with jealousy when he saw you dancing with him," Anna declared with decided amusement. "Only Mitch would walk up to a total stranger and tell him how beautiful he thinks the man's date is."

"Since you know him, I wish you'd tell him to leave me alone." Susan sighed.

"Does he bother you?"

"It's embarrassing to have him following me around. I mean, I'm engaged."

"Don't ask me to believe you don't find him attractive." Anna smiled widely. "No woman is immune to his looks and charm."

Susan tipped her head to the side, gazing at her friend with curious speculation. "Including you, Anna?"

Nonplussed, the blonde glanced away. "That's a question that requires a delicately phrased answer from a married woman. I'm not immune to Mitch," she sighed ruefully. "He can still make me feel like I'm very much a woman, but not in that special way that Frank does. I'm totally in love with my husband and I wouldn't trade him for anyone else even if I could."

"But you and Mitch were more than just make-believe cousins once?" Susan voiced the impression she had received earlier.

They entered the guest room being used as a powder room for the party that evening. Susan paused near one of the mirrors, waiting for the response to her half-statement and half-question. Anna lowered her voice so she couldn't be overheard by the other chattering women in the room.

"There was a time," she acknowledged, frankly meeting Susan's gaze, "when I was infatuated with Mitch. In love? Sure, if I'd received the slightest encouragement. But he let me down easy, never once hurting my feelings or damaging our friendship."

Feeling guilty at having pried into something

that was none of her business, Susan looked away. "I'm sorry, Anna. I had no right to ask that. You should have told me not to be so nosy."

"I don't mind." Anna shook her head, absently watching as Susan retrieved her spring coat. "Mitch has been racing for several years now. Well, actually he's been racing cars since he was in high school, but only winning consistently in the last few years. With his looks and personality, the press automatically tagged him as the bachelor playboy of the circuit. But he isn't a shallow person, Susan. He's very warm and very sincere and very intelligent. Frank says Mitch has an uncanny knack for making the right investment and a very astute business mind."

"Why are you telling me all this?" Susan frowned.

"Because . . ." Anna shrugged uncertainly, "because of the attention he's paying you, I guess."

"I'm flattered, of course, but—"

Anna interrupted. "What I'm really saying is that if I'd received the encouragement you have, I'd already be in love with him."

Nervously Susan turned away, her fingers fidgeting with the lining of her coat. "You're forgetting that I'm already in love with Warren and we're going to be married in August."

"Yes, I suppose I was," Anna said with self-conscious brightness. "Speaking of Warren, he's probably worried that Mitch has waylaid you somewhere."

Draping the light coat over her arm, Susan turned, an equally false smile on her face. She didn't like the vague stirrings of uneasiness she felt.

"We'd better be getting back," she said simply.

As the two women retraced their path to the veranda, Susan spied Mitch standing in the far corner of a room talking with two men. His gaze flicked to her at almost the same instant. There was an almost imperceptible nod of his head to acknowledge her look but no flashing smile to make her heart quicken.

When Susan walked through the room again at Warren's side, she refused to let her gaze be drawn to that corner of the room. Mitch Braden was physically attractive, but there was room for only one man in her life and that was Warren. She didn't intend to complicate things by encouraging Mitch, however unconsciously.

In the car she snuggled close to Warren, needing his nearness to chase away the shivers of apprehension that danced over her skin. When the car was started and they were on the road, he slid his arm around her shoulders and nestled her closer.

"Love me, Susan?" he asked, taking his attention from the road long enough to brush a kiss against the side of her hair.

"You know I do, darling," she answered fervently, and wondered why she was so desperate to convince Warren of the fact.

Chapter Four

Warren bent over Susan's desk, adding the typed notes she had given him to the stack of papers clipped together in his hand. He barely glanced at her as he issued instructions with a preoccupied air.

"I'll probably be with my father all afternoon. Hold all my calls unless Con Anderson phones. Put him straight through," he ordered crisply.

"I will," Susan acknowledged.

Warren straightened. "I'm beginning to look forward to my father entering the hospital tomorrow." A sardonic smile lifted the corners of his mouth. "Maybe the office will settle into some semblance of routine again."

A faint, agreeing smile appeared briefly on her lips, but Warren was already gathering his papers together and starting for the hall door.

Susan sighed and glanced at the small desk calendar, offering a silent prayer of thanks that the long Memorial Day weekend was only two days away. She would welcome the time to recover from this hectic pace that seemed to require a constant juggling of appointments and schedules.

The hall door closed behind Warren as Susan swiveled to her computer, reaching for the keyboard. The ringing of the telephone checked her movement.

"Warren Sullivan's office," Susan answered in her courteous, professional voice.

"Hello, beautiful," was the immediate response.

Susan froze, unable to breathe or speak. It couldn't possibly be Mitch Braden. He would never call her at work, would he?

"Did you wish to speak to Mr. Sullivan?" she asked coolly.

"Hardly," Mitch chuckled.

The hall door opened and Susan quickly placed her hand over the receiver mouthpiece as Warren strode into her office. "Forgot my Palm Pilot," he said in explanation, walking to her desk and retrieving the small device. He glanced at the telephone in her hand. "Is that for me? Find out who it is. I might not be in."

"No," she said hurriedly. "It's for me." A curious light entered Warren's dark eyes. It was a rarity for Susan to receive a personal call at the office. "It's . . . it's my mother," she lied. "She wants me to pick up some things at the store on my way home."

With a satisfied nod, he turned to the hall door. "Give her my regards," he tossed over his shoulder absently.

Susan let out the deep breath she had been holding and slipped her hand away from the mouthpiece of the telephone. She didn't speak until the door was firmly closed behind Warren and she heard his footsteps echoing down the outside hall.

"What was it you wanted, Mr. Braden? I'm very busy," she inquired with cool hauteur.

His tongue clicked reprovingly in her ear. "Lying to your boss is one thing, Susan, but lying to your fiancé? Shame on you!" he mocked.

An embarrassed flush warmed her neck. "If you've merely called to—" she began angrily.

"To invite you on a guided tour of the race grounds tonight," Mitch interrupted lazily, "with a stop for dinner afterward."

"I'm busy."

"Tomorrow night isn't possible, I know," he said with remarkable indifference to her sharp tone. "Tuesday, Thursday, Saturday and Sunday nights are when you have your appointments with Warren."

"They're dates," Susan corrected.

"All right, they're dates," Mitch conceded. "Now, when are you and I going to have a date? It's been four days since I saw you last. Haven't you missed me?"

"Was I supposed to?" The coldness of her voice was to help freeze away the image of his handsome face that kept trying to enter her mind.

"I hoped you would," he replied with a warm huskiness in his voice that made his words almost a physical caress.

Susan swallowed, trying to ease the tightness in her throat. Her pulse was skipping erratically.

"I want to see you tonight, Susan. I promise I'll be a good little boy."

"I told you, I'm busy," she said hurriedly, feeling

the pull of his masculine attraction even over the telephone lines. "I have to wash my hair and—"

"Can't you think of anything more original?" his amused voice laughed in her ear. "No man believes that excuse anymore."

"You're right," Susan said with sudden determination. "I don't need to make excuses. I won't go out with you tonight or any other night, Mitch. I'm engaged to be married."

There was a short pause before he responded in a quiet voice. "Is that your final answer?"

A muscle constricted painfully in her chest. "Yes," she answered, trying to ignore the hurt.

"Okay," Mitch sighed, reluctantly accepting her reply. "Maybe I'll see you around sometime," he said in a shrugging tone that indicated he doubted the possibility. "So long, beautiful."

"Good-bye, Mitch."

Something seemed to be burning her eyes as she hung up the phone. Nervously she ran a shaking hand through her dark silken hair, and blinked rapidly.

Drat the man! Why had he bothered to call? He must have known she would refuse to go out with him. And she had just begun to convince herself that she had heard the last of him. In fact she had even started to forget about him, at least partially, until this telephone call.

Why had she talked to him? she asked herself angrily. She should have hung up the phone the instant she recognized his voice. Or told Warren who was on the phone and let him deal with Mitch.

Since the first time she had met him, Mitch Braden had been disrupting her life, her senses, her emotions, and her relationship with Warren. She wanted to feel the peace and contentment she had known before she met him. Every time she thought she was about to obtain it, Mitch Braden popped up again, disrupting things all over again. Now he had even confused her to the point where she was sorry that she would never see him again. What was worse, she seemed powerless to stop the sadness from invading her heart.

It was a good thing she wouldn't be seeing or hearing from him again. And it was a good thing that the race would be run this weekend and Mitch Braden would be leaving town soon after. Without him around to drive her crazy, her life would settle into its previous pattern. The ripples his unexpected arrival had caused would eventually disappear, without leaving any mark.

The logic didn't cheer Susan.

Her dark hair was caught in a French braid, secured with a ribbon that matched the silk of her blouse. The wide legs of her white slacks swung about her ankles as she walked down the hospital corridor with Warren, the raised heels of her sandals clicking loudly in the hushed building.

"I told Dad we might stop in this afternoon after our picnic," said Warren. "He's been waiting for me to bring you each time I've come to see him. I would've suggested it before, of course, but the doctor thought it would be best to keep visitors at an absolute minimum the first couple of days after the operation."

"I thought you said the operation took less time than expected and that your father had come through it in excellent shape." Susan frowned.

"He did, but he is elderly and it was still a shock to his system. We didn't want to take any risks of complication," he explained. "Here's his room."

He indicated a door ahead and to Susan's right. She waited for him to open it, then walked into the semiprivate room. Robert Sullivan was reclining in his bed, wire-rimmed glasses perched on the end of his nose. He peered over the top of them and closed the magazine on his lap. He looked pale but otherwise in good health.

"Hello, Susan." He extended his hand toward her and she walked to the side of the bed to accept its firm clasp. "You certainly are the picture of a summer's day!"

Surprised by the rare compliment from the usually taciturn man, Susan smiled. "Thank you. You're looking well, too. How are you?"

"Stiff, sore, and uncomfortable, but that's to be expected, I guess," he replied, releasing her hand and turning to his son. "Hello, Warren."

Susan knew she had been dismissed and moved from the side of the bed to an armchair that stood near the foot. The partitioning curtain was drawn, concealing the second occupant of the hospital room, although the loud playing of a radio from the other side made Susan doubt that the other patient was sleeping.

"That radio's awfully loud, isn't it?" Warren frowned in the direction of the curtain.

"Yes," his father sighed heavily. "I wish he'd turn the volume down."

"Would you like me to ask him to do it?"

"No, no." Robert Sullivan impatiently waved aside the offer. "The man's half deaf. He can't hear it if he turns it any lower. Besides, I've already told him I didn't object. He doesn't have it on very often.''

With that explanation, Warren's father shifted the conversation to an article he had just been reading concerning a recent Supreme Court decision. Susan wondered if he had any interests outside of his profession.

It didn't really matter, she decided, glancing at Warren and smiling to herself. They had had a wonderful time on their picnic. Warren had brought along a bottle of wine to go with the meal she had packed. He had taken her to a secluded spot alongside the rapids of a river. The setting had been idyllic, just the two of them alone, talking about their plans for the future.

Susan had been so contented lying on the blanket in his arms. She had hated it when they had to leave. Yet the rosy afterglow of the moment was still with her, maybe the aftereffects of the wine she had drunk.

Leaning back in her seat, Susan relaxed, not minding now that she wasn't the sole object of Warren's attention. From the other side of the curtain, the radio was being tuned to different stations, jumbling music together until it was finally stopped at the sound of a radio announcer's words.

''And now we'll go trackside with Jim Jensen and a report on the status of the Indianapolis 500!''

There was a roar in the background, followed by a second man's voice. ''Hello, ladies and gentlemen, this is Jim Jensen, bringing you up to date on the Indy 500. It will be no surprise to you racing fans out there when I say that the leader is none other than Mitch Braden.'' Susan clenched her teeth in frustration. She wanted to rush over there and turn off that radio. The mere mention of the man's name was enough to destroy her contentment.

"He's been leading the pack since almost the beginning of the race," the radio announcer continued. "But for the first hundred miles Braden and another veteran driver, Johnny Phelps, jockeyed for the lead before Braden took command. He's been ahead by a winning margin ever since."

Trying to close her ears to the broadcast, Susan concentrated on the rainbow colors flashing from her diamond engagement ring. But her hearing only seemed to grow more acute.

"The yellow caution flag has been out three times, but except for those three minor mishaps, the race has been free of accidents. Twelve cars are sidelined with mechanical malfunctions, but none of the drivers of those twelve cars were expected to be among the front runners today.

"If Mitch Braden does receive the checkered flag today," the announcer's voice raised slightly as the background roar of racing engines grew louder, "he's going to have to give a lot of credit to the outstanding performance of his pit crew today. They've been phenomenal. I say that because I see Braden is heading into the pits now. Let's take a few seconds to time him, and ladies and gentlemen, with that crew, a few seconds is all it's going to be."

Suddenly the pitch of the man's voice changed. "Braden is in the pits, slowing—An accident! In the pits!" Susan's eyes widened in alarm. "It happened so fast! Braden was coming in, just starting to slow down, when Mark Terry, who was well back in the pack, accelerated out of his pit area. He couldn't have seen Braden coming in! His car ran right into the side of Braden's and rolled up on top of it!" Her heart was in her throat, all the blood leaving her limbs until she felt chilled to the bone. This couldn't be happening! It wasn't really true!

"Terry has scrambled out of his car, seemingly unharmed, but there's no sign of Braden!" The announcer continued his eyewitness account in a fever-pitched tone. "Emergency vehicles are already on the scene and I can see the familiar blue uniforms of Braden's pit crew. I don't see any sign of fire, but it's impossible to be certain. If Braden is trapped underneath Terry's car—" The thought wasn't finished, to Susan's horror. Her imagination was working much too vividly.

"I can see men working frantically on one side of Braden's car now! Yes, yes, they're pulling him out! He doesn't appear to be conscious. But of course we can't know how seriously he's been injured. That finishes the race for Braden, though. Johnny Phelps is the new leader. What a tough break, fans! Braden's on a stretcher and they're loading him into the ambulance. The Indy officials can be proud of the speed of this dramatic rescue. I—"

"Susan. Susan?" Warren's frowning voice broke in sharply.

"Wh-what?" She looked at him blankly.

"You're as white as a sheet." He walked swiftly to her side. "Are you ill? What's the matter with you?"

She did feel sick. Her hands were cold and clammy when Warren clasped them firmly in his own.

"I—I think I need a breath of—of fresh air," she stammered. How could she possibly explain her reaction to the news of Mitch's accident? It didn't make sense to be so violently upset simply because she knew him.

Warren helped her to stand. "Want me to go with you?"

"No." Her knees were shaking badly. "I'll be all right in a moment, really. It's just a little stuffy in here. Ex-excuse me, please."

She avoided Warren's concerned gaze but caught a frowning look from Robert Sullivan. She managed to force her legs to carry her into the hallway. Out of sight of the door, she leaned weakly against the corridor wall, breathing in deeply to quell the churning of her stomach.

The long gulps of air seemed to bring strength back into her limbs. The nameless terror that gripped her heart started to ease as her knees stopped their quivering.

"Susan?" Warren stood beside her, his eyes anxiously examining her pale face.

"I'm all right." She took another deep breath. "I'm sorry I ran out like that—"

"Don't apologize," he interrupted, circling an arm under her shoulders and drawing her away from the wall. "Let's get you outside in the fresh air."

"I'm all right, really," she protested weakly, but she let his strength carry her along. "I just felt a little faint there for a moment."

"Maybe it was the wine," Warren suggested with a gentle smile.

"Yes," she breathed, taking advantage of the excuse he offered.

The late spring air revived her and returned color to her cheeks. The shock of Mitch's accident had dissipated, but a feeling of sick dread remained. When Warren suggested taking her home, she made only a halfhearted protest.

"Your father—" she began.

"—will understand perfectly. I'll stop by to see him on my way to pick you up this evening, if you're well enough to go out," he said, helping her into his car. His solicitude made her feel even more guilty for not telling him the real cause of her upset state.

When they had driven out of the hospital parking lot, Susan glanced hesitantly at his carved profile. "Do you mind if—if we turn the radio on?"

"Of course not." He smiled at her crookedly, a frown of curious confusion drawing his dark brows together as he reached out to switch on the radio.

A news broadcast was on and Warren started to tune to some music. "No," Susan rushed to stop him, "That station is fine."

Warren shrugged and left it there. Crossing her fingers in her lap that the news hadn't been on very long, Susan listened to a synopsis of world events and swallowed when the announcer changed to the local scene. Forcing a stoic expression into her face, she listened to a shortened account of the accident minus the terrifying adjectives. A cautious glance at Warren caught him listening interestedly, too.

"No report yet on the extent or seriousness of the injuries to Mitch Braden," the announcer said. "A paramedic did say that Braden had regained consciousness in the ambulance. When we have more information, we'll pass it on to you."

Susan's lashes fluttered down in temporary relief.

"Well, our Indy man seems to have had some bad luck," Warren commented dryly.

Susan winced. "Don't be flippant, Warren, please!"

"I didn't mean to sound callous." He slid a questioning look in her direction. "I may not like the man, but I certainly wouldn't wish him any crippling injury."

Her heart catapulted into her throat. She hadn't considered the possibility that Mitch might be maimed or paralyzed. Her initial fear had been for his life. The prospect of that vital, handsome man chained to crutches or a wheelchair or a bed sent more sickening chills over her skin.

"I know you don't, Warren," she replied, suppressing a shudder.

She leaned her head against the back cushion of her seat, closing her eyes and trying to achieve the indifferent interest Warren displayed.

"We'll be home soon," he said, misinterpreting her action and wanness as another sign of the dizziness she had suffered in the hospital and not connecting it with Mitch Braden's accident. He changed the station.

Soft music from the radio filled the silence. The soothing melody didn't penetrate Susan's thoughts, however. Her mind was replaying her last conversation with Mitch. She had been so sharp and so cold with him.

It hurt unbearably now to think that those might have been the last words she would exchange with him. She could have gotten the same message across with politeness and humor instead of being so indignant and rude.

The motion of the car stopped. Susan blinked her eyes open, recognizing the graceful old brick home, and swung her head to look into Warren's dark eyes. He was half-turned in his seat, studying her quietly, his arm resting along the top of the cushion near her head.

With his forefinger, he reached out to touch her elegant braid and its unraveling ribbon. "You look more like a little girl who's had too many treats at the fair than a woman who's had too much wine," he mused, then tilted his head in concern. "Are you sure you're going to be all right?"

"I'll be fine." She smiled stiffly.

"You wait here," Warren ordered, "while I get the picnic hamper from the back."

Susan did as she was told, remaining in the car until his supporting hand helped her out and guided her to the front door of her home. Only when they were inside did Warren release his hold.

"Oh, Susan, it's you!" Her mother appeared in the hallway, from the direction of the kitchen, wiping her hands on a towel. "I didn't expect you home so soon."

"Susan isn't feeling well, Mrs. Mabry," said Warren.

"It's nothing, Mom, really," Susan murmured quickly as Beth Mabry walked forward with concern in her brown eyes.

"You do look a bit pale, dear." She pressed a hand against Susan's cheek. "You don't seem to have a temperature, though."

"You two are making a fuss about nothing." Susan tried to laugh. "It's just a little headache and dizziness. If I lie down for an hour it'll go away."

"I'll call you about six-thirty to see if you feel up to going out tonight," Warren said. "If she isn't feeling better in an hour or so, Mrs. Mabry, I hope you'll have your husband take a look at her."

"I will," Beth Mabry promised. "Let me take that picnic hamper for you, Warren. And Susan, you go and lie down."

"Do as she tells you," Warren added, touching Susan's cheek with his hand in a good-bye caress.

Susan stared at the front door for several seconds after Warren had closed it, wishing that she could have shared some of the anxiety she was feeling with him. But he wouldn't have understood. For that matter she didn't understand it very well herself.

"Would you like an aspirin or something, Susan?" Beth Mabry noticed the unusual expression of melancholy on her daughter's face, and wondered about it.

"No, nothing," Susan refused absently, and started toward the stairwell leading to the second floor.

A car pulled into the drive, the sound followed immediately by the slamming of doors and footsteps approaching the front door. Susan turned toward it, her hand poised on the banister. Her brother walked into the house ahead of his father. Greg's chin was tucked into his chest, hands shoved in his pockets and shoulders hunched forward.

In Susan's shock and subsequent worry, she had completely forgotten that Mitch had arranged for complimentary tickets to the race today and that her father and brother had attended.

"Simon?" her mother exclaimed with some surprise. "Is the race over already?"

"No," he replied, glancing with concern at his son's bowed head. "There was an accident at the track. Mitch Braden has been taken to the hospital."

"No!" The single word held astonishment and fear.

Amy appeared at the top of the stairs, a hairbrush in her hand. "Mitch is hurt?"

"I'm afraid so, kitten," her father affirmed grimly, and Susan noticed the tightness of his mouth. For all his outward control, Simon Mabry was upset, too. In his short acquaintanceship, Mitch Braden had managed to touch all their lives.

"Was it . . . was it very bad?" her mother asked in a voice barely above a whisper. Susan guessed that she was envisioning a flaming crash and remembered her own surge of terror at that imagined picture. "Is he seriously hurt?"

"It was bad enough," Simon answered. "He was trapped for a short time under another car. We heard a radio report on the way home that he had regained consciousness before reaching the hospital, but nothing about any injuries."

"If something happens to him," Amy wailed, "I'll just die!"

Greg shifted his feet uncomfortably and Susan wanted to walk over and put an arm around his shoulders to say that she felt the same miserable pain he did. Fear of the unknown was eating at her heart, too.

"I think I'll turn on the radio," he mumbled. "Maybe they'll know something else."

"Wait a minute, son," Simon laid a hand on

Greg's shoulder. "Maybe I can cut through some of the red tape."

"What are you going to do, Daddy?" Amy raced down the steps past Susan, the long auburn hair that Mitch had admired shimmering like fire.

"I'm going to call the ER and see if I can't find out something," he answered in a decisive tone.

Susan gasped back the little sob that tried to escape and followed the others as they hurried after her father. In the study, they all huddled around his desk.

"I think Kate Johnson's on the ER rotation today," he said as he punched in the buttons for the hospital number. "She's an excellent surgeon."

It seemed an interminable time before anyone answered.

"This is Dr. Simon Mabry," her father identified himself. "I'd like to speak to Dr. Johnson." There was another pause, filled by the drumming of her father's fingers on the desk top. "Kate? Simon Mabry here. What? . . . No, no, I'm not bringing anyone in. I was calling about Mitch Braden, the race car driver they brought in from the speedway . . . I guessed that, but can you tell me anything else?"

Studying her father's expression intently, Susan didn't move, but waited motionless like the rest of her family. He listened quietly to the surgeon on the other end of the phone, his silence occasionally punctuated by understanding mm-hms.

"Thanks, Kate," he said finally. "I appreciate this." Then he said good-bye and hung up.

"Well?" Susan probed anxiously.

"So far," he breathed in deeply, lifting his head to meet the eyes centered on him, "they know he has a broken arm, some cracked ribs, and a concussion. They're still checking for internal injuries and the like.''

A sigh of relief seemed to come from all of them. Susan only knew she wanted to cry, her knees buckling slightly before stiffening to support her.

"I knew all the time he would be all right," Amy declared brightly.

"He's tough," Greg agreed with a tight smile, manfully trying to conceal his emotions.

"I'm so relieved." Beth Mabry shook her head as if astounded to discover how tense she had been. "Every year you hear about a crash of some sort in the Indianapolis 500, but this is the first time we've ever known anyone involved, as more than just a name, I mean."

"I think we all understand, Beth." Simon Mabry glanced warmly about him at the smiling, relieved faces of his children.

Susan swallowed the tight lump in her throat and turned away from the group. Her fingers were still pressed against her stomach, but the nauseous churning had stopped. Mitch was going to be all right, said a joyous voice from her heart.

"Susan, in all the excitement," her mother exclaimed, "I forgot you were supposed to be resting."

"Resting?" her father questioned. "Aren't you feeling well, Susan?"

"I—I had a headache," she answered self-consciously, not quite meeting her parents' eyes. "It seems to have gone away, though."

Which was the truth.

"With all the distraction, you probably forgot to

feel ill." Her mother smiled. "Warren was certainly worried. He'll be glad to hear you're all right."

"Yes," Susan agreed, with a faint answering smile.

Now that she was feeling better there was no reason not to go out with him that evening. But the dinner was an anticlimax. Susan couldn't seem to recapture the peace and contentment she had experienced earlier in his company.

Warren naturally blamed her restlessness on the lingering effect of her headache, and Susan let him, since she couldn't explain to herself why she couldn't find that previous sensation of closeness to him.

Chapter Five

Nervously adjusting the collar of her peach-colored jacket, Susan paused in the hospital corridor. Her palm was faintly damp and she pressed it against her skirt before clutching the leather case a little tighter. She looked ahead at the open doorways of the hospital rooms in the hall as she started forward again.

"May I help you, miss?" a female voice inquired behind her.

Susan turned with a start, smiling self-consciously. "No," she answered quickly, glancing at the leather case in her hands. "I was just bringing some papers to Mr. Robert Sullivan."

The uniformed nurse, an older woman with beautiful waving white hair and twinkling eyes, smiled and nodded. "His room is three doors down to your right."

"Thank you." Susan turned away, her moving

gaze flicking to the open doorway on the opposite side of the hall. There was a rustle of movement from the room.

"Hey, beautiful! Is that you?" Mitch Braden's voice rang out clearly into the hall.

A red blush of embarrassment filled Susan's face as she turned instinctively toward the door in answer and caught the amused, raised eyebrow of the nurse.

She hesitated for only a second before entering the room. She told herself she wouldn't stay more than a couple of minutes, just pop in to wish him a polite get-well.

"Susan?" his inquiring voice called again as she walked through the open door of his hospital room. He didn't see her immediately. He was trying to push himself into a more upright position in the bed with one arm. There was a wince of pain and his face went pale before he slumped back.

"Lie still," Susan ordered quickly, walking swiftly to his bedside.

The blue eyes opened and Mitch simply looked at her for a long moment. "Hello," he said softly, lean dimples appearing in the tanned cheeks.

Her chest constricted at the dark glow in his eyes. "Hello," she returned with equal softness, a faint smile on her mouth.

"I heard your voice in the hall." His compelling gaze refused to let her look away. "I didn't think you would come in to see me."

"What were you going to do?" she teased gently. "Come racing after me?"

She fought an urge to reach out and smooth the tousled gold-brown hair falling across his forehead.

Susan moved away from the bed before she succumbed to it.

"I might have. My legs weren't injured, only this," Mitch tapped the cast on his left arm, "and a few ribs and a bump on the head."

"Well, it didn't knock any sense into you!" She let her hand trail over the foot of the bed and close over the rail, balancing the leather case containing the papers for Robert Sullivan beside it.

"Did you think it might?"

She could feel his eyes watching her. The intentness of his gaze began to affect her breathing and she shifted uncomfortably. Somehow the conversation had become too intimate. She had intended only to make an aloof, polite inquiry about his health, and here she was trading a kind of soft banter with him.

"I don't know." She shrugged, and stared at the diamond ring on her left hand.

"Well!" Mitch breathed in. "Have I lost track of time? Isn't this Tuesday? Shouldn't you be working?"

She was almost grateful for the change of subject. "It's Tuesday and I'm working. Warren's father is here in the hospital recovering from an operation. I was bringing him some papers to study."

"I see." He paused. "Were you at the race? I looked for you, but I only saw your father and Greg. I sent enough tickets."

"Yes, I know you did," Susan answered nervously. "I know they would want me to thank you for them too. Warren and I had already made plans to go on a picnic."

A wry smile tugged the corners of his mouth. "It's probably just as well the two of you weren't there. Warren probably would've cheered when he saw the crash."

"That's not fair," she protested. "All of us were upset when we heard about the accident."

"Were you?" He shot her a piercing blue look.

Susan glanced away, afraid he might have some way of getting inside her mind and finding out how upset she had been. "Of course," she answered curtly. Tossing her head back, she let go of the railing and hugged the leather case in front of her. "I really have to be going, Mitch. Mr. Sullivan is expecting me. I . . . I hope you're feeling better soon."

"Wait." His voice checked her movement toward the door. She glanced warily over her shoulder. "You haven't autographed my cast yet." He flashed her a smile that made her heart turn over.

Susan hesitated as she watched Mitch reach for a black pen lying on the table beside his bed. With a resigned sigh she walked back to the bed, taking the pen he extended toward her. The briefcase was awkwardly in the way and she set it on the bed. She bent slightly over him, the pen poised above the cast as she tried to decide what to write.

"You could put down 'All my love' or 'Love and kisses,' " Mitch suggested with a twinkle.

As quickly as the pen and cast would allow, Susan scrawled "Get well soon" and signed her name. Straightening, she held the pen out to him, reaching for the case with her other hand. But instead of taking the pen, his right hand took hold of hers.

"Susan?" Her startled eyes met his earnest gaze. "I'd like you to come see me again," he said, almost humbly.

"I'm afraid that's not possible." She tried to withdraw her hand, but he wouldn't release it.

"Please, I—" He stopped, glancing down at her hand. "It gets monotonous being confined in this room hour after hour. Most of my friends are guys at the track, and they're pulling out for other races."

"I'm sorry. I—" Susan frowned, wondering if it was loneliness she saw flicker across his face, so handsome and proud.

"I don't expect you to make a special trip to see me." Mitch smiled ruefully, his thumb caressing the inside of her wrist in what appeared to be an unconscious motion. "But if you have to come to the hospital to bring Warren's father any more papers, would you come in and say hello?"

His blue eyes held her mesmerized. "I . . . I suppose I could." She surrendered to their spell.

"Thank you." He carried her fingertips to the soft firmness of his lips, making them tingle from the intimacy of the caress.

There was a rustle of a starched uniform behind Susan, followed by a brisk female voice. "It's that time again, Mr. Braden."

Susan pulled her hand free from Mitch's hold, hiding it guiltily behind her back as she turned toward the nurse she had met in the hallway.

"Madge, your timing stinks." Mitch sighed and made a face.

The nurse winked broadly at Susan before answering. "We nurses pride ourselves on being a nuisance."

"I'd better be going." Susan quickly gathered up her briefcase as the nurse determinedly held out a thermometer.

"You won't forget to come again?" Mitch held her wavering gaze.

"No," she admitted in a low voice, wishing she hadn't agreed as she hurried from his room.

There was too much of a risk that word might somehow filter to Robert Sullivan and from there to his son that Susan had seen Mitch Braden, for her to attempt to conceal the visit from Warren. His lips thinned with displeasure at the news, when she told him at dinner that evening.

"Did you really think it was necessary to see him?" he asked coldly.

"It wasn't necessary," Susan admitted, studying the rounded chunks of ice in her water goblet rather than meet his censorious dark gaze. "But since I was right there, it seemed a bit unfeeling not to look in and wish him a speedy recovery."

"Perhaps," Warren said grudgingly, "but considering that man's lack of manners, I wouldn't worry about doing the polite thing."

"Well, that's not a reason to behave the same way," she replied patiently. "After all, the man has no family here and his friends are mainly people from the racetrack. If they haven't gone already, they'll be leaving town in the next day or two. It's lonely, confined to a hospital room without any visitors."

"Braden, lonely?" The disbelieving words were followed by a short, contemptuous laugh. "I'm sure he has droves of female visitors flocking to his bedside. Does my fiancée have to be among them?"

"I did not rush to his bedside!" Her nerve ends frayed at the edges. "I think it's insulting of you to insinuate that I did!"

"I didn't mean to imply that you deliberately

did, but I don't doubt that Braden and others would look at it in that light," Warren retorted. "Considering the way he's flirted with you so boldly in the past, your visit is a sign of encouragement to continue."

"I did not encourage him," Susan responded tautly.

Yet, remembering the light kiss on her fingertips, she wondered if unconsciously she had. And she had foolishly said she would see him again.

"Not intentionally, but he's conceited enough to believe that you did. That's what I've been trying to explain," he said with impatience.

"All right, you've explained, so let's stop arguing about this."

"I'm not arguing." His imposing, masculine features were tense with controlled anger. "I'm simply forbidding you to see him again."

Her eyes widened in astonishment, their soft brown color flaming into a snapping fire of temper. Her strong sense of independence asserted itself with a rush. Warren had just pushed her too far. Being willing to please the man she loved and planned to marry was entirely different from being ruled by him.

"Forbid me! Of all the arrogant—" Susan closed her mouth abruptly, choking on the anger erupting from inside. Ignoring the interested looks from the other people in the restaurant, she pushed herself out of her chair. "You may ask me not to see him again, Warren, but nobody *forbids* me to do anything!"

Without a backward glance, she stalked from the table, disregarding his low-voiced command to return. The girl in the cloakroom had just handed her her coat when a glowering Warren appeared at her side. Susan turned to him, lifting her chin defiantly.

"Are you going to take me home, or shall I call a taxi?" she challenged.

"What do you think you're doing, making a scene like this?" Warren muttered angrily.

Susan pivoted away. "I'll get a taxi."

Her elbow was seized in a rough grip and she was propelled toward the outer door. His hold didn't lessen as he nearly forced her to his car in tight-lipped silence. The crackling tension remained through the entire journey to her home with neither of them uttering a sound. When the car stopped in front of her house, Susan reached for the door handle.

"I—I believe I owe you an apology, Susan." Warren seemed to have difficulty in getting the words out.

"I believe you do," she answered coolly, turning slightly to give him a measuring look.

His hands tightened on the steering wheel as a muscle twitched in his jaw. "All right, dammit, I'm sorry," he snapped.

Despite her irritation at his reluctantly offered apology, Susan smiled. The dimness of the car concealed it from Warren.

"And I'm sorry for walking out like that," she said gently, meeting him halfway.

"The whole argument was silly," he murmured, taking her into his arms and crushing her tightly against his chest.

"It hurt that you didn't trust me," she whispered.

In answer, Warren kissed her long and hard as if to drive away the memory of their angry words.

Susan responded with equal intensity to show him that all was forgiven, if not totally forgotten. Afterwards she lay curled contentedly in the hollow of his shoulder while his hand absently massaged the soft flesh of her arm.

"Please, darling," Warren said in a low, husky voice, "I'm asking you not to see that man anymore."

Tensing slightly, Susan had the uncomfortable feeling that his apology and the subsequent kiss had been designed to lull her into the sense of security she was now enjoying. The end result would be that he would achieve the very thing he had set out to.

A tiny frown of uncertainty touched her forehead. "I—I'm sorry, Warren, but I can't give you an answer. I simply won't promise that I might not see him again," she murmured, venturing a cautious glance at his impassive face.

For an instant his expression seemed to harden and Susan thought the argument was going to begin all over again. Then he relaxed his mouth into a dry smile.

"The fact that you love me is the only answer I need, I guess," he said softly.

Susan mentally chided herself for her mean thoughts about his motives. She had hated accusing him of trying to use underhanded methods to extract a promise from her.

"Thank you, darling," she whispered.

He placed a quick kiss on her lips. "Come on," he said, dislodging her from her comfortable nest in his arm. "It's time you went in the house. You have to be at work in the morning and you know what a tyrant your boss can be."

"He's a regular monster." Susan laughed as she moved to her own side of the car. Opening the car door, she glanced over her shoulder at his smiling face. "Good night, darling."

"Good night," Warren responded, his voice a gentle caress.

The next day the necessity arose again for Susan to transport some important documents to Robert Sullivan at the hospital. The words were there in Warren's eyes, asking her again not to see Mitch Braden while she was there. Susan looked away, unable to give him the answer he wanted.

All night and for the better part of the day she had been trying to come to a decision. As she walked down the hospital corridor to Robert Sullivan's room, she knew she had reached it.

After she had given the papers to Warren's father, she would see Mitch—and tactfully tell him that it would be better for all concerned if she didn't see him anymore. After telling Mitch she would look in, she was going to look in; she simply could not do it without explaining why.

Keeping her gaze averted from the door to Mitch's room, Susan intended to walk straight by. First she wanted to see Robert Sullivan, then she would go to Mitch.

"Susan!" Mitch's delighted voice interrupted her plan.

She paused glancing over her shoulder to see him standing in the doorway. He looked disturbingly attractive in a knee-length robe of camel brown, one sleeve empty and the bulge of the cast beneath the tied front.

"Hello, Mitch." She swallowed and managed a taut smile. "I was on my way to Mr. Sullivan's room with some more papers. I—I was going to stop in to see you on my way out."

"I somehow didn't think there would be any errand that would bring you back today." He smiled slowly.

"It came up suddenly."

"I'm glad."

"Yes . . . well." Susan breathed in deeply, bowing her head to break away from the blue glitter of his eyes.

"Would it upset everything if you came here before going to his room?" Mitch asked, gesturing down the hallway with his right hand.

Susan hesitated indecisively. "No, no, I don't suppose it would."

But she walked very slowly toward Mitch, not quite knowing what she was going to say to him now that the moment had arrived sooner than she had anticipated. He stepped aside to let her pass, meeting her nervous sideways glance with a faint dimpling smile.

A few steps inside the room, she stopped short, meeting the curious and speculating gaze of the brawny man sprawled in the chair beside the bed.

"Excuse me," she stammered, turning quickly to Mitch. "You should have said you already had a visitor. I'll come back later."

Mitch blocked her path to the door with casual ease. "Stay," he insisted. "Mike was just leaving, weren't you, Mike?" Mitch glanced pointedly at the man with the thinning dark hair.

The man's mouth turned up at the corners, smiling at some secret as he pushed himself out of the chair.

"That's right. I was just leaving." He didn't leave, but stood there expectantly waiting for an introduction.

"You needn't go on my account," Susan said quickly.

"Honestly, miss, I was about to leave before you came," the man assured her in an amused voice. Still he waited.

Out of the corner of her eye, Susan saw Mitch shake his head in resignation. "Susan, this hairy-chested Irishman is Mike O'Brian, my pit boss and sometimes my friend. This is Susan Mabry, Mike."

"I'm pleased to meet you, Mr. O'Brian." Her hand was lost in the hugeness of his.

"Mike," he corrected her formality with a friendly smile. "I recognized you, Susan." At her blank look, he added, "From the restaurant."

Her cheeks warmed as she realized he must have been one of the men who had joined Mitch the first time she saw him. A swift glance at Mitch caught the narrowing look he gave Mike, warning him into silence.

Mike released her hand. "It was nice meeting you." Then he turned to Mitch. "We'll be pulling out in the morning, so take care."

"I will," Mitch nodded. "Don't enjoy your vacation too much. I won't be in this cast very long."

"You wait until the doctor tells you to take it off or I'll break it again for you!" Mike smiled at his threat.

There was a brief clasp of hands between the two, then Mike left the room. Susan felt Mitch's gaze on her and moved toward the window.

"You're looking much better today," she said to fill the silence.

"The dizziness seems to have gone, so the doctors let me up," he replied. "Now that you're here, I'm feeling much better."

Susan fingered the leather case in her hands. "Don't say things like that, Mitch."

"What did I say?" His voice held false innocence.

"It wasn't what you said but what you implied," she answered, pressing her lips together tightly.

He walked slowly toward her. She could hear his footsteps bringing him nearer, but refused to turn around.

"And you don't like it when I imply that I find the sight of you stimulating to the senses," Mitch said quietly.

"No, I don't." Susan stared at the whiteness of her fingers clenching the case handle. "You can't keep ignoring the fact that I'm engaged."

"I don't ignore it, exactly," he corrected with faint amusement. "But since you don't like me to tell you how very beautiful you are, we'll talk of other things. Greg came to see me last night and your father looked in this morning while he was doing his hospital rounds."

Susan sighed, a crazy kind of misery welling up inside. She turned from the window, meeting his level gaze.

"This isn't going to work either," she protested lamely. "I can't make small talk. I was going to come here today because there was something I wanted to tell you."

His gaze moved to the top of her head. "Do you know when the light hits your hair just right it has a fiery glint, crimson red like flames? Yet your hair is such a very dark shade of brown.''

"Don't try to change the subject, Mitch. I'm serious.''

"So am I,'' he agreed. "In certain lights, your hair is definitely red.''

"I don't want to discuss the color of my hair. That's not why I came.'' Frustrated, Susan turned back to the window.

"I know why you came,'' Mitch said calmly. "You came to tell me you aren't going to visit me anymore.''

Her head jerked toward him in surprise. "How did you know?''

"Call it a calculated guess.'' He shrugged indifferently, and stared out the window. "What happened? Did your jealous fiancé find out that you'd seen me and forbid you to come?''

"He didn't forbid me.'' She wasn't about to tell him that Warren had tried. "And he didn't find out, I told him.''

"You told him and he didn't forbid you to see me? I find that hard to believe.'' He grinned crookedly at her, his bronze features glowing attractively in the sunlight.

"I never said he liked the idea,'' Susan protested as her pulse quickened under his glittering look. "He doesn't altogether understand why I'm seeing you.''

"Do you?'' Mitch taunted softly.

"Yes.'' She looked quickly away. "It's never any fun being in a hospital, and not having any visitors makes it even worse. I—I was trying to be kind and compassionate.''

"I see,'' he drawled with an undertone of amusement. "Now you've decided that to keep peace with your fiancé, it's best not to see me anymore."

"That's what I decided," Susan agreed, unconsciously touching the diamond solitaire on her finger. "I have to be fair with Warren."

"I'm afraid you have a problem."

"What?" She slid a wary sideways glance at his face.

Mitch continued to gaze complacently out the window. "The doctor will be releasing me from the hospital tomorrow morning or Friday at the very latest."

"And?" Susan frowned, not seeing how that news would present her with any difficulty.

"And," there was a wicked light in his blue eyes when he looked at her, "your father has invited me to dinner on Friday night."

"No," she said in a small voice.

"Yes." Mitch nodded firmly.

"But you can't go!" she protested.

"I've already accepted the invitation."

"Then phone Dad and tell him you can't come," Susan insisted. "You can think of some excuse to refuse."

"But I'm not going to refuse," Mitch said patiently.

"You have to."

"Why? I like your family and I'm looking forward to one of your mother's home-cooked meals. I don't see any reason I should deny myself the pleasure simply because you have a jealous fiancé. He's going to have to learn to trust you more."

"Warren trusts me," Susan said defensively.

Mitch chuckled. "Of course, it's me that he

doesn't trust, and with good reason. He knows I want you."

"Stop saying things like that!" She spun away from him, angry at him for not refusing the invitation and for the daring and disturbing statement he had just made. "I'm engaged to Warren!"

"You're beginning to sound like a broken record," he taunted.

"I'll repeat myself a thousand times if that's what it takes before you accept what I'm saying!" Her eyes flashed angrily at his mocking expression.

Sobering, Mitch studied her intently for several long seconds, gazing so deeply into her eyes that she had the uncanny sensation he knew what she was thinking. Then, slowly, his firm male mouth grooved into a smile, carving faint dimples into the smooth, lean cheeks.

"You only have nine hundred-odd times to go," he told her.

"Oh!" Her foot stamped the floor in a childish tantrum. "It's hopeless trying to reason with you! Warren said you were much too conceited, and he was right!"

"Do you mean Warren *isn't* always right?" Her outburst only deepened his mocking smile.

Blinking back the furious tears of rage that scalded her eyes, Susan stalked from the room.

"I'll see you on Friday night." Mitch's parting jibe was followed by a throaty chuckle that whipped her already raw nerves. If she had looked back she might have gained some satisfaction from seeing his immediate grimace of pain because of his cracked ribs.

Almost an hour later, she tapped on the connecting door to Warren's office, waiting for his summons before entering. He glanced up from the papers spread before him, straightening against the tall-backed leather chair as he recognized her.

"Did you get the papers safely delivered to my father?" But his dark, inspecting eyes asked an entirely different question.

"Yes, I did." Susan walked to his desk and handed him the keys to his car.

"Good." Warren nodded, and paused expectantly.

Susan knew she could avoid answering his unasked question. She also knew she could avoid mentioning Mitch's intention to join her family for dinner on Friday evening. Unfortunately, there was an excellent chance that her family, especially her brother, might not be so silent about it.

"I saw Mitch today." Susan tried to make it sound like an unexpected happening that was of little importance. Warren said nothing and waited. "I told him I wouldn't be visiting him anymore."

"Susan!" Warren breathed warmly. He leaned forward in his chair, a smile lightening his imposing and rugged features.

"Wait." She held up a cautioning hand. "There's something else I have to tell you."

His dark head tipped to the side in wariness. "What?"

"My father invited Mitch Braden to dinner on Friday night and he accepted."

"Your father! Good God!" Warren breathed in deeply, a look of anger stealing over his face. "Why?"

"How should I know why?" Susan shrugged with bewildered anger. "I suppose it was a combination of reasons. My family's already met him. My father is a racing fan and I guess he got along rather well with Mitch the last time. And Greg practically hero-worships him. Mother agreed, probably because she felt sorry for him, because of the accident and all. In any case, he's coming to dinner and there isn't anything I can do about it."

"I wouldn't be surprised to learn he did everything but ask to be invited," Warren muttered. "And I'm tied up Friday night. I wonder if he knew about that, too."

"Really, Warren, he isn't omniscient," she chided.

"Sometimes I wonder about that Indy man." He shook his head. "I just don't like the idea of you being alone with him for an entire evening."

"With Greg and Amy and Mom and Dad, I'm hardly going to be alone with him," she pointed out.

"You know what I mean."

"Yes," Susan agreed, knowing that in some way Mitch would make his presence felt. "If I thought I wouldn't have to do a lot of endless explaining to Dad, I would arrange to be out. Besides, I don't want it to look as if I'm running away from him."

"You're right," he conceded. "Then plan to be home. He might as well see that you belong to me even when I'm not around."

Chapter Six

"More coffee, Mitch?" her mother asked.

"No, thanks, Beth," he replied, raising his hand in refusal. "My ribs are already saying I've eaten too much."

Susan gritted her teeth. Less than half an hour after Greg had brought him from his hotel, Mitch had been calling her parents by their first names. The easy friendliness between them irritated her.

"Mom remembered last time that you said Swiss steak was your favorite, so she fixed it especially for you tonight," Amy said. "And I helped."

"I guess I have to divide my compliments to the chef between the two of you." Mitch smiled. "I'm flattered that you remembered, Beth."

"Thank you." Her mother was momentarily flustered and Susan seethed inwardly.

"There's nothing like a home-cooked meal," her father stated.

"I'd forgotten what I'd been missing," Mitch agreed ruefully.

"Yeah, but you lead such an exciting life." Greg glanced at him enviously. "Mom's a great cook, but—" He shrugged his shoulders to indicate that food was not important compared to the adventures Mitch had known.

"I thought the same way when I was your age, Greg." His tone held gentle understanding. "But ten years of living in hotels and eating in restaurants can make a man change his mind about a lot of things."

"Haven't you ever considered settling down?" Beth Mabry asked with maternal concern.

Through his spiky dark lashes, his blue eyes glittered at Susan. She met the look with determined indifference.

"Until recently, I was much too busy." His gaze swung back to her mother. "A time or two I've considered buying a house or renting an apartment so I could say I had a home base. But without someone to share it with, it would have been no different from a hotel room."

"You're a very attractive man. I find it hard to believe you haven't found anyone you were willing to share a home with," Beth Mabry laughed with gentle disbelief.

"You have to realize I'm seldom in one place long enough to really get acquainted with anyone. And the chances of meeting someone—say, like your daughter—" Mitch looked at Susan again, but she kept her eyes downcast, knowing they were flashing with temper again, "is unlikely in my profession."

"And when you do, the girl is probably engaged,

like myself," Susan couldn't resist inserting in sugared tones.

"Exactly," Mitch agreed.

"I still think it would be an exciting life," Greg insisted. "When I get older, that's what I want to do."

"If you live that long," Simon Mabry said dryly.

"You used to drive race cars, Dad. I'm just taking after you," Susan's brother pointed out with a sly grin.

Mitch glanced to her father, his head cocked inquiringly on one side. "You didn't mention that, Simon."

"It was years ago, when I was in college." he shrugged. "At the time it seemed like an easy way to pick up some extra money. When you're young and foolish, you do a lot of things without thinking about the risks."

"Why did you quit, Dad?" Amy forgot her young lady act and curled her feet beneath her on the straight-backed chair. "You could have become a famous racer like Mitch."

"Two reasons, actually." he smiled and glanced at his wife, sitting at the opposite end of the table from him. "The first being the fact that I met your mother. For a while, even after we were married, I rather enjoyed the image of being the dashing adventurer until she told me one night that Susan was on the way. That woke me up to the responsibilities I owed to my future family. I had planned to continue racing until Susan was born so I could have the extra money to pay the doctor and hospital bills. Then one day I was working on my car—I couldn't afford to share my small winnings with a mechanic—and the wrench slipped. I broke all the fingers on my left hand. At that point, I realized that what I really wanted to be was a doctor and I was terrified that the injury to my hand might have finished that dream for good. It didn't. The very next day after the accident, I sold the car.''

"When you get married, Mitch, will you give up racing?" Amy propped an elbow on her knee and rested her chin in her hand.

"No, I don't think so," he mused absently. "Eventually I'll have to, of course. Unlike your father, I want to race cars. It's my life."

"Aren't you being a little arrogant?" Susan said tightly. "What you would be telling the woman you married is that this is your life and she can take it or leave it. Surely she has some say in your joint future?"

A steel blue gaze focused on her, his expression unyielding yet not cold or angry. "I'm willing to take her as she is and not attempt to change her. Is it wrong to expect the same in return? Or even arrogant?" Susan looked away from the unwavering directness of his gaze, her sense of righteous indignation deflated by his reasonableness.

"I suppose not," she admitted with quiet reluctance.

"It would be rather like asking Warren to give up his law practice, wouldn't it?" her mother put in rhetorically. "A woman would learn to adjust to the dangers of your job in the same way that I've accepted the life of a doctor. I never thought of it like that before, but it's true."

"I don't see what all the fuss is about," Amy declared airily, uncurling her legs and rising from the chair. She tossed her head, sending her long hair dancing about her shoulders and catching fire from the overhead light. "I think it would be fabulous to be married to a race car driver."

Greg laughed. "Everything with you is 'fabulous.' The dinner was 'fabulous.' The movie was 'fabulous,' " he mimicked.

"Oh, what do you know about it?" Amy accused, her temper flaring because her brother was making fun of her in front of Mitch.

Beth Mabry rose to her feet. "I think it's about time we started washing the fabulous dishes."

"Come on, Mitch," her father grinned. "That's our signal to leave the room before she ties aprons around our waists."

"It was a delicious meal, Beth," Mitch offered, wincing slightly at the pain in his rib cage when he rose from the chair. Then he winked at Amy. "Prepared by a pair of 'fabulous' cooks."

Amy giggled and quickly covered her mouth with a hand as if wishing she had made a more adult reaction. Susan's mouth tightened grimly as she quickly began stacking the dishes on the table rather than watch her father and Mitch leave the dining room. Her younger sister was dreamily watching him go. He seemed to have her entire family in the palm of his hand, Susan thought disgustedly.

"Amy, would you stop mooning over that man and help clear the table!" Susan snapped.

"I am not mooning over him!" Amy's eyes widened indignantly. "And you don't have to be so grouchy!" Susan bit back an even sharper retort, knowing it wasn't fair to take her temper out on Amy. Her sister was at an impressionable age where her crushes were painfully deep and short-lived.

"Besides," Amy lifted her chin to a haughty

angle, "it's my turn for the dishes and it's your job to clear the table," she declared before flouncing into the kitchen.

Susan glanced at her mother and sighed. "Was I ever that obnoxious?"

"We all were." Her mother smiled faintly, and picked up a stack of dishes, carrying them into the kitchen. Susan followed within minutes carrying more dishes. She opened the door in time to hear Amy ask, "How long will Mitch be staying tonight, Mom?"

"I don't know. I imagine until your father drives him to his hotel. Why?" Beth Mabry replied, adjusting the controls on the dishwasher before loading it.

"Couldn't I do the dishes after he leaves?" Amy pleaded. "I mean, he's just got out of the hospital and all. He might be tired and ask to leave early."

"I'm sure he'll stay until after the dishes are done," her mother answered with a straight face but a decided twinkle in her eyes that countered Susan's look of despair.

"We could leave the dishes altogether," Amy suggested, unwilling to give up. "I promise I'll help you do them in the morning."

"The answer is no, Amy."

"If you would help, Amy," Susan put in with thinning patience, "instead of standing around trying to think of reasons not to do the dishes, we might finish them sooner. Besides, Mitch Braden can survive without your company for a little while."

Amy whirled about. "Just because you don't like him, Susan, that's no reason I can't! And don't tell me what I should do!"

"Susan," her mother said with astonishment, "don't you like Mitch?"

"Of course I like him," Susan answered nervously, "but I certainly don't think he's some Greek god who's come down from Olympus to walk with us mortals the way Amy does. He's just a man."

"But what a man!" Amy retorted smugly. "Compared to him, Warren is a total nerd."

"Mother," Susan breathed in deeply, "if you don't do something about this daughter of yours, so help me, I will!"

"Stop it, both of you!" was the stern response. Returning to the dining room, Susan finished clearing the table. She had resolved not to lose her temper with Amy, then lost it anyway. She herself had felt the force of Mitch's attraction. Amy was so young and vulnerable that it was only natural she should fall under his spell. With the dining room straightened and all the chairs in the proper place at the table, Susan walked back into the kitchen straight to her younger sister.

"I'll finish drying the wineglasses for you," she said, taking the linen towel from Amy's hands. "Go on into the living room." She smiled at the joy gleaming instantaneously in her sister's face. "And I'm sorry for putting you down."

"Oh, Susan, you're fabulous!" Amy hugged her quickly and dashed from the room. Susan could hear her footsteps slow to a more ladylike pace before she reached the living room.

The clean-up went fast and Susan felt compelled by a sense of polite duty to follow her mother into the living room. She chose a chair apart from the others, curling up in a shadowed corner which allowed her an unobstructed view of her family and Mitch Braden.

Despite the armless sleeve and the bulging cast beneath his shirt, he looked leanly powerful, like the coiled muscular shape of a jungle cat. The lampshade kept the light from touching off the golden fire of his brown hair, but a blue light seemed to glow warmly in his eyes.

Her family was so at ease with him. The conversation wasn't stilted as it often was when Warren visited them. She had expected Mitch to dominate the discussion, but he had a knack of drawing others into the conversation. But he seemed to sense her faint hostility. She guessed he had been aware of it all evening and was now leaving her alone.

Fine, she told herself, that was what she wanted, but she felt strangely left out, and it didn't help to remind herself that it was her own choice. The cuckoo clock sang out the ten o'clock hour. Mitch glanced at his wristwatch as if to confirm the time.

"I'm sorry, I didn't realize it was so late," he apologized warmly. "I didn't mean to outstay my welcome."

"You aren't leaving already?" Amy moaned.

"It's late, Red," Mitch smiled, then glanced to her father. "Guess I'll call a cab. Greg doesn't have to drive me home."

"Nonsense," Simon Mabry refused vigorously. "The night air will do me good. I won't hear of you taking a cab."

"I appreciate your kindness," Mitch said with a nod. "And I can't thank you enough for this evening. You've all made me feel very welcome."

"Wish you didn't have to leave," said Greg with obvious sincerity.

"So do I," Mitch agreed as he carefully rose to his feet. "My hotel room is going to seem awfully cold and silent after an evening in your home, Beth. Thank you."

"Why do you have to go back there?" Amy frowned, a faint pout on her lips. "I don't see why you couldn't stay here with us."

"Then I definitely would wear out my welcome." The lines around his mouth deepened with a gentle smile.

Susan breathed a silent sigh of relief at his instant refusal. For a second, she had thought he was going to make some wistful remark.

"That's an idea," her father said thoughtfully and Susan's eyes widened in apprehension. "We do have that guest room upstairs, Beth. Nobody uses it for anything."

"Simon—" Mitch held up his hand.

"He's right," Beth Mabry interrupted. "We would be happy to have you stay with us, Mitch."

"I couldn't take advantage of your generosity that way." He shook his head in refusal.

"You wouldn't be taking advantage of us," Beth insisted. "If we didn't want you to stay, we wouldn't have asked. And one more person in this house isn't any extra trouble. Greg and Amy are always inviting their friends over and I'm used to it."

"It's a tempting invitation, Beth, but I don't think I should accept it," Mitch refused again.

Susan, who had been staring in silent protest, finally spoke out. "We understand, Mitch. We wouldn't want you to do anything you would regret. After all, you're used to coming and going as you please and you would probably feel your movements were restricted, staying here with us."

His level blue gaze focused on her and a sudden merry twinkle came into his eyes. "On the contrary, Susan," he smiled, "I was more concerned that your parents might regret inviting a stranger into their home."

"You're not a stranger!" Amy said vehemently.

"I agree," Simon Mabry added. "Speaking for myself, I feel as if we've known you for a very long time. We'd be happy to have you if you would like to stay."

"Well, if you insist on twisting my arm," Mitch shrugged, smiling crookedly, "I guess I have no choice but to accept."

Amy cheered unabashedly while Susan trembled with impotent rage. How could she possibly live under the same roof with him for the three or four weeks he would be staying? She was filled with the uneasy premonition that nothing would be the same after he left. Her life would be irrevocably altered. Greg scrambled to his feet. "I'll come along with Dad and help you pack up your things at the hotel. You can move in tonight. Wow! Wait until my best buds hear about this!" his voice cracked in excitement.

"No, it's too late tonight," Mitch pointed out. "I'll have everything packed and ready to go tomorrow at noon. That'll give you time to reconsider the invitation. And I promise I'll understand if you change your mind."

"We won't," Amy declared as if making a solemn vow.

Unmindful of the startled looks she received from her family, Susan muttered a hurried "Excuse me" and walked quickly from the room. She had no particular destination in mind. She wasn't even conscious of where she was when she came to a stop in front of the kitchen sink. Yanking open a cupboard door above her head, she removed a drinking glass and filled it with cold water. She was just lifting it to her lips when the kitchen door opened. She counted to ten before turning toward it, expecting to see the reproving face of her mother.

"Do you always sulk when things don't go the way you want?" Mitch asked in a low voice laced with curious amusement.

"How could you do this?" Susan hissed angrily.

"Do what?" he repeated with deliberate blankness. "All I've done is accept a neighborly invitation," he drawled lazily.

"Yes." She was so angry she could hardly speak. "All you did was accept an invitation you did everything but get on your knees and ask for!"

"Are you implying that I tricked your parents into inviting me to stay here?" His hurt, affronted look might have seemed genuine if it wasn't for the sparkle in his eyes.

"Yes," she snapped.

"You really believe I could be that devious?"

"Yes!"

A brow raised briefly in resignation. "Time is running out on me. I have to take advantage of every minute that I can."

"What does that mean?" Susan demanded guardedly.

"You're a smart girl, I think you'll figure it out." He smiled.

"Good night, beautiful. I'll see you tomorrow."

He was being deliberately mysterious to confuse her and sidetrack her from the issue. Her fingers tightened around the glass of water in her hand, then paused.

"I wouldn't throw that glass if I were you," he warned, on the verge of laughing. "I think you'd have difficulty explaining to your parents how dropping a glass splattered water all over the walls and door." He walked out.

The second time the door opened, it was Beth Mabry who entered. Susan raised the glass to her mouth and took a long gulp of water.

"What's the matter?" her mother asked quietly.

"It's just going to be awful." Susan avoided the gentle eyes studying her.

"What is?"

"Mitch Braden living here, that's what." She set the partially empty glass on the counter with an impatient wave of her hand.

"Now, why do you say that?" Her mother's curiosity was tinged with surprise as she walked to the counter where Susan stood.

"Because—" Susan glanced up, trying to control the desperate anger that wanted to erupt. "Because Warren is jealous."

"Jealous? Of Mitch Braden? For heaven's sake, why?"

This time Susan related the exact circumstances surrounding her first meeting with Mitch Braden and the subsequent encounters, not omitting the way Mitch constantly flirted with her.

"Does Warren know all of this?" Beth asked when Susan had finished. Her expression was gentle with understanding, but there was a faint gleam of amusement in her eyes that Susan found irritating.

"Of course he doesn't know all of it. He would

be positively furious if he knew everything. But he isn't going to understand why you've invited Mitch to stay here. For that matter, neither do I."

"Yes, you do." Her mother smiled. "Perhaps if I'd known about the way things were between Mitch and Warren I might have considered the invitation more thoroughly before inviting him to stay here. But we certainly can't retract it now even if we wanted to, not unless you want to explain this whole story to the others."

"Greg would have a field day with it." Susan sighed, running a weary hand through her dark hair.

"Besides, you and Warren are engaged. And since you've done nothing to encourage Mitch," there was a brief pause as Susan suddenly averted her head, "then I think Warren should learn to trust you and to accept that you can handle the situation. Mitch isn't staying forever, just a few weeks."

"It's going to seem like an eternity." Susan sighed.

"You're beginning to exaggerate like your younger sister," her mother teased.

Smiling ruefully, Susan pushed herself away from the counter. "If it wasn't so painful being thirteen, then I'd wish I was Amy's age. Good night, Mom."

"It will all work out for the best, Susan."

"Sure," she answered in a doubting-Thomas voice.

* * *

Early on Saturday afternoon, Mitch moved in bag and baggage. The house was in a gleeful turmoil the entire afternoon. Mr. Mabry had decided the garage had to be cleaned out to make room for Mitch's Ferrari. He had driven it over for him since Mitch couldn't manage the gearshift with his broken arm.

Susan tried to stay out of the commotion as much as she could, but the excitement rippling through the house touched her in spite of her attempts to avoid it.

Each time she caught herself about to join the laughter and chatting voices of her family and Mitch, she would remind herself of Warren's inevitable reaction when he came to pick her up for their date that night.

It was difficult being miserable when everyone else was having fun.

As Susan dressed for her date with Warren, she considered Mitch's attitude toward her that day. He had seemed to pay little attention to her. She had expected him to be smugly triumphant, ready to remind her mockingly of his presence in her home at every opportunity. Yet he had been as friendly with her as he had been with the rest of the family.

It wouldn't last, she just knew it. He was merely biding his time. She couldn't afford to relax her guard even for an instant.

The sound of a car pulling into the drive drifted through the screened windows, opened to admit the warm breeze of the early summer's night. Adding the finishing touch of lipstick, Susan hurried to her room, picking up the crocheted shawl from her bed before hurrying out again for the staircase. Warren was early.

The doorbell rang when she reached the top of

the stairs. Before her toe touched the first step, a voice called out from the living room below.

"I'll answer it!" Mitch said cheerfully. Susan froze, unable to walk down the flight of steps before Mitch reached the front door. Whistling absently, he appeared below her, the empty white shirt-sleeve tucked into the waistband of his trousers.

The door was swung open and Susan could just barely see the dark gray of Warren's trousers. She could visualize the stunned look on his face.

"Hello, Warren. Come on in," Mitch greeted, inviting him in as if he had done it a thousand times before, just as if he was a permanent member of the household. He stepped to one side to allow Warren to enter. turning toward the stairs where Susan waited in dread.

"Susan, it's for you!" Mitch called loudly, then paused as he met her gaze. "Sorry, I didn't see you standing there."

I just bet you didn't, Susan thought savagely when she saw the wicked glint in the blue eyes. She averted her gaze to the steps before her as she finally started down.

"Warren is here to pick you up," Mitch announced unnecessarily.

"I can see that," Susan snapped. One look at the glowering rage in Warren's expression told her in no uncertain terms what he thought of the freehanded way Mitch was making himself at home. Susan hurried her pace, fearing an explosion at any second.

With infuriating calm, Mitch waited at the bottom of the stairs with Warren, his mocking gaze watching her descent and knowing the reason for the flush of anger in her cheeks.

Deliberately she ignored Mitch to look directly at Warren. "I'm ready if you are," she said, reaching out for Warren's arm.

"You two have a nice time," Mitch offered as Warren pivoted sharply around to leave. "Don't keep Susan out too late. She needs her beauty sleep." He emphasized the word *beauty* before he closed the door behind them.

Warren began striding toward his car, indifferent to the fact that Susan had to practically run to keep up with him. "Would you kindly explain to me what he's doing there?" His voice vibrated with checked rage.

"You aren't going to like it," Susan said in a very hesitant voice.

He held the car door open for her, his dark gaze sweeping her apprehensive face, its coldness chilling her to the bone.

"There's nothing about the man that I like, and I have the feeling I'll like this even less."

Susan waited until he was in the car before dropping her bombshell. The response was what she expected and dreaded.

"You can't be serious! You can't possibly mean he's going to be living in the same house with you!"

"I'm perfectly serious," she replied in a forced calm voice.

"Your parents actually invited him to stay!" Warren shook his head in disbelief. "Didn't you tell them what kind of man he is?"

"What could I tell them?" Susan reasoned. "That he pays me outrageous compliments? That he flirts with me? They would have laughed and asked him anyway. They like him."

"So you're just accepting it?" he asked grimly. "You're not making any attempt to change the situation?"

"What do you want me to do, Warren?" The impatience she felt and Warren's lack of understanding about her helplessness to correct the situation made her voice sharp. "Move out?"

"You could at least consider it," he snapped.

"He isn't going to live there permanently, only for a few weeks," she reminded him.

"I have a feeling there's going to be trouble," Warren muttered.

Susan echoed the thought, but only to herself.

Chapter Seven

Susan walked into the kitchen. "Is there anything I can help you with, Mom, before Warren comes?"

Glancing up from the salad bowl in front of her, Beth Mabry cut the last tomato into wedges and put them atop the others in the red mound on top of the lettuce. She surveyed her daughter quickly, taking in the freshness of the yellow sundress with its flirty white polka dots.

"Yes, you can toss this salad while I scrub some potatoes to bake," she answered, drying her hands on a terry dish towel. As Susan moved toward her, Beth paused. "On second thought, you'd better have Greg take the charcoal out and get the barbecue grill started. I think he's in the garage tinkering with his car."

"I'll finish the salad when I come back, then." Susan nodded, and walked toward the kitchen door that led directly into the garage. As she opened the door, she heard Mitch say, "Try it again, Greg."

Her brother was sitting halfway behind the wheel of his car, the door open, and Mitch was bending to look under the hood. Greg turned the key in the ignition. There was a whining growl and nothing happened. With an impatient grimace, Greg stepped out and walked to the front of the car where Mitch was intently studying the motor.

"Greg, Mom wants you to take the charcoal out back and get the grill started," Susan told him, her gaze unwillingly drawn to Mitch, who didn't even look up at the sound of her voice.

He was wearing a pair of soiled overalls in a deep shade of azure blue, the plaster cast on his arm concealed behind the zippered front.

"Not now, Susan," Greg muttered with a dismissing glance. "I'm busy."

"If you want to eat before dark, you'd better go do it now," she replied. "It won't take you that long."

"You might as well." Mitch straightened. "This isn't something we're going to fix in a few minutes."

And still he didn't look at Susan. Ever since Saturday night he had seemed to take her existence for granted, as if her presence in the house didn't warrant any special attention. Mitch hadn't ignored her, but he had treated her no differently than he had the rest of the family. He could have been her older brother.

"Oh, all right. I'll start the stupid grill," Greg grumbled, his lanky frame moving with a long stride to a corner of the garage where the bag of charcoal briquets sat. Picking it up, he roughly shoved open the rear door leading into the back-yard and kicked it shut with his foot.

Mitch started to fiddle with something under the hood and Susan turned to leave, not really certain why she had waited.

"Would you mind lighting me a cigarette, Susan?" Mitch asked absently. "My hand is all greasy. The pack's on the workbench. The lighter should be there, too." He waved in the general direction of the counter built into the rear wall of one side of the garage.

Susan hesitated briefly, then walked to the counter, littered with various kinds of garden and mechanical tools. She took a cigarette from the pack and lit it, surprised to find the hand that held the lighter was trembling slightly. She turned to give it to him as he walked toward her, an absent frown of concentration on his handsome face, but instead of reaching for the cigarette, his right hand removed a rag from the workbench. His head tipped sideways toward Susan, indicating she should place the lit cigarette in his mouth. She did so reluctantly, though he barely seemed to notice her at all.

"Thanks," he offered, speaking through the cigarette between his lips. He tried, ineffectively, to wipe the worst of the grime off his hand. Then he sighed. "How does a man with one hand wash the dirt off that hand?"

"That's a good question." Susan had to laugh a little. The amusement that shone in his eyes made it impossible to take offense at a comment he was directing against himself. "I suppose you'll have to have someone else do it for you."

"I suppose so," he agreed, squinting his eyes

against the smoke before gingerly removing the cigarette from his mouth with two still darkly soiled fingers. He arched his back slightly and winced at the pull the movement exerted on his injured rib cage.

"You really shouldn't be working on that car," Susan said reprovingly, "not in your condition. And you shouldn't be smoking either."

"I'm only giving Greg a hand." Mitch smoothly dismissed the idea that he might be overtaxing himself. "He's doing all the heavy work." He leaned against the counter and ran an appraising eye over her revealing dress. "This is Tuesday night, isn't it? That means you have a date with Warren." It was a casual comment without an undertone of mockery.

"That's right," she admitted cautiously. "He'll be here to pick me up in a little while."

"You don't sound very enthusiastic." He tipped his head to the side, looking at her curiously.

"I—I don't know what you mean." Her chin lifted slightly as if she sensed a need for a defensive attitude.

"The man you're engaged to is going to be here in a little while, and you sound so matter-of-fact about it," he explained with indifference.

"Well, it is a fact," Susan shrugged, a faint look of bewilderment clouding her face.

"Aren't you excited about seeing him again?"

"I just saw him when I left the office at five," she reminded him. "It isn't as though I haven't seen him for a couple of days."

"Of course," Mitch agreed with a wry smile. "Guess I was letting myself be influenced by a lot of romantic nonsense. I assumed that you would miss him no matter how short the time since you last saw him."

"Naturally I miss him," Susan retorted, almost too quickly.

"Naturally?" He arched one eyebrow. "You sound very offhand. Are your dates becoming too routine?"

"What do you expect me to do? Fling myself in his arms every time I see him?"

Mitch smiled. "I'm not expecting anything. I was only pointing out that you don't show much emotion where Warren is concerned."

Her head lifted to a haughty angle. "I save any emotional display for when we're alone," she informed him icily.

"Then the two of you do indulge in a little necking?"

"I don't see that it's any of your business."

"It isn't, not really." The laughing blue eyes moved to her mouth, thinned into a disapproving line.

"Then you shouldn't have brought it up," Susan replied with biting arrogance.

"I couldn't help it. You have a very kissable pair of lips, and I didn't like to think of them going to waste," he mocked.

"I assure you they don't."

Her heartbeat skipped erratically as he studied the movement of her mouth when she spoke. It was unnerving. Susan could feel a warmth start in her midsection and slowly begin to spread through her veins.

"I wonder if anyone taught Warren to share when he was a little boy," Mitch mused, his gaze not wavering from her mouth.

Her breathing became shallow and restricted. She knew she had to escape and quickly. That indefinable magnetism was too much to resist. She averted her face sharply. "I have to go and help Mom in the kitchen."

Taking one step, Mitch moved fluidly to block her way. Behind Susan was the work counter and to one side was the wall. She was very effectively trapped.

"Will you please step out of my way?" But there was a betraying tremor in her voice.

"Bribe me." The grooves around his mouth deepened, faint dimpling lines appearing in his lean cheeks. Susan swallowed nervously and took a step backward. Mitch didn't follow. He didn't have to because there was nowhere she could go to escape him.

"Let me through, please." It sounded more like a plea than the order she had intended to issue.

"Warren will never know I stole a kiss from you unless you tell him," Mitch reasoned, flashing her one of those devastating smiles that made her heart turn over. "What's the harm in one kiss? Neither of you will miss it."

"No!" Susan made a small, negative movement with her head, not taking her wary eyes from him as she considered the chances of successfully pushing her way past him. Any attempt to stop her would be hampered by his injuries.

As if reading her mind, Mitch spoke softly. "It would be a shame if that pretty dress you have got soiled by this combination of grease, oil and dirt. Then you'd have to change clothes and make poor Warren wait. You have a choice, beautiful. You can try to force your way by me, in which case I'll simply take my kiss. Or you can willingly give it to me and not get all messed up."

"You're a blackmailer," she accused in a low voice.

The wicked glint in his eyes only grew brighter. "Which is it to be?"

Wildly Susan searched for a third alternative and couldn't find one. With snapping fire in her brown eyes, she stepped toward him. Mitch obligingly bent his head, suppressing a triumphant smile. Lightly she brushed the warmth of his lips with her own and withdrew immediately.

He shook his head in patient despair. "I said a kiss, not a sisterly peck," he scolded lightly.

Susan breathed in sharply. "That isn't fair!"

"I don't have time to play fair. Are you going to do it right?" Now the blue eyes were daring her to kiss him, silently saying that she didn't have the nerve.

Nibbling uncertainly at her lower lip, Susan wondered if she did. Then she threw caution to the wind and moved toward him again. Her gaze scanned his handsome face, taking in again the challenging glitter in his brilliant blue eyes.

Her lashes fluttered down as her lips trembled against his mouth. Although she didn't draw away, it was still a mock kiss, a stiff touching that only outwardly resembled a kiss.

"Like this, honey," Mitch said against her lips.

His mouth closed warmly over hers, melting the rigidity that had held Susan back. The soft persuasion of his kiss had her yielding before she realized what she was doing, and by then the sensations rushing through her were too firmly in command to try to check.

The sweet possession of his mouth had her reeling. Her hands spread themselves against his chest to steady herself. The beginnings of a fiery response were coursing through her when a door opened.

The sound brought Susan sharply back to reality as she realized what she was doing. Quickly she pushed herself away from Mitch, her head jerking toward the rear garage door. Her fear-widened eyes met Greg's stunned expression before swinging with accusing embarrassment to Mitch's calm face.

Another faintly triumphant smile touched the sensual male lips that seconds before had rocked her common sense. Mitch returned his outstretched arm to his side and stepped back to let her go by him. She stalked angrily away from him.

"Wow," Greg whistled. "Wait until old Warren finds out about this!"

Susan stopped in front of her brother, tears of shame and frustration gathering in her eyes and turning them liquid brown. "If you say one word about this to Warren, Gregory Allen Mabry, so help me I'll . . ."

But no suitably chastising threat came to mind. Her mouth snapped shut and her trembling legs carried her swiftly to the connecting kitchen door.

The memory of that kiss haunted Susan for days. Each time she saw Mitch after that, her gaze unwillingly strayed to his lips, and again the sensation of their touch would flood through her. It was frightening to remember her physical reaction to the essentially forced kiss.

What was worse, Mitch knew she had been disturbed by his kiss. The light in his eyes reminded

Susan of it every time he looked at her, although she made certain no chance would leave her alone in a room with him.

If only she could explain to herself the strange ambivalence of her emotions. She was engaged to a man she loved and respected, yet she had experienced physical desire for another man. How was it possible?

She sighed dispiritedly.

"What's the matter, darling?" Warren probed softly.

"Hmm?" She glanced at him blankly, forgetting for a few minutes where she was and whom she was with. She shook her head slightly, his question sinking in. "Oh, nothing. Just tired, I guess."

"You've been preoccupied nearly all week," he commented, turning the car into the driveway of her home and switching off the engine.

"Nonsense," Susan lied with a smile as she moved contentedly into his arms when he half-turned in his seat.

His mouth closed masterfully over hers. It was an experienced kiss meant to arouse the response that it did. But Susan was disappointed again at the lack of chemical combustion. An ache throbbed painfully in her heart because she couldn't stop herself from comparing Warren's kisses with Mitch's. It wasn't right to do it and she hated herself for it.

"I wish I didn't have to go in," she murmured as he nuzzled the lobe of her ear.

"You're certainly having trouble making up your mind," Warren said. "A minute ago you said you were tired and now you say you wish you didn't have to go in." He drew his head away, gazing at her intently. "That Indy guy hasn't been bothering you, has he?"

"Oh, Warren, don't be silly," Susan said with a brittle laugh. "Of course he hasn't."

"Well, he'd better not." The unspoken threat was obvious and Susan shifted uncomfortably in his arms. "Come on. It's after one o'clock," Warren announced. "You'd better go in or else you'll find yourself getting ready for Sunday morning church without any sleep." He didn't allow Susan an opportunity to express her opinion as he moved her out of his embrace and stepped from the car. She stared at the darkened windows of the house and wondered how she was going to get through the whole of tomorrow—no, today it was now—with Mitch underfoot all the time.

Still silently considering that problem, she accepted Warren's hand out of the car and walked to the front door nestled under the crook of his arm. At the door, he stopped and turned her into his arms.

"I wish we were already married." Susan sighed wistfully as she raised her head for his good night kiss. "Why do we have to wait until August, darling? Why don't we get married now, in June?"

"Because we've already made all our plans with the intention of getting married in August," he said patiently. "Dad will be fully recovered by then and I'll be able to take time off for our honeymoon. Besides, all our friends know of our plans. I respect you too much, Susan, to suddenly throw our plans aside and elope. That would raise too many eyebrows."

"I suppose so," she agreed submissively, and knew she had only been seeking a coward's way out of her dilemma. Mitch would be leaving before the month was out anyway and he would be taking that fleeting physical attraction she felt with him. It was only a matter of time.

"Good night, darling." Warren kissed her tenderly.

"Good night," she whispered when he released her and walked to the car.

She stood in front of the door, lifting a hand in farewell as he reversed out of the drive. Then she reached for the doorknob, the door unlocked as she knew it would be. Stepping inside, she closed the door and leaned against it for a few weary seconds. She breathed in deeply and exhaled a long sigh before straightening and turning to lock the dead bolts. They had just clicked into place when someone rapped lightly on the door.

Susan froze. "Who is it?"

"It's me," a quiet voice answered. "Mitch."

Quickly unlocking the door, she opened it, staring at him with curious wariness. He was leaning lazily with one arm propped against the door frame. Her brows drew together when he failed to walk in.

"What are you doing out there?" she asked.

"Walking and thinking." Susan thought she detected a weariness in his voice. "I wouldn't have bothered you except that I was afraid you would lock me out. I'd hate to wake up the whole household in the middle of the night so someone could let me in."

Glancing at the navy shirt that matched the check of his slim-fitting trousers, Susan noticed that he had worked the long sleeves over the cast on his left arm although it was still held in a sling.

"It's awfully late," she pointed out.

"I wasn't waiting up for you, if that's what you're thinking." Mitch smiled wryly. "I couldn't sleep. My arm was bothering me too much. Healing pains, I guess."

"Oh," Susan replied in a tiny voice. "Would you . . . would you like me to get you something for it?"

"You mean a pain pill? No, thanks," he refused. "The pain isn't so bad that I can't endure it. It's a beautiful night. I'll just wander around out here for a while and see if I can't take my mind off it." He straightened from the door, the moonlight glistening with a silvery sheen on his brown hair.

Sympathy surfaced instantly. "Are you sure there's nothing I can do?" Susan offered.

Mitch hesitated. "Well, you could—" Then he shook his head and stepped away. "No, never mind. You wouldn't want to anyway. Don't lock me out, Susan. Good night."

"Wait," she called hesitantly. "Was there something I could do?"

He shrugged slightly. "I was going to ask if you wanted to walk with me for a while, just so I could have someone to talk to instead of thinking about this throbbing in my arm. But I know you're probably thinking that I had something else in mind. I know you don't trust me, so let's just forget about it."

"What would we talk about?" she asked.

Mitch looked back at her. The expression on the handsomely tanned face was solemn and serious. There was no mockery, not even a suggestion of it lurking anywhere near the surface.

"We could compare the new engine technology

with the last year's," he said indifferently, "or talk about the price of tea in China. It doesn't matter, Susan. Forget I mentioned it."

"We would just talk?" she asked for his confirmation of his earlier statement again.

"I won't promise that." Mitch sighed heavily. "With you, I never know from one minute to the next. Right now all I can think about is the needles stabbing my arm. If you want to walk with me, then all right, let's go. If not—well, I understand why and we'll forget it."

"I'll come," she said quietly, and stepped through the door, shutting it behind her, "for a while," she qualified.

"I'll try to behave." Mitch smiled faintly with a half-promise.

It was a warm summer's night, quiet and lazy. Midnight dew had left tiny diamond drops on the grass and leaves. Crickets chirped in somnolent competition with the cicadas in the trees. The houses lining the streets were dark. There wasn't a moving thing in sight, but the stars shimmered softly, sprinkled over the nearly black sky. The moon, lopsided in three-quarter stage, was a pale gold, changing to silver.

In mutual silence, Susan and Mitch wandered into the backyard where the spreading limbs of a maple tree shaded Beth Mabry's rose garden. Beneath a thick limb was a bench swing, ivory white in the night shade. The scent of roses filled the air.

Susan chose one side of the swing and Mitch the other, with a comfortable space in between. "You were right," she murmured. The quietness was so peaceful that it seemed almost wrong to break it. "It is a beautiful night."

"Thank you. I ordered it specially." Mitch leaned back, an absent smile curving his mouth as he gazed through the maple leaves to the night sky.

"Specially for what?" Susan countered.

"For sleepless nights." The swing rocked gently as he shifted into a more comfortable position, easing the arm sling on to his lap. "Talk to me, Susan."

"What about?" she responded uncertainly.

Mitch slid a sideways glance at her, his mouth curving slightly. "Tell me what it's like to grow up a doctor's daughter."

It was her turn to smile faintly. "I doubt if it's all that different. My childhood was very normal."

But she sensed that it was words he wanted to hear to distract his thoughts from the pain of his healing arm. He was hurting. She could tell by the stiffness of the smile he had given her a second ago, one without warmth.

"Begin at the beginning, then," Mitch instructed, "with your very normal entry into the world."

"Well, let's see." Susan leaned back in the swing, staring into the night sky as Mitch was doing. "The stork brought me the first year that Mom and Dad were married. Dad was still in college. He hadn't begun his postgraduate work in medical school yet. My unplanned arrival on the scene was a hardship for them, I know. But Mom said she never regretted having me. She said she didn't know what she would have done if I hadn't been around to keep her company when Dad was putting in those long hours of internship. She worked, of course, and the landlady, Mrs. Gibson, took care of me. Greg arrived the year Dad started his own practice. Amy came four years later." His eyes were closed when she looked at him. Susan wondered if he was asleep or merely resting. Then Mitch spoke to fill the silent pause.

"I was sure I was going to hear about all the contests you won as a baby," he mocked lightly without really opening his eyes. "You had to have been a teacher's pet at school."

"Pet or pest?" Susan laughed softly.

Quietly she began to relate anecdotes of her childhood in school and at home. While she talked, she studied him. His closed eyes kept her inspection safe from discovery. In repose, his face—minus crinkling laughter around his eyes and the dimpling lines in the smooth lean cheeks—was still extraordinarily handsome. The roguish air was gone.

Indomitable strength was roughly and arrogantly carved in Warren's features. Mitch Braden possessed the same strength, but in him it was tempered with determination and consideration. Mitch did not overpower people with the force of his personality. He charmed them to his side. Concluding a story about a pet rabbit she had received one Easter, Susan noticed his breathing had become quite even and how relaxed his posture had become.

"Mitch?" she murmured.

"Yes," he answered in a clear, quiet voice.

"Did my talk bore you into falling asleep?" she inquired, wryly amused by his drowsiness.

Mitch opened his eyes, blue and jewel-bright, focusing his gaze unerringly on her face and looked at her steadily. "I don't think there's anything about you that would bore me, Susan," he replied quite seriously.

Unnerved by the smooth way he had countered her jesting comment with a disturbing compliment, Susan turned away. The atmosphere of moonlight and roses was too romantic for her to be completely untouched by his statement.

"It's your turn now to tell me about yourself," she said, trying to change the subject.

"What do you want to know?" Mitch asked curiously. "And where should I start? I got into a lot of trouble when I was a kid."

Susan didn't want to know about his childhood. She was reluctant to hear about the personal details of his past life. It was better not to learn too much about him.

"Tell me about racing." She chose a safer topic. "Why do you do it?"

"That's like asking why a man climbs a mountain or why a matador enters the bullring." He chuckled softly at her question. "It's the constant challenge, I suppose."

"What's it like to drive in a race?"

He considered her question for several seconds before answering. "Your heart pounds, adrenaline surges through your system, and your senses are more alert than you can ever remember. It's the high level of energy that sustains you when the gravity force exerted on you in the turns tries to pull you apart. It keeps you going when you're so bone weary and exhausted that you want to drop. There's a crazy kind of peace and freedom you feel when you're out there on the track. I don't know where it comes from," he mused thoughtfully. "It isn't from the cheering of the crowd or the deafening roar of a powerful engine. It isn't even from being the first car over the finish line. It comes from inside, I guess. You're competing with yourself, driving yourself to the limit of what you can endure, then discovering you can go farther."

"Aren't you ever frightened?" Susan asked, suddenly fascinated by the insight into a sport she had never really considered in such a philosophical way.

"A man would be a fool if he didn't admit to being aware of the danger and the risks." Mitch smiled. "But you don't have time to be frightened, not at the speed you're traveling. By the time your mind can concentrate on the thing that frightens you, whether it's a particularly steep bank or the out-of-control car ahead of you, you're already past it or the worst has happened."

His calm acceptance of the hazards made Susan shiver. Her heart was in her throat just visualizing Mitch in the Indy 500. There was the instinctive knowledge that she would live with fear if she ever watched him race.

"I think it's time we went into the house," Mitch announced. "It's beginning to get cool, and you must be tired."

Susan didn't correct his assumption that her shiver had been from the growing coolness of the night air. She accepted the hand he offered to help her out of the swing.

"How is your arm?" she asked. "Still bothering you?"

"Hardly at all now." A lazy smile spread across

his features, crinkling the corners of his eyes. "Thanks to you."

Mitch didn't release her hand as they retraced their steps to the front of the house. The warmth of his grip was comforting. It was as if he was silently assuring her not to worry about him.

Chapter Eight

Inside the house, Mitch released her hand and turned to lock the front door. Susan waited for him a few steps inside. She didn't know why except that it seemed the polite thing to do.

"Are you tired?" He glanced at her inquiringly.

"A little," she admitted. "Aren't you?"

"Unfortunately, no." His shoulders lifted in a rueful gesture.

"Do you suppose your mother would object if I fixed myself some cocoa? I can't stand hot milk."

"Of course she wouldn't mind." Susan hesitated, then added, "I'll fix it for you, if you like."

There was a merry sparkle in his look. "To tell you the truth, I was hoping you'd volunteer. I didn't like the idea of having to poke through the cupboards trying to find things. You'll join me, won't you?"

The boyish honesty and engaging smile were too

much for Susan to combat. Besides, although she was tired, she wasn't ready for the evening to end. She didn't want to examine the reason for that thought too closely.

"Yes, I'll join you," she agreed. "Do you want to have it in the kitchen or shall I bring it into the living room?"

"The kitchen is fine. We'll be less likely to disturb the others there." Mitch started for the hallway leading to the kitchen. "I'll give you a hand. Of course I only have one hand that I can use."

In the kitchen, Susan put the milk on to heat and stirred in a paste of cocoa and sugar. She pointed out the cupboard where Mitch could find the mugs and another one where the marshmallows were kept.

As the cocoa mixture began to simmer, Susan glanced over her shoulder at Mitch. He was walking toward her, carrying the two mugs by a finger curled through the handles.

"There are sugar cookies in the cookie jar if you want a snack," she offered.

"No, thanks," he refused, and watched as she carefully poured the hot chocolate into the mugs and floated a pair of marshmallows in each mug.

They each carried their own cup to the narrow breakfast table in front of the windows overlooking the backyard. Mitch waited as Susan sat down in the chair at the head of the table, then he took the chair to her left.

"How long have you known Warren?" he asked casually.

"Why?" Susan tipped her head to one side, surprised by his unexpected question.

"Just curious." Mitch shrugged.

Susan couldn't think of any reason not to answer his question. "I was formally introduced to him when I went to work for the law firm. Two years ago I became his personal assistant when his previous one left to get married."

"That's quite a long courtship, isn't it?" He grinned crookedly.

"Oh, no," she hurried to explain. "We didn't start dating until after the Christmas party last year."

"Not until then?" He frowned in faint disbelief.

"Well, Warren didn't actually notice me as more than his assistant until then." She sipped self-consciously at her steaming cocoa.

"The man must have been blind." He laughed. "What about you? Had you noticed him?"

Susan stirred the melting marshmallows into her hot chocolate. "Assistants are always in love with their bosses without their bosses being aware of it." She tried to make it a joke, unable to meet the mocking glint in Mitch's eyes.

"I thought everybody knew that."

"And after the Christmas party, it was a case of love at first and very late sight for Warren, is that it?" Mitch inquired with decided cynicism. "I mean, you already believed you were half in love with him."

"I guess it was like that," Susan admitted nervously.

"Then how long have you been engaged?"

"Since April."

"April Fools' Day?" he asked mockingly.

There was a defiant tilt of her chin. "He gave me the ring over the Easter weekend, if you must know."

"I would have thought you would have planned a traditional June wedding," Mitch gazed thoughtfully at the cup in his hand, "instead of waiting until August. But then I guess the idea to marry then wasn't yours."

Warily Susan studied his bland expression, a thought just occurring to her and one that she probably should have had earlier.

"You were hiding somewhere listening to Warren and me tonight, weren't you?" she accused in a low, angry voice.

"Inadvertently," he admitted without apology. "I didn't intentionally eavesdrop. I heard the car drive in and assumed it was you. I wanted to be certain you didn't lock me out of the house. Warren usually doesn't walk you to the door, or at least he hasn't lately."

Susan remembered suddenly that the guest bedroom that Mitch used had a clear view of the front door. He must have been spying on her ever since he had come.

"You could have let us know you were there," she retorted bitterly, trying to remember what she and Warren had said.

"The topic sounded very personal. I didn't think either of you would appreciate my opinion on the matter," Mitch explained, the wicked glitter back in his blue eyes. "Does he make love to you?"

The spoon clattered from her hand on to the table. Fire flashed in her eyes.

"If you're asking whether I sleep with him, then you're just going to have to wonder, because I have no intention of answering!" Her sex life, such as it was, was absolutely none of Mitch's business, she thought furiously.

"Temper, temper, Susan!" He studied her for a long moment. "Obviously the man doesn't."

"Obviously?" she echoed angrily. "Why obviously?"

"There are several things that made me reach that conclusion," Mitch answered lazily. "You might have wanted to set the wedding date ahead because you were becoming frustrated sexually. And everything is so precise between the two of you. Certain nights you have dates. On the weeknights he has you home at a certain hour. Everything fits into a prim pattern. Believe me, Warren isn't a man overcome with passion. He's doing everything by the book, including waiting until the wedding night."

Trembling, Susan stared at him while he casually drank his cocoa. "You sound as if that's something to be ashamed of!" she accused. "Maybe it's my choice to wait."

"Okay," Mitch said. "But wouldn't you feel better if his control broke just once? Wouldn't it make him a little more human?"

"I don't know what you're talking about." She looked away hastily, staring at the foamy residue clinging to the sides of her mug. "Besides, Warren is in love with me, whether you want to believe it or not."

"In his way, yes." He nodded agreeably.

"What do you mean by that?" she asked with an irritated sigh.

"If I were a woman engaged to a man and that man held me in his arms and declared how very much he respected me, I would be insulted," he answered simply.

"I see." Her fingers drummed a war beat on the

tabletop. "What you're really saying is that you wouldn't respect the woman you married. Isn't that right, Mr. Braden?"

"Naturally I would respect her, or I wouldn't marry her." Mitch met the angry look in her eyes with good-humored patience. "But that certainly isn't the emotion I would want to feel when I held her in my arms."

"No, I suppose you would feel lust," Susan retorted sarcastically.

"Why not? I'm a lusty man." Amusement touched his mouth, her barbs bouncing off without inflicting one prick.

"I think you're impossible!" she declared with a frustrated shake of her head as she looked away. Out of the corner of her eye, she saw him rub the back of his neck, with a slight stretching motion of his shoulders.

"And because I would enjoy making love to the woman I want to marry, that makes me impossible?" he chided.

"You make it sound as if it's all your decision," Susan replied. "I should think she might have something to say about it."

"If she loved me, she would be willing." His hand moved to wearily rub his mouth and chin. Susan's stifled gasp of indignant outrage drew his gaze to her. "You don't believe me, do you?"

"I think you're pretty conceited!"

"Maybe," Mitch acknowledged nonchalantly. "But if I were Warren and you professed to love me as much as you say you love him, and if I chose to take advantage of that love—which I admit is what I would be doing—then I could have you in bed with me within twenty minutes and you wouldn't protest."

"Of all the—" Susan sputtered.

But Mitch wasn't listening. His hand was covering a yawn that brought a watery brightness to his eyes. When it was over, he glanced at Susan, sending her a sheepishly rueful grin.

"That's a boastful statement to make, isn't it, for a man who's too tired to back it up," he said with half a sigh. "I guess the hot chocolate did the trick."

Pushing the chair from the table, he rose to his feet and carried his empty coffee mug to the sink. Susan stared angrily at him for a few seconds, then picked up her own mug and followed him.

"Would you like me to help clean up?" Mitch offered when she shoved her mug in the sink and walked to the stove for the pan.

"No thanks," she snapped.

He stood beside the sink, leaning against the counter, and watched the suppressed anger in her movements. But Susan refused to meet his gaze.

"I upset you, Susan," he said slowly. "That wasn't my intention. I should have been thanking you for so considerately spending some time with me. Instead I started needling you about your engagement to Warren. I was jealous—I still am. I suppose that's why I was so brash. I'm sorry, truly."

Susan stood in front of the sink, the pot clutched in her hands. She was aware of his gaze studying her bent head. The sincerity in his voice had taken away most of her outraged anger. She swallowed down the lump in her throat.

Why did he constantly have to confuse her? One minute she was trembling with anger at his taunts and another she would be feeling the force of his attraction. Part of her liked the idea that Mitch was attracted to her and showed it, while the other half was indignant that she should feel that way when she was already engaged to marry another man.

"I accept your apology," she said tightly, not ready to wholeheartedly forgive him for provoking her so. She glanced at the wall clock above the sink. "It's a minute after two. You need some sleep."

"Are you positive you don't want me to help with those dishes?" Mitch repeated his offer, still trying to catch her downcast gaze.

"I'm only going to stack them in the sink and wipe off the counter and stove. I can manage that on my own, thank you." Her clipped voice was deliberately cool and indifferent.

His hand closed over her chin, his grip firm but not harsh. He turned her head so he could look into her face. Resentment still smoldered in her dark eyes as she met the patient blueness of his.

"I'm sorry for making you angry, Susan."

"So you said."

"And I want to thank you again for keeping me company tonight. I appreciate it," Mitch finished in a level, serious tone. Then he leaned forward and lightly touched his lips to hers. "Good night."

He was walking away before Susan could offer a protest at his action. When the kitchen door closed behind him, she touched a fingertip to her lips. They still tingled with the warmth of his light caress. Jerkily she brushed the dark hair away from her temple and set about the task of cleaning up, a minor one that hardly took any time. All the time she kept wondering how long it would be before this physical chemistry between her and Mitch would fizzle out. For the sake of her peace of mind it couldn't be too soon.

Two minutes after Mitch had left the kitchen, Susan followed, making her way up the darkened stairs to the unlit hallway of the second floor. Unerringly she turned in the direction of the bathroom to clean off her makeup and brush her teeth before changing into pajamas. Her steps took her past the guest bedroom.

From inside came a stifled gasp of pain and a few savagely muttered oaths. Her eyes darted curiously to the strip of light beneath the door just as it swung open to catch her in full light.

Mitch's tall frame was in the center of the doorway, his navy blue long-sleeved shirt unbuttoned. He started to stride into the hallway, saw Susan and stopped, a dark frown on his forehead.

"Give me a hand, would you?" It was a crisp demand rather than a request. "I can't get my shirt off with this cast on my arm."

Susan hesitated in the hallway, watching as Mitch impatiently tried to shrug his right arm out of the long sleeve. He glanced over his shoulder, the look in his eyes asking her what she was doing still standing in the hall.

"If you'd hold the sleeve, I think I can pull my arm out of it," he said with a thin thread of patience.

His struggle to remove the shirt was genuine and Susan walked into his room to help. She held the sleeve while he twisted his arm, grunting once with pain.

"Now all I have to do is work the other sleeve over my cast," he muttered, tossing her a disgruntled look. "And to think all this is because I was tired of dangling sleeves!"

"Let me help with that," Susan offered, stepping around to his other side to ease the shirt off the cast. "It'll be easier if we take your arm out of the sling to begin with."

Mitch slipped his arm out of the cradle sling. Together they worked the sleeve material over the plaster cast until his arm was free.

It was difficult for Susan not to look at his naked torso. His chest was as tanned as the rest of him, muscles rippling sinewy strong with curling, tawny gold hair sprinkled over the center of his smooth chest. The flat stomach and slim waist belonged to an athlete.

"Shouldn't you be wearing an elastic support for those cracked ribs of yours?" she questioned, self-consciously turning away to drape his shirt over a chair.

"You mean my corset." His mouth quirked mockingly. "It became more of an irritant than a help, so I took it off."

"I see," she murmured, glancing in his direction without quite looking at him.

At this moment, his virility was like a bright fire on a cold Indiana winter night, drawing her irresistibly to its warmth. Susan forced her aroused senses to settle down. She stood nervously before him, not wanting to leave and knowing she didn't dare stay. "Would you like me to help you with your pajama top?"

A naughty light danced gleefully in his blue eyes. "I don't mean to embarrass you, but I don't sleep in pajamas."

"Oh," she murmured, disconcerted by the

image that sprang into her mind. Lowering her gaze, she noticed the sling strap had become twisted around his neck. Without thinking, she reached upward to straighten it before Mitch slipped his arm into the cradle sling. Her fingers felt cold compared to the fire that seemed to burn beneath his skin.

The top of her head felt the caressing warmth of his breath near it. Her lashes veiled much of her disturbed state as she looked into his eyes. A mask seemed to have been pulled over the brilliant blue, yet the directness of his gaze compelled her not to glance away.

With a certainty that frightened her, she knew she wanted Mitch to kiss her. Her hands had completed their task, but they remained lightly touching the back of his neck. His hand was resting casually on the side of her waist.

"Susan." There was a question in his husky, caressing voice.

"Yes?" she answered, her lips parting in invitation. Mitch slowly lowered his head toward her, prolonging the moment when their lips met as if he expected her to deny the kiss at the last second and was allowing her time to protest.

A sensual thrill quaked through Susan at the tentative possession. His mouth moved over hers, tasting the sweetness of her lips. The stiffness, the unnamed fear began to leave her body, melting under his gentle kiss.

The hardness of the plaster cast was behind her back while his right hand caressed her waist and shoulder. When he released her mouth to begin an exploring search of her face and neck, Susan kept her face upturned, eyes closed by the magic in his touch. A sigh of longing broke from her lips an instant before he claimed them again. This time it was with firm possession, a long, drugging kiss that stole her breath and awakened the sexuality that she had held in limbo.

Her hands twined themselves around his neck, not needing the pressure of his hands to mold herself against his length. Arching against him, she was all too aware of his muscular thighs and the solidity of his bare chest. The knowledge added itself to the buffeting storm of emotions raging inside her, sensations that Susan had never experienced before.

Reeling from the turbulent feeling that rocked her, she wasn't conscious of movement under Mitch's guiding hands. The action seemed part of the whirlwind that claimed her, the result of the hardening passion in his kiss.

Then there was a strange floating sensation. Her legs no longer needed to support her. Again his mouth began exploring the sensitive hollow of her throat, drawing tiny gasps of bewildered, sensuous pleasure from deep within. His fingers spread over the bare skin of her back, igniting fresh sparks with their caress. Absently Susan realized that he must have loosened her blouse from her skirt.

"Now do you see what I mean, darling?" Mitch murmured against her throat.

Her lashes blinked with confusion at the smoldering blueness of his half-closed eyes. "Mean about what?" Susan whispered blankly. The throbbing ache in her voice begged for the words to stop and the kisses to continue.

"Seventeen minutes. That's all it took," he answered teasingly.

"Seventeen minutes?" she repeated, trying to rise above the storm that had made everything so topsy-turvy.

"This is the way it should be, my beautiful one," he stated decisively, and leaned his head forward to nuzzle her ear.

A frown puckered her forehead as she came back to reality. Mitch's head lay on a stark white sheet. In disbelief she stared at him, then at the maple headboard of the bed inches away. "I could have you in bed with me in twenty minutes." The words came back with slapping force. Mitch had said that in the kitchen not seventeen minutes ago. Horror washed over her head as she suddenly realized what he was talking about.

"How could you do this!" she breathed with fear-widened eyes.

"Do what?" he asked with mocking indifference.

"You tried to seduce me!" she accused. The pliancy was gone as she held herself rigid under his continued caress.

"If that had been my intention, you would already have been seduced." Mitch chuckled softly.

"How dare you!" She was on fire with righteous indignation now, not desire.

His arms tightened when she tried to pull away. Struggling and twisting, she succeeded in breaking away from his embrace, uncaring of the muffled cry of pain Mitch made as she accidentally hit his injured ribs.

"What's the matter with you?" he muttered as he tried to follow her.

"You can ask me that!" Frantically, she pushed the end of her blouse into the waistband of her skirt.

"Honey—"

"Don't you honey me!" snapped Susan.

"Keep your voice down." He frowned, but with considerable amusement.

"I'll talk just as loudly as I please." Yet she spoke in a softer and more angry tone.

"Susan," Mitch murmured, in a coaxing, placating voice meant to soothe her growing temper.

"You lured me into your room deliberately just to prove your point, didn't you?" she accused.

"Not exactly," he hedged. "I suppose I could have eventually fought my way out of that shirt, but I admit I did use it to persuade you to come in."

"I suppose you're going to try to convince me now that it was a practical joke," she hissed. "You have a very warped sense of humor, Mitch Braden!" He was standing in front of her now, easily within reaching distance, but his hand remained on his hip, a look of patience on his handsome features.

"My full name is Mitchum Alexander Braden," he told her. "My mother always liked to use all of it when she was really angry with me."

"Well, I'm angry, too, Mitchum Alexander Braden!" she declared with some satisfaction. "I think it was a mean, contemptible trick you played when you know I'm engaged to Warren!"

"That's precisely my point," Mitch drawled. "You aren't in love with him. I tricked you because I was running out of time to prove that you don't love him. You have to realize it before you do something you'll live to regret, like marrying him."

"You're quite wrong."

"I am?" he said with challenging humor. "Tell

me how you love him so much that you can almost allow *me* to seduce you?''

"Did it ever occur to you that I might have been imagining Warren in your place?" Susan retorted, thinking fast.

"No, it didn't occur to me, and it doesn't now," Mitch replied. 'You're only saying that to save your pride. Don't be stubborn by refusing to admit to yourself the truth of what I'm saying."

"Truth! The truth is that I want you to leave me alone!"

"You're angry right now, Susan." Mitch sighed. "Think about what I've said, would you?"

His hand reached toward her and fell to his side as she took a hasty step away. Without saying another word, Susan turned around and walked swiftly from his room.

Several minutes later she was in her own bed, staring at the ceiling. How had she allowed herself to be tricked into that embarrassing situation? Nothing Mitch had said had been true. He had jumped to erroneous conclusions, she assured herself.

She was in love with Warren. She had loved him for almost two years. After that much time, a person didn't stop loving someone in one night. *Not unless,* a little voice said, *you never loved him in the beginning.*

"Impossible!" Susan whispered aloud, jamming a fist into her pillow and turning on her side.

Chapter Nine

"Susan, are you going to sleep until noon or are you going to get up?" Amy demanded impatiently, jiggling her sleeping sister's shoulder.

"W-what?" Groggily Susan blinked open her eyes and brushed away the hand on her shoulder.

"Mom has breakfast ready. Are you coming down or not?"

"Yes." She snuggled deeper into her pillow. Then she realized the action would only make her sleepier and stretched out of her comfortable position. "I'll get dressed and be right down."

Amy waited until she saw her sister throw the covers off before she left the room. A gloomy sense of depression seemed to be clinging to Susan as she reached for the cranberry robe draped over a chair. As she slipped her arms into the sleeves, she remembered last night and the depression grew darker.

How was she going to face Mitch after the way she had behaved, she wondered, as she slid her feet into terry cloth slippers. Where had her common sense been? What could she say to him that would convince him it had all been a mistake?

Mistake! It had been a catastrophe. She simply had to convince him that she didn't want anything more to do with him. But how?

Plagued by her seemingly unsolvable dilemma, Susan ran a hand through her sleep-tousled hair. She scuffled down the carpeted floor of the hallway as she made her way to the bathroom.

Opposite Mitch's room, her gaze nervously strayed to the open door. The room was empty. From downstairs, she could hear voices of her family and guessed that he was down there with them.

Breathing a sigh of relief that their moment of confrontation had been put off, Susan turned toward the open bathroom door. She stopped short inside its frame. Mitch was standing in front of the mirror above the sink, shirtless as he had been last night but wearing a pair of pants, thank goodness. Before she could recover from her surprise and retreat, the fingers of his right hand closed over her wrist and drew her into the room. When she pulled to free herself from his hold, he released her immediately and closed the door.

"Good morning, beautiful." He smiled lazily, his eyes moving possessively over her face. "I didn't think it was possible, but you're even lovelier first thing in the morning."

"I imagine you've seen a lot of women first thing in the morning!" she snapped sarcastically, saying the first thing that came to her mind.

"I do believe you're jealous." He chuckled. "That's good."

"That's absurd!" she said with an impatient toss of her head. "You're so determined to see everything the way you want it to be that there isn't any use trying to explain things to you. Excuse me."

"Wait." His hand reached out again, checking her movement to leave. Susan stared pointedly at the fingers on her arm. "Would you help me a second?"

She warily raised her eyes to his face.

Mitch smiled crookedly. "No tricks, I promise."

"What do you want?" she asked, still not trusting him.

"I've been trying for the last ten minutes to pour some aftershave in my hand and I'm running out of patience," he explained.

Her gaze found the uncapped bottle of aftershave sitting on the counter beside the washbasin. That much of his statement seemed to be true.

He let go of her arm and reached for the bottle, tucking it in a precarious position between his cast and his body, cupping his right hand near the top of the bottle.

"See what I mean?" he said as he tried to tip his body to one side to allow the liquid to run into his hand and nearly dropped the bottle in the process.

Sighing, Susan took the bottle from him and poured a small quantity in his hand, which he quickly rubbed over his freshly shaven face.

His gaze danced to her impassive expression. "I thought you might have wanted to put it on. It would have given you a chance to slap my face."

"Would it have done any good?" she asked cuttingly.

"You're still upset about last night, aren't you?" The crinkling lines around his eyes smoothed out as his expression became gently serious.

Her pulse began behaving erratically under his level gaze. "I don't wish to discuss it with you."

"I've backed you into a corner, haven't I, Susan?" He shrugged ruefully. "And all I meant to do was to bring you out in the open where you could see things for yourself."

His hand lightly caressed her cheek as he tucked a wayward strand of dark hair behind her ear. His hand remained there, cupping the side of her head. Susan felt an inexplicable urge to turn her face into his hand and kiss his palm.

Why did he have to be so gentle? She could have withstood his mockery and his flattery. But this? Her eyes grew misty.

A thumb raised her chin. Too numbed by her inner bewilderment to protest, she remained motionless as his head bent toward her. His mouth lovingly caressed her trembling lips and that crazy whirlwind of emotions came sweeping over her again. It took all her strength to stand solidly in the face of it.

Finally, when Susan thought she could resist no longer, he raised his head, smiling lightly into her eyes with a tenderness as moving as his gentleness had been.

"When are you going to give Warren back his ring?" Mitch asked huskily.

Was there a faint unevenness to his breathing? Susan couldn't be sure. She stiffened away from the hand resting on her cheek.

"I'm not giving it back." She lowered her gaze to the sling holding his arm. "I'm going to marry him."

"Susan, Susan," Mitch sighed dispiritedly. "When are you going to wake up?"

"When are you?" she demanded in a childishly hurt and confused voice. "I keep telling you and telling you, but you won't listen. Why can't you leave me alone?"

"Is that what you really want me to do?" His eyes narrowed into piercing blue diamonds, cutting hard.

"Yes! Yes, it is!" Susan declared forcefully.

"All right." His mouth tightened into an uncompromising line as he stepped away from her. "If that's what you want, I'll leave you alone."

Without another word, he walked out of the bathroom leaving Susan standing there more bewildered and uncertain than she had been a moment ago.

And Mitch kept his word. He left Susan alone.

It was no small accomplishment when they both lived in the same house. Yet he succeeded. Whenever Susan entered a room, he found an excuse to leave. At the evening meal, he avoided addressing any comment to her, however trivially. Never once had she caught him looking at her.

If the family noticed the way they ignored each other, none of them said anything to Susan. For them, life seemed to be going very much as usual.

But not for Susan. She kept reminding herself how wonderful it was that she had finally made Mitch leave her alone. In truth, she was restless, on edge, and troubled. She blamed her overwrought state on Mitch's presence in the house.

When he finally left, then everything would be all right. But she couldn't quite convince herself of that. Her three dates with Warren since Mitch had begun ignoring her hadn't proved to be very enjoyable. Each time he embraced her, Susan began comparing her reactions to what she had felt with Mitch. It became impossible to respond to his kisses when she was mentally checking her pulse and respiration rate.

Warren didn't help matters by constantly chiding her for being so nervous and restless. She had come very close several times to telling him to shut up and leave her alone, too. The whole situation was becoming ridiculous in the extreme.

The names on the wedding list blurred into a jumble of lines. Susan shook her head to clear her vision and tried to find where she had left off before she had become lost in thought.

"Hi!" Amy flounced down on the sofa cushion beside Susan. "What are you doing?"

"Going over the invitation list for the wedding," she sighed, running the eraser end of her pencil down the names, not certain which was the last name she had checked. She wasn't really in the mood to do it, but it was something that needed to be done and it filled the time until she went to bed.

"Are you going to invite Mitch?" Amy asked eagerly.

Susan paused, her stomach knotting at the mention of his name. "I don't think Mitch would be very interested in coming to my wedding," she replied, avoiding a direct answer.

"You would come, wouldn't you, Mitch, if Susan invited you?" Amy's inquiry was directed toward the hallway arch.

Glancing up in surprise, Susan bit into her lower lip. Mitch was standing in its frame, lazily watching her with an unreadable expression in his eyes.

"It would be very difficult to refuse a written invitation from Susan," he said dryly. "That would practically be a milestone."

Her eyes bounced away from his face to the papers on her lap. The cast had been removed from his left arm. Without the cumbersome protective cast, Mitch looked more vitally attractive than she remembered. Susan couldn't think of a single reply she could make to his comment. She didn't want him at her wedding. Even though she didn't think he would come, she still didn't want to invite him.

Fortunately Amy filled the silence.

"I'm going to be one of Susan's bridesmaids." Amy had declared vigorously that she was much too old to be a flower girl. "I'm going to wear a beautiful long gown of emerald green. And Mother said I could go to a beautician and have her fix my hair on top of my head."

"Johnny Chambers had better watch out if you catch that bridal bouquet," he teased.

"Oh, Mitch!" Amy giggled, her cheeks turning nearly as red as her hair.

Susan knew that Johnny Chambers was one of the boys in Amy's class at school and also the object of her latest crush. Mitch was still her idol, though.

Mitch leisurely wandered into the room, pausing beside the sofa where Susan sat. Her hand trembled nervously as she felt him looking over her shoulder.

"Is that the list of guests you're inviting to the wedding?" he asked after several long seconds had passed.

"Actually," Susan wouldn't look him in the eye, "this is my list and this is Warren's list. I have to compare the two to make certain we haven't duplicated any names."

"Amy!" her mother called from another room. "You've left your CDs strewn all over the family room. Come in here and pick them up before they get broken."

"Oh, Mom!" Amy grumbled, and slid off the couch. Shifting her leg uneasily, Susan waited for Mitch to leave. He had avoided her so completely in the past week that she was apprehensive about his reasons for staying.

"Susan." He was asking for her attention, but she refused to look at him.

"Yes," she said carelessly as if she had forgotten he was there.

"Are you really going through with this wedding?"

"Of course," she laughed, pretending she didn't understand why he had asked that question. "Kind of a waste of time to compile all these names if there wasn't going to be a wedding, right?" She knew a retort would be forthcoming, so she didn't give him a chance to respond. "I see the doctor removed your cast this afternoon. It must really be a relief not to have that weight on your arm," Susan commented with forced nonchalance.

Out of the corner of her eye, she saw him flex his left arm as if testing it. "Yes, it is a relief." Mitch allowed the change of subject. "The doctor said it was healing almost perfectly, and it certainly does feel better."

"In a couple of weeks you'll be as good as new," she observed brightly, still not letting her eyes stray from the paper on her lap.

"As good as new," he agreed dryly. "I'll be leaving next week, Susan."

"So soon?" She flashed him a glance of surprise, noting the watchfulness in his blue eyes. Then, feeling she had betrayed something, she immediately added, "I imagine you're eager to be on your way now that you've recovered."

"Eager? I wouldn't say that," he mocked. "But I certainly don't have any reason not to meet the boys at Pocono now that the cast is off."

"A-are you racing?" She frowned.

"I'm entered in the Pocono 500 at the end of the month. The time trials start next week," he told her.

A cold chill ran over her skin. She could hardly keep from shuddering. "I—I'm sure you'll do very well," she said. "As Greg says, you're a totally excellent driver."

Mitch didn't reply to that rather inane comment. His head moved in a slight negative shake as if to say the situation was hopeless. In the next moment he was walking out of the room.

Be glad that he's leaving, Susan told herself. *Now everything will return to normal.* She could begin forgetting him. But there was an awful tightness in her throat.

When she mentioned Mitch's imminent departure to Warren the next night, he rejoiced openly with a scathing comment that it was about time. Susan's murmur of agreement was hollow. She tried, but she simply couldn't make herself be glad he was leaving. Warren's exultation at the news forced her to hide the cloud of depression that had hung over her ever since Mitch had told her.

Bright and early Wednesday morning was when Mitch had decided to leave, choosing the hour before Susan and her father left for work. Her mother cooked an enormous farewell breakfast, but most of the food Susan ate lodged itself somewhere between her throat and stomach. She silently wished that Mitch had stolen away in the night, but he seemed determined to make his departure as big an impact on her life as his arrival had been.

Susan stayed in the kitchen helping her mother clear away the dishes rather than join Mitch's entourage. Her father, Greg, and Amy were all helping him pack the fabulous blue Ferrari now parked in the driveway.

Finally there was no more to be done in the kitchen and Beth Mabry was urging her toward the outer door. Susan didn't want to take part in the lingering good-bye outside. She wished she were a child again so she could run away and hide. Instead she squared her shoulders and marched along beside her mother.

His few possessions were all stowed in the car. Mitch was leaning against the door when Susan and her mother joined the semicircle around him. His gaze touched her fleetingly before he looked away.

"Well," Mitch drew a resigned breath and smiled as he straightened from the car and extended a hand to her father, "I guess there isn't any reason to keep prolonging the moment when I have to say good-bye."

"I wish you could, Mitch." Simon Mabry gripped his hand firmly, an affectionate gruffness in his voice. "We're going to miss you, all of us."

"I can't say anything but thanks, and that doesn't seem like enough," Mitch replied. He withdrew his hand and turned to her brother. "Greg."

Awkwardly Greg shook his hand. "Good luck at Pocono, dude. We'll be cheering for you."

Amy's dark eyes were gazing at him soulfully when Mitch turned to her. She offered him her hand, a slight tremble in her chin.

"Good-bye, Mitch," Amy said in a choked-up voice. Mitch flashed one of those fulsome smiles that Susan had not seen in the last ten days. It was just as potent as it had always been and this time her sister was the object of his charm.

"May I kiss you good-bye, Amy?" he asked with an inquiring tilt of his head. "I don't want Johnny Chambers to be the first."

Amy's auburn head bobbed quickly in agreement, a sparkle of ecstatic disbelief in her eyes. Then Mitch was bending his head and tenderly brushing her sister's lips in a chaste kiss.

With her mother, Mitch didn't ask but kissed her lightly without speaking. Beth Mabry gave him a quick hug in return, a teary brightness appearing in her eyes.

"Thank you, Beth, for letting me be a part of your family for a while," Mitch offered sincerely.

"We're going to miss you," she reiterated her husband's statement.

The last one in the semicircle was Susan. She wanted to bolt and run when Mitch turned to her. For a long second he stood in front of her and said nothing, holding her troubled gaze with the compelling blueness of his. The morning sun danced in his hair, brightening the shadowy brown. He looked so vigorous, so strong and so handsome that Susan felt her breath being ripped away. The image of him at this moment seemed to implant itself in her mind to be remembered and recalled for the rest of her life.

"And Susan," he drawled, a faint smile turning up the corners of his mouth. "I always try to save the best for last."

The emotional scene leading up to this moment had eroded the control Susan had fought to attain. She had hoped to wish him a breezy good-bye and let it go at that. But it was impossible to be casual. Still, she tried.

"Good-bye, Mitch." She spoke in a low tone so her voice wouldn't tremble and politely offered him her hand.

Mitch ignored her outstretched hand. "Aren't you going to kiss me good-bye, Susan?" he asked with complete seriousness, not even the faintest glimmer of wicked mockery in his eyes.

Self-consciously she glanced at the amused expressions of her parents. She appeared to be the only one taken aback by his question. Her hand fell uncertainly to her side.

"Warren won't mind," Mitch added, "not since you're kissing me good-bye. You never know, we might never see each other again. That's one of the risks in my profession." The blood rushed from her face at his words as the agonizing memory of his crash in the Indy 500 came vividly back. She swayed toward him, reeling from the stabbing pain in her midriff.

His hands closed over the soft flesh of her upper

arms and drew her the rest of the way toward him. Her head was tilted back to gaze at the handsome features while her hands spread themselves on the solid wall of his chest. For an instant they were like two statues, motionless in the beginning of an embrace.

Drawing her up on tiptoe, Mitch lowered his head to meet her halfway. A quivering magic raced through her when his mouth claimed her lips, persuasively warm and ardent. A longing filled Susan for the enchanted spell to continue, her breath completely stolen and her heart thudding against her ribs. Almost reluctantly, he ended the kiss.

His back was to the others and he spoke in a low, soft voice meant for her ears only. "You aren't going to forget me. I won't let you." In a louder voice, for the benefit of the rest of the family, he said, "Good-bye, Susan."

Then she was released and he was moving away. The flesh of her arms was cold where his hands had been and the coldness began to penetrate to the bone. Only her mouth still tingled with warmth. Her gaze was riveted to him, mesmerized by the mystical power he held over her that made her respond, body and soul, to his touch.

I'm engaged. I'm going to marry Warren. The words were almost a chant, spoken silently to ward off the bewitching effect Mitch had on her.

Susan marveled at the way he had distanced himself from their kiss of a second ago. She was stunned by it and he was smiling cheerfully and bidding everyone a last good-bye as he slid behind the wheel of his sleek sportscar.

When he reversed out of the drive, Mitch waved, but it was a wave that encompassed them all. Susan wasn't singled out for any last attention. She stood in the driveway with her family until he was out of sight, the hushed silence only deepening her depression.

Susan was the first to turn away, hot tears in her eyes. *I'll forget him,* she declared to herself. *Maybe not tomorrow, but he's wrong. I'll forget him.*

It was a bold thought, born of desperation. Her heart didn't believe a word of it, but her mind wouldn't listen to her heart. There were too many things it might have to admit if it did.

Yet when she arrived at the office that morning, Susan didn't say anything to Warren about Mitch leaving. She didn't think she would be able to listen to his caustic remarks about the Indy man. As often as she had tried, Susan couldn't despise Mitch as much as Warren did. Mitch had disrupted her life, but she couldn't bring herself to hate him for it.

Chapter Ten

"Susan! Warren is here. Are you ready yet?" her mother called from the bottom of the stairs. Rising from the edge of the bed where she had sat for the last ten minutes in huddled silence, Susan walked slowly to the hallway door and then hesitated.

"I'll—I'll be down in a minute," she answered. Why hadn't she phoned him and said she wasn't feeling well? she asked herself for the hundredth time, as she walked to the mirror above the chest of drawers. It wasn't that she was actually sick. She simply didn't feel like going out tonight.

To be truthful, Susan hadn't felt like going out Saturday night or Thursday night or Tuesday night or either of the weekend nights before that. This Sunday evening—the second Sunday since Mitch had left—was proving to be no different.

"That has nothing to do with it," Susan whispered angrily the instant she had the thought.

But she was beginning to believe that it had more to do with it than she wanted. Every room in the house was haunted by Mitch's ghost. She could hardly bear Warren's embraces anymore. They left her feeling vaguely revolted and sick. Warren hadn't changed, so she must have.

With a sigh, because there was no reason to delay going downstairs, Susan turned away from the mirror and walked dispiritedly into the hallway and down the steps. The living room was empty and she guessed that her mother had invited Warren to wait in the family room where the others were.

Following the lower hallway, Susan paused in the open archway of the family room, her troubled eyes going to the man sitting with military erectness next to her father. A second later Warren glanced up, saw her and smiled.

"You look lovely, Susan," he said warmly, but she felt nothing.

"I hope I didn't keep you waiting too long," she said quickly.

"I didn't mind in the least," Warren replied, rising to his feet. "I planned—"

"Sssh!" Greg interrupted loudly, gesturing with his hand for Warren to be quiet while he frowned in deep concentration at the radio he held in his hand and took off the headset.

"What is it?" Her father leaned forward eagerly. "The results at Pocono?" At Greg's nod, Simon said, "Turn it up."

"—Snyder's victory today was marred by a disastrous crash on the hundred and seventy-fifth lap that involved seven cars. The leading cars were lapping the slower traffic when Binghamton lost control of his car in the turn and bumped into

Braden, sending him to the wall. That started a chain reaction—''

"Oh, no!" Susan tried to muffle the cry with her hand, but it rang clearly in the hushed room. Warren stared at her stricken expression, a darkening cloud drawing blackly over his face. But she didn't see him.

"Turn it up!" cried Amy, reaching for the radio and bumping the station dial.

"Leave it alone!" Greg yelled, hurriedly turning the dial back to the station.

"—listed in critical condition. Now to the baseball scores," the sportscaster said.

"Oh, Simon," Beth Mabry glanced earnestly at her husband, "you don't suppose it's Mitch? It couldn't be, could it?"

His gaze moved away from hers as if unwilling to guess. "Try another station, Greg," her father urged. Susan was rooted to the floor, frozen by the cold terror that held her motionless. If her heart was beating, she couldn't feel it, as she prayed that Mitch was all right.

Not even the shattering ring of the telephone in the living room could prod her into action. It was Amy who raced from the room, muttering that Cindy, her girlfriend, had chosen a bad time to call. Warren touched Susan's arm.

"Are you ready?" he asked impatiently.

"Not now!" She looked at him blankly, stunned that he would want her to leave before she found out if Mitch was hurt. "I can't leave now."

"What—" Warren began with biting arrogance.

But Amy's voice interrupted him. "Susan, it's for you. It's long distance."

Susan crossed her arms, running her hands shakily over her elbows. "Who is it, Amy?" she called back.

"Someone named Mike O'Brian. Do you know him?" was the answer.

Her eyes widened in instant recognition of the man Mitch had identified as his pit boss at the hospital. She pivoted sharply around and raced to the living room alcove where Amy stood holding the telephone receiver in her hand. Susan took it and quickly put it to her ear. "Hello?"

"This is Mike O'Brian, Susan," the vaguely familiar voice answered on the other end. "I don't know if you remember me, but I work—"

"Yes, yes, I remember you," she broke in nervously.

"I'm calling for Mitch."

Susan interrupted again. "Is he all right? We heard about the crash on the news a minute ago and—is he all right?" she repeated desperately. Her fingers tightened on the receiver.

"Susan—" the man hesitated. "He's asking for you."

Fear rose to strangle her throat. "How badly is . . . is he hurt?"

Her question was met by another moment of silence. "I think it would be best," Mike O'Brian answered slowly, choosing his words with care, "if you could come right away, that is if you can come."

"Of course I'll come. I'll leave right away." Susan choked back a frightened sob.

"I'll tell him."

"Mike, wait! What hospital—" But there was a click at the other end and the line went dead.

Slowly Susan replaced the receiver, turning to find the anxious faces of her family gathered around her. Behind them was Warren, looking angry.

"Mitch? Is he—" Greg began, and stopped.

"I—I don't know how badly he's hurt." Susan shook her head, trying to elude the nausea that made her want to faint. Her frightened brown eyes sought out her father. "Mike said he was asking for me and wants me to come as soon as I can. I told him I would. Daddy," her voice broke for a second, "I don't know which hospital."

He was instantly at her side, a supporting arm curving around the back of her waist. "Don't worry about it, honey. You'll be able to find that out when you get there. First let's get you there."

"You don't actually intend to go to Pennsylvania, do you?" Warren said accusingly.

For an instant, she could not honestly understand why he was objecting. Mitch needed her and her place was there. Then she realized what that meant.

"Yes, I am going," she answered very calmly.

Her father, with his usual perception, sensed what was about to come and immediately began dispersing Susan's audience.

"Beth, go upstairs and pack Susan's things. Amy, give your mother a hand." He tossed a set of car keys to Greg. "Get my car out of the garage, Greg, and warm it up while I call the airlines and see how soon Susan can get a flight."

During the flurry of orders, Warren continued to glare at Susan, angered that she would think of betraying him this way and arrogantly confident he could change her mind. Despite her fear for Mitch, Susan was feeling a crazy kind of peace.

Nothing Warren could say or do would ever take it away from her.

"As your future husband, Susan, I'm asking you not to go," he said crisply.

At his reference to their coming marriage, Susan glanced down at her tightly clasped hands, turning them slightly so she could see the rainbow sparkle of her engagement ring. She smiled faintly.

"I'm going."

"You're my fiancée," Warren reminded her tautly. "I'm not going to stand by while you rush to another man's side."

"I think you've missed the point." Susan raised her head, serenely meeting the volcanic darkness of his eyes. "I'm not asking you to stand by. I'm just wondering how I could have been so blind these past weeks." She slipped the ring from her finger and held it out to him. "I'm sorry, Warren, that we both had to find out this way."

"You can't mean you're in love with this man!" he demanded incredulously, ignoring her outstretched hand.

"That's exactly what I mean."

"But you're in love with me! You've told me that repeatedly. How can you suddenly say you're in love with someone else?" he said angrily.

A gentle smile of understanding spread over Susan's mouth at Warren's outraged bewilderment. "I was once warned that assistants invariably become infatuated with their bosses, especially when they're men like you. I fell so heavily in love with love that I nearly missed the real thing." It was so amazingly clear now that she marveled that she hadn't seen it before. A cold chill chased away the thought. "I may be too late now."

"I'm warning you, Susan, if I take that ring now, it's all over between us," he stated icily. "Don't expect to come running back to me if you discover that you're wrong."

"I understand perfectly." She nodded.

His mouth tightened into an ominous line. Then he reached out and snatched the ring from her fingers. Without another word he strode angrily toward the front door, slamming it loudly.

Her father appeared in the hallway arch, a bright twinkle in his eyes when he glanced at the front door. Turning to Susan, he winked broadly in approval and she couldn't help smiling back.

"There's a flight that will be leaving in fifty minutes," Simon Mabry told her as he walked to the base of the stairs. "Beth, do you have Susan's suitcase packed? We have to leave for the airport now if we want to catch the first flight."

"I think so," her mother called back, appearing seconds later at the top of the stairs with Amy right behind her. "I do hope I haven't forgotten anything, Susan," she said anxiously as she hurried down the steps carrying the overnight bag.

"We haven't time to go over it now," her father decreed, taking the bag and motioning for Susan to follow him.

"Call us as soon as you can, Susan, and let us know how Mitch is," her mother requested, hurrying out the front door behind them. "And give him our love."

"I will, Mom," Susan promised.

The car was in the driveway, the motor running. Greg hopped from behind the wheel as Simon Mabry walked around the front of the car.

"Boy, was Warren mad when he left!" Greg

declared in a slightly delighted tone. "Did you ditch him, Susan?"

"Yes," she said simply, opening the passenger door and sliding into the seat.

"Don't forget to phone!" Beth called to Susan as Simon Mabry put the car in gear. Susan nodded that she would.

"And tell Mitch he can recuperate at our house again!" Greg added.

They reversed out of the drive and headed down the residential street. As they turned on to the highway, Mr. Mabry glanced at his watch.

"I think we'll make it in plenty of time," he assured Susan with a quick smile.

During all the turmoil, there had not been one question or comment from any of her family. Susan shifted self-consciously in her seat.

"Dad," she began hesitantly, "I think I should explain."

"You don't need to," he interrupted her. "I think I'd already guessed which way the wind was blowing."

"But how?" she frowned.

"If there's one thing more obvious than a couple gazing into each other's eyes, it's two people avoiding each other. And," he said with a shrug, "that good-bye kiss Mitch gave you practically clinched it for me. He's one future son in-law that I'm going to like."

"Daddy," chilling fear crept into her voice, "he just has to be all right."

"He will be." It was almost a promise.

Everything had happened so fast that Susan hadn't been conscious of time. Now the interminable waiting had begun.

The jet plane might have had wings, but it couldn't travel fast enough for her. She alternated between cold dread that she was already too late, that Mitch might have died before she was able to tell him she loved him, and clinging hope that love wouldn't let him slip away. The very fact that Mike O'Brian had avoided telling her how badly Mitch was injured made her imagine the worst.

Tears of relief pricked her eyes when the plane taxied to a stop at the terminal building. She knew she couldn't afford to panic.

First she had to find a telephone and discover which hospital Mitch was in and, she hoped, find out his condition. Then she would need to take a cab. She forced all other thoughts from her mind. She had to take one step at a time, she told herself as she impatiently followed the disembarking passengers ahead of her.

The gate area was filled with other passengers waiting to board the plane. Susan hurried to the counter to ask the airline attendant for the location of the nearest telephone. The words never were uttered as a man separated himself from the other waiting passengers and walked to her side. The golden brown head was wonderfully familiar and so was the bright glow in the blue eyes that crinkled at the corners. "Hello, Susan," Mitch said softly.

For a long second, Susan stared at him in disbelief.

"Mitch?" And he smiled. She took a hesitant step toward him. "Wh-what are you doing here?"

The light in his eyes danced wickedly. "I've been meeting every incoming plane that you could have possibly caught from Indianapolis."

She took another step closer, wildly searching

for any sign of concealed injury, cuts, bruises, anything. "But I thought you were hurt? Mike . . ."

"Mike never said I was hurt," Mitch interrupted complacently. "He only said I was asking for you." His voice lowered to a husky caress. "I've been asking for you for a long while. This time you finally heard me."

"Do you mean this was all a trick?" Susan accused in astonishment. An anger began to build at all the unnecessary anguish she had gone through. "You let me believe you were critically injured just to get me out here. I think that's cruel! It's—it's—"

"It's the mark of a desperate man," Mitch answered quietly, reaching to take hold of the hand she was waving wildly about. "A man who's very much in love and who knows the woman he loves loves him, only he can't get her to admit it. And he's terrified she'll marry someone else. You do love me, don't you, beautiful?"

"Yes!" she snapped.

"What about Warren?" He turned her left hand slightly and saw her bare ring finger.

"He was there when Mike telephoned," Susan answered curtly. "I gave him back his ring."

"He must have been furious." The grooves around his mouth deepened, those engaging, dimpling lines appearing in the lean cheeks.

"He was," she admitted. Under the charm of his smile, she began to feel her anger fade. "Oh, Mitch, what about the accident at the race? The radio said a car bumped yours and sent it into the wall."

"That's true," he agreed, cupping her cheek in his hand. "But I just kissed the wall and continued on with the race. The other collisions occurred behind me. I didn't win, but I finished the race.''

Her love couldn't be held in check any longer and Susan rushed into his inviting arms. He held her against him, burying his head in her hair.

"I was so terrified," Susan murmured against his chest. "I was afraid I'd never be able to tell you that I love you."

"Tell me," he ordered, raising his head and forcing hers up with a thumb under her chin.

With her head tilted way back, Susan gazed adoringly into his face. "I love you, Mitchum Alexander Braden."

The blue eyes smoldered. "Now, repeat after me: Will you marry me?"

"Yes," she laughed gaily.

A smile flashed across his face as he shook his head. "You're supposed to propose to me. I told your father you would."

"When?" she asked with a doubting smile.

"About twenty minutes ago when the airline confirmed you were on this plane. I didn't want your family worrying about me, so I called," Mitch told her lazily. "Now, are you really going to make a liar out of me to your father?"

"Will you marry me?" she asked dutifully.

"I thought you'd never ask," Mitch chuckled. Unmindful of the other passengers in the terminal, he claimed his kiss to seal the bargain. At the moment, nothing and no one else existed except each other.

HOMEPLACE

Chapter One

The Boyer River was frozen over. A blanket of snow covered the pasture ground. Out of the leaden sky came more flakes, gently drifting down like white flower petals on a spring day. The wind was still, although there was a nippiness in the air. Except for the crystalline flakes, the whole world seemed to have come to a standstill. Nothing moved, not even the young woman standing so silently on the knoll above the river.

Her jade-green eyes surveyed the scene, so rich in memories, but Catherine Carlsen refused to cry. She was taking a walk back into the past one last time and she didn't want tears blurring her vision.

Below her, where the river made its sweeping bend, was the place where the gentle rapids began, the place that, as a child, she had been allowed to swim. At the bottom of the hill where she was standing, the water was deeper. It was there that she and Clay used to fish for bullheads and catfish with their bamboo poles and a can of night crawlers unearthed behind the machine shed. Farther on was an island, barely discernible now from the ice-covered river, but that was where they had launched their homemade raft. They had watched their visions of reenacting the adventures of Huckleberry Finn sink with their raft.

The memories were endless. Each place her gaze rested brought more recollections of her childhood days. The lone willow tree lay horizontally, almost covered by the winter blanket. It looked bleak and lonely with its limbs sheared of summer foliage. The tiny spring-fed stream that the willow bridged wasn't visible under the snow, but many times she had quenched her thirst in its icy-cold waters in the height of a hot summer day.

Although the majority of her memories came from the summer seasons, Cathie recalled, too, the ice-skating on the river when the ice grew thick and firm, and sledding down the hill toward the river, always stopping a hair's breadth short of its bank. Or the time the adults built a bonfire at the top of the hill so there would be a place to warm themselves in between trips down the hill on a sled or a shovel. Cathie remembered so well how she had sat with her feet close to the fire so she could warm her freezing toes. She had warmed them, but she had also melted the soles off her brand new rubber boots.

How often had she visualized the day when she would bring her own children out here and show them all the places she had played as a child? Now it was never to be. The land no longer belonged to the Carlsen family. The Homeplace, as it had been affectionately called, was no longer home. And she, Cathie Carlsen, was at that very moment a trespasser.

Something brushed the side of her leg. As she turned her gaze down, Cathie's eyes met the earnest, imploring look of the English shepherd dog, Duchess. No matter what the circumstances, there was always an apologetic look about the dog's face. The sad brown eyes were expressing their sorrow at intruding on Cathie's solitude even as Duchess inched closer for a reassuring caress of forgiveness. Obligingly Cathie removed a gloved hand from her pocket to fondle the red-gold head.

"Hello, Duchess. What are you doing down here so far from the house?" Cathie noticed with sadness the collection of gray hairs around the pointed muzzle. Even Duchess was beginning to show her age, and it seemed like only yesterday that she had arrived on the farm, a frightened and bewildered puppy. "Did you get lonely up there, pretty lady?"

"She misses your grandfather."

Cathie turned toward the man standing a few paces behind her. "Hello, Clay," she said. "I didn't expect to see you here today."

Clay Carlsen studied her thoughtfully, choosing to ignore the vague ring of sarcasm in her low-pitched voice. He silently admired the way the brown fake fur coat enhanced the golden highlights of her honey-colored hair. The shoulder-length cut curled beneath the strong line of her jaw and softened her high cheekbones. Yet her feminine features had a look of strength and determination that was clear in her personality. The saving grace of her femininity was the vivid green of her eyes and their thick, dark lashes and the supremely sensuous line of her mouth. The vision of those lips, soft and yielding under the touch of his own, brought a smile to Clay's previously somber face.

"Like you, Cathie," he answered her quietly, "I thought I would make a sentimental journey over our old stamping grounds."

"Mom and Aunt Dana are up to the house packing the personal things that won't be put up for sale at the auction," she sighed, turning away from him to stare out over the river. "I'm supposed to be up there helping them sort through Grandpa and Grandma's things."

"It's a thankless job, but it has to be done."

"I know that." She flashed him a fiery look.

Her honey-gold hair was a gift from her grandparents' Scandinavian ancestors, but her mother's Irish side of the family got the credit for her jewel-colored eyes and the blame for her quick temper. Clay had never known quite how to handle that spitfire temper even when they were children. He was twenty-six, nearly three full years her senior, yet he had always been the one to bow to her wishes rather than bear the brunt of one of her rages. Normally Cathie was a loving, generous person, and that was the side of her that he adored. Over the years she had learned to control her temper, but it was those odd times when it sprang to the surface that Clay liked to avoid.

"I shouldn't have snapped at you like that, Clay," Cathie apologized, but her voice was tinged with the bitterness that had been building inside her. "I can't get used to losing Grandfather and the farm in less than two weeks."

"Well, maybe it's better that it happened this

way," Clay said. He wished that Cathie would cry and release some of the grief she had kept bottled up.

"Why?" she demanded.

"First, because ever since your grandmother passed away last fall, your grandfather has been lost without her. And secondly, I think it was a good thing that the farm was sold almost the very day it was put on the market. Often it's better that the separation is swift and sure. There's no time left for agonizing and brooding over the coming loss."

"We didn't have to lose it at all," Cathie retorted grimly. Her unseen hands were doubled into tight fists in her pockets.

"You didn't really expect your father to buy the farm, did you?"

"He could have." Her chin tilted upward as she cast him a defiant glance.

"Then what? Did you expect him to give up his professorship at the university? He isn't a young man anymore. He couldn't have managed the farm by himself. Or would you have preferred him to lease it out as your grandfather did and have someone else farm it for him? With no one living in the house, it would have deteriorated in no time." There was an exasperated sound in Clay's voice. "Be sensible about this, Cathie."

"He could have bought it," she repeated. "And after you and I were married, we could have lived here and farmed it ourselves."

"I'm a lawyer, not a farmer," Clay stated emphatically. "I didn't spend all those years in college studying law to throw it aside because of some sentimental nonsense."

As soon as Clay had said it, he realized he had just waved a red cape in front of Cathie. Her reaction was instantaneous.

"It isn't sentimental nonsense! And if you think it is, then I'm proud to be sentimental! The very first plowshare that broke this ground when it was a wild prairie was held by my great-grandfather Carlsen. He was one of the first settlers in this area after the Civil War. Look at this land, Clay. It's one of the richest sections of bottomland in Iowa. The dirt is black and fertile, made to grow food and families. This is where our family began. This is the Carlsen home, our legacy given to us by our ancestors. Doesn't that mean anything to you?"

"Of course it does," he placated her. "All of the family is sad to lose it, your father and myself included. But family farms are a passing thing. And you just can't live in the past anymore, not if you want to succeed in life. It's progress, Cathie."

"Then to hell with progress!"

"Don't swear, Cathie. It isn't worth getting angry about," he admonished her gently, all the while thinking what a bewitching creature she was when she was in a temper, her eyes flashing green fires and her face alive with passionate zeal.

"Why? Is swearing strictly a masculine right? I'll swear if I want to," she exploded. "Sometimes I wish I were a man!"

"Well, I'm glad you're not. Otherwise you wouldn't be wearing my ring on your finger," Clay laughed, attempting to instill some lightness in the overcharged atmosphere. But Cathie deliberately ignored him.

"The thing that angers me most of all is that the farm is being sold to an outsider, someone from the East Coast! He's probably some big business executive who's only interested in a tax deduction. He'll probably send some stupid manager out here to live on it while the farm falls to rack and ruin."

"You're being melodramatic. If he is a business-man, and we know absolutely nothing about him, then he definitely will bring someone in who knows farming so he can get a return on his investment."

"Don't bet on it," she jeered.

"Why are you putting yourself through all this?" Clay sighed, taking her by the shoulders and turn-ing her to face him, his hazel eyes taking in the belligerent and rebellious expression on her usu-ally lovely face. "You can't change the fact that the farm is sold. It's useless to torment yourself with visions of what may or may not happen. Everything always works out for the best. This all was probably what was meant to happen."

"Fate, that's your answer for losing the Home-place." A dullness clouded her eyes as her shoul-ders sagged beneath his hands. "You're probably right, but I'll never accept that it's for the best. It just doesn't seem right that there never will be a Carlsen living on this farm again."

"Do you want to know something?" He lifted her chin with his gloved finger. "You're usually always so practical that it's rather nice to discover again how emotional you can get."

"How angry, you mean." A rueful smile curved her lips. "But I never could stay mad at you for very long, even when we were children."

"That's what made it so nice to be only kissing cousins." Clay Carlsen smiled. "It was always so much fun to make up."

"Kissing cousins" had become a standard joke

between them since they had reached their teens and were able to understand that even though they shared the same last name of Carlsen, the actual blood relationship between them was virtually non-existent. Clay's great-grandfather had been a second cousin to Cathie's great-grandfather. With that knowledge, Clay and Cathie had progressed from childhood playmates to sweethearts and had reached the stage of engagement.

"What's going to be done with Duchess?" Clay asked as the dog whined to attract attention.

"I'm taking her to town with me," Cathie answered, moving out of Clay's hold to kneel beside the dog. "The Darbys offered to take her, but she's getting so old that I think she would have trouble adjusting to new people and a new place, too."

"Do you think she's going to find it any easier living in town? At least with the Darbys she would be on a farm and there would be someone around all the time. You'll be at school most of the day."

"We'll work it out, won't we, Duchess?" The aging shepherd wagged her tail enthusiastically in answer to the crooning voice, but Clay caught the disguised determination that plainly said Cathie intended to keep this last link with the farm.

"How much longer is Mrs. Carver staying on?" He conceded to her unspoken request to change the subject as he inquired about the housekeeper who had remained living in the farmhouse after Grandfather Carlsen's death.

"The real estate man asked her to stay until a date has been set to turn the place over to the new owner," Cathie replied grimly, hating to acknowledge the existence of a new owner. "He didn't want the house to sit vacant."

"Which disproves your theory that the place was going to fall into rack and ruin."

"That was the real estate man's idea, so it proves absolutely nothing," she retorted sharply, rising to her feet, to the dog's disappointment. She looked out over the river's cape, shivering at the chilling reality of the situation.

"It's getting cold. Maybe it's time we were heading back to the house," Clay suggested. He pushed back the sleeve on his heavy corduroy parka to glance at his wristwatch. "Nearly four o'clock. That's later than I thought. I have a couple of stops to make. Which also reminds me, what time do you want me to pick you up tonight?"

"If you don't mind, I'll take a rain check for tonight." Cathie accepted his guiding hand on her elbow that turned her in the direction of the house. "This is my mother's last night. She's driving back to the university tomorrow afternoon, so I think I should spend the evening with her."

"No, I don't mind at all," he said as he helped her negotiate the barbed wire of the pasture fence while Duchess trotted to a small ditch and burrowed under the fence to keep up with them. "Are your parents driving back for the auction?"

"No," Cathie sighed. "And I can't say that I blame them. I don't think I will go either."

"It might be a good chance to pick up some furniture for our house," he ventured, unsure as to how far he should push the issue of forcing her to accept the sale.

"All the good furniture is antique and you know how these antique dealers drive up the prices at farm sales. We couldn't afford to pay that much plus the cost of storing until we find a decent house in our price range." Cathie shook her head with resigned sadness. "The family decided I could have the set of crystal in the way of a wedding present and a few other inexpensive mementos. I'm satisfied with that."

The rutted pasture track had brought them to the farmyard. Cathie refused to let her gaze roam over the various buildings and once more fall in the grip of her many poignant memories. She kept walking toward the two-story house with friendly gray smoke rising from its chimney to mingle with the scattering of snowflakes.

"Are you coming in? I'm sure Mrs. Carver would fix us some cocoa," she offered as they reached the green compact car that belonged to Clay.

"Not this time. I'll see you in church tomorrow, won't I?"

Cathie nodded and lifted her head for his good-bye kiss. He claimed her mouth with the gentleness and tenderness that was so much a part of his nature. Then Clay was climbing behind the wheel of his car. Cathie watched him as he drove out of the yard onto the county road that led to the highway before she turned toward the house, following the sidewalk through the metal gate to the back door of the white structure.

"I'm back," Cathie called out as she walked in the door and climbed the few steps of the inside landing to the sun porch. The snow-white hair atop Mrs. Carver's head caught her eye, drawing Cathie's attention to the kitchen. "Where are my mother and Aunt Dana?" she asked, traversing the narrow width of the sun porch to the large kitchen.

"They're in the back bedroom packing away Mr. Carlsen's clothes for the Salvation Army," the housekeeper replied, not pausing in her brisk stirring of some thick goo in a bowl. The vigorous movement sent her rotund figure vibrating. A sharp eye was turned on Cathie. "Didn't you ask your young man to come in? I was just stirring up some frosting for a chocolate cake I made."

"Clay had some errands to run, so he couldn't stay."

"There you are, Catherine. I thought I heard your voice." Her mother stood in the kitchen doorway, her auburn hair glinting in the artificial light that didn't reveal a trace of gray. "Didn't Clay come in with you?"

Cathie repeated her previous statement to Mrs. Carver as she marveled again over her mother's youthful appearance even though she had passed the forty mark many years ago.

"That's too bad," Maureen Carlsen replied when she heard that Clay had left. "I was going to ask him to carry this box of clothes out to the station wagon. I'm afraid it's too big for Dana and me to carry. I suppose we could scoot it along the floor and down the steps."

Eyes that were nearly as green as Cathie's studied the route that the box would ultimately have to take before her mother nodded to herself that the plan would work. With that problem solved, she turned her attention back to her daughter.

"Well, did you and Clay tramp over all your playgrounds?" she asked with a bright and indulgent smile.

"More or less." Cathie shrugged, not wanting to discuss how unsatisfactory their conversation was. "What's left to be sorted?"

"Men are seldom as sentimental as us women."

Her mother astutely guessed the reason for her daughter's noncommittal reply. "Look at your father. He's so steeped in American literature that he can barely remember our anniversary. But I've learned to accept that the day of our marriage doesn't rank high compared to the early demise of Edgar Allan Poe."

"Dad isn't the least bit absent-minded," Cathie protested with an amused smile. "He always remembers our birthdays and the holidays and he always picks out some wonderful, nonsensical gift for us. I don't believe he's ever forgotten your anniversary either."

"I would hope not! I feed him rice every single night for a week to be sure he gets the message," her mother laughed.

"This is a fine time for you to come back to the house, Cathie," her aunt Dana declared, coming to a halt behind her mother. "Just when we've packed the last box. You can take your coat off. You won't need to run back outside."

Long ago Cathie had learned that no matter how biting the comments of her father's older sister sounded, they were not meant that way. Dana Madison had simply never learned tact. With that knowledge, Cathie let the implied criticism slip by without comment.

"I suppose you also let Clay slip away without thinking to invite him in," Dana continued, taking the brown fur parka from Cathie's shoulders.

"He had some errands," Cathie repeated for the third time.

"Have you two set the wedding date yet?" her aunt asked crisply.

"Not yet."

"Wow, you two really believe in long engage-ments!" Dana exclaimed with scorn. "How long has it been since he gave you that ring?"

"Shortly after he passed his bar exam, which was about a year ago," Cathie answered calmly, exchanging a silent look with her smiling mother.

"Let's see, the first excuse was that you were both in college and that it would be too great a strain financially for you to get married. Then it was that you wanted to find a teaching job." Dana was using her fingers to tick off the reasons why their marriage hadn't taken place. "After that, Clay had to pass his bar examination. At least you got an engagement ring then. What's your reason for waiting so long now?"

"We're trying to find a house. Neither one of us wants to live in an apartment even if there was a decent one available, which there isn't. So far we haven't been able to find a house in our price range that's fit to live in," Cathie attempted to explain their delay. "But in the meantime, we're saving our money so we can furnish the house when we do get it."

"In my day, we got married and moved in with our parents until we could afford something better."

"That wouldn't work for Clay and me since none of our parents live here any more. Besides, we're both enjoying our last bit of freedom without the responsibility of school and all."

"You make marriage sound like a prison," her aunt harrumphed.

"There is a confining side to it," Cathie ad-mitted.

"How old are you now? Twenty-three? Twenty-four?"

"I'll be twenty-four on my next birthday."

"And unmarried. That was practically a crime when our mothers were young, right, Maureen?" The older woman addressed her question to Cathie's mother.

"That was a long time ago," her mother shrugged.

"I don't know if it's for the better," Dana sniffed indignantly. "In the past, the family home was passed from one generation to another but here we are selling the very place where we were born and raised. It's a shame that you and Dorian couldn't purchase it, Maureen. I wanted to put in a bid, but Al put his foot down, insisting that it just wasn't practical for us to buy it either."

"It is unfortunate that none of us was able to prevent the farm from going out of the family," Maureen Carlsen agreed with a note of sadness that was felt by all.

"Did you tell Cathie that the real estate agent called today?" Dana inquired.

"What about?" Cathie prompted, her honey-blond head turning toward the older, graying woman.

"To let us know that the new owner will be taking possession, or wants to take possession, the fifteenth of March."

"So soon," Cathie murmured, a pallor stealing the color from her face. That was just over a week away.

"Yes. I guess it was a good thing we set the date for the auction as soon as we did," her aunt Dana nodded sagely. "The agent is making arrangements for Mrs. Carver to have some sleeping quarters for those few extra days between the auction and the new owner's arrival.''

"What I'm hoping," Mrs. Carver said, bringing her newly frosted cake to the small dinette table in the kitchen, "is that the new owner will keep me on. I just have too much time on my hands to set at home alone. Goodness knows there isn't much call for housekeepers anymore, not around here anyway. Did that real estate man find out anything about the new owner, Mrs. Madison?''

"From what I could gather," Dana replied in her caustic voice, "all he knows is that the man's name is Robert Douglas and he lives in Long Island, New York. The agent never asked if the man was married or single, young or old, whether he intended to farm it himself or hire someone else. I suppose all the agent cares about is his commission.''

"It seems to me that a man who would buy a piece of property sight unseen isn't the type who would make it his home," Cathie stated bitterly.

"Now, I heard that the man flew up here in a private plane the day the real estate man contacted him," Mrs. Carver said, drawing the immediate attention of the rest of the group.

"Did you see him?" Cathie's mother asked, voicing the question that rose in all three minds.

"No." The housekeeper shook her head. "If he actually came out to the farm, he never came to the house."

"That's the first I've heard of any visit," Dana commented, plainly showing her dislike of receiving that piece of information so late. "Who told you that?''

"One of the men from the real estate office when

he came out to make a list of the equipment that was sold with the land," Mrs. Carver replied. "Of course, it might not have been the same man that bought the farm, but that's the way I understood him." The cake knife expertly slashed through the white frosting. "Now all of you have to have a piece of this cake before you leave."

Chapter Two

The school classroom was abnormally quiet. The rows of desks were empty of children except for one boy studiously crouched over his paper. Behind the large desk next to the blackboard, Cathie Carlsen was correcting the last of the fourth grade arithmetic papers. Her blond hair was pulled away from her face and secured at the nape of her neck by a scarf that matched the peacock-blue and jade-green paisley print of her silk blouse. As she placed the last paper on top of the neat stack, Cathie glanced at the large wall clock. Rising quietly from her desk, she walked down the row of desks to where the nine-year-old was sitting. Over his shoulder she read the scrawling words *I will not glue books together* repeated over and over again. The boy turned his freckled face toward her, his sandy-brown hair sticking out in all directions, the result of innumerable cowlicks that defied combs and brushes.

"Can I go home now, Miss Carlsen?" he pleaded, his sparkling brown eyes using their influence to the fullest.

"May I go home," Cathie corrected.

"May I go home?" he sighed, his shoulders slumping at the lack of response to his beguiling look.

Charles Smith, or Charlie, as he was known to his classmates, was the instigator of nearly every misdeed done during the course of a school day. Behind the bewitching innocence of his freckled face was a midget monster who was either in mischief or thinking of it. Today's escapade had involved gluing Mary Tate's schoolbooks together during the lunch period. Mary, who possessed a desire for learning, was one of the more intelligent pupils in Cathie's class, which earned Mary the nickname of "teacher's pet" and the revenge of Charlie for her almost perfect behavior.

"Yes, you may go home now, Charlie." Her acquiescence was followed by slamming books and shuffling papers as Charlie raced to accomplish his escape before Cathie could change her mind and make him stay longer. He was halfway to the coatroom when she called her warning after him. "The next time you get into trouble, you'll go straight to the principal's office."

"There won't be a next time, Miss Carlsen," he assured her, backing slowly but surely toward his coat.

"I hope not."

It was difficult keeping a severe expression on her face. She had long ago resigned herself to the fact that every class had a Charlie Smith. And as long as they kept to the frogs and the spitballs and avoided the destructive mischief, the best course was to mark it up to the exuberance of youth, and especially small boys with their snips and snails and puppy dogs' tails.

A few minutes later Cathie was slipping on her three-quarter-length black leather coat and picking up the case that held her laptop to follow Charlie Smith's path out of the brick schoolhouse. The house that she shared with two girlfriends was conveniently only three blocks from the school, thus eliminating the expense of driving. On blustery days like today, the three blocks were just about all that Cathie wanted to walk.

Two weeks had passed since her visit to the farm. The auction had taken place and presumably the new owner had moved in, since the possession date had gone by. Still, in this the latter part of March, there was still a trace of snow on the ground and March promised to go out like a lion instead of a lamb. Spring was several corners away.

Duchess, the English shepherd, was huddled next to her new kennel. At the sight of Cathie walking up the sidewalk, she rose to a crouching sit, her tail tucked between her legs and her head lowered near to the ground as if the chain attached to her collar weighed too heavily on her neck. Her forlorn, sad eyes watched Cathie's approach.

"How was your day, Duchess?" Cathie asked brightly, trying to ignore the woebegone expression on the dog's face but not succeeding. "I'm sorry I have to tie you up, pretty lady, but you keep running away if I don't."

There was the teeniest wagging of the feathery

red, gold and white tail at the soothing sound of Cathie's voice. As the chain hook was unsnapped the wagging increased, although Duchess remained subdued, attaching herself to Cathie's heels to follow her inside the house. There, the shepherd went immediately to the hallway rug where she could keep an eye on all of the comings and goings of the household occupants and especially her beloved new mistress.

Neither of Cathie's two roommates were home yet. Connie Murchison was a loan officer in the local bank while Andrea "Andy" Parker was a dental hygienist. Since Cathie was usually always the first one home, she prepared their evening meal during the week and the other girls took the responsibility during the weekends. She was in the middle of mixing a meat loaf when Andy burst through the door.

"Oh, there you are, Cathie!" she cried exuberantly, her spiky dark hair ruffled by the brisk wind outside. "You'll never guess who I met today!" In the midst of taking off her corduroy parka, she glanced over Cathie's shoulder. "What's for supper tonight? Ummm, meat loaf. Baked potatoes, too? Oh, with gobs of butter and sour cream," Andy groaned. "And just imagine all the calories! Not everybody is like you, Cathie, and can eat anything they want and not gain an ounce of weight."

"You could eat the baked potato with butter and not sour cream or vice versa." Cathie laughed. Andy was on a perpetual diet in a losing battle to combat her tendency toward overweight.

"I could," Andy agreed, lifting her shoulders in a characteristic acceptance of fate, "but potatoes taste so much better with both."

"What are you doing home so early? It isn't even five o'clock."

"Dr. Roland had a meeting of some kind, so he decided to close the office early. That reminds me, I started to tell you who I met today and we got sidetracked." Enthusiasm once more bubbled to the surface as Andy flung her coat on the chair and danced back to the sink to clean the potatoes for Cathie. "Dr. Roland sent me to the bank to make the deposit after work. When I walked into the bank I saw Connie talking to this gorgeous man. Naturally I went over there to say hello. You could tell she was absolutely furious with me, but she had to introduce me to him just the same. As luck would have it, the very second after she'd introduced us, old Mr. Hammer wanted to see Connie and I was left alone with him."

"Left alone with whom, Andy?" Amused exasperation curved Cathie's lips at her girlfriend's uncanny ability to drag out explanations.

"With Robert Douglas." The way Andy made the pronouncement, Cathie expected a trumpet fanfare to blare from some hidden speaker in the room. During the brief span of seconds before Andy continued her recounting of her meeting, Cathie tried to place where she had heard the name before. "You know," Andy prompted at the blank look she was receiving, "the man who bought your grandparents' farm."

There was an instantaneous rise of antagonism inside Cathie. She had to halt her molding of the meat into a loaf for fear she would mash it into a pie. But Andy didn't pay any attention to the adverse reaction she had received, logically thinking that Cathie would be interested to hear about the new owner.

"He's gorgeous! Tall, over six feet, and buff. He's got thick, wavy brown hair, the kind that you want to run your fingers through, and beautiful brown eyes that just make you melt when you look at him. And talk about a tan! He made everybody look as if they'd been hibernating. Oh, and he was wearing this cashmere sweater that fit his . . . everthing. My guess is that he's about thirty something, thirty-two or three probably. And his voice! Kind of low-pitched and quiet as if what he was saying was only meant for you to hear. I mean, it was really sexy."

"Are you sure you didn't forget something?" Cathie asked caustically, irritated by her friend's enthusiasm for this usurper of her family home.

"Yes!" Andy exclaimed with a gasp, as if she had forgotten the most important thing. "He had a scar. A little inch-long scar near the corner of his right eye. It makes him look sort of—" a dreamy expression crept into Andy's eyes "—rugged and masculine and dangerous stuff."

The oven door banged loudly shut after Cathie jammed in the meat loaf pan.

Andy handed her potatoes she'd just wrapped in aluminum foil. "Here, you can put these in the oven, too. I nuked 'em for six minutes. They'll cook fast. But I found out something else about him that really bites."

Visions of bulldozers tearing down the farmhouse to make room for an ultramodern ranch home sprang immediately to mind. "What?" Cathie breathed, half afraid to hear the answer.

Andy sighed heavily, "He's married. The first

fabulous guy that moves into the area has to be married. Is that rotten luck or what?"

The muscles that had tensed in anticipation of some shocking news relaxed and Cathie laughed in relief. "You didn't just come right out and ask him that, did you?"

A suitably injured expression appeared on the dark-haired girl's face. "I'm not totally lacking in tact, Cathie. Besides—" an impish grin spread over her face "—he had a little boy with him who kept calling him father. I just reasoned that where there was a daddy and a little boy, there had to be a mommy."

"That wouldn't necessarily follow. He could be divorced or a widower." Now why had she said that, Cathie wondered to herself.

"Wouldn't that be wonderful!" Andy clasped her hands together in glee. "Not that it would bother Connie if he was married or not. She's terribly unscrupulous when it comes to good-looking men, and Rob Douglas was all that! Which reminds me, you'll probably meet him yourself. He's enrolling his boy in school here. Naturally I mentioned that my roommate, meaning you, was a teacher and also the granddaughter of the former owners of his farm."

"What grade is his boy in?" A terrible feeling of dread encompassed her as Cathie wondered if she could be objective about a pupil who was the son of the man she already resented for buying the family farm.

A frown creased Andy's forehead. "I don't think he said. I remember telling him that you taught the fourth grade, but I can't recall his answers. And I'm such a lousy judge of ages I couldn't tell you whether the boy was seven or eleven. I imagine you'll find out soon enough." She shrugged, not attaching any major importance to the subject. "What's on your agenda for this evening? Are you and Clay going somewhere?"

"I have choir practice at the church. Clay's meeting me afterward, but just for coffee, nothing special."

"That sounds more exciting than my plans for this evening. I'm going to wax my whatevers, rinse out a few sweaters and watch Letterman. You don't realize how lucky you are, Cathie," the other girl said, wallowing unashamedly in self-pity. "First of all, you have a steady guy, which is a major achievement in itself, and secondly, he's terrific. If I were you, I'd march him to that altar so fast he wouldn't know what had happened. And I sure wouldn't let him anywhere near Connie. She goes after anything in pants. Don't you ever get jealous when she flirts with Clay right in front of you? She reminds me of that character in *Sex and the City*, the one who's always chasing men."

"Jealousy just isn't a part of my nature, I guess." Cathie lifted her shoulders expressively. "Either that or it's just that I trust Clay."

A thoughtful gleam in her eye, Andy studied the blond busily setting the small dinette table. "Why haven't you two set your wedding date yet?"

"No particular reason." Jade-green eyes looked up to meet Andy's curious brown ones. "We've been looking for a house and more or less postponed setting a date until we find one."

"Doesn't Clay object? I mean, does he really want to wait?"

The question caught Cathie off guard. Had Clay

ever voiced an opinion in the matter? She couldn't recall that he had. He had simply always agreed to whatever she suggested. Andy was waiting for an answer.

"It was just something we mutually agreed on," Cathie replied calmly, not letting the sudden flickering of doubt be revealed.

"Don't you love him?" At the startled expression on Cathie's face, Andy hurried on with a further explanation. "I always imagined that when you love someone, really love them, it just sweeps you away in a tide of passion. Yet you sound so coldly practical about it sometimes, unless you . . ." A shy flush of color filled Andy's cheeks as she hesitated before completing her sentence. "Unless you and Clay . . . well, that's none of my business, is it? But are you, like, 'saving yourself,' so to speak, for your wedding night?"

"Andy, you are priceless!" Cathie couldn't keep the bubbling sound of amusement out of her voice. "Saving yourself! What a beautifully old-fashioned expression! Anyway, for me, it's always been Clay. I knew I was going to marry him when I was in the eighth grade, and nothing has changed. And as for getting swept off my feet by a man on a white horse—" a grin teased the corners of her mouth "—I could never picture Clay that way. I would always remember that Halloween costume he wore one year when we were kids. It was a cowboy suit and he had his two front teeth missing. It's not an image that fits well with a knight in shining armor."

"It would tarnish it," Andy declared, laughing at her own humor. "Not that I would know since I never had a childhood sweetheart or a teenage sweetheart or any sweetheart for that matter. The plain fact is I talk too much and no matter what I do I can't seem to keep my mouth shut. And you know how men are. They prefer listeners so they can talk about themselves.''

"Listening isn't so hard to learn.''

"As long as the person doing the talking is saying something interesting.'' Andy headed for the hallway, but paused in the doorway. "I've always had this fantasy that some day the right guy would come along and kiss me just to shut me up. And his kisses would be so terrific that they would rob me of all speech. That's silly, isn't it?'' she sighed, "But I was just born romantic. Which is probably why you're going to marry your comfortable and ever-present Clay and why I don't have a date for Saturday night!''

Andy disappeared into her own small bedroom to change out of her white uniform. With dinner in the oven and the timer set, Cathie filled the bathtub and let the bubbly, scented water soak away the day's tensions while her mind kept wandering back to Andy's conversation. There had been the underlying impression that Andy thought Cathie was settling for second best, which was absurd, because she loved Clay. Admittedly there was no white-hot, searing flame of passion between them, but Cathie considered that an overrated commodity. It wasn't nearly as important as respect and friendship and undemanding affection.

From some unbidden corner of her mind came the thought that it would be nice to feel all of those and an unquenchable desire, too. With a sharp shake of her head, Cathie dismissed it.

"Fairy-tale stuff,'' she murmured to the open-mouthed ceramic fish on the bathroom wall. Fictional accounts of love had never borne any resemblance to reality in Cathie's sphere of experience.

Although she had been positive that she would marry Clay, that hadn't stopped her from dating other men when she was in high school and college, and therefore she had more than her experience with Clay to draw on. Kissing had always been a pleasant experience and some men had more finesse than others, but there had never been any throbbing, heat-filled kisses to carry her off to dizzy heights of desire. Accounts of such happenings Cathie had always marked off as poetic license.

Besides, what did it matter to her if Andy didn't find her relationship with Clay particularly romantic, Cathie thought as she briskly rubbed herself dry with the big bath towel. She was very contented with Clay. From a distant part of her mind, she heard Andy's voice mocking her, "Like a cow chewing its cud?"

Cathie gave herself a mental shake. It was foolish to be suddenly questioning her decision to marry Clay or her own views about love and what it meant. They were beliefs she had held for years and simply because they differed from those of someone else that was not a reason for her to doubt their validity.

Slipping the black sweater vest that matched the plaid slacks over her white blouse, Cathie removed the confining hairband from her head. The oven timer would be buzzing any minute now, so she postponed putting on her makeup until after the meal, pausing only long enough to run a brush through her hair.

Andy was sitting in the middle of the living room floor, painstakingly attempting to roll her short hair around pink plastic rollers.

"I haven't seen rollers like that in years."

"That's because I got them at a garage sale. Now why is it—" Andy pointed to Cathie's hair, "—that if brunettes are supposed to have thick, full-bodied hair, I have this thin, fine stuff and you, a blond, have the thick gorgeous hair?" Her shoulders slumped as a lock of hair slipped out of her grasp. "I have to use a ton of this setting gel to glue this darn hair to a roller!"

A statuesque girl appeared in the doorway, her cool gray eyes surveying the scene with superiority. "Have you ever considered a perm, Andrea?" Long hair that was an unusual combination of brown streaked with blond was swung over her shoulder in a graceful gesture as Connie Murchison entered the room.

"And end up with the frizzies! I might as well dye it green if I want to look that bad," Andy declared.

"Hello, Connie," Cathie greeted her second roommate. "Dinner will be ready shortly. How was your day?"

Connie tightened the sash on her ivory, floor-length silk robe before reclining her lanky form on the cinnamon couch. On cue the robe flicked open from the knee down to reveal her shapely legs and the lacy edge of her slip. "It had its moments." She smiled mysteriously.

"Cathie, you're psychic!" Andy exclaimed suddenly. "Do you remember when you said that just because Mr. Douglas had a little boy it didn't mean he was married? Well, you were right. Connie was just telling me that his wife died last fall. Isn't that tragic? I imagine that's why he moved out here, to get away from all the familiar things and start a new life."

"It didn't appear to me that his wife's death had left him all that choked up," Connie observed, leafing through a magazine as if to hide the knowing gleam in her pale gray eyes.

"How would you know whether a man was in mourning or not?" the dark-haired girl demanded. "Just because he wasn't wearing a black armband or grieving visibly over his loss it doesn't mean he didn't care about her dying."

"I just can't visualize a man who, according to you, is supposed to feel this intense loss for his 'beloved' wife accepting an invitation to a party," Connie replied calmly.

"A party!" Andy gasped in horror, bringing an amused smile to Cathie's face. Poor romantic Andy, she thought, was no match for Connie who launched her siege of any unattached male with the precision and expertise of an army general. "You haven't invited him to a party already! Why, you only met him today!" Andy finished.

"I wasn't about to let someone else snatch him up." A dark eyebrow lifted in mock surprise as if such an action would be traitorous to her nature, which it would. "As I told Rob, it's a small party and he can get acquainted with the local people."

"I think you're disgusting!" Andy declared, never one to hide her feelings.

"Why?" Connie shrugged. "He's a man who knows the score. I didn't suggest anything that he didn't want me to."

"Andy told me he was quite handsome." A spurt of cold anger drove Cathie to take part in the conversation. If Connie ever starred in a TV show, it would have to be called *Sex and the Country,* she thought.

A secret smile played around the corners of Connie's mouth. "I assure you, whatever he is, he isn't a farmer. And if he ever had a little black book of telephone numbers, I'm positive it was filled."

"Why did he come out here, then? Why did he buy the farm?" Cathie demanded, not aware that her hands were clenched tightly at her side.

"Really, Cathie!" A husky laugh sounded from the couch. "I haven't got to the point yet where Rob has confided everything to me. I know he has a very healthy bank balance. Maybe it's like Andy said. He's tired of fooling around and wants a committed relationship."

"Dream on," Andy said sarcastically.

"I will." Connie flashed a saccharine-sweet smile.

The humming buzz of the oven timer acted as a deterrent to further conversation among the trio. Cathie pivoted around sharply to respond to it as Andy hopped to her feet to help.

"I don't think I'm going to like this Mr. Rob Douglas," Cathie muttered. Connie's description of the new owner of the Carlsen farm did not appeal to her.

"You haven't even met the man." Andy turned a questioning look on her. "You aren't going to let Connie's assessment of him influence you? I thought he was charming and friendly. What's wrong with that?"

"Absolutely nothing."

Cathie paused in front of the oven door, a potholder in each hand, and glanced over her shoulder at Andy. "I'm not taking sides for or against the man," she said, forcing her temper to recede. "He means absolutely nothing to me and isn't likely to either."

Chapter Three

The following morning, Mr. Graham, the principal, brought Cathie's new pupil to her classroom. Judging by the sullen expression on the boy's face, Tad Douglas was not any happier with the situation than Cathie was, although she was determined to make the best of it and not let her resentment of his father color her relationship with his son. In a silent admission to herself Cathie realized that it might prove difficult.

Tad Douglas had all the earmarks of a young boy who had been spoiled, his every whim indulged by a doting parent. His hazel eyes seemed to possess only two expressions; one was sullen and the other defiant. The impression he created with the rest of the class wasn't very good either. His sandy-brown hair was longer than that of the other kids. His precisely creased slacks and crisply starched shirt didn't bear any resemblance to the casual sweats and denim jeans of the other boys. Cathie noticed the uneasy fidgeting as she introduced Tad to the rest of the class.

Charlie Smith didn't help. From his coveted back-row seat, she heard him snickering. "Tad, ain't that name short for tadpole?"

The boy sitting across the aisle whispered back, "Tad is a frog!" More giggles followed from behind hand-covered mouths.

The invisible shell around Tad grew harder. His superior, standoffish attitude during the rest of the school day did little to help him make friends. In Cathie's brief tenure as an elementary teacher she had learned there was no way that she could make his incorporation into the class any easier. It was up to Tad and the rest of the class, and neither was eager to take the first step.

Cathie felt sorry for the newcomer's isolation imposed partly by the rest of the class and she was troubled by his apathy. Not once during the entire day did he smile or show any interest in the lessons or the activities. Tad was the last one to leave the room during recess periods and the last one to return when they were over. He wasn't allowing any opportunity for anyone to make an overture of friendliness. There was something in his childish version of arrogance that said it had nothing to do with shyness. Tad Douglas simply did not want to make friends.

When class was dismissed at the end of the day, Tad made a project of slowly stacking his books while the rest of the students made their usual mad dash for the door. The room was cleared by the time Tad was done and ready to put on his own coat. Cathie felt compelled to show some interest in his welfare.

"Will your father be meeting you?" she inquired, forcing a smile to appear on her face.

"No," Tad shrugged, slipping his arms into the tailored overcoat. "He doesn't want to be bothered with me."

Cathie's ire at his unknown father increased, but she concealed it with the utmost difficulty. "I thought since it was your first day at school he might," she said calmly. "Do you know which school bus to take to get home?"

"Yes."

A glumly resigned look flitted across his face to tug at Cathie's heartstrings. If it hadn't been for the fact that walking with him to the school bus would have further alienated him from the rest of the class, Cathie would have done it. As it was she could only nod and add a cheerful, "See you tomorrow, Tad," a statement that earned her another sullen glance.

April and May were two very long months, especially for Tad Douglas and Cathie Carlsen. He proved to be a conscientious, intelligent student, his homework always turned in on time and usually always correct, but he never took part in any discussions or showed a desire to do so. Except on rainy days, the recess periods were held outside, with Tad remaining apart from the rest of the class unless there were organized games or computer labs.

More than once Cathie had heard the chanting, "Tad is a frog! Tad is a frog!" and wondered at the unknowing cruelty of children.

Tad still lingered an extra few minutes at the

end of the day. Cathie was never sure if he did it to avoid the ridicule of the children or if he attached some importance to their brief exchanges.

One day she had asked him how he liked his new home. His small shoulders had made their habitual shrug beneath his expensive oxford cloth shirt. "It's all right."

The lack of enthusiasm in his reply had caused her to add, "When I was a little girl about your age, I used to spend all my summers and most of my holidays on the very farm where you live."

She had expected some gleam of interest, but Tad had merely cast her a blank look and asked, "Why?" as if the farm was the last place in the world anyone would want to be.

"My grandparents lived there. I liked visiting them," Cathie continued determinedly, "and because there were so many fun places to play."

He had given her another look that plainly said she was out of her mind as he ended their conversation with, "I have to catch the bus."

Outside school, Cathie had only seen Tad once. That had been after a Sunday church service. She had changed out of her choir robe and was walking to the car park to meet Clay. Dressed in a blue suit and a striped tie, Tad was leaning against the fender of a new Lexus. A toe of one polished shoe was digging furrows in the gravel.

He looked up at the sound of her approach. "Good morning, Miss Carlsen," Tad greeted her politely.

"Good morning, Tad," Cathie returned. "I didn't know you attended this church." Her seat in the choir didn't give her much of a view of the congregation, so it didn't surprise her that she hadn't seen him.

"It was my father's idea," he said, indicating that the thought was definitely not his. "I did see you in the choir, though."

"Next time I'll look for you." Cathie smiled, glancing around her. "Where's your father?"

"Ah, he's talking to somebody." Tad sighed with the impatience of youth.

At that moment Clay had joined them. "There you are, Cathie. I've been looking for you."

"I stopped to talk to Tad. Clay, this is one of my students, Tad Douglas," Cathie introduced. "This is Clay Carlsen."

"Is he your husband?" Tad looked Clay over with almost grown-up speculation.

"No, he's my fiancé." To which the boy nodded with an indifferent understanding.

"Are you ready to go?" Clay asked as Tad turned his gaze away from them. Cathie had the feeling that Clay's arrival was the reason for Tad's unspoken wish to discontinue their conversation. She had told him good-bye and received a mumbled response.

"So that's your difficult pupil and the son of Rob Douglas," Clay remarked as they reached his car.

"Tad's not difficult," Cathie said. "He just doesn't seem to be coping with his new environment."

"Why don't you discuss it with his father?" Clay suggested practically, opening the car door and helping Cathie inside.

Cathie took her time before replying, smoothing her yellow-flowered spring dress while Clay walked around to the driver's side and slid behind the wheel. She didn't want to get into a discussion with

Clay about Rob Douglas. She knew he would scoff at the dread she felt at the thought of meeting Tad's father. Thus far Cathie hadn't seen him or spoken to him and she considered herself lucky that she hadn't. The opportunities had been there to do so. Her roommate, Connie, had had several dates with him, although none recently. Fortunately, as far as Cathie was concerned, Connie had always been ready the moment Rob Douglas had arrived. Andy attributed that to the fact that Connie wasn't eager to introduce him to any other female. Still, on those evenings when Rob Douglas had been expected, Cathie had kept to her room, using the pretext of school papers to correct.

The very fact that their eventual meeting had been prolonged added to its importance and to Cathie's apprehensions. Rob Douglas was firmly established as the new owner of the Carlsen farm, a circumstance that the passage of time hadn't been able to dampen her resentment about. And his son Tad's vague comments about him had tended to increase her antagonism. Most of all there was her own presentiment that once she met him there would be more catastrophic changes in her life beyond the loss of a piece of land that had been in her family for generations.

All of these feelings she had tried at one time or another to explain to Clay. He hadn't been able to understand or attach any importance to them and their discussions had always ended with Cathie losing her temper. Therefore, when Clay had suggested that she discuss Tad's adjustment to his new life with his father, she had passed it off with, "Tad will adjust in time after the newness wears off," and Clay had been content to accept that.

Like many of the other teachers, Cathie applauded the cries of "School's out! School's out! Teacher's let the monkeys out!" that heralded the beginning of summer vacation.

The increased workload of preparing final exams, grading them and filling out report cards convinced Cathie that the summer vacation was really for the teachers. There was pride in passing all her students on to the fifth grade and pity for Mrs. Gleason, who would inherit Charlie Smith with the rest of the class. Charlie had very considerately brought his pet garter snake to the class picnic, to the horror of the shrieking girls and the amusement of the laughing boys—all except Tad, who maintained his lonely superiority to the very end.

The week after school closed Cathie used to recuperate from her previous hectic pace. Although officially it was still spring, the weather had summer's heat. The first few mornings she slept late and lazed in the backyard, sunning herself to acquire the golden tan that came so naturally to her complexion. Then she indulged in a brief buying spree for her summer wardrobe. It was difficult to keep from remembering that last year at this time she had spent her days at the Homeplace doing some of the heavier housework that her grandmother wasn't able to do anymore and indulging in her grandfather's passion for cribbage.

The rising sun cast a cherry-red glow over the horizon before climbing higher to shine in a cloudless blue sky. In the distance the pealing of bells chimed their announcement of Sunday's services. Her hair had a rich golden sheen as Cathie smoothed the white satin collar over her navy blue choir robe. Then she filed in with the rest of the choir to take her seat. The resonant sound of the organ filled the church as it began the prelude. The congregation stood to raise its voice to sing the hymn "Holy, Holy, Holy" and Cathie's alto voice joined in the harmony.

After resuming her seat, Cathie allowed her gaze to shift over the congregation. Her view was limited, but her eyes casually inspected those within her sight. A tiny smile curved her full lips as she spied the small, smartly dressed boy sitting erectly in the fourth pew. Tad's hazel eyes were scanning the choir, finally coming to rest on Cathie. Even at that distance, Cathie could see the slight nod of recognition he gave her. She did the same in return, her heart swelling with tenderness that this serious little boy wanted to exchange a secret greeting with her. Perhaps she had made some headway with him after all.

"The Scripture reading for this Sunday is Matthew 13:44," the Reverend Mr. Wittman intoned. " 'This kingdom of heaven is like treasure hidden in a field, which a man found and covered up; then in his joy he goes and sells all that he has and buys that field.' "

While Mr. Wittman was speaking, a movement beside Tad attracted Cathie's gaze. As she disengaged herself from Tad's look, she mentally braced herself for her first glimpse of Rob Douglas. Her heartbeat quickened.

His strong, powerful face blocked out all thought of her surroundings as she studied it. His hair was brown as Andy had said, but it was a rich, vibrant shade. Its thickness and wave defied any orderly style, but its casual, almost wayward appearance made the man all the more attractive. Still, it was his face that commanded Cathie's attention. It was lean, with a sharply defined mouth and artfully chiseled nose accented by a strong jawline and firm chin. Dark brows curved above eyes that appeared dark, although at this distance Cathie had to assume his eyes were brown, and above the brows was a wide, intelligent forehead. There was nothing soft about Rob Douglas's face, but there was nothing harsh either.

Yet all the innuendos, the implied but never spoken comments were stamped in his face and in the arrogant tilt of his head. He was the epitome of virile masculinity, the supreme dominating male—the type that Cathie had always loathed. She was further irritated by the fact that all around him people were sitting so stiffly, obviously uncomfortable in their unaccustomed Sunday finery, while Rob Douglas sat relaxed and assured in his impeccably tailored suit.

Cathie saw him glance down at his son, then follow his gaze to the choir. Antagonism welled inside her as Rob Douglas met her gaze. She felt a flush of anger fill her cheeks at the suggestion of amusement in his glance. Determinedly Cathie turned her attention to the minister, although through the rest of their service she found her attention pulled back to Tad's father as if he had some magnetic attraction.

The benediction signaled the close of the service. Cathie's movements were more hurried than the rest of the choir as she hastened to remove her robe and place it on its hanger. There was no pause to brush her hair or retouch her makeup. She simply adjusted the locket around her neck, smoothing her dress before picking up her hand-bag and slipping out through the side door of the church. Escape seemed mandatory and Cathie glanced furtively around for Clay, only to see him cornered by Agnes Rogers. Her high heels tapped the pavement impatiently as she debated whether to walk over to free him from the woman's silly gossip or to retreat to the car and let him make his own excuses.

Before she could make a decision on the best course of action, Cathie saw Tad approaching. Something in his squared shoulders and head told her that the only reason he was coming this way was to see her. Cathie felt guilty for not really wanting to see or talk to Tad at this moment, but the antagonistic sensation she had experienced toward his father was still too strong for her to conduct herself naturally with Tad, his son. As she debated turning away, pretending she hadn't seen Tad, the opportunity to do so evaporated.

The boy stopped stiffly in front of her and without any prelude of greetings said, "Miss Carlsen, my father would like to meet you, please."

If only the request had been made less formally, Cathie thought ruefully. A "Hey, my dad wants to meet you" would have put her so much more at ease.

The words of polite refusal formed. "My fiancé and I were just leaving. Perhaps—" Cathie almost said "another time" when she saw a look in his eyes that pleaded with her to consent. It was so unexpected to see an emotional reaction from Tad that Cathie immediately reformulated her reply for the boy's sake. "Perhaps since Clay is still talking to Mrs. Rogers, I'll have time to meet your father."

"He's over this way," Tad said, reaching to take her hand.

Silently chiding herself for giving in, Cathie followed him through the thinning throng of churchgoers. Rob Douglas was talking to the minister when he spied them approaching. The lordly nod of good-bye that he gave Mr. Wittman as he turned to meet them set Cathie's teeth on edge. It was going to be difficult controlling her temper and maintaining the outward serenity a teacher is supposed to cultivate, Cathie realized.

He had an easy, graceful stride that covered ground quickly without appearing to do so. Now, at closer quarters, Cathie felt the full force of his attractiveness directed at her, the vitality and charm reaching out to pull her into his circle of admirers. Her eyes glittered with emerald green sparks as she resolved that she would not fall victim to his charisma. Let him find out that there were some women in this world who wouldn't hang on his every word, she thought with spiteful amusement.

The atmosphere between them was definitely charged as his velvet-brown eyes acknowledged the challenge in hers. Instead of being put off by it, Rob Douglas seemed to accept it and even find humor in it, which did little to smooth Cathie's already ruffled fur.

"This is my teacher, Miss Carlsen." Tad was taking his duties as introducer seriously. "Miss Carlsen, this is my father, Robert Douglas."

"How do you do, Mr. Douglas." The formal situation seemed to demand that there be a handshake, and very unwillingly Cathie offered hers.

"I'm very glad to meet you, Miss Carlsen." His mouth quirked with amusement as she practically snatched her hand away after only the briefest of contact with his. His voice was very clear and articulate but low-pitched, which Cathie decided was the reason Andy had described it as sexy, although she would only concede that it was pleasing to the ear. "My son has mentioned you many times. I believe he's sorry you won't be teaching him next year."

"Tad is a very good student." It was disconcerting to be at the disadvantage of having to look up because of the man's superior height. Cathie welcomed the opportunity to direct her gaze elsewhere, this time at the young boy standing beside them. "I was happy to have him in my class."

"I believe you're right, Tad. Miss Carlsen does resemble Patience."

The unexpected remark brought her head up sharply. A quizzical look was in her eyes as she brushed a gold lock from her cheek.

"Patience is a little kitten. She has honey-colored fur and green flashing eyes," Rob Douglas explained. The gaze that roamed over her face and hair left her with the peculiar feeling that he had touched her. It was a distinctly unsettling sensation.

"I see," Cathie breathed, turning away from the mesmerizing depths of the brown eyes in favor of the more innocuous hazel ones. "Is Patience one of your pets, Tad?"

"You can hardly get close to her unless you wait long enough. That's why we called her Patience." Tad tilted his head way back to look up at his father. "The other day she let me pet her. She even purred."

"Maybe it's just grown-ups she doesn't like," his father commented. Deep grooves were carved on each side of his mouth as he studied Cathie with open amusement. "Your name is Catherine, isn't it? Mr. Wittman told me. Do your friends call you Cat?"

"My friends call me Cathie, Mr. Douglas," she retorted sharply, her hold on her temper snapping at his implication.

"Your teacher has claws, Tad." Silent laughter vibrated from behind the row of white teeth as his smile widened at the angry blush in her cheeks.

Cathie felt a feline desire to sharpen her so-called claws across his cheekbone and add a few more scars to go with the small one near his right eye. A glance down at Tad's bewildered face halted the biting comment that sprang to her tongue.

"You misunderstood me, Mr. Douglas," she said forcing a smile to appear on her taut face. "But I'm called Cathie, not Cat. If I sounded sharp I suppose that's the teacher in me."

"That's argumentative, but we won't discuss it now." There was still the sparkle of superior laughter in his eyes.

The infuriating presence of Rob Douglas succeeded in making her forget all others in her vicinity. Therefore Clay's greeting, "Hello, Tad, Cathie," caught her completely by surprise. There was a moment of expectancy as both men waited for Cathie to introduce them.

"This is Tad's father, Rob Douglas." She glanced at Clay, who had been studying her heightened color and was now turning his appraising gaze to Rob Douglas, the obvious cause of her anger. Clay smiled at the way the man's eyes were admiring Cathie's upturned profile. There were few men who wouldn't be moved by her unusual beauty. "This is my fiancé, Clay Carlsen," Cathie finished.

Her head tilted defiantly as she faced Rob Douglas again. There was an almost imperceptible raising of one dark brow.

"Carlsen?" his low voice questioned as he accepted the hand Clay offered.

"Cathie and I are distant cousins," Clay smiled.

"This is a very small and tight-knit community. You'll find that nearly all the families that have been here for a period of time are related to each other in one way or another." Cathie was angry with herself for making a further explanation. She and Clay shared the same last name, but there was certainly nothing at all wrong about their relationship.

Rob nodded, a complacent smile remaining on his face as Cathie moved closer to Clay. "Whose grandparents used to own my farm?"

Her teeth grated at his possessive pronoun.

"Cathie's," Clay answered for her.

"It's always belonged to a Carlsen ever since my great-grandfather bought it as unimproved prairie land over a hundred years ago." Angry pride forced her to stake her own claim on the farm that he called his.

A thoughtful look subdued the sparkle in his eyes as Rob studied her. "It must have been difficult to part with it after all these years. It's unfortunate that your grandfather didn't leave it to one of his children."

"My grandparents only had three children. Uncle Andrew was killed in a car accident when I was a child." The feeling of injustice crept into her voice, although Cathie tried to explain the circumstances calmly. "My father is a professor at the university and my aunt's husband is a doctor.

My grandfather didn't feel it was fair to saddle either of them with a farm, which is why he asked that it should be sold and the proceeds divided.''

"Your grandfather must have been a practical man," Rob Douglas stated.

"The same can't be said for his granddaughter," Clay sighed, smiling as he put an arm around Cathie's shoulders. "She tried to persuade her father to buy the farm just to keep it in the family."

"I suppose the two of you could have lived on it once you were married to look after it for him." Rob voiced the same thought that Cathie had, but she found herself springing to Clay's defense rather than endorse his suggestion.

"Clay is an attorney. It wouldn't be fair to ask him to give up all those years of school to run the farm or to try to practice law at the same time as running the farm."

Rob Douglas intercepted Clay's look of surprise. Cathie held her breath in anticipation of some astute comment, but Rob made none.

"Tad and I have kept you two from your dinner long enough and I know Mrs. Carver is waiting for us," Rob said, placing a hand on the shoulder of the boy standing patiently by his side. "It's been a pleasure meeting you, Miss Carlsen, and you, Clay."

Cathie didn't realize how rigidly she had been holding herself until she and Clay were alone. Then a trembling seized her legs as the aftershock of meeting Rob Douglas set in.

Chapter Four

A male cardinal butterfly flitted across Cathie's path, his scarlet body and black-crowned head quickly disappearing amidst the branches of a flowering catalpa tree. Her white cotton sundress intensified the golden tan of her bared skin. She shifted the books she was carrying from one arm to the other. Beneath her leather sandals she could feel the burning heat of the pavement from the hot June sun. The asphalt in the streets was soft and mushy to the step. These were the days to enjoy the burning warmth of the sun before the scorching heat and high humidity of Iowa's July and August arrived.

Cathie was making her weekly trek to the local library, preferring to go in the middle of the week when there were fewer people and she had plenty of time to browse without interfering with anyone else. The last two books she read she hadn't enjoyed at all. Because of her meeting on Sunday with Rob Douglas, Cathie found herself picturing him as the leading male character in the novels, which had made it difficult to concentrate on the plots. She would have preferred to forget she had ever met him, but his image was too potent to wish away.

Her hand closed over the iron railing as Cathie started up the concrete steps that led into the small library. From the corner of her eye she glimpsed a group of children gathered at the end of the block. Their chanting voices pierced her semi-daydream state. Cathie halted midway up the steps as she recognized Tad Douglas in the center of the group. The jeering sound of the children's laughter angered Cathie and she retraced her way down the steps and started walking toward the white-faced boy so determinedly trying to ignore the taunts hurled at him.

But she wasn't the only one who had seen the harassment taking place. As Cathie walked closer to the group, she saw Rob Douglas walk out of the lumber store across the street, his long stride carrying him directly to the scene. He reached the group several steps before Cathie.

His growling demand, "What's going on here?" scattered the children in every direction, while Tad took one look at the scowl on his father's face and tucked his chin against his chest.

"What was all this about, Tad?" His stern words brought no response from the boy. Rob Douglas's hand shot out and turned Tad's face up toward his. "I want an explanation."

Cathie knew that closed, sullen look on his son's face. She had seen it often enough in class.

Although she had the opportunity of turning away and avoiding another meeting with Rob Douglas, she chose not to take advantage of it.

Stepping forward, she said, "The other children were teasing him about his name."

The fiery dark eyes were turned on Cathie and she experienced relief that his anger wasn't directed at her. Rob looked all the more imposing in faded jeans and a tight fitting short-sleeved polo shirt. The muscular physique that his Sunday dress had only hinted at was revealed by his casual clothes.

"What do you mean, his name?" Rob Douglas released Tad's chin, which immediately fell back to his chest.

"Tad, short for tadpole or a frog." Cathie spoke quietly as if the softness of her voice would ease the pain those words had inflicted.

The grim line around Rob's mouth grew even grimmer as he looked down at the sandy-haired head of his son. He inhaled deeply to control his anger and glanced at Cathie. "I appreciate the information, Miss Carlsen."

After a brief nod in her direction, he herded Tad across the street to where his Lexus was parked. Cathie watched them for a minute before turning back toward the library, trying to refocus her thoughts on choosing books, but finding Rob Douglas a potent influence on her mind.

"Aw, come on, Cathie," Andy wheedled. "You said yourself that Clay wasn't coming over tonight, so you have no reason for not coming with us to Black Hawk Lake."

"Really, Andy, I don't feel like going swimming tonight." Cathie refused for about the sixth time, and the second time since their evening meal. "I would rather spend a quiet night alone here at the house."

"There's a whole group of us going. Nobody's matched up with anyone else, so you don't need to worry about Clay getting jealous," the dark-haired girl persevered. "I agree that it's terribly peaceful with Connie on vacation at Okoboji, but it's too beautiful a night to sit around by yourself."

"That's exactly what I want to do," Cathie insisted.

"Well," said Andy, sighing as she lifted her shoulders in a resigned gesture, "if that's what you really want to do, far be it for me to try to change your mind. But you're really going to miss an awfully fun evening."

"I'll survive," Cathie replied drolly as she secured her blond hair behind her head with a tortoiseshell clasp.

A car horn tooted impatiently in front of the house. "That must be Mary Beth!" Andy exclaimed, racing out of the kitchen to the front room where her beach bag and towel were. As she retraced her steps, speeding toward the outside door, she called out to Cathie, "I don't know what time we'll be back, so don't worry if I'm late. Bye!" And the door slammed.

The oscillating fan continued to whir noisily from its position on the kitchen counter, so the house didn't become completely silent at the departure of Andy. Cathie stared at the closed door, her green eyes clouded and without their usual jewel-bright sparkle. Now that she was alone, she stopped fighting the restless feeling that had been nagging at her all afternoon and evening. The true reason she had declined Andy's invitation wasn't because she wanted to spend the evening alone, but because she didn't feel like going swimming with a boisterous and laughing group of people. Nor was she missing Clay's company, even though he was tied up this evening.

It was a strange mood she was in, unsettled, restless. There were plenty of things she could do—read one of the books she had picked up at the library today, write her parents a letter, do some washing. Cathie could think of all the things she could do, but nothing that she wanted to do.

After wandering aimlessly through the house twice and drawing concerned looks from the dog Duchess, Cathie finally picked up one of the library books and settled in an easy chair in the living room. It was a futile attempt because she kept reading the same page over and over without remembering what she had read. The ring of the telephone was almost a relief.

Lifting the black receiver, she said, "Hello."

"Hello. This is Rob Douglas. I wondered if you were free this evening?"

For a moment Cathie's heart stopped beating before it began racing away at an incredible speed. She collected herself before answering. "You must want Connie. She's on vacation. This is Cathie Carlsen speaking."

"I'm aware that Connie is on vacation and I know whom I'm speaking to." There was a suggestion of dry amusement in his voice. "It's you that I wish to see, Miss Carlsen."

"Me? What do you want to see me about?" A

frown creased her forehead as her hand tightened its grip on the receiver.

"There are some personal things I want to discuss with you," Rob answered. "May I come over?"

"What personal things? About your son?" Cathie wanted it clarified before she would consider agreeing to another face-to-face confrontation with him. "Surely we can discuss it over the telephone?"

"Not really. I'll be there in about twenty minutes."

"Just a moment, I—" she began, but the line on the other end was dead. Slowly she replaced the receiver, wishing that she had gone with Andy instead of staying home.

Then cold anger swept over her at his high-handed assumption that simply because he said he was coming over she would be there. He hadn't even waited for her to say whether she was free.

"Duchess, I think it's time someone taught Mr. Douglas a lesson." The dog's tail wagged briefly as if in agreement while Cathie hurried toward the small desk in the living room to retrieve some paper and a pencil. She quickly jotted down a note addressed to Rob Douglas that stated she had a previous engagement, then rummaged through the desk drawers to find some tape.

A wicked sparkle gleamed from her green eyes as she taped the message to the front door. She paused long enough to imagine Rob Douglas's face when he saw it before dashing back into the house for her handbag and the car keys inside it. After several minutes' delay trying to remember where she had left the bag, Cathie found it and sped out of the door to the small garage.

The heavy garage door was its usual stubborn

self, opening halfway, then refusing to budge until Cathie had broken a sacrificial fingernail. Inside the car, she put the key in the ignition, listened to the motor turn over once, then twice, then three times before it finally coughed and sputtered into life. Excitement flushed her face, giving it a glow as she turned in the seat to look out of the back window and reverse the car out of the garage into the drive. Before she could maneuver the car into the street, a bronze Lexus pulled into the driveway, effectively blocking her escape.

Her hand smacked the steering wheel in anger. "Damn! Damn! Damn!" she muttered under her breath.

"Calm down." Rob Douglas leaned down to look in the window on the driver's side. His mouth quirked at the furious expression on her face. It was not a smile, but annoyance touched by amusement at her futile attempt to elude him. "Did you think it would take me twenty minutes to drive that distance? The farm is barely two miles from town."

"If you would read the note on the door, you'll find I have another engagement," she stated coldly. "So if you will kindly move your car, I'll be on my way."

He reached in the opened window, turned off the motor and extracted the key from the ignition, his arm brushing her rounded breast. "You're lying, Cat," he stated calmly. "You don't have any other appointment."

"And just how do you know that?" she demanded, refusing to reach for the keys that were being held just out of reach.

"If you had other plans for this evening, you would have seized on that excuse for not seeing

me immediately. As it is, you only thought of it
after I'd hung up," he smiled. The smile didn't
lessen the hard, uncompromising glitter in his eyes.
"I can't understand why you're so anxious to avoid
me, Cat, especially since I only want to talk to you
as parent to teacher."

"Stop calling me Cat!" She was bristling with
anger as he opened the car door for her. Brushing
away the hand he offered, Cathie stepped out of
the car, seething with fury that he could see
through her pretense so easily. "My keys, please."

Rob Douglas dropped them in her outstretched
palm and Cathie transferred them to her bag. Her
hands clenched the leather bag tightly as she stood
silently in front of Rob, too aware of the way he
towered over her. He always looked so cool and
collected, no matter what. She unnecessarily
smoothed her hair back to where it was caught by
the clasp, fighting to get control of her temper.

"I suppose we should go in the house," Cathie
suggested icily.

"It would be more conducive to a business conversation than the hard cement of your front
steps," he agreed, stepping aside so she could lead
the way, a cool, arrogant gleam lighting his brown
eyes as she stalked past him.

Duchess met Cathie at the door, her tail wagging
until she saw the stranger following her mistress.
A shrinking shyness sent the dog hiding behind
Cathie's legs, the graying muzzle sticking out to
test the air in case it was someone she knew.

"Your watchdog?" Dark eyebrows raised signifi-
cantly.

Cathie wished it were true, then she could have
set Duchess on him. Instead she sighed, "She's just

a pet. She was my grandfather's dog, but she always was shy around strangers, and since I took her from the farm, the poor dear has been even worse." She gave the red-gold head hugging her knees a reassuring pat. "Go and lie down, Duchess."

"She's a beautiful animal, even if she is beginning to show her age. An English shepherd, isn't she?"

"Yes," Cathie nodded abruptly. "Would you prefer the kitchen or the living room?"

"Wherever you think would be most comfortable."

There wasn't any room that would seem comfortable to Cathie as long as Rob Douglas was in it, but since he left it up to her, she chose the kitchen. Its strictly utilitarian atmosphere would not encourage casual conversation. With luck their discussion about Tad would be short and she could send him quickly on his way.

"Would you care for something to drink?" She didn't want to offer him anything, but her ingrained hospitality demanded it of her. "I could make some instant coffee, or I have pink lemonade in the refrigerator."

"Spare me the instant coffee," Rob refused firmly, revealing the same aversion she felt toward it. "But I will have some lemonade, if you don't mind."

"Not at all." Minutes later she set a glass for each of them on the Formica-topped table and drew out a chair on the opposite side of the table from where he was seated. "Now, what did you want to discuss about Tad?" she asked in her most businesslike manner.

"You didn't seem surprised by the episode this afternoon. I take it this has happened before."

"Yes. It's not at all unusual for a child to be teased about his name. Another boy in my class is named Jack, but the children invariably call him Jack Rabbit because his ears stick out. It's something a teacher can't prevent." Cathie didn't have any intention of being blamed for it, though she followed the school rules against bullying to the letter.

His thorough study of her face was making her uncomfortable. "I'm not accusing you of anything," Rob told her, looking unbearably relaxed and in charge. "How does he get along in school?"

"You signed his report card," she returned defensively. "He's an excellent student, as I said before."

"I don't doubt his scholastic ability," he agreed with marked patience. "I'm more concerned about his ability to get along with other children."

"Doesn't Tad talk about what goes on at school to you?" Cathie was unwilling to point out how singularly detached Tad had been from the rest of the class.

"I want your view."

"Okay." She took a deep breath. If he wanted her view, she would give it to him just exactly the way it was without any of the frills of teacher diplomacy. "Tad seemed to be determined not to become a part of the class. He never took part in any discussions, didn't join in any games unless he was forced to, and kept to himself at all other times. He was the straggler, the last one to arrive in the room and the last to leave. He avoided all contact that he could with the rest of the students." Cathie paused, taking in the grim set of Rob Douglas's jaw. He wasn't liking what he was hearing and there was a pleasing sense of revenge that she was upsetting him as much as he upset her. "Even the way he dressed, his expensive clothes, set Tad apart. They weren't right for the rough and tumble play of boys."

"He didn't make any friends?" His gaze hardened and Cathie's eyes were drawn to the small scar, its pencil-thin line making the glitter in his dark eyes appear all the more portentous.

"None."

His hand closed tightly over the glass on the table. "Did you think his behavior was natural?"

"Of course not." An angry frown creased her forehead.

"Then why didn't you notify me of Tad's behavior?"

Cathie knew she had been wrong in that. If it had been anyone other than Rob Douglas, she would have contacted the parent. But she had been too determined not to have anything to do with him. Even now she couldn't admit that she was wrong.

"I believed that, given time, Tad would adjust," she answered primly. "After all, it wasn't just the school that was different. He had moved to a different state, had a new home, and I had heard that his mother died last fall. Those are a lot of changes for a small boy to adapt to, and I didn't think the two months of school was enough time for him to do it."

"But you still didn't think I needed to know what was going on." Rob shook his head in exasperation and anger. "Why?"

"I thought he would confide in you," Cathie flared. "You are his father!"

"Yes." He sighed, leaning against the padded chair back. Grim lines deepened the grooves around his mouth, determination etched in the carved lines. "I am his father."

"You must have had some indication of what was going on?" The somber concern in his face made Cathie unconsciously soften her tone and take the sarcasm out of it.

Rob looked at her sharply from beneath the dark gathering of his brow. "When you were listing the adjustments Tad has to make, you didn't include a father that he doesn't know."

"What?" Cathie breathed, her head tilted to the side in surprise, not quite sure she had heard him right.

"I met Tad's mother when she was only seventeen. She was unlike anyone I'd ever met. Her parents were extremely wealthy and owned a large estate on the East Coast. When she told them she wanted to marry me, it was probably the only time in her life that she'd stood up to them. Since she wasn't of legal age, we needed their consent, and they would only give it if we agreed to live in the small guest house on the estate grounds." Rob continued in a flat, unemotional voice. "I won't embarrass you with the more intimate failures of our marriage except to say that when Yvette discovered she was pregnant, she used it as an excuse to move back to the main house. I stayed on. I thought when our child was born he would tie us together, but her parents, Yvette and Tad became the family and I was the one who was excluded."

In spite of herself Cathie felt a welling of sympathy for him, even though she realized he was too proud a man to accept it, if he ever needed it, which she doubted.

"We were divorced a year after Tad was born. Yvette's problems were the result of an excessively sheltered and controlled life. Her parents' world went only as far as the estate walls, and Yvette saw no harm in raising our child in the same way. At the time I had neither the money nor the power her parents possess, so there was no chance of taking my son away from her. I was refused visiting privileges with Tad unless Yvette or her parents were with me. The last time I saw Tad he was five years old. He sat passively in a chair the whole time, dressed like a miniature preppie, not playing or showing any desire to play. I didn't go back again until Yvette's death last fall. It was worse than the last time I saw him, and I knew it was my last chance to get him away from that oppressive environment. The court hearing took place in February and the judge awarded me custody. Only now is Tad beginning to doubt all those stories he was told about how I didn't care about him, that I'd deserted him and his mother. So you see, that shell he's in is how he protects himself and this teasing by his classmates only serves to reinforce it."

"Why are you telling me all this?" Her voice was tight. She didn't want to know about his past or that of his son. She didn't want to become involved in his life, and yet an inner voice kept telling her she already was, that their paths were already entwined. "You should be telling Mrs. Gleason, his new teacher."

Rob leaned forward to rest both arms on the table and gaze intently at Cathie. "There are three long months of summer vacation. Three months during which you and I together could help Tad take a giant step forward."

"Why me?" she protested, feeling herself being drawn into the whirlpool of his plans and wanting to resist, to shut her ears to his low, persuasive voice.

"Because Tad likes you. Your approval has become important to him. You haven't been subject to the name-calling of his grandparents. He can accept you as you are."

"I don't understand. What could I possibly do to help him?"

His gaze firmly held hers. "You told Tad once that you used to spend your summers on the farm. I can barely persuade him to walk in the barn door, and if it weren't for that little yellow kitten that lives in the barn, I wouldn't get him that far."

"And you think I might be able to talk him into being more adventurous," Cathie finished his thought.

"Let's put it this way. Tad is intrigued by the treehouse in the grove opposite the house. He asked me once if I thought you used to play in it as a child, but he won't venture over there. Several other times he's inquired whether you might have done something or other when you were on the farm."

"So what are you asking? That I take him on a grand tour of the place?" She had to make her voice sarcastic to hide the ache in her heart brought on by her cherished memories of the Homeplace.

"To see it a few times through your eyes might make it seem less alien to Tad," Rob said quietly.

"That won't help him get along any better with

the other children," Cathie pointed out desperately.

"If we can get Tad to accept his surroundings, we might be able to get him to accept the people that live here."

Why did he persist in saying "we"? Cathie thought in irritation. "It's impossible," she said aloud, shoving her chair back from the table and rising to her feet.

"I'm not asking very much, only a few trips to the farm to visit my son." An eyebrow quirked arrogantly in her direction.

Put that way, it didn't sound like very much. How could she refuse? "I'll do it," Cathie agreed ungraciously, "for Tad's sake."

"It never occurred to me that you would do it for any other reason," said Rob, an arrogant look in his eyes. He rose from his chair and walked over to the table near where Cathie was standing. She was looking out the window at the orange dusk laced with streaks of purpling pink, but she turned at his approach.

"Is that all you wanted, Mr. Douglas?" she demanded, glad of the shadows that prevented her from seeing his face clearly, all too aware of the thudding of her heart brought on by the resentment he always generated in her.

"Yes, that's all. I didn't think our discussion would take up so much time. I've really made you late for your so-called appointment now." Amusement lurked in his voice as Rob Douglas recalled her fictitious excuse when he had arrived.

"You know very well I had no such appointment," Cathie retorted sharply and bitterly, taking the now empty glass from his hand.

"You just didn't want my company, is that right?" That knowledge didn't seem to upset him too much.

"Yes, that's exactly right," she agreed, tilting her chin upward in defiance.

"I wonder why? Do you know?" He evidently meant his question to be rhetorical because he continued talking, a hand reaching out to hold Cathie's and examine the diamond ring on her third finger. "You don't have the look of a woman in love," he mused. "When is the wedding?"

"We haven't set a date yet, if it's any of your business."

"What day would you like to come out to the farm?" Rob asked, ignoring the deliberate snub.

He was pinning her down, as if he doubted that she would keep her word to come out. "Would next Tuesday be convenient?" she inquired haughtily, knowing she was delaying the time for as long as she could to give herself an opportunity to gather her defenses around her before she had to meet up with him again.

"Around one-thirty would be fine," Rob agreed, taking his leave of her.

Chapter Five

The wild roses were in bloom along the roadside, their pink petals accented by the green, green grasses. A wild canary flew among the grove of trees, his yellow body like a shaft of sunlight in the shade. The familiar cry of a meadowlark sounded in the distance. There was that indescribable feeling of coming home as Cathie turned her car into the farm lane. Even Duchess recognized it, becoming a whining, wiggling mass of ecstasy from her place in the back seat.

The dog tumbled out of the car the minute Cathie parked it and opened the door. Her russet-gold and white body was a quivering mass of happiness as she raced from the car to the house and back again. Her feathery tail that had seemed to be perpetually tucked between her legs since Cathie had taken Duchess away from the farm was now wagging merrily in the air. A tightness gripped

Cathie's throat because she knew her heart gave a similar leap of joy when she gazed around the familiar and beloved surroundings.

This was her second visit with Tad. The first she had kept short so she could ease out of the role of teacher. Rob Douglas had not mentioned that Cathie was going to visit them, and Tad had been pleased and surprised when she did. Much of his reserve vanished at the discovery that she had stopped to see him and not anyone else. They had taken a short walk around the house and yard with an excursion across the road to the grove of trees where the tree house was, but Cathie wasn't able to persuade Tad to climb the tree for a closer look. She was glad that his father had been out in the fields and she hadn't had to encounter him during the visit. It had made it all the more enjoyable for her.

It looked as if she wasn't going to be as lucky on this visit as Rob Douglas followed his son out of the house. Duchess intercepted them as they reached the halfway point between the house and Cathie. The dog sniffed Tad's feet before greeting the boy enthusiastically, much to Cathie's delight. She had always known the shepherd liked children, but she had particularly been anxious that the dog make friends with Tad. The boy was hesitant to touch the red-gold head until a quiet word from his father prompted the movement. Duchess attached herself proprietarily to Tad's heels and accompanied him to Cathie.

"Good afternoon, Miss Carlsen. Tad told me you came last week," Rob Douglas greeted her smoothly without even a gleam of conspiracy in his eyes.

"How do you do, Mr. Douglas," she returned

before turning to smile at Tad. "Hi, Tad. I see you've met Duchess. I hope you don't mind my bringing her along, but she was terribly homesick for the farm. She used to live here, too."

"She seems to be a very nice dog," Tad observed solemnly, gazing down at the graying muzzle that was turned adoringly toward him.

"If you two will excuse me," Rob broke in, "I have a lot of work to be done and I'm sure you want to plan what you're going to do this afternoon."

Cathie breathed a silent sigh of relief as he walked away. She was always so stiff and uncomfortable around him, as if she were constantly holding her breath in anticipation of something. Besides, he was so infuriatingly male.

"As you can see by the way I'm dressed," Cathie began brightly the minute Rob was out of hearing, "I thought I'd take you on a tour of some of the places where I used to play."

Tad inspected her patched blue jeans and the scuffed tennis shoes, passing over the faded red-checked blouse to stop on her face.

"Do you have some old clothes to change into?" she asked. She could tell from the doubtful expression on his face that the neat slacks and crisp shirt were repeated in the rest of his wardrobe. She could have bitten off her tongue for making such a mistake. "It doesn't matter," Cathie hurried on. "I don't imagine we'll get all that messed up just walking."

"Maybe we can go fishing instead," Tad suggested with marked hesitation. "You told me the last time that you used to do that lots of times and I've never been fishing. Do you suppose we could, Miss Carlsen?"

"School is out, Tad. You can call me Cathie."
The smile on her face was genuine, but it didn't
reassure the boy.

"I was always told that it wasn't proper to call
your elders by their first name," he said solemnly,
his eyes gazing earnestly into the depths of her
green ones.

"That's old-fashioned. Besides, you make me feel
like an old lady," Cathie teased, drawing the smile
from his face that she had been seeking. "And I
think fishing is a great idea. I'm sure my old poles
are still in the garage. I'll go and check while you
run in and ask Mrs. Carver if she has a container
of some sort that we can put worms in."

Tad was off like a flash with Duchess running
excitedly beside him, while Cathie walked to the
large double garage. There, amid the open rafters,
she spied the old bamboo poles that she and Clay
had used so many times before. It took a few tricky
maneuvers before she was able to get them down.
Surprisingly the hooks weren't rusted and the red
and white bobbers, although a little dirty, were
still serviceable. There was a garden spade leaning
against the corner of the garage and Cathie picked
it up and joined Tad in the front yard. He was trying
to appear as calm and self-possessed as always, but
Cathie saw the glimmer of excitement in his hazel
eyes.

"Ready to meet Mr. Worm?" she asked gaily as
Tad proudly held an empty coffee can out for her
to see.

"Where do we find him?"

"In the ground, silly." She laughed. "Out
behind the machine shed is the best place."

"Which one is the machine shed?" Ted asked, glancing around at the buildings in the barnyard.

"That one there by the drive where your dad keeps his tractors and plows." Cathie pointed. They set off toward it with Duchess trotting contentedly alongside.

"What's that big white building next to it?"

Cathie smiled to herself. At last he was expressing an interest in his new home, and she felt slightly guilty for being the person he asked instead of his father. "That's the corn crib. Do you see the weather vane on top of the cupola?" Tad nodded. "The direction the rooster is facing tells us which way the wind is blowing. Today it's from the west. 'When the wind is from the west, the fish bite the best,' " she chanted, remembering the old rhyme that had been her and Clay's byword.

"Do you really think we'll catch some fish?"

"The Boyer has a lot of catfish, bullheads and carp in it. And if we can find us some worms, I don't know why we won't."

"What's the Boyer?"

"That's the name of the river that runs through the pasture," Cathie explained patiently as they rounded the corner of the machine shed. Propping the fishing poles against the side of the building, she carried the spade over to where some old lumber was piled. "Help me lift this plank, Tad."

Once the board was lifted and set on top of some others, she set about digging up clumps of moist, black sod. She smiled to herself as Tad rather hesitantly helped her break up the clumps and capture the quicksilver worms trying to escape.

"I think that's enough," she said, glancing into the coffee can where fat, wriggling worms tried to bury themselves in the few chunks of earth she had thrown in.

"My hands are all dirty." He was staring at them and the slime and dirt that coated them. "I'd better go and wash."

Cathie checked herself just in time from saying that his hands were going to get a lot dirtier. "If you rub your hands together like this," she showed him, "you can get the worst of it off and we can rinse the rest off in the water trough."

Reluctantly Tad followed her suggestion while Cathie knocked the dirt off the spade and set it to the front of the machine shed so she could carry it back to the garage when they returned. It was difficult not to watch his meticulous efforts to clean as much of the grime off as possible. It was a strain on the imagination that here was a boy who didn't like to get dirty, but Cathie kept her amusement concealed.

"Are you ready?" she called, picking up the bamboo poles and resting them against her shoulder.

With a skeptical look in his eye, Tad picked up the can of worms and joined Cathie. Together they set off toward the pasture gate, pausing at the concrete water trough to rinse off their hands. Instead of taking the gate that led into the pasture, Cathie chose to walk the rutted track along the pasture fence line that bordered the cornfield.

"Why aren't we going that way?" Tad inquired, hopping to keep up with her longer strides.

"I was getting thirsty, and if we go this way, we can stop off at the spring for a drink." Cathie was determined to introduce Tad to all the simple pleasures of the farm. "Here's the spring." She stopped, pointing to the sliver of gleaming silver water on the other side of the fence. "You go first, Tad."

Stepping on the bottom strand of barbed wire with her tennis shoe, Cathie held the top strand up for Tad to crawl through. She was a bit more of an expert at dodging the thorny wire and wiggled through on her own.

Clumps of grass were sneaking onto the pebble-strewn area surrounding the tile through which the spring water came, but there was still enough open dry sand for Cathie to kneel on and scoop up handfuls of the refreshing water. She stepped back and watched Tad mimic her movements.

"Mmm, that's really cold," he declared, wiping the droplets of water from his mouth with the back of his hand. "Almost colder than the water Mrs. Carver keeps in the refrigerator."

Tad's grimy hands were forgotten as he once again entered into the spirit of adventure. The dullness was gone from his hazel eyes, making them sparkle with gold flecks introduced by the brilliance of the sun. He picked up the can of worms and set out with Cathie to follow the tiny ribbon of spring water to where it joined the Boyer River. There was an unaccustomed lightness in his walk that brought a satisfied smile to her face.

At any place they could have stepped across the rivulet of water, but Cathie led him to the weeping willow tree whose main trunk lay horizontally over the spring. "Follow me," she ordered, glancing back at the boy behind her as she began her balancing walk across the rough bark of the trunk. A foot or so on the other side of the spring, the trunk began rising upward to the sun, and that was where Cathie hopped off onto the ground.

Tad followed a bit more slowly, but landed on the ground near her with a proud smile of accomplishment on his face. Where the spring dumped into the river, the water was smooth, reflecting the bright sun like a mirror. A multitude of wild flowers dotted the pasture grass with honeybees busily gathering their sweet nectar. Cathie felt incredibly like a child again as she led Tad along the riverbank on one of the many trails the cattle had carved into the hillside.

"The cows won't bother us, will they?" Tad inquired, glancing across the river where a scattered group of dairy cows was grazing.

"No, they're gentle," Cathie assured him in an offhand manner to lend emphasis to her words. They were approaching the singing rapids. "We'll cross the river here, that way we can fish on the other side where the water is deeper and have the sun at our backs."

"How are we going to get across?"

The poles were already lying on the ground as Cathie bent to remove her tennis shoes. "We'll wade. The water is only a foot or so deep. Clay used to be able to cross with his shoes on by hopping from stone to stone. Every time I tried, my foot slipped into the water and I got my shoes wet. Now I play it safe by taking them off."

As soon as her shoes and socks were off and her jeans rolled up, Cathie turned to help Tad, showing him how to tie the laces of his shoes together so he could carry them around his neck. Then the pair waded into the bubbling water racing over the collection of rocks. After his first hesitant steps and exclamations over the water's coolness, Tad enjoyed the refreshing and uninhibited sensation of the swiftly running river curling around his ankles. They paused at the small sandbar sitting in the middle of the river, a partial cause of the rapids, and Cathie pointed out a school of minnows gathered in the protective shallow waters.

The teacher instinct was strong and unwittingly she began turning the excursion into a biology trip, starting with the minnows, then the snails and explaining the functions of other larger fish in the balance of nature in the river. His inquisitive mind readily took to the subject, his questions continuing as they stopped on the opposite bank to wipe their wet feet with their socks and put their shoes back on.

"Where does this river go?"

"It flows on south into the Missouri River north of Omaha, Nebraska. Did you know, Tad, that the state of Iowa has the mighty Mississippi River as its eastern boundary and most of the muddy Missouri River at its western boundary? And the waters from this very river end up in the Gulf of Mexico."

Arriving at the spot where she had decided they would fish, Cathie slid down the steep bank to a lower shelf, then took the can of worms from Tad and helped him down. The geography lesson was set aside as Cathie showed him the fine art of putting a protesting worm on a hook. Her distaste for the job was similar to his but, as she explained, necessary if they wanted to catch any fish. An expert cast was easy with the bamboo poles and soon they were both leaning against the black soil of the bank watching the red and white bobbers floating on the dark waters of the river.

"Once Clay and I decided to make a raft and float all the way down to the mouth of the Mississippi River. We launched it up on the river by that far island." She was resting her chin on her knees as she indicated an island upriver.

"How far did you get? Did you go all the way?" Tad asked eagerly, caught up by the excitement of the idea.

"Clay and I weren't very good boat-builders," Cathie laughed. "Treehouses and huts were more our line. The raft sank the minute it went into the water."

"You must have really had a lot of fun here," Tad sighed, resting his chin on his knees in mimicry of Cathie.

She wanted to convince him that he could have a lot of fun, too, but that was something he had to realize himself. "What was it like where you used to live?" she asked, changing the subject to get Tad's comparison to his previous home and the farm.

"It was different. A lot different." A scowl covered his young face as he concentrated his gaze on the moving bobber. "There were flowers and roses all over the lawns and gigantic trees and hedges all over. It was beautiful, like a painting. I picked some flowers once for my mother, but they were prize flowers or something. Everybody was really mad at me. I don't suppose I could have ever had a treehouse there. My grandfather told me the oak trees were hundreds of years old and very valuable. Most all the furniture in the house was antique, even the bed I slept in. Grandmother was always afraid I would scratch it, but I never did. My mother's room was the most beautiful of all. Some nights she used to let me come in and sit while she listened to music."

"Do you like music?" Hearing Tad's calm acceptance of such a stifling existence, Cathie had to seize on an unrelated subject.

Tad nodded vigorously. "My favorite record that mother sometimes played was the '1812 Overture'. I liked it when the cannons boomed."

At his age, Cathie thought to herself, she probably would have been humming "Found a Peanut" instead of that, but at least he had exhibited a typically boyish reaction in his reasons for liking the song.

The bobber on Tad's line disappeared underwater for a split second before reappearing. "I think you have a nibble," Cathie whispered. "Watch your bobber."

It disappeared again and popped back to the surface. Tad gripped the pole tightly in his hands, glancing excitedly at Cathie, but unsure of what to do.

"Let the bobber go under again and give the pole a hard yank when it does," she instructed.

The bobber went under again and stayed. Cathie knew the fish was hooked and Tad wouldn't have to worry about setting the hook. They were both shouting with glee when Tad flipped the line out of the water and sent a good-sized bullhead flopping onto the grass of the upper bank. Removing hooks from fish mouths had never been Cathie's forte, but she managed to show Tad how it was done. While he rebaited his hook, she found a stick that would work as a stringer for their catch.

Now that the first fish had been caught, Tad set about his fishing in earnest. Their luck was evenly dispersed, with Tad catching two more and Cathie hooking three, one of which she tossed back as being too small. Both of them were enjoying themselves so much that the sound of a pickup truck blended in with the calls of the meadowlarks and crows, the distant babbling of the water over the rapids and the occasional lowing of the cows.

Both were surprised when Rob's voice sounded above them. "I saw you two from the road. Are you catching anything?"

Tad was the first to recover, jumping to his feet and scrambling up the steep bank without any concern for the condition of his clothes.

"I caught three bullheads!" he cried, unable to conceal his delight. "And Cathie caught three, too, but she put one back because it was too small to eat. Show him what we caught."

Quite willingly Cathie turned away from Rob Douglas's brilliant brown eyes to retrieve the makeshift stringer from the shallow water near the bank. She held them up for Rob to view, conscious of her racing pulse and the slight flush in her cheeks.

"Cathie said Mrs. Carver might cook them for supper tonight. Do you think she would?" Tad asked after Rob had complimented his son on the size of the fish.

"I think we can persuade her," he nodded, turning an impersonal smile of gratitude on Cathie at this change in his son. "Don't you, Miss Carlsen?"

"I think so," Cathie agreed, only to be interrupted by Tad.

"She said to call her Cathie because Miss Carlsen makes her sound like an old lady," he announced, correcting his father, while Cathie cringed inwardly, especially in the light of the laughing look in Rob's eyes.

"I think it's only fair that you call me Rob," he

grinned. Cathie nodded agreement with a resigned smile, experiencing a flash of temper for ever agreeing to his proposition to show Tad around the farm. Immediate chagrin replaced her anger at the happy look on Tad's face. So far the experiment had been successful. "By the way," Rob went on, "I brought a bottle of lemonade and some cookies down with me just on the off chance that you two might be hungry or thirsty."

Since no one would suffer by her refusal but herself, Cathie accepted the offer of refreshments, knowing the effects of the sun and the soaring temperature had reduced her mouth to a cottony state.

"I didn't think to bring any glasses," Rob remarked, uncapping the quart bottle of lemonade and passing it to Cathie. "So it will have to be a community jar."

The sweetly tart liquid was truly thirst-quenching as its tangy coldness soothed her parched throat. "Mmm, that's delicious," Cathie sighed, handing it back to Rob.

"Where were you going, dad?" Tad asked, after he had taken a giant swig of the lemonade.

"Out to cheek on the new calves," Rob replied. "You haven't seen them yet, Tad. Would you like to come along?"

His son didn't reply, but turned instead to Cathie. "Did you use to do that?"

"Clay and I could hardly wait until the calves were born." All the other times she had referred to Clay that day had been because of the many childhood episodes they had enjoyed together, but this time Cathie knew his name was a defense mechanism to prevent Rob from drawing her more tightly into his family circle. "My grandpa always let us name them."

"Then you would be interested in this year's spring crop." Rob's dark gaze held hers as she swallowed nervously. "Since Clay isn't here—" there was a mocking twitch at the corner of his mouth "—you and Tad can name them."

"What about the fish?" his son interrupted, much to Cathie's relief.

"We can pick them up on the way back." Rob smiled down at the boy. "The five you caught are a pretty good size, just right for tonight's supper. So there's no need to catch any more. They'll wait there until the next time you go fishing."

His father's explanation assured Tad and he said, "All right, we'll go."

Cathie pressed her lips tightly together as Rob's head turned toward her. She was being cornered into going with them and she didn't like it one bit.

"I'll have to pass," she said, smiling falsely into the velvet-brown eyes that were regarding her with amusement. "It's getting late and I really should go."

"It won't take more than a few minutes to check the calves." Rob's voice was soft and ultimately persuasive, but it only made Cathie harden her resolve. "And it will save you a walk all the way back to the house."

Her mouth opened to emit a polite refusal when she spied the stricken look on Tad's face. His shoulders were beginning to sag. Instead of their afternoon ending on a high point, her refusal was bringing back the boy's brittle shell.

"I'll go," Cathie gave in, tossing her head like an

unruly filly as she glanced angrily at the handsome man looking so smugly back at her.

"Let's go, then." Rob smiled at his son, sending Cathie a sideways glance. "Everybody in the truck."

"May I sit by the window?" Tad's exuberance had returned as he hopped around to the passenger's side of the cab.

Cathie inhaled deeply before agreeing, knowing that would place her in the middle beside Rob. But it was a typical request and she had no cause to deny Tad the window seat. If only she hadn't become so fond of the boy, she thought to herself, none of this would be happening.

The close quarters of the truck were stifling. It was impossible with the three of them in the seat for Cathie to avoid coming in contact with the driver. The brushing of his arm and thigh against hers transmitted a throbbing heat to her. Her pulse had quickened as Cathie held herself rigidly in the seat. The intriguing aroma of aftershave lotion mingled with his earthy, masculine scent to form an intoxicating combination. She stared straight ahead, trying to keep from bouncing into Rob as the truck made its slow, bumpy way over the uneven pasture ground.

The Boyer River snaked through the L-shaped pasture, its waters dividing it into two halves. A small herd of stock cows were occupying the far end of the L, and Cathie blinked in relief as the ivory-white hides of the Charlois-Angus herd came into view. Rob stopped the truck some distance away so as not to upset the quietly grazing cows and the trio climbed out of the cab. Cathie stayed near Tad while Rob walked closer, studying the cows and the calves. Several minutes later he walked back to them, his face a study in concentration.

"I have a calf missing," he announced. Now his eyes were diamond bright as they swept over the herd.

"Are you sure?" Cathie asked, knowing it was not uncommon for rustling to occur even in this day and age, although usually in numbers of more than one.

"Yes, I'm sure," Rob nodded. "The cow's probably hidden it somewhere."

"What are you going to do?" Tad inquired, his curiosity aroused by this interesting development.

"Find it, I hope, son," he replied, clasping the boy's shoulder warmly. "Want to give me a hand?"

"Sure," Tad nodded eagerly.

Rob turned to Cathie. "It will only take a few minutes. Will you help?"

"Yes," she answered. She was too much of a farm girl to refuse, especially for something as undemanding as finding a calf.

"We can be fairly sure the cow didn't hide the calf near the river because the cover isn't very good there. And she didn't hide it in this general area or she would have showed some interest when we drove up. That leaves the stretch of ground by the fence," Rob declared. "We'll fan out. If she starts following one of us then we'll find out where she's hidden the calf." He glanced down at Cathie. "I'll take Tad with me."

"Okay," she said, finding herself in complete agreement with his suggestion which, by its very thoroughness, let her know that he wasn't an inexperienced city-dweller.

The trio walked together for several yards until

they reached the designated stretch of pasture. Then they split up with Tad and Rob veering to the left while Cathie changed her angle slightly toward the right.

"The cow's noticed us," Rob called. Cathie glanced over her shoulder to see the beige-white cow alertly watching them. "She's concentrating on you, Cathie. The calf must be in your direction."

Maintaining the direction of her steps, she kept a close watch on the cow, anxious to find the exact location of the calf but cautious of incurring the wrath of the mother. Another glance over her shoulder saw the cow following her at a slow but interested pace. Cathie kept studying the terrain in front of her, trying to catch some sign of the calf without any success. A sound behind her drew another glance. The cow was trotting now, still several hundred feet away but coming closer. Quickening her pace, Cathie adjusted the direction in which she was walking so she would reach the fence in a shorter time.

But the change of direction was a mistake that she learned only after she had committed herself. The pace of the hoofbeats behind her increased and Cathie broke into a run, heading for a gap in the fence where the wires sagged. She kept telling herself not to panic, that there was no danger of the cow catching her as she ducked beneath the wires into the tall weeds on the other side of the fence.

Instantly the ground exploded beneath her. The air was rent by Cathie's shriek of surprise and the frantic bellowing of the calf she had just stepped on. As she dove headlong into the bull nettle, the calf made a hasty exit back into the pasture and his mother. The low, rolling sound of Rob's laughter intermixed with the more shrill sound of Tad's. Trying to avoid the prickles of the nettle bush, Cathie rolled into a cocklebur plant. When she finally regained her feet with the prickly burrs encased in her blouse and hair and the sting of the itch weed on her bare skin, she was livid with rage at the laughing pair walking toward her.

Chapter Six

"Are you all right?" Rob asked, trying to hide the chuckle in his voice with concern, but the laughter danced out of his eyes.

"A cow chases me through a fence and I land on the calf, fall into some itch weed and then a cocklebur patch and you ask if I'm all right!" Cathie snapped angrily.

"You were so funny," Tad giggled behind his hand.

She glanced from one to the other before looking down at her grass and dirt-stained pants and blouse. Her sense of humor was too strong now that the shock of the situation was over.

"It must have looked pretty ridiculous," she conceded with a slight smile.

"I don't know who was more surprised, you or the calf." Rob grinned as Cathie broke into laughter. Tad immediately joined her, no longer holding back the giggles that were shaking his slender body.

As she imagined the comedy episode viewed from their eyes, tears of laughter blurred her vision as she tried to scramble back through the fence. Without the threat of the cow breathing down her neck, she got hung up on the barbs and Rob had to help her.

"Here, let me pick some of those burrs off you," Rob offered once she stood safely on the other side.

The laughter had at last subsided, leaving her short of breath. "I must look a sight." Cathie put a hand to her disheveled hair and encountered a prickly burr.

"I think you look beautiful," Rob said huskily from his position near her right shoulder.

She turned her brilliant jewel-green eyes up to his face, meeting the enigmatic expression in the fire of his dark eyes. No one had ever looked at her like that before probing, somehow sensuous. Her heart hammered against her rib cage as she watched the hypnotic darkening of the brown eyes. This was just a reaction from the cow chasing her, Cathie told herself, although she didn't really believe a word of it. An ever-reddening flush filled her cheeks as she turned abruptly away from him.

"You sure found that calf in a hurry," Tad commented, his previously reserved face transformed by a grin that spread from ear to ear.

"I sure did," Cathie agreed, discovering it was hard to squeeze the words out through the lump in her throat.

"I think we could use some more of that lemonade, Tad. Why don't you run back to the truck and get it?" Before Cathie could suggest that they all go back, Rob directed his next order to her. "Stand still. I almost have all the cockleburs off your blouse.''

Tad was speeding away and she was left alone with Rob. "Have you got them yet?" she asked, wishing he wouldn't stand so close to her. His nearness seemed to be having the oddest effect on her breathing.

"There are a few in your hair. I'd better get them out before they snarl these spun-gold locks of yours.'' There was a teasing quality to his voice that added to the small tremors running through her body. His touch was electric as he carefully worked the spiny burrs free from her hair. She could feel the caressing quality of his breath against her neck, a decidedly pleasing sensation that Cathie closed her eyes tightly against. "You have very beautiful hair, Cat," Rob murmured from somewhere near her ear. "Long hair has always seemed so totally feminine to me.''

Some magic spell had wrapped its charms around her so she couldn't even take offense at the diminutive "Cat." As she felt herself about to capitulate completely to him, Cathie took a firm hold on herself. She was behaving like Andy would.

"Have you got them all out yet?" she asked in a voice that wasn't as shaky as she felt.

There was a hesitation before he answered. "Yes, that's the last, unfortunately."

"Here comes Tad with the lemonade." From her side vision, she had seen the boy approaching. Cathie willingly used him as an excuse to step away from Rob, nervously brushing the hair away from her face. "I can definitely use a cold drink after this.''

After each had taken a drink from the jar, the

trio started back to the pickup, with Cathie walking with Tad a step or two ahead of Rob. She was more grateful than she could say when Tad offered her his seat by the window and he took her place in the middle. She was much more at ease with the breeze from the opened window playing over her face as opposed to the burning touch of Rob Douglas. He stopped at their fishing hole and tossed the poles and bait in the rear of the truck while Tad took possession of their catch.

Duchess had long ago returned to the yard and barked a welcome at their arrival. Cathie was all set to climb in her car and leave, but Rob had noticed her idle scratching of her bare arms and insisted that she come into the house and wash in a solution of baking soda and water to take some of the sting away from the nettles.

"There's no need. I'll take care of it when I get home," she protested, sidling toward her car door.

His hand reached out and imprisoned her upper arm. "I insist," he said with a half-smile.

Her muscles stiffened and his grip tightened in response. It was a test of wills that Cathie would have fought to the finish if Tad hadn't been looking on. The fire of battle was in her eyes for Rob to see as she agreed.

Mrs. Carver was standing at the head of the steps as they entered the house. "Telephone for you," she told Rob. "It's that man from the lumberyard about that material you ordered."

"Cathie fell in some nettles. I brought her in so she could wash off with some baking soda," Rob explained as he excused himself to answer the phone.

"Those nettles can really make you itch." The

housekeeper clucked her tongue in sympathy, although Cathie had only noticed a mild reaction, probably because her mind had been so occupied with Rob Douglas and escaping his attention. "You wait here on the sun porch."

It was something of a relief to find the sun porch hadn't changed very much. The furniture was different, with a plumply cushioned, blue-flowered chaise lounge near the windows and an assortment of similarly cushioned wicker furniture painted white. But the room ostensibly maintained the same airy atmosphere as when her grandparents had lived in the house. There was even a cribbage board on one of the small tables.

The door leading into the living room was closed, so she had no way of knowing what changes had been made there, if any. Naturally the kitchen remained the same. Of course it had already been modernized several years ago, which only left the repainting of walls or new curtains.

Mrs. Carver was back in a matter of minutes, carrying a washbowl, cloth and towel. The solution eased the mild, stinging itch as Rob said it would. By the time Cathie had dried her arms with the towel, Rob still hadn't returned, so she asked Mrs. Carver to pass on her good-byes and scurried out of the house.

Tad was in the yard playing with Duchess, tossing sticks that she was obligingly returning. "Are you leaving?" Taking the stick from the shepherd and holding it in his hand, Tad studied her sadly.

"It's time I went home." Cathie nodded, adding with a smile, "but I'll come back another time."

"Would you like to stay for supper and have some of the fish we caught? I'm sure Mrs. Carver

wouldn't mind." There was so much adult politeness in his invitation that Cathie almost wished she
could stay to keep bringing out the little boy in
him.

"No, not this time." She shook her head firmly.
"Come on, Duchess," she called to the dog. "It's
time for us to leave."

The shepherd trotted obediently to her side, but
as they walked toward the car, Duchess lagged farther and farther behind. When Cathie opened the
back door for the dog to climb in, Duchess stopped
completely, her tail tucked between her legs and
her pointed nose almost touching the ground.

"I don't think she wants to leave," Tad spoke.

At the sound of the boy's voice, Duchess slunk
toward him, casting furtive glances behind her
when Cathie ordered her back. The back screen
door slammed. Cathie, who had been walking
toward the dog hiding behind Tad's legs, glanced
up to see Rob striding toward them. Duchess also
saw the two adults converging on her and decided
that the small boy didn't offer much protection.
With a spurt of rebellion, the dog ignored the
commands from Cathie and raced for the comparative safety of the little-used front porch and
squeezed through a hole in the foundation.

"She won't come out from there until dark."
Cathie sighed in exasperation.

"I guess she still considers this her home." Rob
glanced down at her troubled expression, his
innate awareness sensing her nervous desire to
leave quickly.

"I'm afraid so."

"Does that mean we can keep her?" Tad piped
up from behind them.

"Duchess belongs to Cathie, Tad," Rob corrected his son gently.

In her heart, Cathie disagreed, knowing that the dog belonged to the Homeplace, the farm. "Perhaps in the morning you'll be able to catch her," she said aloud.

"I'll bring her to you when I do," Rob assured her.

"Thank you. I'm sorry to put you to this trouble, but I never dreamed this would happen when I brought Duchess out here. She's never been disobedient."

"It's no trouble." Cathie wasn't capable of meeting his gaze. Her nerves were too raw from their encounter in the pasture. The noncommittal look in his eyes told her he knew it as he held her car door open. "It will be a pleasure," he added.

Any softening in her attitude because she felt she was inconveniencing him was immediately erased by the infuriating realization that he could somehow read her mind. An eyebrow arched haughtily above a jade-green eye.

"You seem to forget, Mr. Douglas, that I'm engaged," Cathie reminded him none too gently, while making sure the ring on her left hand reflected the rays of the afternoon sun.

"No, I haven't forgotten, Miss Carlsen." Rob's mouth moved in a semblance of a smile as he shut the door and stepped back. "Have you?"

His reflection remained in her rearview mirror until Cathie made the turn out of the driveway onto the country road. He was absolutely insufferable, she told herself, so sure of his attraction that he thought every woman would fall at his feet.

His casual flirting with her when he knew she was engaged added more fuel for her fiery temper.

There was only time for a hasty shower before Andy and Connie arrived at the house from work. The kitchen was stifling hot and Cathie knew it would be unbearable if she cooked anything on the stove. There was a fresh head of lettuce in the refrigerator, some leftover ham and chicken, a small bowl of hard-boiled eggs and two tomatoes. Add to that some cubes of cheddar cheese and she would have an adequate salad for their meal.

Later, after her roommates had returned home and the meal had been eaten, it was Connie who first commented on Duchess's absence.

"I see you've finally got rid of that mongrel," she observed, stepping into the hallway where the dog usually laid while Andy began the task of clearing away the dishes. "I was constantly finding dog hairs on my clothes, not to mention the odor that clung to everything."

"I haven't got rid of Duchess," Cathie corrected her sharply.

"You should," Connie sniffed, walking briskly from the room.

"Where is she?" Andy asked. "Is she sick?"

"No, nothing like that." Cathie hesitated, finding herself unwilling even to confide to Andy exactly where Duchess was. But lies had always caught up with her in the past. "I went out to the Homeplace today to see Tad. I took Duchess along and she hid from me when it was time to come home."

"Oh, no! So what are you going to do? You can't leave her out there."

"Tad's father is going to bring her back tomorrow."

"The poor dear probably thought she was going home for good," Andy commented, turning on the taps and filling the sink with soapy water. "What time is Mr. Douglas coming?" There was a happy twinkle in her dark eyes. "Now that he's evidently dropped Connie I might chase him myself!"

"I imagine he'll bring her back in the morning," Cathie answered, anxious to get off the subject of Rob Douglas.

"Naturally he'll come when I'm at work," Andy moaned.

Rob Douglas didn't bring Duchess back in the morning or the afternoon. Cathie had decided that they hadn't been able to catch the dog and was toying with the idea of calling to find out when Clay arrived to take her out to the theater.

"Are you ready to go?" he queried, dropping her an affectionate peck on one cheek.

"In a minute." She smiled, walking toward the telephone. "I was just going to call out to the farm to see if they've caught Duchess yet."

"The farm? Do you mean the Homeplace?" His forehead became creased with a curious frown. "What is Duchess doing out there?"

"I took her out there yesterday for a run when I called to see Tad," she answered calmly as she picked up the receiver.

Cathie knew Clay was averse to her decision to visit the boy now that school was out. Feeling that Rob had told her of his past marriage in confidence, she hadn't mentioned the true circumstances to Clay. He felt it was no longer her concern how the boy adjusted since he wouldn't be in her class in the autumn.

"He's here!' Andy squeaked, bounding into the living room via the kitchen hall. "He just drove up this minute!"

"Who?" Clay asked, but Cathie already knew.

"Rob Douglas," Andy informed Clay.

Cathie had already replaced the receiver and had turned toward the door. "Does he have Duchess with him?" she asked, wiping the nervous sweat that had suddenly collected in the palms of her hands on the sides of her pink linen dress.

"Yes, I caught a glimpse of her in the back seat of his car," Andy told her, tagging along behind Clay and Cathie.

Rob was just getting out of his car when the three walked out the front door. A hand raised in greeting to them before coaxing the reluctant shepherd out of the car.

"Duchess doesn't seem very happy to be back," Clay commented when Cathie took the leash from Rob and nearly pulled the dog toward her.

"If you think she's unhappy, you should see Tad." Rob smiled, taking the hand that Clay offered in greeting. "He was practically heartbroken when I put the dog in the car."

If that was supposed to make Cathie feel guilty, it succeeded, combined with the very slight wag of the dog's tail when she petted the shepherd. "I appreciate you bringing her back," she said, unable to put any warmth in her voice.

"I'm sorry I didn't bring her back earlier," said Rob, without a trace of regret in his voice, "but she and Tad were having such a good time that I didn't see any hurry, especially when I had work to do in the fields.''

"Thank you for bringing her anyway," Cathie repeated, feeling the hint was broad enough for anyone to see that she was anxious for Rob to be gone.

"Not at all," he replied blandly, his brown eyes mocking the coolness of her expression. His gaze flicked to the glistening curls of her shoulder-length hair. "I'm glad to see that your hair didn't suffer from the cockleburs."

"Cockleburs? What's this about the cockleburs?" Clay picked up the subject immediately, despite the glaring look from Cathie.

"Didn't she tell you?" Rob looked innocently at Clay. "Cathie took a header into some itch weed and cockleburs when she was out at the farm yesterday. It took a while for me to get the burrs out of her hair and clothes."

If looks could kill, Cathie would have sent Rob six feet under. She bit her lower lip to keep the scathing retort from slipping out, aware that under the tan, her cheeks were taking on a rosy hue.

"No, she didn't mention it to me." Without looking, Cathie could feel the inquisitive eyes of her fiancé turn on her.

"It was hardly important." She shrugged.

"Oh, it could have been." A mocking smile curled one corner of Rob's mouth. "Especially if that beautiful honey-colored hair of yours had had to be cut to free it from the burrs." He glanced from one to the other. "You two are obviously going out somewhere, so I won't keep you any longer. I just wanted to return your dog."

After Rob had driven away, Cathie wasted no

time in chaining the unhappy shepherd to her kennel. Andy winked at her broadly as Cathie walked past her to Clay.

"What was all that about?" Clay inquired when they were both in his car and en route to the theater.

"What?" Cathie asked, deliberately playing ignorant.

"That episode yesterday with Douglas."

"Just what he said. I tumbled into some weeds and got a few cockleburs in my clothes and hair."

Clay turned his attention away from the road ahead of them to survey her with a particularly amused look. "It didn't sound quite as simple as that the way he told it."

"You can't go by what he said," she declared sharply.

"Why not?"

"Don't be silly, Clay. It's not worth arguing about," she insisted.

"Who's arguing?" Clay asked. After one more thoughtful glance, the subject was dropped . . . to Cathie's relief.

Chapter Seven

A satisfied gleam lit her eyes as Cathie fluffed the short curls on top of her head. She hadn't realized how hot and heavy her long hair had been in the summer's heat. The small rectangular mirror in the choir's changing room confirmed the compliments she had received from her friends that the new, shorter style was attractive. What she couldn't see for herself was that the long hair had emphasized her youth while the perfectly shaped gamine style of gently waving curls made her appear more womanly and alluring.

Clay, who often got upset with her but never angry, had been on the verge of it the night before when he had picked her up for their regular Saturday date. Cathie had always known he was old-fashioned and had more than once stated his preference for long hair, but she never dreamed he would attempt to dictate how she wore her own hair. It had been a totally unpleasant evening.

In all honesty, Cathie knew she hadn't been indulging in a mere whim when she had gotten her haircut. The original decision had come from a defiant desire to show Rob Douglas that his compliments meant nothing to her. If he liked her hair long, then she disliked it. Clay might have put the wrong conjecture on such reasoning, so she hadn't confided in him.

It had been a disappointment in church this morning to discover that Rob Douglas wasn't in his usual pew. She would have enjoyed seeing the expression on his face when he saw her cropped-off hair. That moment of satisfaction would have to come another time, Cathie decided, smoothing her simply styled, jade-green dress.

She was one of the last to leave the choir room. Clay wouldn't be waiting for her this Sunday. He was visiting his parents, and after last night's near argument Cathie had decided not to go with him. She didn't know quite what she would do since she couldn't remember the last time she had spent a Sunday without Clay.

As she reached the pavement, she was toying with the idea of driving to Black Hawk Lake for an afternoon swim when she heard someone call her name. Cathie glanced back toward the church and saw Rob Douglas walking toward her. His lithe, athletic stride automatically called attention to him and she could feel the questioning eyes of the remaining members of the congregation turn toward her. Cathie could almost read their thoughts as she felt herself reddening that Rob Douglas had singled her out in front of everyone. They had probably all noticed Clay's absence.

To make matters worse, Rob took her by the

elbow and led her aside so they wouldn't be blocking the pavement, then retained the light grip on her arm. His eyes flicked over her hair and then alighted on her face.

"That's quite an improvement," he commented dryly.

"I thought you liked long hair," Cathie declared without thinking.

That half-smile curved his mouth as he looked down at her with lazy amusement. "I don't like long hair just for the sake of long hair. This style suits your personality a bit more. It's a little cheeky and sophisticated, very much like a feline."

This wasn't turning out the way she intended it at all. "What did you want to speak to me about?" she demanded, wanting a quick end to the conversation.

"I found a small trunk tucked away in the corner of the attic that must be your grandparents'. It's filled with old clothing and such, from what I could tell. Since it's rather heavy, I thought if you could come out to my place this afternoon I could help you load it into your car and take it home."

Cathie had expected him to bring up something to do with Tad. She was at a loss for words when she discovered that he was only attempting to return something that quite evidently belonged to her family now.

"Yes, I can come out this afternoon," she replied, blinking up at him in confusion.

"Around three?" Rob asked with the complacency of a man who knows the answer is yes.

"I'll be there." Cathie nodded.

His hand left her elbow as he stepped away, raising his voice almost deliberately for the benefit of the onlookers to say, "I'll see you this afternoon, then."

Cathie's teeth ground tightly together as she saw the speculating looks appear in the men's eyes while the women regarded her with disapproval. How many times had she joked that in a small town something was no sooner done than said, but she had never thought she would be the object of the censure. They surely couldn't believe that she was arranging an assignation with Rob Douglas on the church lawn? Well, the damage was done, Cathie thought to herself, and idle talk never hurt anyone. If only that nagging feeling would leave that Rob Douglas had known all along that this was going to happen.

The short walk from the church to her house was completed in record time as anger lent impetus to her pace. Once there, Cathie debated whether to change into a pair of casual slacks and blouse before deciding that if she still wore the green dress and her high-heeled sandals she would be less likely to be talked into staying by Tad or Rob.

Her original plans for the day called for eating her midday meal out and Cathie stuck to it, choosing a leisurely drive over the back roads of the farmland to pass the time before her appointment with Rob Douglas at the Homeplace. When her grandparents were alive they had spent many a pleasant hour doing the same thing. Her grandfather, even though no longer able to farm himself, was always interested in the condition of his neighbor's crops. Cathie could almost hear his comments as she drove past the neat, symmetrical fields of corn and wheat.

"Arthur has a good-looking field of soybeans

there," or "That corn crop of MacDuff's is a disgrace. Just look at the weeds in the field!" Corn had been Grandfather Carlsen's favorite subject. He had always been extremely proud that Iowa was known as the Tall Corn State. Cathie smiled as she remembered how he used to tease her slightly plump grandmother that she had been corn bred and corn fed, just like the succulent Iowa beef.

A hen pheasant dashed across the road in front of her, forcing Cathie to slow down. Wavelike rows of young corn bordered each side of the road, freshly disced so that the rich, black soil contrasted sharply with the green of its stalk and leaves and the burgeoning tassels on top. When she had been a child, the measuring stick for a good corn crop— barring bad weather—had been if it was knee-high by the Fourth of July. With all the agricultural improvements that had been made, it was usually hip-high by that time.

As a meadowlark exposed his yellow throat to the sun from his perch on a fencepost and trilled his song to the country, Cathie arrived at another intersection in the graveled road. She made the turn, experiencing the desire of an old carriage horse to hurry the last mile home. There, on the small hilltop on the other side of the Boyer River, sat the farm buildings that until Rob Douglas came had always constituted the Homeplace.

The memories had closed around her and it was hard to bring herself back to the reality of a new owner without bringing resentment back, too. Ten minutes early, her gold watch told her as she made the turn off the county road on to the short lane. But it wasn't only resentment that was making her uneasy about this visit with Rob Douglas. There was something else that made her apprehensive to be around him that had nothing to do with his owning her grandparents' farm.

A strange car was parked in the driveway in front of the yard. As she drew closer, Cathie recognized the man behind the wheel as Charlie Smith's father. If it hadn't been that he had already seen her and was waving, she would have turned and driven right back out. Stop feeling so guilty for coming out here, she chided herself, parking the car a few feet away from his.

"Good afternoon, Mr. Smith," she called cheerfully as she stepped out of her car. The screen door banged at the house and Cathie glanced around to see Charlie and Tad walking down the path followed by Rob.

"How are you, Miss Carlsen?" Charlie's father replied, tilting his straw hat back to reveal the white band around his forehead in contrast to his sunburned face. "Chuck and I were planning on doing a little fishing down at the river. We just stopped up here to make sure it was all right with Mr. Douglas."

"Hi, Miss Carlsen," Charlie greeted her before turning to his father to babble excitedly. "Tad knows a real good place to fish so I invited him along. He says we'll catch lots and lots."

"Come along, then, Tad," the man said, waving airily. "Grab your pole and climb in."

Tad glanced anxiously from Cathie to his father, his expression revealing that he was unsure whether to leave now that Cathie had arrived.

"Run along, Tad," Rob prompted gently. "Cathie only came out this time to pick up a trunk that was left behind in the moving."

After a quick "hello" in her direction, Tad dashed off for the garage and his bamboo pole. Cathie murmured a quiet greeting to Rob, letting her gaze slide away from the look of lazy amusement in his dark eyes. She stood silently by as Rob introduced himself to Ray Smith and listened to their brief exchanges about the weather and the crops until Tad came sprinting back with his pole in his hand.

Charlie urged him into the back seat of the car and Cathie found it hard to believe that Charlie had been the one to lead the rest of the class into chanting "tadpole." Although there was still an unmistakable air of reserve around Tad as he sat next to Charlie, there was still the triumph of being able to show another boy where to catch fish which had an equalizing effect. Despite all Charlie's mischievousness, even to starting that horrible chant, Cathie knew there wasn't a malicious bone in his body. Everyone was his friend.

"Tad has been fishing every day since you were last here," Rob stated after the Smith car had left the driveway.

"Being with Charlie will do him good," Cathie commented. "That's one boy who's all boy. Tad will probably learn a lot that you'll regret."

"Snakes in the pocket and that sort of thing," Rob chuckled. The throaty sound was a pleasing accompaniment to the gentle rustle of the breeze in the cottonwoods. "I eagerly await that day."

Cathie didn't want to get into any discussion about his son. She was already too involved in their affairs, so she had to swallow back that shared feeling of victory that she and Rob had coaxed Tad out of his shell.

"I appreciate you letting me know about the trunk," she said, deftly changing the subject. "I can't imagine how mother and Aunt Dana missed it."

That knowing look came across his face and the small crescent scar near the one eye almost made it look as if he was winking at her inability to behave normally with him. But Rob smoothly slipped into the new conversation.

"The attic is very dimly lit and the trunk was in the far corner, so it's not inconceivable that they overlooked it. It's in the house," he said, stepping to the side so Cathie could precede him.

Her heart was skipping beats as she walked along the path to the house with Rob right behind her. His arm brushed hers as he opened the back door for her and followed her inside. Her sandals made a tapping sound on the linoleum steps up to the sun porch with the more solid sound of Rob's shoes right behind her. She hesitated at the top, glancing around for some sign of the trunk and, more importantly, the reassuring presence of a third person, namely Mrs. Carver.

"I left the trunk upstairs," said Rob, walking ahead of her to open the almost full-length door leading into the living room. "I thought you might want to go through it. As I said, there seemed to be mostly old clothes on top and I have a box of Tad's clothes I was going to give to the Salvation Army. You would be welcome to include whatever you didn't want to keep in with it." A crooked smile was tossed over his shoulder. "That way the trunk wouldn't be quite so heavy to carry down the stairs."

"Where's Mrs. Carver?" she asked.

"Visiting her daughter," Rob replied.

Cathie just wanted to take the trunk and run, then chided herself for being so cowardly. So she didn't trust Rob? Apart from the way he so arrogantly mocked her sometimes, there was no reason to feel that way. And she was quite able to take care of herself. Besides, there was that glint of amusement in his eyes that said he knew very well that she didn't want to spend an extra minute in his company. Her blond head tilted back defiantly as she gazed coolly at the brown head leading the way. She would show him that she was totally immune to his supposedly irresistible charms.

Cathie paused in the living room, ignoring Rob, who had reached the door leading to the stairwell. Her green eyes glanced around the room, taking in the large hooked rug that covered the floor and the comfortable, overstuffed furniture in warm yellows and browns with a sprinkling of persimmon for color. It filled the room with old-fashioned ease and down-home warmth. She spitefully wished that the room would have been redone in those ugly modernistic furnishings that she disliked instead of this style that fitted so well into the simple farmhouse.

"Well?" Rob said softly from the stair door. "Do you find any drastic changes?"

"It's very nice," she said grudgingly. Her gaze trailed around the room again, stopping at the partially opened double doors that led into the parlor. The slight opening revealed unfinished wood shelving on a wall that had always been bare. "Are you remodeling the parlor?" Without waiting for an invitation, Cathie walked to the walnut-stained doors and pushed them open.

The parlor, that lovely old-fashioned room that had always sprung to life at Christmas time when a huge evergreen tickled the ceiling and brightly wrapped presents tumbled all over the floor, was no longer. Rows of shelves filled the entire north wall of the room, framing the large window in the center. The mint-green paint of the rest of the walls had been covered by rich walnut paneling. The floor space in between was a jumble of boxes and crates. Two overstuffed chairs were draped with white sheets that still had fragments of sawdust clinging to the cotton cloth.

A computer was set up in one corner, and a state-of-the-art printer in another, and beside it was a desk cluttered with papers and books. Somehow, in the middle of the mess, was a long cylindrical roll of carpeting waiting patiently for the floor to be cleared so it could take its place. A vibrant dark gold color peeped from the ends as tufts of thick pile escaped the roll.

"I suppose it's somewhat of an understatement to say that the room is a mess right now," Rob commented from his place behind her left shoulder. "Mrs. Carver swears it will be autumn before I ever get it done."

"Are you making this your . . ." Cathie glanced around the partially redecorated room, wanting to feel resentment for the destruction of the parlor and all its old memories, but her mind's eye was visualizing the room as it would appear in its completed state. She knew it would be a room she would like. "Are you making this your office?" she finished.

"Office, den, study, whatever."

She could feel his shrug of indifference at placing

a label on the room. A package of books rested on top of a large box, partially opened with two books sticking out. Their vividly colored jackets attracted her and Cathie stepped over to pick one up. The name Robert Douglas leaped at her where the author's name was written. Her startled expression turned to Rob.

"Are you a writer?" she gasped. The question itself was almost an insult since she was holding one of his books in her hands.

"Is that an accusation or a question?" Laughter danced from his eyes at her chagrin.

The discovery had caught her off guard as Cathie fumbled around for the words to cover her confusion. "I didn't mean it to sound like that. I just didn't know . . . No one has ever mentioned that you wrote books."

"Now my secret is out. Or at least, you hold it in your hands."

"Is it a secret?" Her jade-green eyes rushed to his face, trying to read the impenetrable expression that mocked her so openly.

"Since I don't use a pseudonym when I write, I don't see how it could be," he replied calmly, turning his attention from her to survey the room.

"Then why doesn't anyone know?" she asked, puzzled by this suggestion of modesty that didn't fit in at all with her conception of him.

"It didn't seem necessary to broadcast it to the world. I write mystery thrillers—that's my latest." Rob turned back to her, his gaze racing over her face with penetrating thoroughness. "Some of them even sell," he said wryly, "but I don't have false beliefs in my own importance."

Cathie glanced down at the book and opened

the cover. The inside leaf contained a list of other books by Robert Douglas, and glowing reviews from national newspapers. "Why are you here? Working in the fields and remodeling rooms when you could be writing?"

"I told you the truth when I said that I had moved here to Iowa for Tad's benefit. I know you'll find it hard to believe, but I was brought up on a farm and I remember what a wonderful time I had roaming the countryside, helping with the planting and harvesting." The surprised expression on Cathie's face drew an open laugh from Rob. "What's the matter, don't I look like your typical farm product because I don't have a band of white on my forehead where my hat sits?"

"We were told you were from Long Island, New York. How could any of us know that you might have been brought up on a farm?" she defended herself.

"There were plenty of working farms on Long Island when I was growing up."

"I had no idea," she replied, avoiding his eyes. "Are you still going to write?"

"Of course," he nodded. "I have the evenings in the summer and the long winters here will give me quite a few free hours. Writing and farming will blend well together, with just about the same amount of satisfaction." Rob inclined his head toward her in mock deference. "Now, if I've satisfied your catlike curiosity, would you like to see the trunk?"

"I wasn't trying to pry in your private life," Cathie retorted, drawing herself up to her full height which still left her several inches shorter than Rob.

"Of course not, you were just curious," he

agreed smoothly, leading her again into the living room and to the stairwell door.

Cathie held tightly to the smooth banister railing of the stairs, her nervousness increasing with each step. All her preconceived ideas of Rob were being eliminated one by one. She had preferred thinking of him as an egotistical Easterner, far removed from rural community life. It made him easier to dislike.

"Tad has the room at the head of the stairs and Mrs. Carver sleeps in the bedroom over the kitchen," Rob spoke, climbing the steps ahead of Cathie. "The middle bedroom is so large I don't know what we'll ever use it for, since I'm using the large bedroom off the study downstairs."

"My grandparents intended to have a large family when they built the house, but there ended up being only three," Cathie felt the need to explain the reason for the spacious upstairs. "There were always plenty of relatives to keep it filled, though."

The middle room was virtually empty with only a few boxes sitting around and the trunk that had brought Cathie here. It was difficult to step into the room and not expect to see the large four-poster bed on one side of the room and the single feather bed where she had slept as a child or the picture on the wall of a shepherd boy guarding his flock by moonlight. Before the memories crowded too close around her, Cathie walked quickly toward the trunk, opening the lid to lift out the men's clothing packed on top. The gentle scent of lavender clung to the tweeds and wools.

"Here's the box I was putting Tad's old clothes in," said Rob, carrying a cardboard box over to the trunk where Cathie was kneeling.

"Thank you," she murmured absently, placing the clothes in the box knowing they would be of no use to her.

Below the men's clothing was a horsehair blanket. With a gasp of happy surprise, Cathie shook it open, running her hand over the silken fineness of the dark brown and white spotted hide.

"I remember this!" She turned excitedly to Rob. "It's the hide from Uncle Andrew's horse, Pal. When the horse died, he sent the hide off to a tanner in Minnesota to make a blanket out of it. In the old days, they used them as buggy blankets. When I was a little girl, Grandma used to let me put it on my bed."

"Then I'm glad I found the trunk." Rob watched lazily as she fingered the green velvet material on the reverse side of the blanket.

Cathie lovingly folded the blanket and set it to the side, turning to the layers of tissue in the trunk. As she carefully lifted them away, her hands touched satiny material.

"It's grandmother's wedding dress," she breathed, very gently pushing away the tissue and holding the ivory and lace dress up. Her grandmother had been several inches shorter than Cathie and was quite small as a young girl, judging by the tiny waist of the dress. "I wish I were that small," she grinned. "I would wear it for my own wedding."

"Have you set the date, then?" Rob asked, his gaze flickering from the dress to her.

"No, not yet." Cathie shook her head, arranging the dress back in the bottom of the trunk surrounded by the protecting layers of tissue. There was something in the way that he asked the question that put her on the defensive.

"You and Clay grew up together. Did you know all along you were in love with him, or did you just discover it all of a sudden?" His head was tilted inquiringly to one side as he studied her.

"I knew when I was in high school, but Clay discovered it when I followed him into college." Her reply sprang easily to her lips. It was her standard answer to similar questions that friends and relatives had asked over the years.

"How long have you been engaged?"

Cathie touched the cluster of small diamonds that adorned the ring on her finger. "Clay gave me my ring after he passed his bar exam a year ago."

"And you aren't married yet." There was a note of disbelief in his voice. "What are you waiting for?"

"We're trying to find a house we like. As soon as we do, we'll get married."

"You're a patient woman, Cathie." Humor etched itself in the tanned lines around his eyes and mouth.

"Why?" A trace of temper added a sharpness to her words. "Because we're being practical? Because we didn't dash to the altar the minute we decided we were in love? Just because we had the good sense to wait until Clay could get himself established in a good law practice and we could find a nice home to live in isn't a reason to doubt the way we feel toward each other."

"Haven't you ever wanted to just give in to impulse?" The sharpness of his gaze refused to allow her to look away. "Let your heart take over?"

It took Cathie a full second to understand the point of his question. Her back stiffened. "You're confusing lust with love. They aren't the same thing at all.''

"I wouldn't begin to argue that they are." The daggers she flashed at him couldn't find any opening in his smooth and mocking countenance. "But desire is a part of love, isn't it? And passion?"

"Well, our love is based on friendship and companionship. Desire . . . well, that would be quite far down on our list of reasons to get married," Cathie declared icily.

"Did you ever date anyone other than Clay?"

"Of course," she said huffily, closing the trunk and securing the latches. "I went out with several other men before I was engaged."

"Did you kiss them?"

"Yes, I kissed them," she answered in a tight voice of barely repressed anger. "This conversation is ridiculous. None of this is any of your business."

"I never said it was." Rob shrugged. "I was just curious how an attractive woman like you could remain so unmoved by one of the pleasanter and more satisfying aspects of being in love. It crossed my mind that maybe you'd never been properly made love to."

"Kissing is a little overrated," she snapped, now knowing how prudishly sure of herself she sounded. "It's pleasant and enjoyable, but there's certainly no heart-pounding or earthshaking revelations, as those romance books lead you to believe."

There was a fluttering like butterfly wings in her stomach as Rob appeared suddenly closer to her, although he hadn't moved. A glitter of mischief lit up the depths of his velvet eyes as his gaze settled on her mouth. Cathie moistened her lips nervously, then swallowed, conscious of the triphammer beat of her heart.

"There's some truth to that," he agreed blandly. "Would you object to testing your theory?"

"How?" Cathie demanded, eyeing him with marked distrust.

"By kissing me."

His calm statement jolted her. "I will not!" She retorted indignantly. "How could you even suggest such a thing?"

She moved to step past him, but the mockery in his expression halted her. "Probably because I knew you wouldn't do it," said Rob, lowering his voice to a jeering taunt. "You haven't got the nerve to really kiss me."

Angry words of biting denial formed on her lips until she intuitively realized that that was exactly what Rob was expecting. She would show him! A falsely sweet smile settled on her pink lips. Then instead of stepping past him as she had intended to do, she stepped toward him. Cool green eyes stared up into the amused brown ones. Her hands rested lightly on his chest to balance as she raised herself on tiptoes to reach the sensuous line of his mouth.

Chapter Eight

Cathie's legs were trembling as she drew closer to the smooth, close-shaven face, the delicate lingering scent of lavender from the trunk mingling with the potently intoxicating aroma of masculine cologne that clung to Rob's tanned cheeks. An electric tingling vibrated through her at the joining of his lips against hers. His mouth was warm and mobile, persuading but with a firmness that demanded and received a response.

Cathie had a strange feeling of unreality, of being slowly sucked into a dangerous pool of quicksand without a single attempt to save herself. She was being pulled down, down . . . His strong arms circled her waist and drew her against the burning warmth of his muscular chest, arching her to the thrust of his hard body. Cathie found herself totally surrendering to this embrace that was half heaven and half hell. Her hands moved to the back of his neck, letting the hair curl over her fingers while she molded herself closer to his outline. Rob's kiss was consuming her, wholly and completely, melting the last vestiges of resentment and inhibitions, making her aware of the true differences of the sexes and what making love meant.

Then their lips parted slowly and Cathie was being gently set away, her feet seeming to be placed on solid ground, free of the treacherous depths of the quicksand embrace. Her blood was singing a wild song of ecstasy in her ears as she fought to bring her breathing to a regular rate. Her eyelids fluttered open, revealing shimmering pools of green reflecting the disturbance Rob had caused. Her gaze eagerly examined his face to see if he had been as moved as she, but there was only the slightest irregular beat in the vein running near his temple.

"Sometimes it can be like that between two people," Rob said calmly.

He had just turned her world upside down, made all her firmly held beliefs vanish with one fiery kiss, and he was acting as if it was the most natural statement to make. She had never felt this drowning sensation when Clay kissed her, only a tender, loving desire to give and receive. There was no overwhelming sensuality between them such as she had just experienced with Rob.

But with Clay there was that precious feeling of security, Cathie argued silently with herself. She wasn't drawn to the brink and then plummeted into some whirlpool of passionate longing. The first emotion would last forever. How long would the second last? she asked herself and shuddered inwardly at the frightening thought. She mustn't allow herself to fall in love with Rob Douglas, to be caught up in the spell he was trying to weave.

His dark eyes were still regarding her, waiting for her to comment, to admit that it hadn't been a casual kiss. A glittering light of anger flamed in her eyes as she studied the tall, arrogant man standing so calmly in front of her. Rob Douglas, the new owner of the Carlsen farm—the Homeplace that was so precious to her and had always been so much a part of her life. He was living here now where he had no right to be, regardless of any signatures on legal documents. His presence had already destroyed one long-held dream of hers to live on the farm and raise her family. She wasn't about to let him destroy her relationship with Clay. For nearly six years she had planned to marry Clay and she was not going to allow one kiss from this usurper to change her mind.

"Did you expect me to melt at your feet?" Cathie asked scornfully, tilting her head back so he could see the contempt written in her face. "I concede that you're quite skilled in evoking a response from a woman, but the effect doesn't last."

Her scathing words only brought a sparkle of indulgent amusement to his eyes. "I have half a mind to make you eat that pride of yours," Rob grinned without the slightest dent to his ego.

He moved toward her and Cathie took a quick step backward, tripping over the trunk and nearly falling. His quick reaction kept her upright although the touch of his hands on her back sent fresh goose bumps up her spine. Rob knew it, knew that part of her wanted to taste the wild honey of temptation again.

"Let me go!" she ordered, surprised, at how

convincing her voice sounded with his mouth so hypnotically close.

She expected him to disregard her demand and force her to submit to another embrace. She had to hide her surprise and regret when Rob did as she asked and let her go.

"You can sheathe your claws, Cat." He smiled. "Patience is one of a writer's most valuable virtues. I've learned that waiting only increases the pleasure."

The fuse to Cathie's temper took fire and raced away. "Then you'd better pray for a major catastrophe, Mr. Douglas," she exploded, "because I wouldn't look at you unless you were the last man on earth, and even then the sight of you would still make me sick!"

He laughed outright at that, like an adult at a child's spiteful words. "Is that the way you're reasoning away that funny feeling at the pit of your stomach? Oh, my little green-eyed Cat, you have a great deal to learn."

"You won't be teaching me," she said determinedly, trying to ignore the twisted knots in her stomach.

Rob sighed almost contentedly as he finally turned his diamond-bright gaze from her. "I know you're anxious to run away. Would you like me to carry the trunk down to the car for you?"

The trunk? Cathie touched her forehead, feeling the short blond curls tumbling about her head in disarray. That was why she had come here in the first place—for the trunk. That seemed an eternity ago.

"Yes, please," she said stiffly, watching with grudging admiration as he picked up the heavy old trunk with ease and carried it through the door toward the stairwell.

After the trunk had been safely stowed in the back of the car, Rob turned toward Cathie, her car keys still in his hand. She reached out to take them, but his fingers closed over them.

"I can't let you leave without offering you something cold to drink," he said. At the expression of refusal leaping into her face, Rob continued before she could voice it. "We could sit over there underneath that big walnut tree by the cornfield. If you don't feel like carrying on a civil conversation, we can sit and listen to the corn grow."

Cathie inhaled sharply at his last statement. She couldn't count the times she had heard her grandfather make the same comment. The walnut tree had been his choice, too, for those lazy summer evenings when even the crickets' and cicadas' songs were slow and somnolent. Often Cathie had sat with her grandfather and listened to those soft crackling sounds which he had assured her was the corn growing in the nearby field. And now this intruder was saying the same thing, not laughingly as Clay had always done, but sincerely like her grandfather.

"No," she breathed quickly, her eyes widening as her blond head made a negative movement. "No, I don't care for anything, I have to go."

"Tad will be sorry he missed you," said Rob. His gaze narrowed, not guessing how close his casual comment had come to piercing her shield of angry pride, but knowing for a moment she had been vulnerable to his suggestion.

"Yes, well," Cathie stumbled, "he knows there'll be other times. May I have my keys?"

Rob handed them over to her and she slid quickly behind the wheel of her car before some traitorous part of her would agree to stay. As she drove out the lane, Cathie made a silent promise to herself that she would begin breaking off her connection with Tad. It would have to be done slowly so he wouldn't feel she was deserting him, but if his afternoon fishing expedition with Charlie was successful it wouldn't be too difficult to accomplish. The sooner she avoided all contact with the Douglas family the better off she would be.

Cathie was determined that she never wanted to be trapped in a situation like today where she was tricked into kissing Rob Douglas. Never again did she want to lose control of her emotions and be swept away on a rising tide of pointless desires. Her mind reached the decision with cool and calm calculations, which made the tears on her cheeks come as a surprise when their salty taste reached her lips.

There was the whoosh of another rocket leaping into the midnight-blue sky, then a sudden explosion of color drawing sighing "ahs" from the crowd gathered around the open athletic field. Tiers of stars in layers of red, green and blue gently fell toward the earth as another rocket made its ascent. Cascading spirals of glittering gold whistled their way down to make room for more brilliant shooting stars. Elsewhere around the fields was the rat-a-tat of a string of firecrackers being set off to accompany the more spectacular fireworks display.

The Fourth of July was marked all over the country by traditional celebrations such as the one

Cathie was now watching, where the shattering, vibrating boom of the cannon rockets was softened by scattering showers of make-believe stars. And Cathie still felt the same mixture of awe and excitement as she had when she was a child. The colorful illumination of the sky revealed the memories of past happiness in her eyes when her gaze was drawn to a pair of young children waving the magic wands called sparklers. They were dancing on the blanket their parents, like Cathie and Clay, had spread on the ground.

Another group of children was racing around the parked cars. Cathie recognized Charlie Smith as the leader and was surprised to see Tad among the pack. She glanced furtively around for his father to find him quietly studying her several yards away. Rob Douglas was leaning against a car parked beside Clay's with several other people, one of whom was Connie. His head dipped in a silent greeting to her and Cathie spun around to concentrate on the fireworks display, feeling a burning heat rush over her cheeks.

She had been so successful at avoiding any contact with Rob the past two weeks that she had truly believed her luck would last. She might have known he would bring Tad here tonight to see the fireworks, but Cathie had been confident that the secluded corner of the field where she and Clay were would be off the beaten track.

"Hello." Rob's voice came from Clay's side of the blanket. "Do you mind if we put our blanket next to yours, Clay?"

"Help yourself," Clay smiled. "The ground is free."

"Hi, Clay. Hi, Cathie," Andy declared pertly,

forcing Cathie to turn in Rob's direction in order to greet her roommate.

It wasn't just Rob and Connie as she had first thought but Andy and three others. The fair-haired man she knew because she had met him at the house when he had come to pick Andy up for a date. The third girl was a nurse a few years older than Cathie and the man with her was a new vet who had just moved into the area. There was a brief flurry of introductions to make sure everybody knew everybody.

"It sure is hot tonight, isn't it?" Andy commented once the group was settled on the blankets with Andy and Rob spilling over onto Cathie's and Clay's—at Clay's suggestion. "The temperature must still be in the nineties and it's so humid," she continued, adding stress to the last word. "Don't you just feel sticky all over, Cathie?"

"It is uncomfortable," Cathie agreed, keeping herself well back in Clay's shadow to conceal herself from Rob's eyes.

"What an understatement!" Andy exclaimed. "All I do is move my arm and I sweat like a horse!"

"Do you remember what your grandmother always used to say?" Clay tilted his head toward Cathie with a confiding look.

"How could I forget?" she replied, widening her eyes in agreement. "I'll have you know, Andy, that horses sweat, men perspire, and ladies glow. At least, according to my grandmother they did."

"Well, I am glowing!" Andy announced firmly, drawing chuckles from the small group.

Before the subject could be carried further, Tad catapulted himself into the group, followed by a panting Charlie Smith. His cheeks were flushed and his sandy-brown hair clung to the perspiration on his forehead. Tad looked like a typical boy, grinning and excited.

"Charlie asked me if I could stay overnight with him," he said breathlessly to Rob. "Can I, please?" His bright hazel eyes darted over to Cathie. "Hi!"

"Hello, Tad." She smiled, happiness filling her heart at the genuine warmth in his eyes. No matter how she felt about his father she couldn't hold anything back in her affection for his son.

"Do your parents know about your invitation, Charlie?" Rob inquired, turning from the eager face of his son to the shifting, impatient boy anxious to be away from the constricting adults.

"Yes, sir." The freckled face bobbed quickly. "I've got six brothers and sisters and my mom said another boy for one night wouldn't make any difference. Can he come? He can wear some of my clothes and pajamas."

"Please," Tad inserted when Rob still hesitated to give his approval.

Andy's friend Dennis had engaged Clay in a conversation which left Cathie free to listen in on this exchange between father and son. Tad was joining in, becoming a part of other children his own age. Her jewel eyes gleamed with the success of his transition while she waited breathlessly in case Rob wouldn't agree. Rob must have sensed her anxious gaze resting on him. As he turned, his eyes silently asked her opinion. Her blond curls moved in a barely perceptible nod of agreement, and the velvet-brown eyes smiled back before Rob turned away.

"You can stay overnight, but—" the qualifying word halted the two boys in midflight— "I want you to take me to your parents, Charlie, so I can make arrangements to pick Tad up tomorrow when it's convenient for them.''

Cathie watched the trio walk away, Rob's supple stride keeping pace with the two boys trotting hurriedly ahead of him. Some part of her was walking with him because of that strange, intimate look they had exchanged—a look that Cathie would rather forget, but its warmth was too fresh. Instead she turned to Clay, seeking his closeness to overshadow Rob's.

"Don't you think this fireworks display is better than last year's?" Cathie asked as another golden cascade of swirling spirals drifted downward.

"You sound just like my aunt." Andy laughed before Clay could reply. "She says the same thing every year."

"You know Cathie is just a small-town girl," Clay said to Andy in a definitely teasing tone. "The Fourth of July is the most exciting evening in her life outside of Christmas."

"That doesn't speak very highly of you as my escort," Cathie retorted with impish humor, glad of the light-hearted conversation that diverted her thoughts from Rob.

"Oh, look!" Andy exclaimed, directing their attention to the fireworks. "They're lighting the flag. That means the end to the fireworks for this year."

All eyes turned to the large rectangular framework at the far end of the field. Like falling dominoes, the spark raced along the frame touching off white stripes, then red stripes, the field of blue and finally the stars. It was the grand finale, the close of the Fourth of July celebration until next year. As the flag display began spluttering out, the general exodus from the athletics field began.

"Let's wait until the crowd clears out," Clay suggested. "It's cooler sitting here in the open than being stuck in the car waiting on traffic."

In mute agreement the small group remained sprawled on their Indian blankets, chattering idly until Andy popped to her feet. "I know what let's do," she declared. "Let's all go to Black Hawk Lake and swim. It's a perfect night for it."

"Sure," Dennis joined in. "My folks have a cabin there. We can have something to drink and everything. They won't mind."

While the others were voicing their approval, Clay glanced at Cathie and quietly asked her opinion. "What do you think? Do you want to go?"

"If the water were in front of me right now," she sighed, "I would probably go jump in it with my clothes on. It feels hotter now than when the sun was up."

There was a flurry of voices as arrangements were made for swimsuits to be picked up and a meeting place agreed on. In less than half an hour they were all back at the athletics field, the chosen meeting ground, with their swimsuits, towels and robes. But another member had joined their party, and Cathie felt a pinprick of doubt about the excursion as she gazed at Rob Douglas.

Andy was standing next to her as the men debated whether to drive their own cars or ride together in just two. "Is he going with us?" Cathie asked, keeping her voice low so it wouldn't carry.

"Who?" Andy's dark brows knitted together.

"Rob Douglas."

"Yes." A blank expression of surprise covered

Andy's face at Cathie's unexpected question. "You don't mind, do you? I mean you've gone out to the farm to see him, you couldn't possibly still dislike the man. All the gossips in town are talking about it."

"I went out to the farm to see Tad, not his father." A decidedly defensive note crept into her voice. "I couldn't care less whether he goes with us or not," Cathie lied, knowing she would be self-consciously aware of him. "He just wasn't here when we made the arrangements."

"He came back later, I guess," Andy shrugged. "And you know Connie is still trying to get her hooks into him, so she was bound to invite him along. He doesn't seem too keen on her, though, not that I blame him. Outside of being beautiful, what has she got that I haven't? I wish I were a teacher like you, then I could talk to Rob about his son like you do. He might notice me then."

Cathie was saved from commenting by Clay walking toward her. "We decided to each drive our own car," he told her. That was welcome news since she had been dreading the prospect of Rob and perhaps Connie riding with them.

As the gathering broke up to get into their respective cars, Cathie couldn't keep her eyes from straying to Rob, only to color furiously when he glanced her way and nodded, the knowing light in his eyes mocking her irritation. Dennis and Andy led the small caravan in his car while Cathie and Clay brought up the rear. They rode in silence for several miles.

"What are you so quiet about?" Clay finally asked, his hazel eyes turning their gaze from the road long enough to glance at Cathie. Her head was turned away from him so he could only see her honey-colored hair.

"I have a slight headache," she said, touching her temple to emphasize her words. "I don't know that I really feel like going swimming."

"It's probably the heat," Clay said, brushing aside the problem. "Once you get in the water and cool off you'll feel better."

"I doubt it," she replied caustically, directing her spite at Clay since Rob wasn't there. "With everybody splashing and yelling, it will probably get worse."

"What's the matter with you lately?" Clay demanded. "You're constantly changing your mind. Two weeks ago you wouldn't go with me to visit my parents because you were singing in the choir at church. Then last Sunday, you took off to visit your parents. Earlier tonight you could hardly wait to go swimming, and now, not even an hour later, you don't want to go. This isn't like you, Cathie."

How could she begin to explain to Clay what the source of her real problem was? How could she tell him that she wanted to avoid any contact with Rob Douglas? It was something she couldn't even explain to herself, except that ever since he came to this town, her world had been changing. Nothing was the same as it used to be as much as she tried to make it so. The slight drumming in her temples wasn't bothering her as much as the building tension at spending time with Rob Douglas.

Cathie rubbed the back of her neck and stared into the black curtain of night outside the car windows. "I don't know why I'm so moody lately," she murmured, drawing a deep breath. "But you're probably right. Once I get in the water, my head-ache will more than likely go away."

What else could she say? Any more protests about going swimming would have meant more questions, and if Clay asked more questions, he might just find out the truth. Besides it was silly, Cathie told herself, to let the presence of Rob dampen her evening.

Chapter Nine

"Oohh, the water is cold!" Connie said shivering, her feet dancing away from the gentle waves that lapped along the sandy shore.

"No, it's not," Andy called from where she was treading water. "It's really warm once you get in it."

"Come on." Clay grabbed Connie's arm and pulled her into the lake, laughing at her shrieks of displeasure as he firmly immersed her in the water.

Cathie needed no prompting as she waded into the cool water until it was nearly touching her white bikini, then submerged to swim toward the raft anchored several yards from shore. Through water-spiked lashes, she saw Clay swimming beside her, his grin challenging her to a race. He was already lifting himself onto the raft when she reached it. The rest of the group had gathered there too, with the exception of Connie and Dennis. But it was Rob's hands and not Clay's that reached down to help Cathie onto the floating platform.

Under the glow of the moonlight, his tanned body glistened like a bronzed statue, muscular and smooth, naked except for his black trunks. She kept her eyes averted from his face, feeling an attack of breathlessness that had no basis in exercise overtake her as she inadvertently glanced at him, her senses traitorously ignited at his touch. The second her balance was established she eluded the firm but not restraining grasp of his hands and moved away toward Clay, her only refuge from the magnetic pull of Rob's nearness.

"Rob, give me a hand up," Connie called imperiously from the water near the raft. Cathie was thankful to have the attention diverted from her; she needed the time to regain her composure.

Dennis came drifting past the raft, lolling in an oversized rubber tire while propelling himself with his hands. A duplicate of the tire was floating a few feet behind him along with a pair of yellow air mattresses. There was a scramble from the raft into the water to see who could lay claim to the floating objects which ended in laughs and shrieks as one swimmer after another was capsized by the rest. Cathie joined, finding safety in numbers.

It was several minutes later while the others were engrossed in their water game of King of the Mountain that Cathie slipped away from the noisemakers, taking one of the forgotten air mattresses. There was too much body contact in that game, and Cathie knew that sooner or later it would include her and Rob. Agilely she slipped onto the mattress, reclining on her back as the gentle rocking motion of the water carried her quietly away from the robust crowd.

The smiling face of a silver-dollar moon illuminated the lake, chasing the dark shadows away to hide under the trees that gathered near the shore. It was peaceful lying here on this soft cradle, Cathie thought, relaxing as the waves carried her farther from the group and closer to the shore.

There was no sound or movement to betray the presence of another person, but all of a sudden Rob's head appeared beside her. His brown hair, curling and wet around his forehead, gave him a rakish look to match the fiery blaze in his eyes.

"What are you doing so far away from the rest of us? We're operating according to the buddy system tonight. There's to be no separation unless it's in pairs."

The initial shock was over and the blood was again starting to pump through her heart. "Where's Clay?" Cathie slid off the mattress into the water, using it as a shield against the penetrating gaze that had thoroughly raked her skimpily clad body.

"You cling to him as if he were a security blanket," Rob mocked. Like Cathie, he was using the natural buoyancy of the air mattress to keep him afloat without treading water. "What is it you're afraid of?"

"I'm not afraid of anything," she asserted, pushing her wet curls away from her face as she eyed him with false boldness.

His hand reached out and captured her arm, pulling her easily through the water to him. They had drifted close enough to shore so that Rob, because of his superior height, could touch bottom. Cathie could feel it just out of reach of her tiptoes. Without its support, struggling was wasted effort. He brought her close to him, his hands burning her flesh where they touched the nakedness of her waist. As he drew her tighter into the circle of his arms, Cathie tried to hold herself away, yet needing to cling to him to keep her head above water.

One of his hands moved to the back of her hair, holding her firmly while his head, framed against a star-spangled sky, began its slow descent. The feel of his sleek body pressed against hers was a potent sensation as the heat from him generated a different fire in Cathie. Shudders of sweet ecstasy quaked through her when his mouth closed over hers, expertly arousing the desire that she had always before kept suppressed. Rob was an irresistible force that she had to resist. It was a supreme test of will to keep her arms from encircling the hard smooth shoulders and mold herself closer to his body. In that Cathie succeeded, only to have her lips betray her and part under the sensually demanding and experienced request of his.

It was torturous bliss, wanting this kiss and despising herself for that want. It was Clay she was going to marry, not Rob. It was Clay who should be making her respond physically like this. When she thought she couldn't stand not giving herself wholeheartedly to the embrace, his mouth moved away from hers. Rob still held her tightly against him, his mouth moving softly against her golden hair. Cathie's head rested weakly against his shoulder, her breath silent sobs in her attempt to regain control. Shame and humiliation inflamed her because she had responded to a man who was not her fiancé. Yet she wanted to feel the hard pressure of his mouth on hers again.

"You're trembling like a frightened little cat," Rob murmured. "You're afraid, but you're afraid of the wrong thing."

Tears burned her eyes and she held them tightly shut. "Let me go!" she demanded in a tense voice that cried to be silenced by his lips.

"Is that what you want?"

"Yes." She knew she was lying.

As Rob let her drift away from him, he kept a steadying grip under her arms that loosened as she began treading water on her own. It was all she could do not to swim back to his open, inviting arms. Cathie glanced over her shoulder at the laughter and splashing horseplay of the rest of their party. She was suddenly cold, terribly cold and unwilling to face Clay as though nothing had happened. The darkness of the tree-lined beach beckoned and after casting Rob a condemning look, she struck out toward it, her arms cleaving the water with sharp, vigorous strokes.

Blinding hate enveloped her as she walked the last few yards to shore and strode toward the over-sized blue beach towel she had left on the sand. At that moment Cathie hated Rob Douglas with a violent, sickening rush of emotion. The ache at the pit of her stomach told her that he was awakening her to the needs of the flesh as only her future husband should. Rob was changing her. Even Clay had noticed it. And she hated Rob for that, for disrupting her safe, secure world.

With hard, vigorous movements, Cathie scrubbed every clinging droplet of water from her skin, the harsh rubbing chastising the weakness of her flesh.

When the fury of her rage passed, she slung the towel around her shoulders and sank to the ground in the darkness of an overhanging tree. Gazing out at the glacial moon and the brittle silver of the stars, she shivered, then caught a flash of yellow flame out of the corner of her eye.

"Here." Rob stood above her, his approach muted by the traitorous cushion of the sand, holding a cigarette toward her.

"I don't smoke," she said icily, but he pushed it into her hands anyway. It was something for her trembling hands to hold on to, so she kept it. He was obviously impervious to the coolness of the night as he lowered himself to the sand beside her, his naked chest glistening in the pale moonlight. "I didn't ask you to join me." The frigid sarcasm of her voice lashed out at him while she wished she could do the same with her hands.

A cloud of cigarette smoke hung in the air between them, as Rob lazily reclined on one arm. "I know you didn't," he replied with infuriating calm.

"Do you have any idea how much I despise you?" Cathie demanded, her green eyes shooting fiery sparks as she glared at him. "You are the most loathsome, disgusting man I've ever met! How could you be so brazen and make love to a woman when the man she's engaged to is not twenty yards away?"

"Why didn't you call out to him to rescue you from my barbaric person?" he retorted smoothly, a glint of retaliatory anger in his dark eyes. Cathie's sharp intake of breath was an admission that he had found the vulnerable chink in her defensive armor. "You may call that an engagement ring, but it's nothing more than a friendship ring. You can't love him and kiss me like you just did."

"I'm going to marry Clay," Cathie declared, a hollow ring to her voice.

"Then I pity both of you."

"Pity?" She turned her puzzled, angry face toward him. "Why should you pity us?"

"I pity Clay more than I do you," said Rob, inhaling on his cigarette. "Because he'll end up with a dissatisfied unhappy wife and won't know why."

"And you do, I suppose." She turned away from him to study the grains of sand at her feet, his words cutting more deeply than she cared to admit.

"Yes. Would you like to know what's wrong with you?" he asked, an arrogant smile on his face.

Her mouth was compressed in a tight line. "Not particularly," she said with a dismissive shake of her head. "But I have the feeling you're going to tell me whether I ask you to or not."

Rob leaned forward and rested his arms on his knees as he contemplated her profile thoughtfully. "You haven't grown up yet, little kitten." He smiled as she gave him a startled look. Many things she could be accused of, but at that moment she was more aware of herself as a woman than she had ever been. "You're still living in some fantasy world that you built when you were a romantic teenager. You mapped everything out to enclose yourself into a cocoon of security. You chose Clay to marry because he was a link with your childhood happiness. With him, there would be no secrets or surprises because you'd grown up with him. But your plan included the farm where your idyllic marriage would be acted out. That's why you and Clay have kept finding excuses to keep from getting married, because you wanted the proper setting. My arrival disrupted your world before you even met me.''

Cathie nodded numbly in agreement, uncaring of the glittering fire of satisfaction that lit his brown eyes. His words were so close to what had actually happened that it frightened her, casting doubts as to how genuine her affection for Clay really was and more doubts as to why she was marrying him.

"Tell me, Cat," Rob continued, "did you just ignore the physical aspect of a man-woman relationship or was it something you were going to endure in order to have the children who would one day discover all the magic of the farm? Why did you become a teacher? To maintain your connection with your childhood?"

His arrows of speculation were coming too fast for her to ward off. She cupped her hands over her ears so she wouldn't have to hear any more. "Stop it!" Cathie cried. "I don't want to hear any more of your stupid theories!"

With her eyes shut she didn't see his hands reach out to grasp hers and pull them away from her ears. At his touch, she struggled wildly until she had no more strength and submitted to the bruising hold he had on her wrists. But her eyes remained wide and rounded, reflecting the glittering anguish and fear that she would once again succumb to his charisma.

"I don't mean to hurt you." Rob's voice was low and soothing as if he were trying to calm a frightened animal. "There isn't anything wrong with having dreams or even trying to make them come true, unless it goes against your heart. Don't fight me any more, Cat, because of a dream."

The moonlight beamed down over his shoulder

lighting her face and hiding Rob's face in its shadow. "I'm twenty-four years old," she protested weakly. "I'm not a child anymore. I know what I want."

She could see the flash of his teeth that signaled a smile, indulgent or mocking she couldn't tell. "There's always some part of all of us that remains a child."

"I love Clay." Cathie blinked at the tears hovering at the edge of her lashes, one last protest against her growing emotion for Rob. "I've always loved Clay."

"Of course you love him. But as a brother or a lover?"

"Why do you care?" There was a pleading, protesting tone in her voice. "What difference could it possibly make to you?"

His hesitancy was a tangible thing. Unconsciously Cathie was holding her breath in wary anticipation of his reply. There was an overpowering feeling that his answer was of supreme importance, her future happiness hinged on it.

"I don't come into it at all, Cat." Rob finally spoke and her heart plummeted to her toes. He didn't care for her. "It's your relationship with Clay that's in question." He released her wrists and rolled to his feet to stand and look down at her. "Think over what I've said . . . for your own good."

The next instant he was several feet away, briskly toweling his wet hair. Cathie couldn't help watching him, studying the wide shoulders and the narrowing waist and hips. But the only thing she could feel was a lonely, aching emptiness somewhere in the region of her heart. She had told herself before that it would be foolish to fall in love with Rob. And she had finally done it.

"Cathie, what are you doing here?" Clay trotted out of the water, a happy grin of exhaustion on his face as he made his way toward her. He barely even glanced at Rob. "I wondered where you'd got to." As he walked past Rob, Cathie noticed the sharp contrast between Clay's almost white skin and the deep tan of Rob's. Clay collapsed on the sand beside Cathie, a wet arm playfully snatching her towel away. "You missed a lot of fun. What have you been doing, anyway?"

Cathie examined the clean lines of Clay's attractive face, not finding the strength and maturity that were etched so indelibly in Rob's face. "Rob and I were talking," she replied.

"Hashing poor Tad over again, huh? Or was he bringing you up to date on the changes at the Homeplace?" Clay grinned.

"No, actually we were just talking man to woman." Her statement didn't even bring a glimmer of surprise, much less jealousy, to Clay's face. He merely shrugged and began recounting how Connie's swimsuit top had accidentally came unhooked.

"Clay, I'm cold," Cathie interrupted impatiently. "Let's go home."

The rest of the party was just coming out of the water and Rob was walking to meet them. Connie had separated herself from the group to rush forward to meet him. And Cathie didn't like the twinge of pain that attacked her midsection at the burst of laughter from Connie at some unheard comment from Rob. Jealousy wasn't part of her nature, she had once bragged, but that was before Rob. She shivered.

"Hey, you're covered with goose bumps!" Clay exclaimed, running a dry but cool hand over her arm.

"I told you I was cold," Cathie snapped angrily, pulling the towel from his hands and wrapping it around her as she rose to her feet. Clay was forced to follow suit.

"Hey, where are you two going?" Andy called out as Cathie started toward the place where they had parked their cars.

"Cathie has an attack of chills. We're going to go ahead and leave now," Clay shouted back, lifting a hand in good-bye, but Cathie kept walking, not wanting to meet Rob's glance.

"Don't you want to stop and change clothes before we drive back?" Clay asked as Cathie slid into the passenger seat of his green compact car.

"I want to go home," she repeated determinedly.

"You don't have to be so touchy." He frowned as he slipped a blue cotton T-shirt over his head and took his place behind the wheel. "I only thought that if you were cold you might feel better in some dry clothes."

After he had reversed the car out of the parking space and was on the road leading back to the highway, Cathie voiced the thought that had been uppermost in her mind. "Clay, would you like to get married? Right away, I mean."

"You mean not wait until we find a house? To simply get married on the spur of the moment, like that?" He snapped his fingers and gave Cathie a look that doubted her sanity. "That wouldn't make sense, to throw away all our plans."

"But what if it takes us another year to find the house we want?" she persisted, gazing straight ahead, her voice calm and unemotional.

"Then it takes another year," he replied, lifting his shoulders in a dismissive shrug.

"And after we find the house, it will take time to get it decorated and fixed the way we want it?"

"We've already talked all this out and figured it into our plans." There was a bewildered frown on his forehead as he studied the pattern of his headlights on the concrete road.

"And after that, what kind of an excuse do you suppose we'll come up with to postpone the wedding?" Her eyes widened with false innocence as she turned them toward Clay.

"You aren't making any sense at all."

"What I think I'm asking is, do you really want to marry me, Clay?"

"Of course I do." There was a desperate note in Clay's confused voice as if he couldn't find the words to convince her. "Isn't that what we've been planning to do?"

Cathie sighed heavily, turning her troubled gaze away from him. "Planning and planning and planning, but never doing."

"Well, what do you want to do?" he demanded, half angrily. "Do you want to run off and elope tonight? Where would we live? I don't have enough cupboards in my apartment to hold my own clothes, let alone yours. You aren't suggesting that I move in with you, Connie and Andy, are you?"

"No, I'm not suggesting anything like that," she answered. Her shoulders sagged with the confusion of her own thoughts.

"Then explain to me what this conversation is

all about," Clay sighed, glancing at her with exasperation. Automatically he made the turn that would take him to Cathie's house. There was a moment of silence as he pulled into the driveway and turned off the engine. He turned sideways in his seat to study her.

"Clay, weren't you the least bit jealous when you found me with Rob?" Cathie had to swallow the lump in her throat before she could get that question out.

He cocked his head to the side, taken aback by her question and uncertain how to answer it. "Why should I have been jealous? You told me yourself that all you did was talk."

"He kissed me, too, Clay. And it wasn't the first time." The two bright spots of color on her cheeks didn't appear because she was embarrassed about telling him what had happened; they were there because of the way she had responded to those kisses. Her head lifted boldly to meet his gaze. There was surprise on his face, not anger or jealousy. "You aren't even upset now, Clay."

Inhaling deeply, he turned away to tap the steering wheel with his fingers, finding a lot of unanswered question in himself that suddenly needed answering. They were so close, Cathie thought to herself as she watched the silent soul-searching Clay was going through. She did love him deeply, but she knew that it was more the love of a sister or a friend.

"Have you fallen in love with Douglas?" Clay asked quietly.

"At the moment I don't even think I know what love is," she replied with bitter amusement, resting her tense neck against the back of the seat. "I'm learning what it isn't. We've been so close all our lives, Clay. It seemed so natural and right that we get married. Now, I'm beginning to wonder if we both reached that conclusion for the wrong reason."

"I care about you more than any woman I've ever met. I love you, Cathie," Clay declared earnestly.

"I feel the same." Pain tightened its hold around her throat. "We both need time to think this over. We're too confused to be sure of our own emotions and what we really feel."

He eagerly seized on her implied suggestion to postpone the discussion. He needed time to think coherently over these sudden doubts. "It's late," he agreed, not seeing the cynical smile that turned up the corners of Cathie's mouth. "Things will look different after a night's sleep. All this talk will turn out to be premarital nerves, a lot of smoke without any fire."

"I hope you're right," she said, opening her car door and climbing out. "Don't bother to see me to the door, Clay. Let's just call it a night."

Cathie was in the house with the door closed and locked behind her before she heard the car motor start. She glanced down at the ring on her finger and knew she wouldn't be wearing it much longer.

Chapter Ten

Cathie's premonition had proved correct. Her finger was bare. Clay's attempts on the evening following the Fourth to dissuade her from returning it had been halfhearted and lacking conviction.

The termination of her engagement was a mixed blessing. Now Cathie was free, but free to do what? To fall in love with Rob Douglas? When she had been engaged, her thoughts had never been far from him. Now, they were always centered on him. Besides, Rob had made it clear the night at the lake that he didn't enter into her life at all. She had been a method of amusement for him, a mild flirtation.

Over a week had passed, a week of staring into space while the minutes dragged by, a week of being the object of understanding looks from the people she knew. They thought her melancholy abstraction was caused by her broken engagement. They couldn't know that Cathie was seeking ways to bump casually into Rob and inform him of the current change. That desire was mixed with dread. Rob had been the one to point out the error of her emotions. Would he applaud her break with Clay or mock her inability to make the discovery on her own?

Her heavy sigh broke the stillness of the room as she turned her gaze away from the window and the golden twilight signaling the approach of night. The coo of a mourning dove matched the sad, silent sounds of her own heart. Andy glanced sympathetically in Cathie's direction before returning her attention to the book on her lap.

Clay had wanted to keep on seeing Cathie, but she had been adamant in her refusal. There was the fear that because Rob didn't care, she and Clay would drift back together in their old pattern and they would both suffer from it. But right now, Cathie would have been glad of his company. Anything to relieve these tortuous moments of wanting to see Rob and not having the courage to carry out her desire.

The shrill ring of the telephone was a welcome interruption and Cathie sprang to her feet to answer it. Perhaps it was Clay. If it was, she would invite him over for coffee and they would talk over old times and alleviate this tormenting thought of Rob. With that occupying her mind, it was a shock to hear Mrs. Carver's voice on the other end of the line.

"Is that you, Cathie?" Rob's housekeeper demanded.

"Yes. What's wrong?" she breathed quickly.

"My daughter Sharon just called me. They've rushed my grandson to the hospital. Appendicitis," she explained with a rush. "She wants me to come just as soon as I can."

For one terrifying minute Cathie had thought something had happened to Rob before she soberly realized that Mrs. Carver wouldn't have thought to notify her if there had. "Do you need a ride? I'm not busy. I can be out there in a few minutes."

"No, I have a car. I called because Mr. Douglas had to drive to Omaha and won't be back until late this evening. And I can't go off and leave Tad here alone. As late as it is, I can't take him to the hospital with me because heaven knows what time I'll be back. I didn't know of anyone else other than you I could call on the spur of the moment to stay with Tad. The two of you are quite good friends and he trusts you."

Cathie paused. "You want me to stay with Tad?"

"Until Mr. Douglas comes back or I come back from the hospital. Would you, Cathie? I'd feel so much easier knowing you were with Tad. I'm sure Mr. Douglas wouldn't object."

"Of course, I'll come," Cathie agreed, her spirits lifting at the prospect of possibly seeing Rob. Besides, the need for her to go to the farm was genuine. There was nothing engineered about it. And Cathie knew she was the likely choice to watch Tad. She was in full agreement with Mrs. Carver that he shouldn't be left alone or carted off to the hospital.

"Thank you." The housekeeper's gratitude flooded over the line. "I'll ring Sharon at the hospital and let her know I'll be leaving as soon as you get here.''

"I'll leave immediately," Cathie assured her before exchanging good-byes.

As Cathie walked into the door of the farmhouse, Mrs. Carver walked out. Tad was quite delighted at the change, finding Cathie a willing listener to the tales of his escapades with Charlie Smith, who was now his best buddy. Patience, Tad's half-grown yellow kitten, had become a houseguest and Cathie was duly introduced to him.

Although she tucked Tad into his bed at the top of the stairs at ten o'clock, it was a half hour later before he actually fell asleep. There was nothing worth watching on television. Cathie's thoughts were too preoccupied with Rob's eventual return. At last she flicked the set off, her gaze shifting to the closed parlor doors. She couldn't help wondering how much farther Rob had got in his remodeling of the room into a den.

Opening the heavy walnut double doors, Cathie gasped at the complete transformation of the room. The satiny sheen of the walnut paneling and shelves gave the room a rich glow, echoed by the vibrant carpeting. The two overstuffed chairs that had been previously hidden by protective sheets were covered in a rich gold and brown plaid that suited the masculine room. Books lined the shelves and as her fingers trailed over the titles, Cathie saw they ranged from reference books to reading material.

Her glowing eyes roamed admiringly over the room. She felt no remorse over the loss of the parlor. The room had been used only once a year at Christmastime. This was a room a person would want to be in all year through, a cozy room that beckoned one to come and sit. As she lifted a mystery book from the shelves bearing the author's name of Robert Douglas, Cathie longed to do just that, but she decided to forgo that pleasure in favor of the sun porch where she could view Rob's eventual arrival.

The night was sultry with heat lightning dancing across the southern skies. Although the walls of the old farmhouse were thick to keep the house cool in the heat of the summer and warm in the cold of the winter, the sighing southeast breeze that filtered through the open windows of the sun porch was a refreshing addition. Cathie propped herself on the blue-flowered chaise lounge, flicking on the switch of the overhead reading lamp.

With each page she turned, she became more and more engrossed in the suspense-filled mystery. The fluttering of a moth outside the window as it beat its wings futilely against the screen was unnoticed. The rasping screech of the crickets' song was ignored along with the drone of the cicadas. Not even the eerie hooting call of a hunting owl drew her attention away from the printed pages.

It was two in the morning when Cathie finished reading, the closed book remaining in her lap. Stifling a yawn, she glanced at her watch, surprised by how quickly the time had passed and understanding why she had such difficulty focusing her eyes on the last pages. She gazed out the window at the galaxies of stars sprinkled over the blue-velvet sky and wondered how much longer it would be before Rob came home.

The merry songs of sparrows, robins, flickers and thrushes all blended together, their melodic sounds broken by the crowing of a rooster. Cathie's eyes opened slowly to focus on the golden kiss of dawn. Morning—it couldn't be! Cathie blinked the last of the sleep from her eyes. Her blond head turned swiftly away from the windows as she realized that Rob hadn't come back.

A momentary shaft of fear struck her until she saw the man sleeping in the chair, his feet stretched out on an ottoman and his head propped against his arm in an uncomfortable position. A blue sports jacket lay over the back of the matching wicker chair while his tie remained loosely knotted around his neck and the white shirt unbuttoned revealing the smooth column of his throat. Rob looked so peaceful, his hair attractively disheveled as if he had raked his fingers through it before falling into an exhausted sleep. Cathie had no idea what time Rob had got back. Not a sound had disturbed her sleep, yet the light above her head had been turned off.

Very quietly she rose to her feet, setting the book that had been on her lap on a nearby table, and tiptoed into the kitchen. The wall clock showed it was a few minutes before six o'clock. Making as little noise as possible, Cathie put the coffee on before making her way to the bathroom, purse in hand. After sleeping in her clothes, she knew she was a rumpled mess. She washed her face and applied lipstick and mascara before running a comb through her tousled short curls, hoping the wrinkles would somehow disappear from her clothes.

Pleased by her reflection in the mirror, Cathie walked back into the kitchen, her steps as light-hearted as her spirits. There was supreme contentment in knowing Rob was in the next room. The electric percolator was just emitting its last sighing pop when she walked in. She sniffed appreciatively at the fragrant steam as she filled a mug from the cupboard.

"Would you pour me a cup of that coffee, too?"

A wild leaping of her heart followed Rob's words as she spun around to stare at the tall, imposing figure framed in the kitchen doorway. "I . . . I didn't mean to wake you," Cathie stumbled before recovering her poise.

"You didn't." He smiled, walking farther into the room. "It was the aroma of that coffee. It sends out its own wake-up signals."

She reached in the cupboard for another over-sized mug and filled it with coffee, then carried both to the dinette table where Rob was now sitting. "I didn't hear you come in last night."

"I know." His brown eyes moved lazily over her face with that velvet quality that was soothing yet so disturbing. "What happened to Mrs. Carver?"

"Her grandson was rushed to the hospital last night with appendicitis, and she asked me to stay with Tad," Cathie explained, choosing a chair opposite Rob.

She was hesitant to meet his eyes squarely, afraid that her inner excitement would be revealed. No other man had ever been able to make her senses so conscious of his presence the way Rob did. This was love and not fleeting physical attraction. And there was the realization, as she sat across the table from him with the dawn just breaking outside, that she had always loved him, almost from the first day she had met him. A fine line divided love and hate, two equally explosive emotions. Cathie had looked on Rob as an enemy, a usurper, but with a secret smile she knew it was because he was stealing her heart and not the Homeplace. Still, it was impossible to admit any of this to Rob.

Her gaze moved unconsciously from the dark liquid in her cup to the equally dark but shadowed and enigmatic expression in Rob's eyes. It was then that she realized a silence had descended on them. The unreadable look in his eyes made her uneasy.

"It must have been quite late when you got back," she said, wrapping her trembling fingers around the cup. "I know it was after two when I dozed off. You should have wakened me when you came in." Although she was unutterably glad he hadn't.

Rob sipped his coffee, lowering his gaze from her face. "It was nearly four in the morning. It didn't make any sense to wake you from a sound sleep to send you home to try to go back to sleep."

There was such a natural vitality and alertness about him that Cathie found it hard to believe that he had only had two hours sleep himself. Yet he looked refreshed and rested. She wanted to suggest that he catch a few more hours of sleep, but she didn't know of any way to word it without sounding oversolicitous.

"I don't need any more sleep." A crooked smile touched his mouth as he perceptively read her thoughts. "But I could eat some bacon and eggs. How about you?"

With a self-conscious laugh, Cathie agreed, assuring him that she wasn't a novice in the kitchen. Once she had the bacon sizzling in the pan, she began setting the table while Rob excused himself to wash up.

"You didn't mention how you liked the book," Rob commented, walking back into the room with his hair combed and in place and bringing the clean scent of soap.

"Oh, I enjoyed it," she said fervently, then laughed. "That sounds offhand, doesn't it?" she asked, tossing him a smiling glance over her shoulder. "I just realized how hard it is to sound sincere when you're talking to the person who actually wrote the book you just read. But it's true. I honestly couldn't put it down until I'd read the last page."

"That's sufficient praise for anyone." He stood near the stove watching as Cathie broke two eggs and slid them into the hot melted butter in the pan. "I like my eggs over easy with toast and jam on the side."

Over their breakfast meal, Rob explained that he had driven to Omaha to meet a representative from his publishing firm who had stopped over en route to Los Angeles. Cathie received the impression that this representative was also a personal friend, but Rob didn't reveal if it was a male or female. She shifted the conversation to his past life, lightheartedly matching reminiscences of their childhood growing up on a farm.

"How did you get that scar near your eye?" Cathie asked when Rob mentioned his tour of duty in the armed forces.

"The truth?" His eyes gleamed with wicked mischief. He touched the scar lightly as he grinned. "I received this when I fell off my bicycle at the age of six. Not a very adventurous story, is it?"

Cathie laughingly agreed, and began the task of clearing the table. It was a pleasant surprise when

Rob joined her. With the two of them, it took almost no time at all to wash up.

"What time does Tad get up?" Cathie asked as she put away the dishcloth and hung up the dish-towel Rob had been using.

"Around eight. Luckily he's not like me. A bowl of cereal and some juice can carry him until lunchtime," Rob said, shrugging and pouring them each a cup of coffee and carrying it onto the sun porch. After they were both comfortably seated in wicker chairs, he turned his gaze toward her with bland watchfulness. "What have you been doing with yourself lately?"

Cathie took a deep breath. This was her chance to tell him she had broken her engagement to Clay. "Not really very much. I'm getting kind of anxious for school to start again so I can have something to do." There was a pause while she stared at the shimmering liquid in her cup as it caught the sunlight that streamed through the win-dow. "Clay and I broke up."

"I know you did," he said, meeting her startled look easily. "You forget this is a small town. The local grapevine passed that message around the day after you gave him his ring back."

A very small "oh" came from her lips.

"What now? Are you trying to find someone else to fill the empty niche in your fantasy?" There was a sharp, biting note in his voice.

"What do you mean?" Cathie asked in a tight voice made weak by the constriction in her throat.

"You don't have Clay around any more. Surely you must be looking for another partner to act out your childhood dream. I imagine as the new owner of the Homeplace I would be a likely candidate."

His gaze was penetrating and harsh. Cathie couldn't meet it squarely.

The Homeplace. How strange! A few months ago it was all so important to her. Every room held some precious memory, and yet last night the only thing she had been conscious of was how much of Rob's presence was in every room. From the outside, it still looked like the farm home of her grandparents, but on the inside where the living was done, the house was unmistakably Rob's. No, Cathie could honestly say to herself that Rob's ownership of the Homeplace had nothing to do with her love for him. One look at the grim expression on his face told her that he didn't believe her.

"You would be a perfect choice," she agreed, pride making her lift her chin, forcing her to ignore the tears rising to intensify the green of her eyes. "Except that I've made a pact with myself that I'll only marry the man I truly love."

One eyebrow flickered into an arch before settling back to match the other. "Do you mean you've given up your dream so easily?" The disbelief in his voice mocked her.

"It wasn't easy." Gratefully she let her gaze slide from his to glance around the room and outside to the cornfields at the edge of the lawn and garden. "I'll miss this place. Some of my happiest moments were here." Including those with you, she added silently. "But I think I have my priorities in the right order now, and it doesn't include a marriage of convenience anymore."

"That's good." Cathie felt his gaze narrowing on her as she continued to look away. An indignant anger and hurt pride were making themselves felt, generated by the pain in her heart. "You wouldn't have found me to be as easy as Clay," he added.

That remark was pretty much the last straw. Cathie rose to her feet. "I really think it's time I left. I'm sure you're capable of looking after your own son when he gets up."

Rob was on his feet, towering over her until she was robbed of her breath. His gaze was so penetrating that she felt sure he must guess the truth of her feelings.

"I appreciate you coming out here last night on such short notice," was all he said

"I did it for Tad," Cathie declared vigorously.

"I never have thanked you for the time you spent with him."

"Don't bother." The tears were so close to spilling over her lashes that Cathie grabbed her purse and bolted for the door.

It was heartbreaking to discover there was no way mere words could ever convince Rob that she could care for him as a person and not as the owner of the Homeplace. Even if she could, he gave no indication he was interested in accepting the heart she would give him so willingly. No, she was only of use to him because of Tad. And now that Tad had adjusted to his new life, Rob didn't care about her anymore.

Chapter Eleven

"You've been unaturally quiet, Cathie." Andy glanced curiously at her. "All through lunch you didn't say two words except to nod your head yes or no to whatever I said."

"Is that so unusual?" The brittle smile couldn't reach the dull green eyes. Cathie sighed, turning her gaze away from her roommate's probing eyes to study the rolling, dark gray clouds slowly billowing over the entire sky and the incredibly still trees with not a breath of wind stirring their leaves. "I don't know, maybe it's the weather." Or Rob Douglas, her mind added, sending a twisting dagger of pain to her heart.

"Well, the forecast said thunderstorms." Andy's brown eyes turned skyward, too, as she plucked at the nylon uniform clinging stickily to her skin. "And those clouds look as if they're going to burst any minute. It'll probably be raining when I get off work tonight, since I left my umbrella at home."

When they neared the corner where they would separate, Cathie to go home and Andy to return to the dental office, the first fat raindrops splattered on the dust-covered pavement. Andy's palm turned upward to assure herself it was raining.

"It isn't going to wait until this afternoon," she declared, looking at the droplet on her hand. "I'm going to make a dash for the office before I get drenched." She was already moving away from Cathie at a brisk pace. "I'll see you tonight."

Cathie returned the wave, making her steps swifter as she crossed to the other side of the street. The rain was falling faster now as the air around her became more muggy but with a fragrant cleanness. For several blocks, the rainfall was steady and gentle, like a tepid shower. Cathie couldn't bring her feet to hurry despite the growing dampness of her peasant top and jeans. There was no desire to return to the emptiness of the house that she had done her best to avoid these past four days. She wanted no time to think about Rob Douglas, or the torment of her situation would be more difficult to bear.

Thunder rumbled as darker clouds rolled overhead, accompanied by darting tongues of lightning. The air became slightly cooler, stirring up a sighing breeze that gradually grew into a wind. As Cathie made her turn half a block from her house, the drops began falling closer together, driven now by the wind. Common sense made her sprint the short distance to the door rather than risk a complete soaking. At the closing of the door behind her, a fiery flash of lightning split open the clouds and sent torrents of water to ricochet off the ground.

The gusting wind was whipping the rain through the open windows. Cathie scrambled hastily to close them before the water could do more than dampen the floors and furniture. After she had wiped the small pools under the windows, she turned the towel on herself, blotting away the few drops that were still clinging to her skin. There were few gaps between the roaring thunder and the streaking lightning. She felt a kinship with the violent storm as if its fury was unleashing her own pent-up emotions and bringing some measure of relief.

Curling up on the sofa with her arms wrapped around her knees, Cathie stared out the window at the angled sheets of driving rain. It hammered at the quaking leaves of bushes and trees and beat down the drowning blades of grass. The birds, squirrels, rabbits, and all the rest of the little creatures had taken shelter from the deluge. Cathie's head came up with a start. Duchess! There was no covering flap on her kennel and the rain would be beating unmercifully. Cathie raced toward the door, pausing only to take the clear plastic umbrella from the closet. Paying no heed to the buffeting rain, she headed straight for the kennel, scolding herself for forgetting the aging shepherd.

"Duchess! Come on, girl," she called coaxingly before dropping to one knee beside the small dark opening. The sky had darkened ominously, making it difficult to see in the dim interior, but a searching hand ascertained that Duchess wasn't inside. The metallic gleam of the chain half hidden by grass caught her eye, and lifting it, Cathie saw the rusty broken link and knew that Duchess had run away.

There was no telling how long she had been gone since Cathie couldn't remember seeing the dog when she had dashed in the house a quarter of an hour earlier. And she had been gone all morning, which gave the shepherd ample time to break free and run off.

Cathie debated whether or not to go in search of the dog, whose final destination, she knew, would be the farm. The question was, had Duchess already reached it or was she en route? Cathie tried to convince herself that the dog would take shelter, but visions of soft, trusting eyes and the graying muzzle wouldn't go away. It was foolish to try to find Duchess in a storm that showed no signs of letting up. Cathie argued with herself all the way to her car.

The windshield wipers had little effect on the onslaught of rain as the car crept along the highway with Cathie peering out of the rain-streaked windows for a glimpse of the dog. At every place that offered any sort of protection for the shepherd, she rolled the window down, ignoring the biting spray on her face to search for the telltale red-gold color. The big tree loomed ahead of her at the intersection of the county road and the highway. The Homeplace was only a quarter of a mile west on that graveled road.

Cathie inhaled deeply. "Well," she sighed aloud, "I've come this far, so I might as well go all the way."

Her car tires slushed onto the sodden gravel road. The air rumbled with repeated rolls of thunder that seemed to match the quaking going on in her own body. She parked the car near the machine shed, wishing there was a place where it would be out of sight. Snatching the umbrella from the passenger seat, she scrambled out of the car to dash toward the corn crib. The soaking wind tore her pleading calls for Duchess from her throat, drowning them in the fury of the storm. Faintly she heard an answering yelp. There, framed in the machine shed doors, sat Duchess.

Cathie dashed into the rain, her sandals slipping and sliding in the mud. The remnant of the leash was still attached to the shepherd's collar. Cathie had but one thought—to get the dog from the machine shed to the car. But Duchess had an entirely different idea as she retreated farther away from her mistress into the dark recesses of the shed. With a diving grab, Cathie caught hold of the leash and began the thankless task of dragging the reluctant dog to the doorway.

The umbrella had to be abandoned since Cathie couldn't manage the dog and the umbrella at the same time. She paused in the doorway to catch her breath and assess the distance from the shed to the car. Through rain-spiked lashes, she studied the path that was quickly becoming a quagmire and wondered how much of a fuss Duchess would put up between here and there. If only the dog were human, she could explain why she didn't want to stay in the shelter of the machine shed. Why it was so important to leave before Rob discovered she had been here.

A blinding flash of electrically charged fire raced jaggedly across the sky, momentarily darkening the pupils of her green eyes. Her gaze scanned the clouds. With a sharp intake of breath, she saw the dark finger snake out of a cloud, its weaving funnel dancing above the ground before disappearing back into the clouds. She had lived in Iowa too long not to recognize a tornado, however far away it might be. Duchess whined and pulled backward on the leash, and instantly Cathie fell to her knees and threw her arms around the dog's neck.

"What are we going to do? We can't leave now!" Closing her eyes tightly against the panic that leaped in her chest, she buried her head for a moment in the damp fur of the shepherd's neck.

"I thought I was seeing things when I spotted your car parked down here!" an angry voice barked above her head.

Cathie remembered to keep a hold on the leash as she jumped to her feet, her wide frightened eyes turning on Rob while her heart hammered away somewhere in the area of her throat.

"Don't just stand there!" He reached out to grasp her wrist. "Didn't you see that funnel cloud? We have to get under cover."

"Duchess," Cathie murmured protestingly, foolishly thinking of the shepherd instead of herself. "I can't go without her."

Rob cursed silently under his breath as he picked up the whimpering dog and ordered Cathie to go ahead of him. "Go to the root cellar behind the house!" he shouted.

Without the shelter of a roof, she was drenched by the pounding rain in seconds. Widened green eyes kept scanning the clouds, knowing that at any second another funnel might be born. Blocking out the sound of thunderous claps and explosive fireballs, she tried to keep her ears tuned for that terrifying sound of a hundred jet engines. Cathie was gasping for breath when she reached the slanted wooden door that led down to the root cellar. Rob was at her heels, the sodden dog limp and quivering in his arms. It took all her fear-weakened strength to lift the door for Rob to precede her. The small electric bulb shining at the bottom of the steps was a beacon leading to security and safety. Cathie tumbled down the stairs toward it, letting the door slam shut overhead.

The scent of potatoes, apples and pears all mingled with the odor of the musty earthen walls. Duchess didn't bother to shake the water from her saturated coat but scrambled beneath the jar-laden shelves the instant Rob set her on her feet. Now that the race to safety was over, Cathie's legs were no longer capable of holding her up. She forced them to carry her to an upright crate where she collapsed with quivering relief.

"Where's Tad?" The thought of the boy somewhere out there in the storm struck fear in her heart.

"With the Smiths," Rob answered calmly in spite of the angry frown creasing his stern features. "I called over a half hour ago when I heard the tornado warning on the radio. They're all safe in their basement. And Mrs. Carver is at the hospital with her grandson. What were you doing out in this?"

Cathie wiped the excess water from her forehead that kept trickling down from her hair. "Duchess ran away and I couldn't face the thought of her being out in the storm. I knew she'd come here."

"Of all the stupid . . ." His mouth clamped tightly shut on the rest of his words. "Didn't you even have the radio on in your car?"

He was standing above her, the summer shirt

plastered to his wide shoulders accenting every rippling muscle. At the brief negative movement of her head, he sighed in exasperation and raked his fingers through his curling hair.

"How long do you think this will last?" Cathie asked, involuntarily flinching as a resounding crash of lightning made itself heard through the thick earthen walls that muffled all but the loudest sounds.

"Half an hour, an hour." Rob shrugged dismissively as if time was of little consequence. "It depends on how large a cell this storm is."

As he walked toward the stairwell, Cathie noticed the portable radio and flashlight sitting on the shelf near the exit. Rob flicked the radio on to a local station, and the serene melody of a popular ballad filled the air.

Impatiently his gaze slid over her. "I didn't think to bring a towel or blanket to dry ourselves with."

A burning rush of color flamed in her face, and she knew that her own cotton top was just as revealing in its wetness as his had been. "I don't mind," she murmured.

Water dripped from the ventilation shaft, sounding much louder than the steady hammer of rain on the wooden door. The shepherd was still cowering under the shelves, her ears flat against her head and her eyes, wide and frightened by the violence outside. Cathie silently wished that Rob would stop pacing back and forth like a caged panther. The small muggy cellar was becoming charged with an unbearable tension, and she knew her racing pulse no longer had anything to do with the storm taking place outside. Trivial conversation was impossible for Cathie. She was too conscious of Rob as the man she loved and not as a fellow human being trapped by the storm.

The explosive report of striking lightning threw the dimly lit cellar into complete darkness. Cathie leaped to her feet. The shriek torn from her throat was generated more from surprise than genuine fear. Before she could recover her wits, Rob's arms were around her, drawing her against the firmness of his body.

"The power went out, that's all," he murmured, holding her in the protective circle.

For a moment Cathie couldn't move or breathe, so overwhelming was the desire to slip her arms around him and lift her head from his muscular chest for his kiss. His previous rejection of her made the natural impulse impossible to carry out, another humiliation more than her pride could bear. Unwillingly she held herself away, his arms not letting her escape altogether, but she was free from the hypnotic beat of his heart beneath her head. A quivering sigh raced over her body.

"You're cold," Rob observed, his voice coming from somewhere near the top of her head.

"So are you," she answered quickly, her fingers still touching the cool dampness of the shirt that clung to his muscular body like a second skin. "It's ... it's these wet clothes."

"As soon as this storm eases, we can change into something dry."

Cathie was grateful for the darkness that concealed the torment his nearness was causing. "Yes," she agreed, attempting to shift out of his arms.

But he tightened his hold. "It would be best if you stayed close to me to ward off the chance of a chill."

"No, no, I'm all right," she protested, pushing ineffectually against his chest.

"Don't turn female on me, Cat," he said angrily, pulling her roughly against him. "I'm not going to try to seduce you."

She had not the strength or will to fight him as he maneuvered through the darkness to the crate, easing her down to the earthen floor so the two of them could use if for a backrest. Weakly Cathie let him cradle her in his arms, the burning warmth of his body sapping what little opposition remained. For an eternity of minutes they remained there, with Rob never commenting on the rigidity of Cathie's slender frame.

Rob moved slightly, lifting his arm from around her shoulders. "The rain seems to have let up. I'm going to check to see what it looks like out there." He reached above their heads for the flashlight, mercifully not shining it on Cathie's pale, strained face.

The beam of light picked out the path to the wooden steps. As the hinges creaked on the overhead door, the radio announced that the worst of the storm seemed to have passed. With the cellar door opened, partially illuminating the underground room, Cathie could tell the falling rain had a more gentle patter to it. At the sound of Rob's shoes descending the stairs, she rose to her feet inhaling deeply and attempting to wipe the nervous strain from her face.

"It's safe to go inside now," said Rob, his face shadowed by the gray light coming over his shoulder from the opened door.

As if in confirmation of his words, the cellar light came back on, only to be switched off by Rob as

Cathie walked past him to the steps. Duchess was much more reluctant to leave their shelter, consenting only after several repeated commands. Then the shepherd raced around the house, heading for the comparative safety beneath the front porch. Rob's swinging stride brought him abreast of Cathie as they walked swiftly toward the back door. Stealing a glance from the corner of her eye, she watched him run an appraising look over the farm seeking signs of the storm's damage to his property. None was visible except for a few broken tree limbs. Cathie couldn't help wondering if the Smith farm and Tad had fared as well.

Once they entered the house Rob made straight for the telephone, and Cathie knew his thoughts were on his son. She waited anxiously while he put the call through. After a brief exchange of words, the grim lines around his mouth eased into a smile which he cast over his shoulder to Cathie, signifying that Tad was all right. She smiled tremulously back, her heart singing that Rob should be so perceptive of her thoughts.

"No damage at the Smiths' either, and Tad is fine," Rob said, turning to her after he had replaced the receiver. "I talked to Ray. From what he's been able to find out from his neighbors, the few tornadoes that were sighted all stayed in the air, although the accompanying winds did take a few trees."

"That's a blessing," Cathie agreed, blinking at the acid burning of tears in her eyes for caring so much about what happened to Rob's son. But the subsequent shuddering of her shoulders was from relief at knowing Tad was safe and unharmed.

"There's a robe hanging on the bathroom

door," Rob said, misinterpreting her shiver. "After you get out of those wet clothes, you'd better take a hot bath."

"What about you?"

"I'll use the shower downstairs." Cathie started to turn away, feeling foolish for voicing her concern for his well being. "Set your clothes outside the bathroom door," Rob added, "and I'll toss them in the dryer in the basement. It shouldn't take more than a few minutes to get them dry."

Cathie hadn't realized how chilled she was until she slipped out of her wet clothes, wrapped herself in the large terry cloth robe and set the clothes outside the bathroom door while the tub was filling with water. She knew she should have insisted on leaving immediately rather than prolong her stay with Rob, but it had been so much easier giving in to the authority in his tone. As she crawled into the tubful of hot water, she was glad she had stayed. The water was a balm to her raw nerves as it eased the aching tension of her muscles held so tightly in check when she had rested against Rob. She lay in the tub gaining strength from the soothing caress of the water until she heard Rob moving around in the kitchen.

There was a rap on the door. "I've poured you a cup of coffee," Rob called out from the other side.

"I'll be out in a minute," she answered, stirring herself into mobility even though she could have used a longer respite from his presence.

Rob barely glanced up when she padded into the room minutes later, the robe securely belted around her waist. "Sit down." He motioned toward the table, sliding a glance in her direction over his shoulder.

He looked just as sexy in dry clothes, she noticed—but maybe that was because all her senses had been electrified by the big storm. When he turned away from the counter carrying her cup of coffee, she veiled her look with dark lashes. He stopped beside her chair, brushing her arm as he set the cup down and causing a renewed fluttering in her stomach. Involuntarily she drew away.

"Your clothes will be dry in a few more minutes," Rob said abruptly, moving away to lean against the kitchen counter.

There was a burning intensity to his brown eyes as he studied her lowered head. Cathie took the cup of coffee in her hand, seeking to divert her attention from his magnetic attraction. She took a healthy swallow and began coughing and sputtering, not from the heat of the coffee but because of the liberal lacing of whisky it contained.

"Why didn't you tell me?" she demanded hoarsely. Her eyes were watering from the potency of the liquor. The choking sensation remained as she rose from her chair and walked to the sink to pour the remainder of the liquid in the cup down the drain.

"Because I presumed you would do exactly what you just did," he answered sharply. "This way you drank at least some of it down." His dark eyes raked her form, still shuddering from the aftereffects of the drink. "As shaky as you were out there in the cellar, trembling like a half-drowned kitten, I thought you needed it."

"Storms like that don't terrify me. I grew up with them." Her knuckles were white from the way she was gripping the cup so tightly. "You were imagining things."

"Then why were you quivering in my arms?" Rob demanded with a derisive laugh.

Now it was her chin that was trembling as Cathie tried to salvage a bit of her pride and self-respect. "Maybe I just couldn't stand to have you touch me," she spat out sarcastically, needing to deny the havoc his touch caused in her.

The angry fire in his gaze seared over her as his arms shot out to imprison her shoulders. "Damn, but I'm tired of you always lashing out at me! Am I supposed to take your insults without any protest?"

He drew her roughly against the rock hardness of his chest. Her arms were pinned against him by her own body and the iron strength of his arms held her there. Twining his fingers in the golden curls of her hair, Rob forced her head up, staring into the eyes sparkling with diamond tears.

"Please, please let me go," she whispered. The hard contours of his body were destroying all her weakly constructed defenses, the desire to surrender almost impossible to withstand.

The soft, persuasive velvet look was gone from his eyes, replaced by anger. "You really are a cat, aren't you?" Rob mocked. "Aloof when it suits you, other times hissing and showing your claws." His gaze narrowed on her lips, moistly parted and tremulous. "It's time I heard you really purr."

"N-no!" Cathie breathed, already being brought closer to the sensual line of his mouth. But there was only the barest glimmer of a smile on his lips before they took hers captive.

There was no place to withdraw to, away from the feverish heat building under the consummate kiss. Her head was pressed back against his shoulder, the short honey-colored curls clinging to the silk shirt while the sweet savageness of his mouth received the response it demanded. Here was a sensual storm as tempestuous as anything the heavens could create. Cathie was swept away by the sheer power of his embrace.

Her arms that had been crushed between their bodies found their way around his neck, bringing her still closer to him. The caressing movements of his hands on her back molded her tighter, the combustion of her surrender changing his lips from demanding to possessive. Rob's breathing, too, was ragged as he explored the sensitive cord in her neck and the tan hollow of her shoulder.

"Rob," she murmured, aching for the feel of his lips against hers again and moving her head until she found them. It was agony when he dragged his mouth away again.

"Damn you," Rob muttered into her hair as he crushed her tightly against him. His breath fanned her ears before he moved his head away to stare into her questioning, hurt eyes. "I swore I wouldn't let you bewitch me. But you have!"

"Rob . . ."

"I've fallen in love with you," he declared grimly, unmindful of the disbelief in her eyes. An eyebrow arched at the look of dismay. "Where's the triumphant smile, Cat? You win. I lose."

"Rob, you don't understand. I never loved Clay," Cathie began earnestly, "not like I love you." Her fingers covered the cynical curl of his mouth. "It has nothing to do with the Homeplace, the farm. It never did, except at the beginning when I hated you for buying it." She swallowed nervously at the still doubting look on his face. "How can I make you understand that I'm telling you the truth? You can sell the Homeplace, burn it to the ground, do whatever you want, and I'll still love you. You can take me to New York or the Arctic Circle. All I want is to be with you." Her hands moved lovingly over his face, savoring each line of the handsome features. "All I want is to be yours."

His fingers bit into her shoulders as his dark eyes examined her face. "It's true," she breathed again, letting all the love she had tried to conceal shine in her eyes. "I do love you."

"Then why . . ." His eyes raced over her face. "Damn it, Cat, what took you so long?"

"The hardest thing to realize was that I loved you. When I finally admitted it to myself you made it clear that you expected me to pursue you in order to get the farm." A small smile curved her mouth. "A girl has some pride, you know, and until this moment I didn't believe that you actually cared for me."

"Oh, Cat!" He laughed exultantly. "I do!" He swung her completely off the floor to rain kisses on her face, before finally settling on her mouth in one long, breathtaking kiss. They were both stunned by the passion-charged minutes when Rob lifted his head some time later. "I think you'd better go and get your clothes out of the dryer and put them on damp or dry, or I'm not going to be responsible for my actions," he murmured huskily.

With a laugh of pleasure, Cathie slipped out of his arms, the feverish color of her face revealing that she was truly his to command. There was a sharp intake of breath from Rob at the love radiating so openly from her green eyes, eyes that she knew would never tire of looking at him.

"Go," he ordered gruffly, and she dutifully glided toward the stairwell to the basement. As her bare foot touched the first step, his voice halted her. She turned to drink in the sight of the lean frame a few steps away. "Did you mean it, Cat, when you said you would go back to New York with me?"

"Yes," she replied without any hesitation.

"What about the farm?"

She smiled widely, understanding his need to be reassured of the genuineness of her love. "I'll miss it because basically I'm a country girl. But my homeplace is where ever you are, Rob. It's the most important thing in the world to me for you to believe that."

"I do," he said nodding, a possessively tender light shining from his eyes.

Cathie wanted to cross the space that separated them and feel again the heady excitement of being in his arms. But considering the present state of their emotions that was too dangerous. Instead she turned and floated down the stairs, changing into her dry clothes in record time. Rob was standing in front of the windows in the sun porch, a cup of coffee in his hand, and staring out the window when she ascended the last flight.

"Look," he said, darting an admiring glance in her direction before motioning with his head out the window. She walked swiftly to his side and was immediately nestled against his shoulder as she looked out the window. A rainbow was arching out of the dissipating clouds, shimmering with jewel-like beauty. The entire countryside was etched in sharp relief, the air washed clean to vividly reveal the rolling fields of corn, wheat and hay, dotted by trees and buildings.

Cathie sighed. "It will be hard to leave all this beauty."

"Who said we were?" Rob's gaze turned tenderly to her bemused face.

"You did." Her eyes widened with blinking bewilderment.

"No," he smiled. "You brought it up. I only made sure that if I asked you to leave the farm for New York, you would. I have no intention of ever leaving here."

"That's too wonderful to be true!" Cathie gasped, covering a little sob of happiness. "I feel I should give up something I cherish to prove that I love you and not what you own."

"I have a better idea. Why don't you spend the rest of your life proving that you love me? That would truly be heaven on earth."

His head was moving to take her up on the invitation written on her parted lips when the back door slammed. They turned in unison as Tad raced up the steps. He showed not the slightest surprise to see Cathie as he greeted them together.

"Hi, dad. Hi, Cathie. Mr. Smith brought me home so you wouldn't be worried about me. Boy, that was some storm!" His words were tumbling over each other in his excitement. "Me and Charlie saw a tornado! But it never came down out of the sky."

"We saw it, too," Rob said, nodding and holding Cathie tighter when she would have moved away. "I'm glad you're home, son. I wanted to ask you what you thought about Cathie and me getting married." A teasing light danced over her flushed cheeks. "I have to get my proposal in to make it official."

"Really?" Tad's hazel eyes grew enormously large. "That would be terrific!" Then he stopped, a smile running from cheek to cheek. "Especially since you won't be my teacher next year."

"We'll go see your parents this weekend," said Rob, gazing into her tremulous expression. "That is, if you are going to marry me."

"Yes," Cathie breathed.

"I forgot to tell you," Tad inserted. "When we drove past the pasture, I saw where the wind had uprooted the willow tree over the spring."

Cathie tore her gaze away from Rob's handsome features to look at Tad. The willow tree, that special living bridge over the spring, had been in some strange way a link with her childhood. Now it was gone, destroyed by the storm that had brought her Rob. Then a smile came back to her mouth. It was more than an even trade.

"I'm sorry, Cat," said Rob, gently touching her cheek. "That was a special tree. Tad told me about it."

"I don't mind, darling," she replied, turning her head to brush a kiss in his palm. "Not anymore."

Chapter Twelve

Sunlight shimmered on the smooth surface of the jade stone, making the diamond brilliants on either side of the green gem sparkle while turning the circling band into molten gold. Their simple church wedding had taken place in August and Cathie still studied her wedding rings, unable to believe her good fortune. Harvest time was already nipping at the heels of summer. School had been in session for three weeks, not sufficient time for Cathie's heart to stop leaping every time one of her students addressed her as Mrs. Douglas.

She smiled up at the Saturday morning sun. She hadn't known that loving a man could bring such utter contentment and bliss. Even during the mundane tasks of making beds, fixing meals and washing dishes, she would glance in Rob's direction and feel that rush of warmth that made their relationship so special, night or day. Her temper was still with her, rising to the forefront when some minor irritation became more than she could bear, but Rob wasn't passive like Clay and gave as good as he got. And they always ended up laughing about it later, or better yet—loving.

"Cathie!" Tad's voice pulled her out of her daydream.

There was more satisfaction for her watching the slender darkly tanned boy racing across the lawn to where she was reclining on a lawn chair. His bleached brown hair was tousled by the wind, his face was streaked with dirt and perspiration, his denim jeans all patches and grass stains. The Tad who stopped breathlessly in front of her bore almost no resemblance to the aloof, withdrawn child who had walked into her classroom those many months ago.

"Dad wants you to help him." A happy grin split his face. There was open affection in the way his hazel eyes glowed when they looked at Cathie.

"Where is he?" she asked as she rose to her feet, glancing down at her clean clothes and hoping the help Rob wanted didn't involve a greasy tractor.

"Out in the pasture," Tad replied, reaching for her hand to hurry her along.

A sad light dimmed the brilliance of her eyes, but she quickly chased it away. Cathie still couldn't get used to walking down to the pasture and not seeing the willow tree by the spring. The little ribbon of water looked so lonely without it. Of course she hadn't told Rob that. She didn't want him to think she attached that much importance to an old tree.

"Has something happened to one of the cows?"

she asked, dodging the muddy Duchess who was rejoining Tad.

"No," Tad assured her, grinning over his shoulder with an impish twinkle in his eyes that puzzled Cathie. Usually such excitement from Tad heralded the arrival of a baby animal, but to Cathie's knowledge there was none expected.

Tad hustled her to the barnyard, taking the short cut past the concrete water tank and out the pasture gate. Near the bottom of the hill where the spring flowed into the Boyer River, Cathie saw the red and white pickup truck parked. Tad raced ahead to join his father, who had watched Cathie's hurried progress down the hill.

"Here she is!" Tad announced, fairly dancing with excitement.

"What is all this about?" Cathie asked, puzzled by the conspiratorial look exchanged between the two. Rob's brown eyes swung back to her, then he reached out to take her hand and lead her around to the opposite side of the pickup.

Tears sprang to her eyes as she looked at the sapling lying on the ground and the open hole almost in the exact spot where the old willow had been. The sapling was a willow, too. Her voice couldn't get past the lump in her throat as she looked from the baby tree to the warm, loving light in her husband's eyes.

"It's a surprise." Tad spoke up, gazing curiously at the tears trickling down her face. "Aren't you happy?"

"Yes." A sobbing laugh finally permitted speech. "I'm very happy, Tad." She felt Rob's arm around her shoulders. "How did you know?" she asked, lifting her gaze to his face.

"Oh, Cat," he smiled, tenderly wiping a tear from her cheek, "I saw your chin trembling the day we burnt the last of the dead limbs. I know you tried not to let me see, but I know you too well."

"Thank you," she whispered.

"I didn't do it for you, you know." The velvet eyes gleamed with mischief. "It'll be years before this willow can grow big enough for you to climb. I'm planting it for our grandchildren."

Tad took no notice of the blush in Cathie's cheeks. "We've figured it out," he said importantly, "that if we tie a string on the trunk of the sapling and anchor the string on the other side of the spring, we can make it grow across on the other side just like the old one."

"No, Tad." Cathie shook her head, wiping the tears from her face to smile down at him. "Let's not do that. You see, you can't force things to be the way they were in the past. Let's let the new tree grow the way it wants to."

Tad didn't seem too excited by her suggestion, but accepted it willingly. The gentle pressure of Rob's hand on her arm brought Cathie's face around.

"You really have given up your dreams of the future," Rob murmured, gazing into her love-starred eyes. "All those plans you made to keep everything the way it was."

"All but my dream of living the rest of my life with you," she nodded.

Their lips met in a kiss that was boundless in its pledge of love.

Author's Note

In 1876 Eli Haradon came to the Boyer River Valley of Iowa and erected a blacksmith and wagon shop in Sac County around which the settlement of Early, Iowa grew. The railroad was built through the county in 1881, and the town moved two miles north to it. The old town site and surrounding acreage became the Haradon farm.

Eli Haradon was my great-grandfather. The first thirteen years of my life were spent in and around the town of Early with the most memorable and precious times on the Haradon farm. There, my cousin David and I built tree houses, huts and disastrous rafts. Hours were spent sitting on the banks of the Boyer reading comic books and watching the red and white bobbers on our bamboo poles floating on the river.

Years ago, after nearly a century as the family home, the farm was sold out of the Haradon family. I took a last, nostalgic journey over my beloved farm this spring. As I paused near the remains of the willow tree that once bridged the spring flowing into the Boyer, I knew this farm—my "homeplace"—would become the focal point of this novel. All the characters and incidents in this story are fictitious, but the farm is real, as are my memories of my own idyllic days where the wildest dream was no farther out of reach then the top limb of my favorite climbing tree.

Janet Dailey

Here's a preview of
SHIFTING CALDER WIND by Janet Dailey.
A June 2004 paperback
from Kensington Publishing.

———————————

A blackness roared around him. He struggled to
surface from it, somehow knowing that if he
didn't, he would die. Sounds reached him as if coming
from a great distance—a shout, the scrape of
shoes on pavement, the metallic slam of a car door
and the sharp clap of a gunshot.

Someone was trying to kill him.

He had to get out of there. The instant he tried
to move the blackness swept over him with dizzying
force. He heard the revving rumble of a car engine
starting up. Unable to rise, he rolled away from
the sound as spinning tires burned rubber and another
shot rang out.

Lights flashed in a bright glare. There was danger
in them, he knew. He had to reach the shadows.
Fighting the weakness that swam through his
limbs, he crawled away from the light.

He felt dirt beneath his hand and dug his fingers
into it. His strength sapped, he lay there a moment,
trying to orient himself, and to determine

the location of the man trying to kill him. But the searing pain in his head made it hard to think logically. He reached up and felt the warm wetness on his face. That's when he knew he had been shot. Briefly his fingers touched the deep crease the bullet had ripped along the side of his head. Pain instantly washed over him in black waves.

Aware that he could lose consciousness at any second, either from the head wound or the blood loss, he summoned the last vestiges of his strength and threw himself deeper into the darkness. With blood blurring his vision, he made out the shadowy outlines of a post and railing. It looked to be a corral of some sort. He pushed himself toward it, wanting any kind of barrier, no matter how flimsy, between himself and his pursuer.

There was a whisper of movement just to his left. Alarm shot through him, but he couldn't seem to make his muscles react. He was too damned weak. He knew it even as he listed sideways and saw the low-crouching man in a cowboy hat with a pistol in his hand.

Instead of shooting, the cowboy grabbed for him with his free arm. "Come on. Let's get outta here, old man," the cowboy whispered with urgency. "He's up on the catwalk working himself into a better position."

He latched onto the cowboy's arm and staggered drunkenly to his feet, his mind still trying to wrap itself around that phrase "old man." Leaning heavily on his rescuer, he stumbled forward, battling the woodenness of his legs.

After an eternity of seconds, the cowboy pushed him into the cab of a pickup and closed the door. He sagged against the seat and closed his eyes, unable to summon another ounce of strength. Dimly he was aware of the cowboy slipping behind the wheel and the engine starting up. It was followed by the vibrations of movement.

Through slitted eyes, he glanced in the side mirror but saw nothing to indicate they were being followed. They were out of danger now. Unbidden came the warning that it was only temporary; whoever had tried to kill him would try again.

Who had it been? And why? He searched for the answers and failed to come up with any.

Thinking required too much effort. Choosing to conserve the remnants of his strength, he glanced out the window at the unfamiliar buildings that flanked the street.

"Where are we?" His voice had a throaty rasp to it.

"According to the signs, there should be a hospital somewhere ahead of us," the cowboy replied. "I'll drop you off close to the emergency entrance."

"No." It was a purely instinctual reply.

"Mister, that head wound needs tending. You've lost a bunch of blood—"

"No." He started to shake his head in emphasis, but at the first movement, the world started spinning.

The pickup's speed slowed perceptibly. "Don't tell me you're wanted by the law?" The cowboy turned a sharp, speculating glance on him.

Was he? For the second time, he came up against a wall of blankness. It was another answer he didn't know, so he avoided the question.

"He's bound to know I was hit, so he'll expect me to get medical attention. The nearest hospital will be the first place he would check."

"You're probably right about that," the cowboy agreed. "So where do you want to go?"

Where? Where? Where? The question hammered at him. But it was impossible to answer because he didn't know what the hell town they were in. That discovery brought a wave of panic, one that intensified when he realized he didn't know his own name.

He clamped down tightly on the panic and said, "I don't know yet. Let me think."

He closed his eyes and strained to dredge up some scrap of a memory. But he was empty of any. Who was he? What was he? Where was he? Every question bounced around in the void. His head pounded anew. He felt himself slipping deeper into the blackness and lacked the strength to fight against it.

He simultaneously became conscious of a bright light pressing against his eyes and the chirping of a bird. Groggily he opened his eyes and saw filtered sunlight coming through the curtained window. It was daylight, and his last conscious memory had been of riding in a truck through night-darkened streets.

Instantly alert, he shot a searching glance around the room. The curtains at the window and the rose-patterned paper on the walls confirmed what his nose had already told him: he wasn't in a hospital. He was in a bedroom, one that was strange to him.

His glance stopped on the cowboy slumped in an old wicker rocking chair in the corner, his hat tipped over the top of his face, his chest rising and falling in an even rhythm. Surmising the man was his rescuer from the night before, he studied the cleanly chiseled line of the man's jaw and the nut brown color of his hair, details he hadn't noticed during the previous night's darkness and confusion. The man's yoked-front shirt looked new, but the jeans and the boots both showed signs of wear.

He threw back the bedcovers and started to rise. Pain slammed him back onto the pillow and ripped a groan from him. In a reflexive action, he lifted a hand to his head and felt the gauze strips that swaddled it.

In a flash the cowboy rolled to his feet and crossed to the bed. "Just lay back and be still. You won't be going anywhere for a while, old man."

He bristled in response. "That's the second time you've called me an old man."

After a pulse beat of silence, the cowboy replied in droll apology, "I didn't mean any offense by it, but you aren't exactly a young fella."

Unable to recall who he was, let alone how old he was, he grunted a nonanswer. "Where am I, anyway? Your place?"

"It belongs to some kinfolk on my mother's side," the cowboy answered.

He studied the cowboy's blue eyes and easy smile. There was a trace of boyish good looks behind the stubble of a night's beard growth and the sun-hardened features. A visual search found no sign of the pistol the cowboy had been carrying last night.

"Who are you?" His eyes narrowed on the cowboy.

There was a fractional pause, a coolness suddenly shuttering the cowboy's blue eyes. "I think a better question is who are you?"

"Maybe it is," he stalled, hoping a name might come to him, but none did. "But I'd like to know the name of the man who quite likely saved my life last night so I can thank him properly."

"You dodged that question about as deftly as a politician." Blue eyes glinted in quiet speculation. "But I don't think that's what you are. You strike me as a man used to asking the questions rather than answering them."

"Now you're the one dodging the question."

"My friends call me Laredo. What do your friends call you?"

His head pounded with the strain of trying to recall. Automatically he touched the bandages again.

Observing the action and the continued silence, the cowboy called Laredo guessed, "You can't remember, can you?"

"I—don't you know who I am?"

"Nope. But I'll tell you what I do know—the material in that suit you were wearing wasn't cheap, and those were custom-made boots on your feet. It took money to buy them, which leads me to think you aren't a poor man. There's no Texas drawl in your voice, which tells me you aren't from around here, at least not originally."

"We're in Texas?" he repeated for confirmation. "Where?"

"Southwest of Fort Worth."

"Fort Worth." It sounded familiar to him, but he didn't know why. "Is that where we were last night?" he asked, recalling the city streets they had driven through.

"Yeah. In Old Downtown, next to the stock-yards."

"There's an old cemetery not far from there," he said with a strange feeling of certainty.

"You couldn't prove it by me," Laredo said with an idle shrug of his broad shoulders.

He fired a quick glance at the cowboy. "You aren't from around here?"

"No. I'm just passing through. Now that it looks like you're going to live, I'll be leaving soon."

"Not yet." He reached out to stop him with a suddenness that sent the room spinning again. Subsiding weakly against the pillow, he swallowed back the rising nausea.

"I told you to lie still," Laredo reminded him. "That bullet gouged a deep path. It wouldn't surprise me if it grazed your skull."

He fought through the swirling pain, insisting, "Before you go, I have to know about last night. The man who shot me—did you see him?"

"I guess if you don't know who you are, you don't know who he is either, do you?" Laredo guessed. "I'm afraid I can't help you much. All I saw was the figure of a man with a scoped rifle. I couldn't tell you if he was old or young, tall or short, just that he didn't look fat."

"Tell me what you saw." He closed his eyes, hoping something would trigger a memory.

After a slight pause, Laredo began, "I'm not sure what it was that first caught my eye. Maybe it was the car door being open and all the interior light flooding from it while the rest of the parking lot was so dark. You were standing next to it facing another man. His back was to me so I didn't get a look at him. It took me a second to realize you were being robbed. He did a good job of it, too.

You don't have a lick of identification on you—no wallet, no watch, no ring. Nothing. He even took your spare change. Right now you don't have a cent to your name."

"But this robber wasn't the man who shot me." He recalled Laredo mentioning a man with a scoped rifle. He couldn't imagine a common thief carrying one.

"No, he wasn't. The shot came from behind you. The second I heard it, I knew it didn't come from any handgun. You dropped like a rock. Your robber jumped in the car and hightailed it out of there."

"I half remember hearing a vehicle peel out. Somebody yelled. Was that you?"

"Yup. I wanted your sniper to know somebody else was in the area. About the same time I saw you moving so I knew you weren't dead. He snapped off a shot in my direction. I saw the muzzle flash and fired back."

"Do you usually carry a gun?"

Amusement tugged at the corner of his mouth. "Like I said, we're in Texas, and the definition of gun control here is a steady aim."

He managed a brief smile at Laredo's small joke. "What time was this?"

"Late. Somewhere between eleven and midnight."

He wondered what he was doing there at that hour. "Aren't there some bars in the area?"

"A bunch of them."

From somewhere outside came the familiar lowing of cattle. "Are we in the country?"

Laredo nodded. "The Ludlow ranch. It's a small

spread, not much more than a hundred acres. It hardly deserves to be called a ranch."

"Why did you bring me here?"

"I didn't have many choices. I probably should have taken you to a hospital like I first planned. But with you being unconscious, I couldn't just drop you off at the door. Taking you inside meant fielding a lot of questions I didn't want to answer. So I brought you here." He allowed a small smile to show. "I figured if you died, I could always bury you in the back forty with no one the wiser."

"Except the Ludlows."

"I wasn't worried about Hattie talking."

"Who is Hattie?" The hot pounding in his head increased, making it difficult to string more than two thoughts together.

"Since Ed died, she owns the place." After a slight pause, Laredo observed, "Your head's bothering you, isn't it?"

"Some." He was reluctant to admit to more than that.

"No need in overdoing it. Why don't you get some rest? We can talk more later if you want. In the meantime, I'll see if I can rustle you up something to eat."

"Did you say you were leaving soon?"

"I did. But I won't be going just yet." Moving away from the bed, Laredo crossed to the window and lowered the shade, darkening the room.

He closed his eyes against the pain, but it wasn't so easy to shut out the blankness of his memory. Who the hell was he? Why couldn't he remember?

"What happened, Laura? Did you forget to
look where you were going?" The familiar-
ity of Tara's affectionately chiding voice provided
the right touch of normalcy.

Laura seized on it while she struggled to collect
her composure. "I'm afraid I did. I was talking to
Boone and—" She paused a beat to glance again at
the stranger, stunned to discover how rattled she
felt. It was a totally alien sensation. She couldn't
remember a time when she hadn't felt in control
of herself and a situation. "And I walked straight
into you. I'm sorry."

"No apologies necessary," the man assured her
while his gaze made a curious and vaguely puzzled
study of her face. "The fault was equally mine." He
cocked his head to one side, the puzzled look
deepening in his expression. "I know this sounds
awfully trite, but haven't we met before?"

Laura shook her head. "No. I'm certain I would

have remembered if we had." She was positive of that.

"Obviously you remind me of someone else then," he said, easily shrugging off the thought. "In any case, I hope you are none the worse for the collision, Ms.—" He paused expectantly, waiting for Laura to supply her name.

The old ploy was almost a relief. "Laura Calder. And this is my aunt, Tara Calder," she said, rather than going into a lengthy explanation of their exact relationship.

"My pleasure, ma'am," he murmured to Tara, acknowledging her with the smallest of bows.

"And perhaps you already know Max Rutledge and his son, Boone." Laura belatedly included the two men.

"I know *of* them." He nodded to Max.

When he turned to the younger man, Boone extended a hand, giving him a look of hard challenge. "And you are?"

"Sebastian Dunshill," the man replied.

"Dunshill," Tara repeated with sudden and heightened interest. "Are you any relation to the earl of Crawford, by chance?"

"I do have a nodding acquaintance with him." His mouth curved in an easy smile as he switched his attention to Tara. "Do you know him?"

"Unfortunately no," Tara admitted, then drew in a breath and sent a glittering look at Laura, barely able to contain her excitement. "Although a century ago the Calder family was well acquainted with a certain Lady Crawford."

"Really. And how's that?" With freshened curiosity, Sebastian Dunshill turned to Laura for an explanation.

An awareness of him continued to tingle through her. Only now Laura was beginning to enjoy it.

"It's a long and rather involved story," Laura warned. "After all this time, it's difficult to know how much is fact, how much is myth, and how much is embellishment of either one."

"Since we have a fairly long walk ahead of us to the dining hall, why don't you start with the facts?" Sebastian suggested and deftly tucked her hand under his arm, turning her to follow the other guests.

Laura could feel Boone's anger over the way he had been supplanted, but she didn't really care. She had too much confidence in her ability to smooth any of Boone's ruffled feathers.

"The facts." She pretended to give them some thought while her sidelong glance traveled over Sebastian Dunshill's profile, noting the faint smattering of freckles on his fair skin and the hint of copper lights in his very light brown hair.

Despite the presence of freckles, there was nothing boyish about him. He was definitely a man fully grown, thirty-something she suspected, with a very definite continental air about him. He didn't exude virility the way Boone Rutledge did; his air of masculinity had a smooth and polished edge to it.

"I suppose I should begin by explaining that back in the latter part of the 1870s, my great-great-grandfather Benteen Calder established the family ranch in Montana."

"Your family owns a cattle ranch?" He glanced her way, interest and curiosity mixing in his look.

"A very large one."

"How many acres do you have? I don't mean to sound nosy, but those of us on this side of the

Atlantic harbor a secret fascination with the scope and scale of your American West."

"So I've learned. But truthfully we don't usually measure in acres. We talk about sections," Laura explained. "The Triple C has more than one hundred and fifty sections within its boundary fence."

"You'll have to educate me," he said with a touch of amusement. "How large is a section?"

"One square mile, or six hundred and forty acres."

After a quick mental calculation, Sebastian gave her a suitably impressed look. "That's nearly a million acres. And I thought all the large western ranches were in Texas, not Montana."

"Not all." She smiled. "Anyway, according to early ranch records, there are numerous business transactions listed that indicate Lady Crawford was a party to them. Many of them involved government contracts for the purchase of beef. It appears that my great-great-grandfather paid her a finder's fee, I suppose you would call it—an arrangement that was clearly lucrative for both of them."

"The earl of Crawford wasn't named as a party in any of this, then," Sebastian surmised.

"No. In fact, the family stories that were passed down always said she was widowed."

"Interesting. As I recall," he began with a faint frown of concentration, "the seventh earl of Crawford was married to an American. They had no children, which meant the title passed to the son of his younger brother." He stopped abruptly and swung toward Laura, running a fast look over her face. "That's it! I know why you looked so familiar. You bear a striking resemblance to the portrait of Lady Elaine that hangs in the manor's upper hall."

"Did you hear that, Tara?" Laura turned in amazement to the older woman.

"I certainly did." With a look of triumph in her midnight dark eyes, Tara momentarily clutched at Laura's arm, an exuberant smile curving her red lips. "I knew it. I knew it all along."

"Knew what?" A disgruntled Max Rutledge rolled his chair forward, forcing his way into their circle. But Boone stood back, eyeing the Englishman with a barely veiled glare. "What's all this hooha about?"

"Yes, I'm curious, too," Sebastian inserted.

"Well . . ." Laura paused, trying to decide how to frame her answer. "According to Calder legend, Benteen's mother ran off with another man when he was a small boy. If the man's name was known, I've never heard it mentioned. He was always referred to as a remittance man, which, as I understand, was a term used to describe a younger, and frequently ne'er-do-well, son of wealthy Europeans, often titled."

Sebastian nodded, following her line of thought to its logical conclusion. "And you suspect your ancestor ran off with the man who became the seventh earl of Crawford."

"Actually, Tara is the one who came up with that theory after she found some old photographs."

Taking Laura's cue, Tara explained, "Back when I was married to Laura's father, I was rummaging through an old trunk in the attic and came across the tintype of a young woman. At that time, the housekeeper, who had been born and raised on the ranch, told me it was a picture of Madelaine Calder, the mother of Chase Benteen Calder. I'm not sure, but I think that was the first time I heard the story about her abandoning her husband and young son to run off with another man. Needless to say, I was a bit intrigued by this slightly scandalous bit of family history. And I became more intrigued when I happened to lay the tintype next to a photograph taken of Lady Crawford. Granted, one was a picture of a woman perhaps in her early twenties, and the woman in the other photo was easily in her sixties. Still, it was impossible to discount the many physical similarities the two shared, not to mention that the young woman had been called Madelaine and the older one was known as Elaine. I just couldn't believe it was nothing more than a series of amazing coincidences. I've always suspected they were pictures of the same woman, but I have never been able to prove it."

"And if you could, what would that accomplish?" Max challenged, clearly finding little of importance in the issue.

"Now, Max," Tara chided lightly, "you of all people should know that sometimes there is immense satisfaction to be gained from finding out you were right about something all along."

Max harrumphed but didn't disagree with her response. Boone remained a silent observer. Something about the way he looked at Sebastian Dunshill spoke of his instant dislike of the man.

"You say there's a portrait of Lady Elaine displayed at the earl of Crawford's home," Tara said, addressing the remark to Sebastian.

"Indeed there is. A splendid one."

"I'd love to see it sometime."